THE LAND WHERE THE SUN DIES

Henry Carlisle

Also by the author
VOYAGE TO THE FIRST OF DECEMBER

THE LAND
WHERE
THE SUN DIES

G. P. Putnam's Sons
New York

For Olga

Justice to a nation who are dying need never be expected from the hands of their destroyers; where injustice and injury are visited upon the weak and defenceless, from ten thousand hands—from Governments—monopolies and individuals—the offence is lost in the inseverable iniquity in which all join, and for which nobody is answerable, unless it be for their respective amounts, at a final day of retribution.

—George Catlin

My children, we are strong, we are numerous as the stars in the heavens, and we are all gunmen.

—Thomas Jefferson

Eliza

COLD wind swirled the fallen snow in the avenue where their hired cab passed. The sky to the east was black, to the west the sun blazed between lowering clouds and the gentle hills they had traveled that afternoon, casting brilliant light on the white government buildings, some still fire-blackened above the windows, others under construction with scaffolding and piles of numbered stone before them; enough, it seemed to the girl, for the Pyramids.

Her father, opposite her beside her mother, was looking out at these sights quite as a visitor should do. He was dressed in his best and looked as prosperous as any gentleman she saw in the vehicles they passed. Her mother, in her bonnet and Sunday dress, wore an anxious frown, and when the sun crossed her face she seemed to the girl incredibly aged.

Then, as he had done many times before, her father unconsciously touched the pocket where he carried the letter, and the girl, whose name was Eliza Hutchins, looked away quickly, fearful that the letter would only bring disappointment to her father. It had been her doing, the reason they had come here: a sheet of paper scrawled by the man Eliza had called "Uncle Jackson" for as long as she could remember, General Andrew Jackson. The letter introduced to his friend, President Monroe, "my kinsman John Hutchins, a man of excellent character having experience dealing with the Cherokees" (mercifully omitting mention of the Nashville dry goods trade) and recommended him for a post in the War Department's office of Indian affairs. Apart from their belongings in the trunk over their heads and the few

9

remaining bank notes of doubtful discountability, the letter and the hope it represented were indeed all they had in the world. Nor could Eliza even share her apprehensions with her parents then because her father did not know of the part she had played in suggesting to Aunt Rachel that Uncle Jackson write the letter and her mother did not credit it, believing as she did that no proper-bred young lady of seventeen could in the nature of things accomplish any act of consequence. So Eliza bore her fears in silence.

What a harsh people, she thought as she looked out at the city, who punish a man so cruelly for uncalculating trust in his friends and neighbors. She looked again at her mother, who tried a little smile, and for the first time Eliza realized that her mother was perhaps suffering the most because she could not begin to conceive why these things were happening to them. Eliza smiled back and touched her mother's hand, fighting against her own sense of helplessness.

Then she experienced a murderous rage against the British for burning the city.

It was dusk and a lamplighter was at his work when the cab drew up at the door of William O'Neale's tavern and boardinghouse; as the door opened and a servant hurried down the steps to assist with their trunk and Eliza heard the convivial din from within the taproom, it was then that she felt most despondent; for in the upside down world of insolvency whatever is most welcoming and desirable becomes most icily forbidding to those who must count each dollar as if it were an hour of life. Then why had they come to William O'Neale's? Again the perverse workings of the debtor's bleak universe: Uncle Jackson, unmindful of the seriousness of her father's plight, had determined that no other establishment in Washington could possibly do for them. Had not his young friend, the newly appointed Senator from Tennessee, John Eaton, written that O'Neale's had become the preferred rendezvous of the great and ambitious men of national politics? They would meet persons of consequence there, the general told them, persons in positions to render service to her father. So just when they were nearing the end of their resources they were to sleep in warmed feather beds and dine on oysters in the company of the nation's eminent men.

Eliza wondered how she could climb the stairs to the door.

William O'Neale, a red-mustached, florid-faced Irishman of ready wit and even readier laughter, in no way dampened by his knowledge of his new guests' kinship with General Jackson, did not simply greet John and Mary Hutchins and their quiet, dark-haired daughter, but fairly enfolded them bodily into his establishment, introducing the "relations of General Jackson" to whatever Senators, judges, or Congressmen impeded their progress through the common rooms to find—as it was indispensible to do at once—Mrs. O'Neale.

But then, in the center of a circle of gentlemen where the talk and laughter were loudest, Eliza saw the most beautiful young woman she had ever seen in her life. Her hair was deep chestnut, her eyes dark and quick, her skin apple-white, her lips full; she was simply gowned in fashionable French calico, for no frill or ornament could have enhanced the voluptuous perfection of her form, full-bosomed, slender-waisted, seeming always in liquid motion. She was laughing at the instant Eliza first saw her, and then with breathtaking grace she touched the ringlets at the back of her head, saying something that made the men laugh. Eliza could not take her eyes off the belle. All the Nashville girls she knew were trained and frightened into womanhood, but this girl, a year or two older than her, and endowed by nature with great beauty, seemed truly to delight in herself, and in her sex, and therefore was more beautiful, Eliza thought, even than nature. Feeling herself plain, burdened, and travel-worn, she ached with envy.

Whoever she is, she is who I would be, Eliza Hutchins told herself.

And just then she saw the girl glance in their direction,

11

suddenly excuse herself, cross the room to William O'Neale, and shelter herself under his arm—smiling at Eliza with softened eyes that seemed to see through to her thoughts.

"My daughter, Margaret," said their host with mock displeasure that did not conceal his pride. "The bane of an otherwise happy life. Mr. and Mrs. Hutchins, dear, and—their daughter. Relations of General Jackson."

"Eliza," said Eliza, as the beautiful girl kept her eyes on her a moment, indeed an exceedingly long moment, before greeting Eliza's mother and father. Then abruptly she broke free of her father's embrace and to accept the arm of a very collected-looking young gentleman who was approaching them. Upon their host's astonished discovery that the relations of the general had never met the good friend of the general, he presented their new Senator, John Eaton.

"A pleasure to meet you," said Eaton in a voice fully as composed as his appearance, "and to repair the omission of our not having met in Tennessee."

As her father replied with similar courtesy, Eliza stared at Margaret O'Neale (as she supposed her name was), but now Margaret could look at no one but John Eaton, hanging prettily on his arm as if gauging how well they set each other off, appearing now quite oblivious of Eliza, who wondered if something about her displeased the older girl, who had seemed so especially interested in her moments before. Had that strange, thrilling look meant nothing? How could it have meant nothing when those softened eyes had made her blood swim with pleasure as they dared her not to look shyly away? Yet without another glance at her, Margaret let John Eaton lead her into another room, and Eliza wondered how such a spirited and beautiful young woman could care for such a collected young man as John Eaton, Senator though he was and, she had heard, a man of large property. Eliza promised herself that she would again draw Margaret's attention, for she had no doubt now that there was some secret reason she had not once looked at her again.

When Mrs. O'Neale, a large lady of refinement and measured cordiality, arrived to show them to their rooms, Eliza realized that for five or ten minutes she had not thought once about her father's circumstances.

The next morning she awoke again to reality. Outside it was crisp and clear. At breakfast in the warm tavern her father said, "It will be all right," when her mother's smile seemed about to shatter.

Margaret was nowhere in the common rooms.

All morning Eliza walked with her mother through the barren expanses of the damaged city; when they grew cold they stopped at another tavern for tea, and her mother, to sustain their spirits, told her for the hundredth time how the McKitchens had left Virginia and crossed the hostile mountain wilderness, using Indian trails when they dared; and Eliza saw her mother's eyes come alight as she told of the dangers they had faced from the invisible enemy, infinitely wily, whose presence was told in the sway of a branch at the darkest edge of the forest; but they had made it through, the McKitchens, with the help of God they had made it through.

So would they now, Eliza had told her mother, praying it to be true.

When they returned to O'Neale's her father was already there. He told them that the President had taken cold and was receiving no one. Mr. Calhoun was not in the city. Through an assistant, President Monroe had tended his respects to Mr. Hutchins, informing him that he would advise Mr. Calhoun of General Jackson's letter the moment the Secretary of War returned, four, perhaps five days hence.

By making small economies, they had resources enough for five days at O'Neale's.

Those next days were excruciating for Eliza. Now the jovial hospitality William O'Neale showered upon "the general's relations" seemed threatening; Mrs. O'Neale's thin, appraising smiles seemed to account their estates, the fine fare at the dinner table choked her; and worst—and

13

best—she lived in delicious dread, and longing, of suddenly entering a room where Margaret would be. So when her mother primly had told her that Miss O'Neale was not Miss O'Neale at all, but Mrs. Timberlake, having married at a very young age a naval officer who was now at sea, and that therefore her flirtatious attentions to her father's guests, especially to Senator Eaton, were in the most generous view indecorous, Eliza told her mother sharply that they of all people had no business criticizing others. Almost at once she regretted her outburst and apologized (thinking of Margaret now as being hopelessly unreachable) but the damage had been done and her mother was hurt. And in those several days Eliza never once found herself alone with Margaret Timberlake, who slept through the morning, vanished in the afternoon, and was constantly in attendance to her parents' guests in the evening. And when she did take notice of Eliza it was as if nothing had passed between them at all.

Then on Friday, the fourth day, a messenger came to the tavern with a note from the office of Mr. Calhoun informing John Hutchins that the Secretary would be pleased to receive him at four that afternoon. By then however he and his wife and daughter were incapable of distinguishing promising news from continued bad, so he told them that he expected Mr. Calhoun was receiving him only as a perfunctory courtesy to the general.

When he did not return by suppertime Eliza began to fear that despair might have driven him to some dreadful decision.

At seven he appeared in their rooms, smiling at their anxious expressions.

"All is well," he said, taking her mother's hand. And he told them that Secretary Calhoun had that very day appointed him a subagent of the Creek Indians. Within six months, a year at most, they would be free and clear of debt.

"Thank God," said her mother. "Thank God."

"Thank Uncle Jackson too," said Eliza, feeling relief that the letter had achieved its purpose, but feeling too a new

14

dread she could not account for when she tried to imagine what lay before them. She asked where they were to live.

"Georgia—first," her father said. "Perhaps later—it is quite possible—south of Georgia."

To their questioning John Hutchins replied that Secretary Calhoun had hinted at momentous events in the making: At this very moment their kinsman was leading his army into Spanish Florida for the purpose of pursuing the Seminole Indians.

"The Secretary says the Spanish should be finding the climate in Florida unusually warm this spring," John Hutchins said.

"The Indians must too," said Eliza sharply. "Uncle Jackson will see to that."

"Eliza!" said her mother.

She saw her father's sad smile and knew that he and her mother were thinking back to a certain summer evening at the Jacksons' Tennessee plantation, the Hermitage. She could recall every detail. The single downstairs room of the main log house was filled with guests, mostly kin, gathered to celebrate the birthday of the hosts' adopted son, Andrew Jr., just turned six. After a festive supper the boy sat on Aunt Rachel's knee listening wide-eyed to Uncle Jackson, standing by the fireplace, speaking of the treaty he had made with the Creek Indians following his campaign against them. Firelight wavered on the faces of his audience. Parson Blackburn, his fat white fingers laced over his tightly stretched watchchain. Eliza's father and mother. Her cousin Laird Caffrey, just her own age, glancing her way now and then, once catching her eye and smiling the sudden smile that made the girls of the Nashville Female Academy swoon. She had looked away quickly. John and Mary Donelson and next to them in a chair of her own, their nine-year-old titian-haired daughter, Emily Tennessee, listening as gravely as the adults. Next to Emily, sitting very erect, was her seventeen-year-old cousin Andrew Jackson Donelson, called Jack, beloved ward of Uncle Jackson and Aunt Rachel, themselves childless in a house they had filled with children. And on the floor near Rachel and Andrew Jr. another ward, five-year-old Lincoyer, the Creek Indian boy the general had found on the battlefield at Horseshoe Bend near his dead mother and sent home to the Hermitage to be raised as another son. Eliza had wondered then whether the boy understood anything of what his foster father was saying.

By the treaty the United States had gained twenty-three million acres of his people's land in Georgia and Alabama.

"Dismal business," he had said, adding with a nod to Aunt Rachel, "Your humanity would have been touched, my dear."

And as Aunt Rachel shook her bonneted head at the sadness of it, Eliza had suddenly spoken up: "Then why was it done, Uncle?"

In the dead silence that followed she had seen her mother's pained look and felt her father's pride in her. She glanced quickly at Laird Caffrey, gratified by his stare of utter astonishment. And when she met Uncle Jackson's sharp blue gaze he said, "Because it was necessary, girl. At Fort Mims Weatherford's braves had massacred men, women, and children like you without mercy. They had to be taught a lesson."

"But the lands are theirs!" she had said, as a sigh filled the room.

"Land comes to those who work it, settle it, fight for it," the general replied harshly, turning to her father and the others to show Eliza that he was through talking with her. "The time will soon come when all the Indians will be packed off west—for their good as well as ours. By the Eternal, it must be!" He looked down, meeting Lincoyer's eyes, adding, "For their good as well as ours."

"It's God's will," Aunt Rachel said gently.

"Amen," Parson Blackburn echoed.

Near tears Eliza had then seen Laird Caffrey exchange a certain look with Jack Donelson and she promised herself that she would never forgive either of them ever. Delicate

Little Emily Tennessee was watching her in a solemn, judicious way, as if Eliza were a stranger to be pitied.

Since the evening of what she called Eliza's lapse, Mary Hutchins had made a practice of relating to her daughter every atrocity and outrage committed by Indians in the history of her family and that of other western Tennessee families she knew of, and she garnered from the columns of newspapers items describing Indian raids and telling of tortures that could not be described; she came to dote on the subject far in excess of the requirements of Eliza's education, until it had become a fascination, an obsession, and finally—after John Hutchin's bankruptcy—a solace to her. Several months before their arrival in Washington, when the gravity of their situation was first plain, she had read Eliza every word of the massacre of Lieutenant Scott's party on the Apalachicola River in Florida: forty men, women, and children set upon by Seminole Indians and brutally tomahawked, except two men who escaped by jumping into the water and one woman who was taken captive; but worst of all, most incredible, was the fact, stated in the papers, that they had battered the children to death against the sides of the captured boat. Eliza could not understand such cruelty. How could human beings treat infants of their own species so? Were the Seminoles what her mother said, unfeeling animals?

"Human life isn't sacred to them, like it is to us," Mary Hutchins told her.

So, troubled, she went to her father, knowing of his respect for the Cherokees and their respect for him, and asked him about the killing of the children; he explained to her that certain Indians believe that murder must be avenged a man for a man, a woman for a woman, a child for a child if the spirits of their dead are to find peace in the other world, and he said that he had heard of terrible atrocities committed against the Seminoles by white borderers and militiamen, even by the regular army.

17

Eliza asked if they murdered Indian children.

John Hutchins reflected, then said, "I don't know. People do terrible things when they are afraid." And he told her how the hostility between white Americans and Indians had grown on the borderlands; how a century or more ago the Seminoles—the "broken-away people"—had come to northern Florida, separatists from the Creeks of Georgia and Alabama, and had lived in peace in the jungles and hammocks and flat riverlands below the border, untroubled by the Spanish authorities to the east and to the west. But their peaceable life was threatened from the very beginning by their hospitality to runaway blacks from the neighboring slave states, for they were slow to comprehend that the American claimants clung to their property rights with a grasp that was stronger than reason or death, and breaking it was to strike at the heart of their pride. And when they did understand this truth clearly enough to give it voice around their council fires it was too late, John Hutchins said, for they could not yield up the ghosts of the first runaways and they would not yield up their living progeny who were by then—though in some cases their nominal slaves—their allies, councillors, interpreters, and oftentimes kin. So by their heedless policy the Seminoles continued to attract more runaways until they had made themselves the quarry of Georgian slave-hunting parties, militia raiders, and now, when they had retaliated, of the American army, whose power they could not calculate.

Now a match had been set to this powder keg.

Certain British agents and adventurers were going among the Indians offering friendship and arms and inciting them to commit warlike acts against the American settlers. Their names were Colonel Nicholls, Major Woodbine, William Arburthnot, the last a trader with close ties with the Indians, and an adventurer called Ambrister.

"I have heard Uncle speak of such men," Eliza said. "He says that no punishment is too harsh for those who stir up Indians to violence, and I agree with him. He should punish *them*, not the Indians."

18

"Still," said Hutchins, "perhaps it's best that the Seminoles—and the Spanish—be taught a lesson now. Our settlers have the right to peace on their own lands. The raids must stop. Perhaps it's better that the Indians learn of our power now or they'll oblige us to destroy them."

Father and daughter looked at each other without speaking.

"It must be," he added, and the image of her uncle saying "By the Eternal" sprang to her mind. "Mr. Calhoun wishes our policies accomplished with the greatest possible humanity. He was clear on that point." When she did not answer he said, "Great events are preparing, dear, and great opportunities."

That evening, alone in her room before a tall oak-framed mirror, Eliza Hutchins resolved never again in her life to care about anything. It was too lonely, caring. It was a part of childhood that must be left behind. In the real world grown-up people lived in, it was neither pretty nor fashionable; it was ugly, for the secret of fashion and beauty was a carefree spirit. Caring only gave one lines; it spoiled one's chances for love. And in a graceful gesture Eliza swept up her dark hair and held it high in back, like Margaret Timberlake's. She smiled and made her eyes grow wide and bright. Then, for no reason she could ever tell, she wept uncontrollably.

Laird

En route from West Point to
Caffrey Station, Davidson County, Tennessee
June, 1818

ALL the way down the Ohio he had been admiring her, wondering how to make her acquaintance, when by the greatest luck, downstream from Cincinnati, a piece of soot

19

lodged in her eye and he had offered her his handkerchief. She was about his own age—eighteen—pretty, with blond pigtails, freckles. Scandinavian, he guessed. Traveling with her parents.

"Where're you bound?" he had asked her, smiling because she was pretty and because of the way she looked at him, a little surprised and openly pleased, taking in his cadet's uniform, not missing the huge chevrons which meant that he was captain of his class.

"Fort Memphis." Slight accent.

"Settling there?"

"Expect to," she told him. "We've relations there—least we did when they last wrote. Where're you bound for?"

"Home," he said. "Near Nashville."

She sighed, then turned to the railing looking out over the water, the canebrakes, cottony clouds reaching to the horizon. Strange, he thought, he had never been partial to girls with freckles before.

"Wonder if I'll ever be able to say 'home' like that, so proudly," she said.

"Sooner than you think, most likely. Where're you coming from?"

"Pittsburgh last. Before that—" The whistle drowned out her words as another packet, steaming upstream, came into view. She put her hands to her gingham bonnet to shut out the sound; when the answering whistle had died away she said, "General Jackson lives in Nashville."

"East of it," he told her. "Just log buildings on the place now. They figure someday soon—"

"You are acquainted with General Jackson?"

"Ought to be. Our place is two hills over." He did not add that through his Donelson side he was related to the general's wife, Rachel. She might have taken it for bragging.

"I do admire General Jackson very greatly." Somehow she had moved closer and was looking up at him surprisingly unshyly.

"We all surely do."

20

"I'm Astrid Nelson."

"Laird Caffrey," he said. The sudden feeling of apprehension he felt then to be flirting with this complete stranger lately from Pittsburgh was decidedly pleasurable.

"I wonder if I might ask you a very special favor, Mr. Caffrey?" Her voice was gossamer.

"Certainly, Miss Nelson. If it's in my power."

He had to bend close to her lips to hear her reply.

"Could you possibly ask General Jackson for just the smallest lock of his hair?"

When he left the packet with the other Nashville passengers at the landing at the mouth of the Cumberland, he waved to her from the wharf, promising himself that he would obtain and send a lock of Andrew Jackson's hair to her relatives' last address at Fort Memphis if it was the last thing he did on earth. He was never to do so.

The sidewheeler which would ferry the Nashville passengers the 193 winding miles up the Cumberland was half the length of the packet, twice her age, half her speed, in every way a humbler vessel, except in name, which for some time had been *Victory*. Painted on her wheel housings in bold red letters, that name formed a semicircle over a crude profile bust of Andrew Jackson in military uniform and, below, the legend NEW ORLEANS—1815.

As Laird boarded he looked up at the pilothouse, flanked by outsized twin stacks with fancy cinder traps, and there observed the master of the *Victory,* one Bill Hollis, raising a green bottle to his broad red face. Below, at the firebox, the only crew was stoking the fire, a lean, wiry boy who was the riverman's son by a Knoxville woman who some twenty years before had shared his cabin under the bluff at the Nashville landing, before decamping. Little Will he was called, known to Laird as the youngest veteran of General Jackson's New Orleans campaign, singled out by the whole town for his small size and warlike appearance at the victo-

21

ry celebration in Nashville three springs ago, as Laird, then fifteen, looked on, envying the little militiaman, hardly older than he and two heads shorter. Now as Laird came on board, the veteran stopped his work and with a settled grin looked the cadet over from head to toe—until his father yelled down for him to get moving and Little Will spat leisurely into the fire and went back to his stoking.

That afternoon, steaming up the Cumberland under a windless blue summer sky on the final leg of his first homeward journey, Laird daydreamed of the Donelson party some forty years before, of his grandfather and grandmother Caffrey passing these dogwood- and redbud-flecked stands of ancient trees, then concealing Indians; poling, rowing, striving to keep close to the other flatboats and dugouts of Colonel John Donelson's flotilla on their last, harrowing stage of the thousand-mile river journey from Fort Patrick Henry, Virginia, to meet James Robertson's overland party at the cedared bluff which would become Nashville, Tennessee; four months of almost constant harassment by Indians during which a number of the party, including women and children, had been wounded or killed when the steersman ventured too near leafy banks or when boats had grounded or broken up in rapids and the Indians had fallen on them. Some who survived that voyage were alive in Davidson County today, Laird's father among them, and Colonel Donelson's son, Captain John, and daughter, Rachel, who a decade afterward had married a newcomer named Andrew Jackson from Waxhaw Settlement straddling the Carolinas' border. In forty years the survivors and their descendants had largely accomplished the original goal: They had settled the Cumberland Valley, held off and finally subdued the Indians who had hunted there, increased their slave holdings to clear and cultivate the rich land; they had repaired their fortunes handsomely; and in the process they had become a new breed, as different from Virginians as Virginians from Englishmen: Cumberland people, hardened by fighting for what was theirs, bound

22

together by the memory of that first river voyage, that heroic speculation.

Not all the emigrants had fared so well as the Donelsons and the Caffreys, and the Caffreys' kinsman John Hutchins was one. A babe in arms on the journey, he had grown up on the plantation his father had torn from the virgin land, working right along with his few slaves at first, sometimes fighting off Indians, ready to face hell itself to mend their estates. The son remaining a babe in arms figuratively because while his father was killing himself, not at all figuratively, raising the log buildings, worrying about sun, rain, crops, debts, John Hutchins had somehow managed to grow up with his head in the clouds, a taste for books, and no idea of why his father was laying down his life for 400 acres. As a young man he had gone off and lived among the Cherokees for a time, as assistant to a government agent. On his return, it was true, he had worked hard to help his widowed mother keep the plantation and its log houses, but in spite of his late-born efforts the land eventually was sold to pay off the creditors. When he set up in trade in Nashville everyone said at the time that he was born to be a preacher.

And when, that winter, Laird Caffrey had learned of John Hutchins' failure and departure for Washington City with his wife and Eliza, he wrote to his cousin assuring her of his affection no matter what distance separated them, a romantic letter, in retrospect a trifle on the flowery side but heartfelt; for what had before been only a boyhood fancy of some day bringing Eliza to Caffrey Station as his bride had then, with the news of her father's trouble and her departure, suddenly seemed destined to be—one day he would return her to where she belonged. The three years of West Point still ahead seemed like forever—and Little Will Hollis' eye on him reminded him that he was a long way from making his mark in life.

In fact all the time Laird Caffrey had been sitting on a packing case forward of the pilothouse letting these reflections drift among his impressions of the river under the summer sky, Will Hollis, sitting near the firebox, had been studying the cadet with more than passing interest—while his father in the pilothouse, who from his coarse, puffy face and small red eyes would never be suspected of possessing a very keen sense of observation, appeared to be aware of his son's attentiveness to the cadet and indeed increasingly perturbed by it.

That afternoon the *Victory* put in at Birdwell's Landing, and Will Hollis, veteran of Jackson's campaigns, was employed loading on wood from a pile on the dock. His father approached Laird.

"That boy," he said loudly, nodding toward Little Will, who was boarding with about a half cord of split wood balanced on his narrow shoulder, "he's in the military business himself." The speaker waited until the wood rattled into the bin by the firebox, then continued, speaking more to his son than to Laird. "'Pears General Jackson don't make a move without him. How many redskins you getcha', boy?"

Will Hollis looked at his father with a faint smile as he returned down the gangplank to the woodpile.

"Half horse, half alligator," Bill Hollis called after his son, "leastwise when it comes to dreamin'. Couldn't tell it for looking at him, Mr. Caffrey, but that boy's so high and mighty he's like to bust wide open. You just wouldn't credit the notions he's got in his head."

Little Will, returning, passed his father without a glance, dumped his second load of wood by the firebox in a way to show that it was no further concern of his, turned to Laird, then slowly approached him, coming up close, putting on some kind of show, saying nothing, only studying him with the same faint smile and narrowed gaze Laird had felt on him since he boarded the *Victory*.

"Here, mind your place, boy," Bill Hollis called over.

"Got no place, Pa," Little Will said, adding to Laird, "His whole life Pa's looking to own a nigger and all he could do for himself was a bastard."

24

"Shut your mouth!" Bill Hollis warned.

Then Will spoke to Laird in another voice, fervent and quiet, so that his father could not hear. "Laird Caffrey, I'm going to haul out of this river someday, and when I do you're going to see something."

"I surely wish you luck," Laird answered, uneasy about the way the other said his full name and spoke as if there were something between them. Little Will pulled a plug of tobacco from his pocket and bit at it.

"Do you, Laird Caffrey? Do you honest?"

He went back for another load of wood.

During the afternoon of the third day on the Cumberland the *Victory* reached the Nashville landing, which was still decked out with the red, white, and blue bunting that had welcomed General Jackson home from Florida a week before. The Caffrey carriage was waiting at the square on the bluff, and by sundown, just as the bell was calling the hands in from the fields, Laird was home. As the carriage drew up before the columned portico, he saw his father through the parlor window rising from his chair, silhouetted against the window beyond, the violet hills to the west beyond the fields; and suddenly all the impressions of his first year at the Academy and the return journey were part of another world.

Monroe

The President's House, Washington City
July, 1818

THE French gold clock on the mantelpiece was striking five as, in the mirror behind it, the President, standing at his desk, watched the double doors close slowly behind the six men.

The Cabinet meeting was over five hours after it had begun, five sweltering hours for the fourth afternoon.

He turned to the tall windows open on the steamy summer glare and gazed out over the unfinished city—and in his mind the country southward. Florida. Then, mindful of the delicate task still to be done today he sat again at his desk and took up the letter from the man who in those four days had never been long out of their thoughts, and he read it over, arranging in his mind the facts of the extraordinary campaign which had caused him to call a Cabinet meeting in such a season.

It had indeed been a most interesting action, swift, ruthless, provocative; it was pure Jackson; and while his own first response to the startling reports had been that of the majority, upon reflection he had come to see the Florida events in a much larger light. Of course in taking the Spanish strongholds General Jackson had exceeded his orders and weakened his case. The President took a pen and placed a mark at the phrase ". . . the incompetency of an invisible boundary to protect us from the enemy. . . ." That would not do. As long as there was a boundary claimed in Madrid and acknowledged in Washington, that boundary, invisible or not, must be respected by the government if not by General Jackson. Here and elsewhere the general's impetuous language must be improved.

The President then read over the note from the Spanish minister to Secretary Adams. It was short and unequivocal: "In the name of the King, my master, I demand prompt restitution of St. Marks, Pensacola, and all other places wrested by General Jackson from the Crown of Spain. I demand furthermore indemnity for all injuries and losses and the punishment of the general."

And soon undoubtedly there would be outcries from England over the executions of the trader Arburthnot and the adventurer Ambrister. Well, he thought, let England keep her treacherous agents out of the Western Hemisphere. Jackson had done well to make an example of those two for

26

inciting the Seminoles to commit hostile acts against the United States.

But he would have to justify his order.

James Monroe looked around the semicircle of Boulle chairs he had bought in Paris—they were good pieces and he had paid fair prices for them—and he recalled the perspiring faces of the six who had just occupied them. Five of his cabinet had argued that the administration must disavow the seizures of the Spanish posts and the executions of the Englishmen, that Jackson had exceeded his orders, John Calhoun protesting most vehemently, calling for the general's punishment, because the orders were his and his vanity was stung (never before had Monroe sensed the reach of his Secretary of War's pride and ambition). Alone the dour New Englander John Quincy Adams had urged that they back General Jackson, his metallic voice growing harsh and edged with anger as he took them to task for their irresolution. They must stand firm, he had said. The law of nations justified all the general's actions, and he would deal personally with the Spanish minister. What else had they expected from Jackson? Adams had demanded.

What else indeed? In the larger light the general had served his country's deepest interests handsomely. But he had done so on his own responsibility.

The President recalled the precise words of Jackson's pledge: "Let it be signified to me," he had written, "through any channel (say through Mr. Rhea) that the possession of Florida would be desireable and in sixty days it will be accomplished."

The general had asked for a sign and the President had given him a sign, exactly that, nothing more: a verbal message passed to him by Congressman Rhea instructing him to conduct the campaign in Florida as he saw fit, but with never a word spoken or written committing the administration to a course of aggression against Spain. The President had been careful on that score. Fresh pursuit of the hostile Seminoles and their blacks, protection of the harassed bor-

27

derers were the stated objects of the government; so, unquestionably, Jackson, in taking the Spanish posts and executing the Englishmen, had exceeded his orders.

The President now realized that he had always expected he would.

That was what Adams could not understand. Instead— surprisingly because he was a New Englander with no kin or constituency of Southern settlers or slaveholders to satisfy—the Secretary of State had insisted that they stand behind Jackson because he had obeyed the spirit of the orders if not the letter, and all that had been done was justified by necessity and the law of nations. Were they to treat the general as Queen Elizabeth had treated Raleigh: benefit from his services and then destroy him? In the end was not the question for Adams, intelligent and statesmanly though he was, one of conscience? Did he truly not understand the delicate game that was being played?

Great interests were at stake, very great interests; and voices in Congress—Henry Clay's the loudest of all—were crying that the administration was leading the country to war, that the Constitution was set at naught by General Jackson's invasion of foreign soil without Congress' assent; so the administration therefore had to steer its present course with the greatest possible care. But not meanly! Adams was right there, certainly. In the sodden heat of the late afternoon the President thought back to Madrid, years before, also in the full heat of summer, remembering his mission there, when he had been kept waiting in ministry anterooms, treated more like a petitioner than an emissary from a sovereign nation, and his ignominious return empty-handed. He recalled other defeats and he remembered the feeling of always being given impossible tasks to perform. But there had been triumphs too: his negotiations for the purchase of Louisiana with Napoleon himself. He remembered his staunch friends in Virginia, Jefferson and Madison among them. They had always stood by him. And he thought of his greatest hour during the second war with

England, when after humiliating defeats on the northwestern frontier, with Washington City invaded and burned, and with troops who had fought with Wellington massing in Cuba, he had cast his lot and that of his country with the one man he had known might turn the tide: Andrew Jackson.

In a single day at New Orleans the general had revived the country's pride and hopes; and James Monroe, who as Secretary of State and of War had given his full authority and every resource the stricken government could provide, was never again to feel that the United States need defer to any foreign power.

Andrew Jackson.

He knew that the fiery Tennesseean thought him cool and pliant, lacking his own hair-trigger nature. He had listened as Jackson described his vision of a West cleared of the red man from the Appalachians to the Mississippi, a vast domain opened to peaceable settlement and commerce. Florida would be annexed as well, and never again would a foreign nation preside over a jungle sanctuary for fugitive blacks and murderous Indians. If Spain persisted in her refusal to sell or cede Florida, then, said Jackson, let her deliver up the Negroes and keep their Indians off the warpath or he personally would do it for her. This was, he said, the inevitable course of Progress and for that matter the will of the Almighty. The President had listened carefully. He understood. He and the general were of one mind— except that while Jackson imagined that he was goading the President to action the President was learning how to use his general.

For James Monroe, at sixty, had for many years known another, older and wiser man's far greater vision of the Western lands: the philosophical fancy of Thomas Jefferson of unending Western settlement, breeding states, then whole ranges of states spreading under a single sky and a single flag to the Pacific shore. And Monroe recalled (dimly, for that had been long ago) Jefferson's idea that in the course

29

of this flow of settlers westward the Indian would be educated to the white man's law, set to farming lands of his own, learning respect for property rights, and eventually integrated as useful citizens side by side with the whites. This had been his humanitarian plan. But other, more pressing trials facing the young country had prevented Jefferson as President from ever implementing (eventually from even remembering) his project for the Indian—who in any case had proved less amenable than he had thought.

So Monroe had seen Jefferson's plan for the Indian come full circle.

When France, Spain, and England had threatened the frontiers to the north, south, and west, the response, Jefferson saw, was swift American settlement of the outland territories. There was no time to school and integrate savages; their lands were needed for the security of the nation. Those to the east must be induced or compelled to emigrate westward and westward again as white settlers poured in around them.

Their lands must be had by any means.

For the security of the nation.

So let the Indian agents know that their usefulness to the government depended on their securing Indian territory; let them understand that they would be rewarded accordingly. So had Jefferson written to Andrew Jackson in 1803.

Let them know that the methods used in securing large tracts were of no concern to the President, only the end result. So in the same year had he written William Henry Harrison.

And let the government's trading posts induce the Indians to buy more and more goods on credit, so that when the debts exceeded their ability to pay, the government might accept, at its price, their lands in liquidation of the debts. So also had he instructed Harrison in the same year.

Monroe had seen Jefferson's dream for the Indian change from a white cloud driven by winds of State to a looming black thunderhead threatening all red men.

He had responded to the true and deep desire of the nation. To the will of the electorate. And in 1806 he had told Indians visiting Washington, in words adapted to their understanding: "My children, we are strong, we are numerous as the stars in the heavens, and we are all gunmen. Yet we live in peace with all nations; and all nations esteem and honor us because we are peaceable and just. Then let my red children be peaceable and just."

And now Jefferson was an old man living out his years in the grand, odd, decaying house he had built on a breezy hilltop near Charlottesville, a house called Monticello, designed by himself to suit his wishes, and there he lived with his books, his gardens, and his few slaves, receiving visitors. He was deep in debt; an old man in a stained robe tinkering with his clocks, tending his shrubs and flowers, corresponding with the great and learned; the Sage of Monticello, indulged by his creditors out of respect for his past services to his country.

Monroe suspected that no intimation of failure on the account of the Indian disturbed Jefferson's retirement. Had not his life been as rich in great achievement as a man's can be? Beyond a doubt his old dream that the Indian was any more amenable to civilization than ordinary men believed had long ago been driven from his mind by the practical truth that the Indian must go West or face grief and destruction in the East.

James Monroe too had reached the view that national interest and popular will would best be satisfied by the removal of the Indians westward. Even now John Calhoun was at work on such a plan to be submitted to Congress, a humane plan depending on rewards and inducements rather than force. And should it fail there was always Jackson, ready to drive the red man to the setting sun at sword's point.

He had demonstrated his readiness in Florida.

But the Florida adventure was only part, a beginning of a far larger scheme than even Jackson could imagine.

President Monroe intended that under his administration Florida would become part of the United States.

And beyond was a greater goal: to make it known to all European powers, to the whole world, that henceforth the United States intended to dictate the law of nations in the Western Hemisphere.

The hostile Seminoles were serving a useful purpose.

So was General Jackson.

And, knowing Spain, he knew that now the King must be allowed precisely that measure of vindication which would permit his minister to negotiate with honor; so in that steamy room this day, over the protests of Adams, whose voice had grown hoarse urging them to adopt a more aggressive stand, the President and his Cabinet had decided to return two of the three Spanish fortresses—keeping one, as a symbol of the nation's resolve to exercise what power it saw fit on its own continent.

Now it was Monroe's task to inform Andrew Jackson of his decision and at the same time to placate him, being tactful and even flattering—yet leaving no question in the end about who was in the service of whom.

It was dusk when he finished the letter, a breeze stirring the heat in the room. He read it over with satisfaction, then folded it precisely, heated a stick of sealing wax, turning it slowly in the lamp's flame, sealed the letter, then pressed the wax with his onyx signet ring.

Great events were indeed in progress and he would leave his mark on them not like the blood-red drops falling on the paper but like the crest of his ring on the cooling wax; his greater, lasting mark.

His task done, the President started to arrange the papers on his desk and his eye fell on a list of names over Calhoun's signature: new appointments to the War Department's Bureau of Indian Affairs. Yes, he thought, they would need good men to implement the government's new policies toward the red man, honest, intelligent men who could explain the necessity of these policies to the Indians and show them that their own interests lay solely in compliance with them; able, humane men. He noticed a familiar name on the list.

John Hutchins, Esq. Subagent.

But how was it familiar?

Then he remembered: This was the kinsman of the general. Calhoun had taken him. He glanced at the sealed letter, thinking for a moment that he would write a postscript on the outside of it. But then he decided that there would be time enough to mention Mr. Hutchins' appointment in person to General Jackson, letting him know, directly, that he was always delighted to be of service to him.

Eliza

Savannah
September, 1819

HER arm in his, Eliza stood with her father in the crowd massed along the riverfront; the band struck up, the steamer's great paddle wheels began to turn, hawsers slashed the churning water, the steamship's whistle wheezed then stunned the river with a blast that sent white gulls veering from the pilings; on the speakers' stand the mayor waved his tall hat and the crowd cheered, waving hats, arms, handkerchiefs, under a large blue banner proclaiming BON VOYAGE. S.S. SAVANNAH. SAVANNAH–LIVERPOOL.

As the steamer began to move, Eliza dared glance again at the young man who had caught her attention during the mayor's speech. His vantage point from which to view the ceremony was the taffrail of a black-hulled brig at the berth neighboring that just vacated by the Savannah, and though he was indeed young (though not quite so young as Eliza imagined) and casually dressed in a black sea jacket, loose gray ducks, wearing no cap, she judged by his appearance of being altogether at home on the afterdeck that he was master of the vessel whose name and home port carved and whited in the gleaming black stern, dancing with broken light, were *Northern Star,* Bristol, Rhode Island. The youthful mariner (whose face, though rather fuller than an ideal face, was still passably handsome) was watching the departing steamer, puffing at a pipe clamped between his teeth; but what especially struck Eliza about him was that for all his possessive manner he appeared to be entertaining interesting thoughts about the scene they were observing, at least thoughts which she would be curious to know.

"The beginning of a new age," her father declared at her side.

"I do hope so," she said, doubtfully, "but with all that smoke they have barely cleared the pier."

John Hutchins waved his hat. "They will make the crossing. The Atlantic will be conquered by an American steam vessel."

He looked at her then with a distant smile, proud of the steamship, proud of his daughter in the new green dress and bonnet he had bought for this day, her nineteenth birthday. Again the whistle sounded, John Hutchins applauded and called out "Hooray!" and suddenly she was uneasy about his high humor, for she had learned that such moods were often followed by fits of depression.

Indeed the two years since their harrowing arrival at O'Neale's had not been easy ones. Mary Hutchins had never fully recovered her spirits after the shock of their uprooting from the Cumberland; her health had suffered and, as Eliza had lately come to suspect, perhaps even her will to recover. For the first year they had remained in the capital; complications within the War Department had delayed Hutchins' assignment to the Creek Agency and he had been obliged to work at the Indian Bureau performing the duties of a clerk. By careful economy he managed to reduce his Nashville debts, but the new burden of physicians' bills and medicines had delayed their liquidation. Meanwhile Eliza

34

had devoted herself to caring for her mother in their rented back rooms in a large brick house in Georgetown, whose owner, a Revolutionary widow, had taken a liking to Eliza and permitted her to borrow books from her library.

Then, one evening in early February, 1819, John Hutchins had returned to their lodgings in a state of elation. Andrew Jackson's Florida campaign, it seemed, had jogged the Spanish King into ceding all of that territory to the United States—and his kinsman John Hutchins was to be the first agent to the Seminole Indians there. Was it not a splendid turn of events? For there were indeed great opportunities in Florida, he assured them. Until the cession of Florida was concluded they would be residing in Georgia where he would represent the government in negotiations with the divided Creek nation and the Georgia commissioners; he would travel at once, they would join him as soon as he had found a new temporary home for them—and surely, he said, the southern climate would be more beneficial to Mary Hutchins' health than winters in the capital; indeed, there was every reason to believe that the long-awaited move south would be a blessing. And Eliza, sitting at the foot of her mother's bed, saw the invalid's pallid features fill with dismay as her husband destroyed her last hope that somehow they would return to their Cumberland home.

Rather, her worst fears were being realized, for to Mary Hutchins Florida meant banishment into an eerie wilderness inhabited by murderous Indians and fugitives. Leaning forward in his chair, refusing to see what appeared so plainly in his wife's eyes, John Hutchins spoke again of "opportunities" and "prospects" which were already very much on the minds of their kinsman and certain of his friends. As the wind murmured at the windows, the flame on the nightstand between them wavered and Eliza saw her father's earnest eyes harden. She felt a sudden anger against him.

"And what of the Seminoles?" she had asked. "What are their opportunities and prospects now?"

"Don't speak that way," her mother admonished.

And Hutchins had smiled at her as if she were a child, saying, "They will be treated with all possible consideration. Calhoun himself has assured me that this is the government's intention. We shall deal with them with persuasion—for their own interests—but never with force."

After their move to Savannah—as negotiations with Spain dragged on—Hutchins had traveled to the border areas, conferring with the state commissioners and with Andrew Jackson's friend James Gadsden. Contrary to his expectations, his wife's health had declined during the first miasmal summer in Savannah—a circumstance which positively convinced John Hutchins that she would improve rapidly during the fall and winter months.

When the steamer cleared the rows of piers and headed downriver to the open sea, Eliza and her father started to stroll along the riverfront in the direction of their lodging. Just then the mariner in the black jacket was descending the gangplank of the brig; then to Eliza's surprise he nodded to her father and made his way toward them through the crowd. Suddenly the same young man whose thoughts only moments ago had aroused her curiosity was setting her own thoughts tumbling in confusion.

"Who is he?" she asked quickly.

"Extraordinary man," was all her father could reply before the stranger was with them, greeting him.

"Liza, Captain Richard Wolfe, owner and master of the *Northern Star*."

"An honor, Miss Hutchins."

"Mine, sir," Eliza said, wondering at the captain's youth—she guessed him to be still in his twenties—and even more at the strength she felt in his calm gaze.

"Memorable day," John Hutchins remarked, gesturing after the steamer, now far down the river. "Amazing times."

"Indeed," the captain said, relighting his pipe, "if only our progress were not confined to steam engines." He smiled at Eliza, adding, "I'm a sailing man."

Before she could reply—except with a look as direct and appraising as the captain's own—the *Savannah*'s whistle sounded in the distance, scattered cheers went up, a band of boys scrambled to tear down the blue banner. Of one accord John Hutchins, his daughter, and Wolfe started down the riverfront, past the brick warehouses, Hutchins taking up the cause of Progress over Wolfe's quiet dissent and Eliza's uncustomary silence.

Soon they were part of another, harder-looking crowd, and Eliza saw where it was converging.

In the shade of a roof supported by wooden columns an auction of Negroes was under way, the first such spectacle she had ever seen. A powerfully formed young black dressed in cotton cloth the color of soapy water stood on a platform, a woman with a child in her arms looking on as the trader extolled the young Negro's strength, endurance, and skills to a circle of idlers and a few buyers.

"Seven hundred," the trader called as they approached. "Come, gents, do I hear seven hundred?"

Eliza felt a sudden revulsion, less from the scene itself than from the buried memory it stirred: of her father returning to their Cumberland house, then stripped of its furnishings, and telling them that since no buyer could be found in Davidson County for their Sam, Jessie, and their daughter Sally, the bank was obliged to order them sold in New Orleans to satisfy the creditors. How many times had Eliza tried to imagine what had befallen Sally, whom she had grown up with, and her parents. But worst of all was the memory of her father's look when, instinctively and only for an instant, she had glared at him in condemnation; only an instant but long enough to last them both a lifetime, and she wondered if he was remembering that time now, in the merciless sunlight of the curtainless house.

When they came abreast of the auction platform, Captain Wolfe stopped, bade good-bye to Hutchins, turned to Eliza who, having realized that the captain meant to attend the auction, made no effort to hide her feelings, which at that moment were seething; but if the mariner observed her sudden change toward him he showed no sign of it as he parted from them.

As Eliza and her father moved on, she heard Captain Wolfe call out a bid for the Negro.

"So that's his idea of Progress," she said indignantly.

John Hutchins smiled. "How like my daughter to jump at conclusions. I'd no chance to tell you, but Captain Wolfe doesn't trade Negroes into bondage—he buys them into freedom."

And as they strolled into the town he explained that the *Northern Star* had been one of several slavers owned by Wolfe's grandfather, who had amassed a fortune in the trade, and how the grandson, a foe of slavery, now spent his share of that fortune taking aboard free Negroes and purchasing the freedom of others, in Charleston, Savannah, St. Augustine, Mobile, New Orleans, and transporting them to Philadelphia, New York, and Boston, where members of the American Colonization Society saw to their needs until the day when land would be found for a permanent home in their ancestors' continent.

They started along the street leading to the jessamine- and bay-scented square their rooms overlooked.

"It's your future we must be thinking about," John Hutchins declared after a time.

"Not today, please, Father."

"What better time?"

"We talked about my future yesterday. And twice last week."

"But with nothing settled, no—"

"—no plan," Eliza finished for him, smiling.

"See here," Hutchins said, "don't think for a moment that my wish for you to return to the Cumberland has only to do with the question of marriage."

"With Laird Caffrey."

"With someone *like* Laird Caffrey," he corrected her firmly.

38

She took his arm. Since last spring when Rachel Jackson had invited her to stay at the Hermitage her father had decided that she must accept at once, as if there were no good reason for her being with them any longer, for their sake or hers.

"Who would look after Mother when you're away?" she asked.

"She'll soon be recovered. Thank God, she's blessed with a strong constitution."

Eliza thought, *And who will look after you, Father?*

Then she thought of Captain Wolfe, wondering whether he had bought the slave and started him on his way to freedom.

Rachel

Pensacola
July, 1821

EVEN the chair she sat in was rickety in this heathen land. The balcony creaked when she shifted her weight. The town she beheld was Babylon come up before her. The sea itself was menacing. As the morning freshness yielded to sodden heat she sat as still as possible not to perspire, a stout plain woman, whose skin under her lace cap was sunbaked the color of bread crust, looking out over the crowds milling behind the lines of soldiers to the place where she would first see the general.

Near her, on a wicker stool, sat her young mulatto maid, now and then waving a reed fan uselessly through the air.

Rachel knew she would see the general first at the edge of town, riding out in front of his aides, and he would pass toward her between the soldiers, Spanish across the street, American below her, and the silent crowds behind them, and he would surely look up at her as he neared the wisteria-tangled balcony, perhaps wave, and then he would ride into the plaza where the main body of American troops stood in ranks facing the Spanish guards on the steps of Government House. Then there would be a long ceremony before he would be with her again.

"When he come?" the mulatto asked, looking sulkily and now apprehensively down the street.

"Ten," Rachel replied. "Ten sharp." The girl began to fan her slowly but now in earnest.

Rachel Jackson knew the kind of hurt the girl felt; you felt it mostly from the top of the head through to the cheekbones and it stayed and stayed, but she had had no business acting as she had done, flirting with her eyes and her skirts right out in the street with her, turning the heads of the Spanish and the colored and even an Indian in this Godless place. Maybe she should not have told the general, knowing as she did that he could not abide disrespect toward her, that he would kill the man or punish the slave who even appeared to demean her, so much did he care for her; but she had told him. And he had meant it when he swore he would have Mr. Blair (the owner who had kindly lent her) give fifty lashes on her bare back or he would buy her himself and administer them himself. Now Rachel would have to ease him into forgetting the vow. How he did care for her, that man.

"Never see'd so many foreign peoples." The mulatto spoke scornfully, and Rachel knew that the girl was taking the first difficult step to placate her.

"It's Babylon," she said, thinking of Parson Blackburn and what he would think of the abominations she had witnessed on her walks. "We have seen Babylon." And the words of the psalm came back to her: "By the rivers of Babylon there we sat down; yea, we wept when we remembered Zion."

If only Parson Blackburn were to come here, for if ever a place needed Gospel it was Pensacola.

The girl's voice was syrupy when she said, "We see'd Babylon in New Orleans; 'n' in Montpelier."

40

Rachel took up her long-stemmed pipe and packed tobacco into the bowl. "Everywhere, child," she said. "Everywhere south of Nashville."

She lit the pipe and puffed on it, finding little comfort in the smoke, remembering the question of the Prophet: "How shall we sing the Lord's song in a strange land?"

Would he come at ten? There had been so many delays already. Perhaps he was ill. He had looked so pale and peaked when she had seen him last, five days ago at the encampment north of town. *God grant him health,* she prayed.

Never had separation been so painful to Rachel as in this place of noxious beauty, where from her balcony she saw rank garden growth bursting over sun-scored walls of barbarous hues, rose, pale blue, ocher, the palest yellow; where vagrant perfumes mingled with the acrid odors of urine and horse dung left to bake and scatter in the sand, and with the smells of the spiced food her stomach would not take. It was truly Babylon. And beyond the plaza over the roofs the sea standing sparkling blue under the morning sun more than anything else made her long to be back home with the general in Tennessee.

Dear Lord, how she did miss home! The fine new brick house, still scant of furniture, only the few plain pieces and rugs from the old log houses they had lived in so many years, her vast garden laid out and barely planted yet, a thousand things requiring her attention: goslings, chickens, curtains, preserves, and all the people who belonged to the place, especially the children. In the next room her little Andrew Jr., as dear to her and the general as any children of their own could have been (dearer perhaps), lay sleeping feverishly, but at the Hermitage were Jack Donelson, little Lincoyer (now sorely missed by Andrew Jr.); and gentle James Earl, though a grown man still a child, plying his paintbrushes (he knew gardens but not how Rachel wanted the new one to be); and all the others, nephews, nieces, wards, connections, friends. Her elder brother, Captain John Donelson, might look out for the working of the plantation, supervising the harvest and the sale, and his wife,

Mary, would look out for household matters requiring female judgment, the older nieces were handy with the young ones, her own Hannah was a taskmaster over the other house servants, and dear Parson Blackburn would look in and hold service on the Sabbath, but it was not the same with her and the general gone; there were so many who needed her, so many she joyed to look after; and now there would be one more. By end-summer Eliza Hutchins would be coming to stay for a time at the Hermitage and Rachel regretted that she would not be there to meet her in Nashville and take her home. No doubt the girl could look after herself; since she was a child she'd always been the strongest of the three of them (now two with poor Mary gone), independent, fonder of books and horses than the girlish intrigues of the Nashville Female Academy; a proud, lonely thing, with long burnt-chestnut hair and blue eyes that never let you stop knowing who she was; not even shy of speaking up to the general on occasion, and the general admired her for it, as he would, though she puzzled him. Rachel loved this distant niece she hardly knew, in ways perhaps as much as she loved her blood niece Emily Tennessee—because something about Eliza made her remember the girl she herself had once been. . . . Now it was high time she was coming back where she belonged and could marry, start a home, and raise children, the Lord willing. As a young girl her private ways had scared off beaux but never her cousin Laird Caffrey—and he would be home from West Point. . . . Rachel swayed in her creaking chair wishing she were home too.

Then suddenly she thought of John Hutchins, recalling his highborn-looking, expectant face; surely here was a man starred for some other time and place, not the Cumberland, a good man but too high-minded to be practical; God help him now with the Indians in Florida.

As for the general, she had known from the first that he should never have come here. His first instinct had been the right one: When the letter from the President had come asking him to preside over the transfer of Florida and to serve as its first American governor he had at once, with her blessing and encouragement, sent off his refusal. But then the delegation had come clamoring to the Hermitage with messages from John Eaton and other friends in Washington City urging him to accept—for their sakes, they had said, for the nation's sake—and over her protest he had let his letter be retrieved from the post office and wrote a second one accepting. Now he regretted his decision and wished he had listened to her, but he would never go back on his word and would do what he had come here to do no matter what the obstacles.

Rachel fought back the growing fear that some calamity had befallen him.

The nation's sake, indeed! Behind the appointment, she suspected, was Mr. Monroe's skulduggery; she had never trusted the man or been fooled by his buttery Virginia ways. And had not the general already done enough for the nation, more than almost anyone? Circuit judge, Congressman, Indian fighter, and then commanding general at New Orleans, when the United States lay besieged and apparently forsaken by the Lord. (How they had feted him when they had passed through that city of perdition and unholy riches; they had greeted him like a Caesar.) And had he not defeated the hostile Creeks at Horseshoe Bend and personally obtained most of their lands for the United States? And Florida? Who had won Florida for the country? Certainly not Mr. Monroe, with his fancy French furniture.

For the dozenth time she looked down the street to where her husband would come. She closed her eyes and prayed that he was all right, that the delays, the quibbling, the bad faith of the silken-mannered Spanish had not planted a canker in his spirit that had spilled its poison into his body; he had looked so white and poorly. "Dear God," she prayed aloud, "protect him in this treacherous place!"

Down the street four men came rudely elbowing a drunken path through the crowd, singing as they came. Georgians, most likely, thought Rachel; already acting as if they'd taken title to the lands they coveted; it was a good thing that gentlemen like John Eaton and her cousin had already bought sizable tracts before this ruck swarmed in. Or perhaps they were office seekers. Well, let them stand in line; the general had his own people to consider. Oh, she could feel for the Spanish today—some, she saw, watched the carousing Americans with glowering looks while others, even grown men, turned away with moist eyes; it was a hard day for them and Rachel could harbor no hatred for the Spanish; they were born idolatrous and devious; and some did have a sort of dignity; and their black-eyed women, some, were handsome and graceful (though God only knew how fallen from Grace); but she had to allow in fairness that the Spanish soldiers, lined up facing the Tennessee boys, were puny and ridiculous. It was a hard day for the Spanish of Florida but it was a judgment too. For with the girl she had walked these streets and seen the abominations with her own eyes. Whores of every color brazenly walked the dirty sand or lounged along the decaying walls, luring every sort of ruffian and degenerate. Drinking and gaming dens were in full swing all day and all night. She had seen fighting and heard such blasphemy that she wondered that the Lord did not let the waters rise to destroy Pensacola. Worst of all, no one observed the Sabbath. Business went on as on any other day, and there was if anything more drunkenness, more dancing, more gambling, and, she had no doubt, more fornication.

As these thoughts were in her mind she suddenly recognized, in the street, staring up at her, the outlandish black man with the silver necklace.

She had seen him before on one of her walks, and he had looked at her then as he was looking at her now, with an intense, unwavering gaze, as no other colored man had ever looked at her in her life.

The man was tall and his strong, his heavy body was garbed in an open buckskin jacket, an ornamented buckskin skirt, rawhide leggings, moccasins, and across his chest the three silver crescents of his barbaric necklace. Blair's girl—who at night had gone prowling among the blacks of the town—had said he belonged to the Indians that the Spanish let run wild in the jungles to the east—the Seminoles.

He was a fugitive sure, thought Rachel.

God lend John Hutchins strength and judgment to deal firmly and compassionately with the lawless heathens in his charge; she would have rested easier with a military man in his place.

The Negro in Indian dress passed with the crowd under the balcony out of her sight.

If the general had seen the way he had looked at her he would have had the man publicly whipped to within an inch of his life.

Oh, there would be a new day soon in Florida. The great whore Babylon would be destroyed and a New Jerusalem would rise in the ashes. Yes, she felt compassion for the mournful Spanish she saw; but they had had a controversy with the Lord and had fallen away from Him. There would be a new day now and God's work would be done. The general had come down on them like an avenging angel. Now if only Parson Blackburn could follow in his path bringing Gospel to the city and to the wilderness—and to the general.

Rachel looked far out over the heads of the crowd to where the green wild land began. No longer, she thought, would that jungle shelter fugitive blacks and hostile red men. As the sea would give up its dead, and death and hell give up its dead so the jungle would give up the strayed souls and heathens sequestered in it.

And through her whole body Rachel felt a great compassion for the Indian.

It was her humanity the general praised her for.

Silently she prayed that the Seminole would see the Light of God and walk in the city with walls of jasper.

45

Anxiously now, she looked down to the end of the street—just as the clock on Government House began to strike the hour.

"Ten now," said the girl.

"Then he'll be coming now," Rachel declared, adding to herself, "If God wills."

And before the tenth chime a roll of drums at the edge of town announced the arrival of the general and his retinue, while all up and down the street and in the plaza the soldiers came to attention and the crowds pressed close behind them; and Rachel felt great happiness as she first caught sight of him riding toward her between the rows of soldiers.

He was all right after all. His coming at the hour was the answer to her prayer.

As he came Rachel gave thanks to the Lord, again and again, not knowing she was speaking aloud, and tears blinded her as she swayed in the wobbly chair, saying, "Thank You, Lord. Oh, thank You, Lord."

Then, as he approached—handsome John Reid on his right, fiery little Dr. Bronaugh on his left, two other aides flanking him, all looking so fine in their full-dress uniforms and splendid mounts—she stood up and went to the railing (hardly noticing the dark glares of the old Spanish couple in the window opposite), and he saw her and waved up to her, his gaunt face haggard, white, and set as if he were overcoming pain; then he passed beneath the balcony and into the plaza.

Before the steps where, now, the governor stood he dismounted and, to a second roll of drums that set up a great din, he strode up the stairs, offered the governor his hand, then turned to face the crowd. The drums stopped, and there was such silence that Rachel could hear chickens squawking a street away; then the guns of the American warships in the bay began to thunder in salute, as a band in the plaza struck up "The Star-Spangled Banner," and she saw the royal flag of Spain slowly descend, while on a second halyard, the Stars and Stripes rose until it hung alone proudly at the top of the staff. And through her tears Rachel looked beyond to the shimmering sea. It was no longer alien.

The general would soon be with her again.

Eliza

AS she felt the mare's gallop become a dead run she gave the horse its head. She heard Laird Caffrey shout but did not look back, knowing only the red clay rushing beneath her stirrup, the road raining leaves, the strength of the running animal with whom she was one.

"Liza," he called again, "pull up!"

Around the turn she saw the carriage lumbering ahead but still she did not check the mare's run; Laird shouted again, closer now, and they pounded past the carriage, heard the driver shout and glimpsed the startled faces of the tall-hatted men inside and the four shying grays. A quarter mile farther, within sight of the Hermitage gates, he was beside her, reaching across for the reins.

"Let go!" she shouted, trying to break his hold, but he managed to check both their mounts to a rough canter and finally to a halt.

The carriage passed them, the grays' ears perked warily forward, driver and occupants staring at them, then turned into the Hermitage drive.

Eliza caught her breath. "Just what are you doing?"

Wearing the pale blue uniform of a second lieutenant of the Cavalry, sitting his skittery chestnut gelding like the born rider he was, Laird looked consternated. Then his strong face settled into a squint-eyed grin.

"Looked like you were running away."

"Well, I wasn't," she told him. "I was plain running—and just beginning to enjoy myself at that."

"Guess there's no way you'd be run away with." He smiled. And fearing that, the way he meant it, it was true, knowing only that she could not accept her cousin's twice-offered proposal of marriage, not yet if ever, she said, "There might be," and was pleased to see his face go slack with puzzlement.

"Thought Eliza Hutchins always spoke her mind," he said, recovering his grin. Without answering she drew the reins across the mare's neck, spurring her, and all the way to the stables she thought, as she had often done through the summer, that she must not stay on here much longer.

By the box stalls they dismounted and handed their sweating horses to the stableboy to be walked. She started for the main house, but he touched her arm, and when she stopped, took her in his arms and kissed her.

"Eliza, marry me."

"No, Laird."

"Why?"

They walked on toward the house.

"I don't belong here anymore." She was thinking of another, smaller white house twelve miles away where she was born, a house vandalized by the pain of having to pack up and leave it to a bank and strangers. "Maybe I never did."

"I'm not asking you to marry the Cumberland, I'm asking you to marry me."

She smiled. They had reached this point before.

"Anyway," he said, "I'm not half done soldiering. Might be some time before we'd come back here. By then—"

"By then?"

He smiled broadly again, shaking his head. "That's why I love you—nothing gets past you."

"Do you love me?" she asked.

"Just said so, didn't I? Marry me, Liza, and you will belong here because I'll make it so. You'll belong to the Cumberland all right, and one day to Caffrey Station."

"And to you."

"Could all be if you'll let it be."

48

For all her feeling that she must not marry him she knew that he was right. It could all be, so easily. It was in the air that she would be his wife, since spring when Aunt Rachel had stopped talking to her about beaux and about her own first marriage to the jealous man who had made her so miserable. It was time for her to marry, her father and everyone at the Hermitage seemed to be settled on that point; and her husband was to be Laird, who was of good stock and would one day be rich enough, she guessed, in land and slaves; with childbirth, she would shuck off whatever in her made her different from her kin. It could be easy. Andrew Jackson Donelson and his cousin Emily Tennessee Donelson were plighted and both were younger. Indeed, it could take little to become the Cumberland wife that people and the place would season until the untried person in her would hardly be a memory.

"I'll be leaving soon," she said.

"Back there?"

In her mind she saw the river near the agency where black water ran and bright-plumaged birds screeched in the branches of the cypresses and live oaks and down the shadowy tunnel of foliage where the river wound cottonmouths with hell-window eyes nested in cypresses knees and alligators dozed on the banks. She remembered her mother dying and her father waving good-bye when she left with the trader and his family for Pensacola, neither she nor John Hutchins finding much to say.

"Yes."

"Your father ask you back?"

"He wants me back."

"I thought John Hutchins'd be too sensible a man to have his daughter growing up in the jungle. Here I'm offering you to share a whole life together and you favor wild Indians and alligators."

"And my father," she replied sharply.

"I was surely making no reference to him," he answered solemnly.

"It's not all jungle," she continued after a moment, and

49

in a different voice. "There are lakes and savannas, rivers and islands of thick woods they call hammocks." And some deviltry made her add, "It's a sight more beautiful than Tennessee."

"To some eyes maybe," Laird spoke sharply. "Anyway it's no place for a female. Indians aren't cleared out yet."

"I'm not afraid of Indians," she said, remembering the council when she had stood with the Seminole women at a distance from the semicircle of chiefs and braves her father was addressing, remembering the smells of tobacco and wood fire.

"Bet you're not at that," he conceded. Then, as they approached the Hermitage, "A girl who'd stand up to Uncle Jackson. . . ."

She did not answer. Somehow Laird's remark summed up all the reasons she was so ready to leave Davidson County, leave him, at least for now, chancing her fate rather than sealing it by marriage. Since she had lived at the Hermitage the old tale of her "speaking up" to the general had been her badge, the moment in her whole life by which she was known here. At the dinner table Andrew Jackson had sometimes regaled his visitors with that story, how as a mere caution of a girl she had demanded, yes demanded, to know why the Creeks should not be permitted to keep their lands, her uncle always insisting on the honest feeling of the question and the spirit in which she asked it, and she knew that he was looking to give her some cachet in his house, to see her acknowledged for her contribution to its legend, to have her known for a childlike defiance the very story of which told in her presence would testify to its extinguishment. She believed that he meant to extol her as a person of tender feelings, as praiseworthy in her sheltered sex just as he praised Rachel's humanity; so she would smile along with the guests' amusement at the disparity between the poised dark-haired young lady they saw and the scamp her uncle pictured, all the time imagining herself quietly pulling the tablecloth and bringing New Orleans crystal, china, silver, victuals to the floor in a crash that would commemorate her faithfully.

"I meant every word," she told Laird.

"I know you did. That's what made it so fine. Uncle Jackson was fit to be tied. I mean I guess it makes a man sort of wonder, when he's just taken twenty-three million acres of Creek land for the country. I guess it does at that."

She stopped and turned to him. Men descending from a second carriage and going up on the portico noticed them.

"I still mean it."

"Mean what?"

"That it's wrong to take Indian land." She was comfortably mad now, and madder still when her cousin's face went empty-eyed and reasonable.

"People need the lands," he insisted. "They'll get them somehow, sooner or later. Can't stop folks from doing what they're going to do anyway. Might as well get it over quick."

"My father's told me what *folks* are doing," she argued. "They make the Indians sign papers they don't understand. They get them drunk and cheat them!"

Now she saw righteous anger in her cousin's slow smile.

"John Hutchins wouldn't have anything to do with things like that," he reproved her gently.

"He certainly wouldn't!"

"Uncle Jackson's seen Indians up close enough too," Laird said then. "Course he feels different about it. Feels the country's meant for Americans, not for redskins. Sees things in a simple way." He nodded toward the men going into the house. "That's why all these people are here trying to get him elected President."

She walked away from him and went up on the portico and into the hallway where glances told her that she was living up to her reputation as a spitfire. Judge John Overton ventured to approach her, confident of his Virginia-style manners and the position accorded him by his old friendship with the general.

51

"Day, Miss Liza. Been out riding with that fortunate young man, I see."

Seeing Laird watching her from the doorway, she smiled at the judge and said yes, she had been riding, yes, with that fortunate young man, only she didn't guess he was all that fortunate today; and soon others awaiting the general's arrival for Nashville came to pay their respects to his young kinswoman.

After a few minutes, observing that Laird was talking with Emily Donelson, she excused herself and started for the staircase when Senator John Eaton was suddenly before her, contemplating her very collectedly, his head held back as if to escape the large collar that flared up from an impeccable tangle of cravat stuck with a pearl stickpin, contemplating her as if he had been doing nothing else for a quarter of an hour, though in fact the general's younger friend and political adviser had in that time engaged in a dozen very useful conversations, paid several elaborate compliments, and bent his ear to a number of interesting pieces of information—but contemplating her in a way she did not like. He seemed to presume that some bond of understanding existed between them, not necessarily an amicable one, at best a truce. The weak late-afternoon sun, filtering through Aunt Rachel's muslin curtains and the smoke in the noisy west parlor, failed to reveal anything more in his steady brown eyes.

"Dear me, Miss Hutchins," he said. "Your lovely eyes are fairly flashing. I trust all is well?"

"Quite well, thank you, Senator."

"For if any man in this house has offended you—by a single word—"

"None has yet, sir, and though I appreciate your kindness I am accustomed to looking out for myself in this house."

"Admirable," said John Eaton with a smile. "Admirable indeed."

Why did she feel such antipathy toward him? Perhaps it was childish jealousy of him, from the first time she had seen him with Margaret Timberlake; but she also sensed condescension on his part; after all, in his scheme of things he was a wealthy planter, a Senator, she no more than a poor relation of the Jacksons whose father had been rescued from penury by a minor government post—or was it her imagination?

Just then there was a movement toward the entrance and the south windows, the clatter of a carriage rolling up to the door, a cheer went up. As the cheer became an ovation the Senator excused himself and pressed through the throng. From the first landing she watched the general enter amid his exultant following, shaking hands, his gaunt features unsmiling, accepting the acclaim as a sign of the gravity of his responsibilities; then, followed by Eaton, Laird, Overton, Major Lewis, Jack Donelson and others pressing close behind them, the general entered the dining room where toasts would be given. Only then did she realize that Rachel was not downstairs.

Passing her own room, she saw the letter propped on her dresser. Her father's graceful cursive hand. Eagerly she tore it open, reading the first lines for the message she hoped to find; but there was no reply to her last letter to him, their letters had crossed. The pages described a treaty talk with the Seminoles. Then—at the very last page. . . .

She hurried on to Rachel's room.

She found her rocking in her chair by the window, an open Bible in her lap, listening to the toasting and cheering downstairs. When her aunt smiled Eliza saw that she had been crying.

"It's God's will," she sighed as Eliza closed the door behind her. "That's some little comfort, ain't it?"

In the two years Eliza had seen her aunt's delight at returning with the general to the Hermitage wither into dread that he would be called away again to serve the country.

"Yes, Aunt Rachel, it is some comfort," she said, and they talked awhile, then she told her that she had decided to return to Florida and live with her father.

"Ain't our horses good enough for you, child?" asked

Rachel. Then she seemed to remember something and frowned. "What about you and Laird, honey?"

"I'm not meaning to marry Laird, Aunt Rachel. Not now anyway."

Rachel shook her head.

"Guess you know what's best for you. Not always easy. Laird's a fine boy and the Caffreys are good stock, but I guess you know best."

"I'm not sure I do, Aunt Rachel. I'm fond of Laird but I don't feel like the wife he's looking for."

"Your father is a good man," said Rachel then, "but not a lucky man—except in having you around to look after him now—'cause that's the way it's always been, even when you were little." She reached out and took Eliza's hand, and her eyes showed the intensity of her thoughts. "Don't throw your life away, child. Worst thing you can do. Easier than you'd think too. Why, if it wasn't for Uncle Jackson I don't rightly know what I'd have done." Tears rose to her eyes and she smiled. "Don't pay no attention to an old woman, honey. I do believe you're one who knows her mind. Go on, better start getting your things together and we'll find some way to pack you down to New Orleans. Florida! Why, Lord Almighty, I guess each one of us sees things a little different in this world. Go on, now."

Eliza kissed Rachel's cheek and left her rocking, shaking her head, looking past the curtains to the fields, her plain, rough features showing traces of her youthful beauty in the coppery autumn light. When Eliza closed the door behind her the house was filled with John Eaton's voice.

Hutchins to Eliza

The Indian Agency
(Undated)

MY very dear Eliza,

You must forgive me for not writing, but for three weeks I was journeying through Seminole country persuading the chiefs to gather at a place on the coast at Moultrie Creek to hear the "talk" of their Great Father delivered by Mr. Gadsden. It was a melancholy business. More than 400 came, stern and proud in appearance, wearing plumed headdress and silver crescent gorgets, all their finery, but the wretched state of the women with them, emaciated and ill-attired, betrayed the true condition of this blighted and bewildered people. For two seasons now, since the Spanish ceded us the Territory, many villages besides those near us have let their fields grow back to wilderness, for they too say they do not know where they will be at harvest time or who will reap their crops. Two years they have lived in uncertainty, not knowing our intentions toward them, for indeed until Moultrie we have proclaimed none; and the lands around theirs are claimed by settlers who loathe and fear them. So they came, beating drums and uttering yells as they approached us on the first day. After the usual salutations and pipe smoking Mr. Gadsden spoke, telling them that their past misconduct had angered the Great Father and made him send General Jackson to punish them, and that if he chose he could send him again to destroy them. Mr. Gadsden declared then that the Great Father was nevertheless merciful and would forgive his children but that they could no longer range over the entire Territory and must soon stay on lands assigned them, southward and inland. When the chiefs murmured he said, "Will the hatchet stay buried and the musket remain

55

stacked?" Clearly Mr. Gadsden will prove an effective spokesman for the government if he does not drive these desperate people to a suicidal war against us. The Indians replied eloquently but in the end they signed the treaty almost as Mr. Gadsden dictated it, though with what feelings in their hearts one can only guess. By this agreement the Florida Indians have surrendered their claim to the whole of the Territory, agreeing to move to the designated four million acres in the central area, and to prevent the habitation of runaway slaves there.

Now it is my duty to see the terms of the treaty carried out—and to protect the rights of the Indians. It is an uneasy task. Once my "knowledge of the Cherokees" and my sympathy for the red man were assets to the government, now they are liabilities and I am at odds both with the settlers and with the Indians. The worst is that I feel my compassion for them hardening into callousness. There is finally our own welfare to reckon with. And there are great opportunities here.

I miss you sorely, Eliza. My consolation in your absence is the certainty that you are among friends and connections under the hospitable roof of our illustrious kinsman and his incomparable Rachel. I do not speak of L—— C—— for fear of bringing a frown to your brow, nor of rival beaux unknown to me but perhaps too well known to Mr. C. Were you not in such company (I refer to the Jacksons) I would be tempted to invite you back for a visit. Further to test my resolution not to steal you—even for a few months—from what I am confident is a full, rewarding, and pleasurable existence in our Cumberland home, there is a captain of my acquaintance, James Sedley, master of the *Fairwind*, Savannah, sailing from New Orleans mid-November and calling at St. Augustine when I shall be at that place. But I say nothing more of this.

I am, your affectionate father,
John Hutchins

56

Jackson

IN his firm, slightly reedy voice, the general sang the words
of the hymn with expression, but his thoughts drifted from
their meaning. He was content. During the past fortnight
he had dined with rivals, forgiven enemies, attended an
endless round of formal affairs, given and received a score of
toasts, and quite confounded those of the press and the capital's Society who would portray the new Senator from Tennessee and (as his friends insisted) the People's next candidate for the Presidency as an ill-bred warrior chieftain. As
governor of Florida, it was true, his temper had been set
boiling by Spanish bad faith during most of his brief incumbency in that exasperating office—which Rachel had *wisely*
advised him not to accept, and which friends had even hinted might be James Monroe's way of keeping him out of national politics; yet on his return to the Cumberland he had
soon felt at peace again and truly had no ambition in the
world but to spend the rest of his earthly life with Rachel at
the Hermitage surrounded by family, servants, friends, and
visitors.

But soon the call had come, the People's call, faint at
first, then unmistakable—as John Eaton and his other Tennessee friends assured him beyond the shadow of a doubt—
the one summons which, regardless of personal welfare, he
must answer. And having accepted the duty to contend for
the Presidency he had applied himself wholeheartedly to
the campaign, because it was the People's will that he win.

And now to be sitting in a warm parlor with a storm outside on the Lord's Day, resting from his efforts, singing sacred songs in the company of old friends, was happiness indeed. His cares and the pains of his body had been eased by
a single, now-uncustomary whiskey punch and a glass of

claret with supper, and his spirit refreshed by the hymns Margaret Timberlake was playing on the piano—her hands, which this morning at church he had seen folded at lips moving softly in prayer, striking the chords with a force that bespoke the strength of her faith. And as he sang he thought of Rachel at the Hermitage, wishing that she could be one of this congregation of friends now, singing the hymns she loved, hoping that she was not missing him too sorely.

Close to one another in the small parlor they sat in a semicircle around Margaret, her back to them at the piano: her father, singing lustily and well; Major Lewis, who had no musical ear; Margaret's excellent mother, singing, as she did all things, with piety; Captain Richard Call, singing stoutly, though perched on a chair far too fragile for his burly person; and John Eaton, singing a fine clear tenor that blended charmingly with Margaret's soprano. (For an instant the general thought of John Timberlake, now somewhere across the sea in naval service. A handsome, amiable man was Margaret's husband, of aristocratic Virginia blood but unfortunately a perfect fool about money and by some quirk of fate serving his country as a purser.)

Sleet rustled at the windows.

If only Rachel were here. As a young woman she too had been such a natural young creature, full of life and spirit, governed always by unwavering virtue. . . . A wave of anger seized him as he suddenly thought of the anonymous scoundrels who ridiculed her as a coarse frontierswoman— the same vicious breed as those who scorned Margaret because her father kept a public house.

By the Eternal—

Aware of John Eaton's restraining eye on him he *willed* his spirit to be at peace again—and indeed it was at peace when they sang Amen.

That night in the room he shared with Eaton (his younger friend having gone for his usual late stroll) he wrote to Rachel: "In the evening Mrs. Timberlake, the married

58

daughter whose husband belongs to our Navy, plays the piano delightfully, and every Sunday entertains her pious
mother with sacred music. . . . Accept my prayers for your
happiness and believe me your affectionate Husband."

Eliza

SEVENTY-FIVE miles southeast of St. Augustine, near the
northern extremity of that inland territory designated by a
treaty made at Moultrie Creek as the Seminole preserve,
stood a cluster of log structures in a clearing of oak forest,
the Indian agency of eastern Florida. The most prominent
building, its logs barely weathered, was a two-story house
with an appended kitchen; downstairs a living room with a
stone fireplace; across the entranceway the agent's office;
upstairs, his bedroom, and across the stair landing the room
Eliza had occupied during the two years she had lived here.
Across the compound from this building was a one-room
cabin designated in Bureau of Indian Affairs records as the
Indian School, although it actually served as lodging for
passing visitors and a jail as the need arose. At the east of
the compound was a paddock and pigpens; on the west a
combined storehouse and smokehouse and, next to it, the
cabin occupied by the servants, Delia and Abel.

On this morning Eliza awoke at daybreak hearing the
birds in the oaks (the howling of wolves in the night now a
memory); and as she did every day now, since her return
from Tennessee, she felt alert to the natural world in a way
she had not since she was a child. From the north window,
through an opening in the trees, she watched the first rays
of the sun grazing the forest that descended into a vast, gentle valley, then rose to a distant blue ridge that reminded
her of the sea's horizon. To the west the forest thinned and

the valley gave way to rolling hills beyond which were the first Seminole villages. She arose and dressed in her long buckskin riding skirt, boots, a cotton blouse, and buckskin jacket; then combed, wound, and pinned her hair. Below her windows she heard Delia passing, humming in doleful argument with her familiar spirits.

As she served breakfast Delia's silence spoke even more expressively then her doomsday crooning. Even the measured motion of her big body was eloquent. Something was wrong. She wore a dress of the brightest trader's stuff and a calamitous frown.

"Whatever's the matter, Delia?" Eliza asked finally.

"You goin' again."

"I'll be back before nightfall."

"Know what your father say."

"He doesn't forbid me from visiting the villages, Delia."

"He don't like it none, 'specially when he's gone. Course he don't forbid nothin', Mass' Hutchins don't. Now if it was me I'd say, chile, just stay 'way from them Sem'noles."

"And would I obey you, Delia?"

"Likely not. Miss Liza—"

"What is it?"

"I told you we see'd Mr. Solano."

"In one of your dreams? Ben Solano's not supposed to be on the preserve."

"No dream, Miss Liza. Like I said, me and Abel was berryin' down by the spring when we heard the horses and we hid behind the bushes and see'd him ride by on the trail north—with two other white men, one of 'em leadin' a poor fugitive; and the wonder is he didn't cotch us too; he got the power to know we was hidin' there—just plain luck he was thinkin' of somethin' else."

"Delia, if it was Ben Solano he has no supernatural powers and what's more he's not going to take you and Abel. He wouldn't dare."

"Yes'm," said Delia, setting up a great clatter of pots in the fireplace.

"Mr. Solano's an evil man," pursued Eliza when the din

had subsided. "He preys on Indians, steals their Negroes, sells them whiskey, tries to scare them off their lands—but he has no magic powers and you needn't be so afraid of him." For the briefest instant she glanced at the rifle standing in the corner of the room near the door.

"Bullet ain't made'll kill Mr. Solano," Delia responded at once. "Oh, he knows, I tell you—and I ain't the only one who knows he do."

From past conversations Eliza understood that the unnamed confidant was Legba, the West African herald of the spirits who was Delia's informant about the world beyond her ken. And the confidence Delia shared with Legba was that she and Abel were neither freemen nor slaves but legal ghosts in human form. Born on the same Georgia Sea Island plantation, manumitted at the death of their master, who had been kind enough to free them but not enough to send them a hint from the other world of how they were to provide for themselves, they had been driven from place to place, threatened by whites when they sought the company of freedmen who were settled in miserable existences but somehow settled, until they made their way to the southern border near Fort Scott and there acquired a small homestead on the Flint River. But at the end of the first year the Mikasukis burned their cabin and crops and because their papers were destroyed in the fire they were now fair game both for the red and the white hunters. John Hutchins had found them soon afterward, believed their story, and offered to keep them and pay them wages. Now Legba had told Delia that the slave catcher Ben Solano somehow knew all this and Delia believed him because only Legba had the knowledge that made sense of their lives.

"If you're so worried about Ben Solano," said Eliza then, "tell Legba I'll wait to go to the villages until Father comes back."

"He knowed it right along," Delia replied.

John Hutchins returned that evening at sundown weary after almost a week of touring the northern part of the Seminole preserve, the first four days in the company of Commissioner Gadsden and Governor Duval. Now fifty, Eliza's father still had the look of a young man in whom signs of age appeared like a disguise; he was quite tall and still more lean than stout, his hair more brown then gray, though thinner; his features were still sharp and gaunt, though less so; his coarse complexion sun-browned; and his gray eyes were as she had always remembered them: earnest, expectant, at once intelligent yet bewildered, youthful yet haunted. The moment he walked into the house that evening she saw that he was troubled.

"Eliza," he announced as they sat down to supper, "this trip has made up my mind—it's time you were leaving. Letting you come back here was selfish and ill-considered, and it's high time you were home for good."

"Father, this *is* home."

"It's not safe for you—and there can be no more riding alone to the villages."

"We'll talk about that when you're rested," she said, adding, "now tell me about your trip."

John Hutchins shook his head, though in truth he was as ready to close the subject as his daughter, for as she knew very well, he did not really wish her to leave.

"A poor land we're bringing them to," he told her, "and small wonder so many refuse to come. Duval said it was the poorest land he'd seen in Florida, and Gadsden admitted that, even with the few hundred acres of good fields around the old villages it is not likely to sustain them. But when Duval said, 'By God, we must have the government extend the boundary to the north'—and I agreed, Gadsden answered, 'They won't be here for long—no sense in letting them get to like it too well.'"

"James Gadsden's own treaty gives them twenty years!" Eliza exclaimed.

Her father smiled sadly.

"He says that since so few had come, they've not lived up to their end of the bargain. They stay where they are, plant-

62

ing nothing and thieving from the settlers when they get hungry—and giving rascals like Ben Solano open season on them." Eliza decided at once that it was no time to tell her father what Delia and Abel had seen. "To that, Duval said that the Seminoles must be made to move here, but that they must be given more decent land, because as long as he was governor he would not hear of Indians starving in the Territory; and he would not have whites preying on them. Duval is a fair-minded man, Eliza, but as determined as any to make his fame and fortune in Florida—and who can blame him for that?" He paused, looking at her with a challenge to which she did not reply. "As for Gadsden, when it comes to Indians he and Andrew Jackson see eye to eye." He now looked at her searchingly. "In the end, Eliza, Gadsden, and Duval agreed on one thing: That it's my job to see the law's obeyed by red man and white—especially the slave laws—with no help from the army, no weapon but persuasion and promises. It's no kind of work for a man, Eliza!"

"Yes, it is, Father," she responded. "It's exactly that!"

That night lying in bed hearing the wolves and, once, to the west where she would ride the next morning, the roar of a panther, Eliza fell asleep remembering Uncle Jackson as she had once seen him, strolling in Rachel's sunny garden naming the flowers for the Creek boy Lincoyer.

Laird to Eliza

Caffrey Station, Davidson County,
Tennessee, May, 1825

DEAR Eliza,
I received your favor this morning, a clear Tennessee morning full of promise—but there was no prom-

63

ise in your letter. I acknowledge that you have given me little reason to look for any, but I do; my hopes will not admit themselves whipped, but are perhaps as stubborn as your refusals. You say you could never be the sort of wife I expect, that I wish for you to be someone you are not; and in this I stand condemned without trial, for what do I expect that you, Eliza and no other, will be mine, to love and care for and protect "till death do us part"? Is this such a selfish desire? You say I would wish to change you. To this charge I plead guilty, for I would wish—and would strive with all my forces—to bring you a happiness you have never known before for the rest of our lives together.

You cannot imagine the excitement at the Hermitage, indeed throughout the Cumberland, when the general returned from the capital. Anyone would have thought he was coming back as a victorious hero, not as a defeated candidate, and surely his popularity among the People has soared to new heights following the connivery of Mr. Adams and Mr. Clay to deprive them of their choice. No one here doubts that four years hence the general will enjoy a sweet revenge, and that Nashville and the Nation will have their rightful President.

With his return the Hermitage was lively enough, but no sooner had the lord and lady seen their trunks unpacked than frantic female plans were afoot for the reception of Lafayette and his party. All young ladies were for weeks aflutter with preparations for the festivities. On the appointed day the sun shone bright and when the old Hero's boat swung into view a great shout went up, "Welcome, Lafayette, friend of the United States!" Flags waved. Children pranced. Little Will Hollis had his steamboat all decked out with pennants, saluting the arrival with toots of his whistle. And when the honored visitor stepped ashore Uncle Jackson greeted him warmly but with great dignity and escorted him to a carriage, in which, preceded by a mounted color guard led by your correspondent and followed by a great press of citizenry, they rode slowly up to the town between the ragged ranks of our redoubtable militia, by contrast with which we regulars were said to appear very grand and martial.

When will you return? You write that your work on behalf of the Indians of Florida occupies you fully but what of your own life? Is it to be spent ministering to aboriginals, wretched though they may be? There is a home for you here, as my wife, and that you will soon claim it is the devoted wish of your friend

Laird Caffrey

P.S. My good regards to your father.

Hutchins

The Indian Agency
December, 1825

HE sat at the table, bare but for the half-gone whiskey in front of him, watching through the rippled windowpanes the four men riding into the council ground, Ben Solano at their head. Eliza was at the stove, her back to the window, fixing supper. As the men dismounted by the hitching rail Hutchins saw that one was a short hefty man he didn't recognize. The setting sun in the trees behind them, flaming in the undulating glass, cast their long shadows on the ground as the four approached the house at a ceremonious amble that showed the importance of their coming, the more because for three of them it was the second visit that week. They were halfway to the house when John Hutchins spoke.

"New one with them this time."

Eliza set a baking tin on the stove and crossed to the window.

"Ruck!" she said.

"Our people, Liza." He took a swallow from his glass. "I'll hear their grievances. It's what I'm here for."

"You're here to see to the Indians. Not Ben Solano and his slave catchers!"

Eliza glared out the window at the men coming up on the front stoop, then she went to the chair by the unlit fire, took up her knitting and sat, rocking furiously.

"You'd better let me do the talking, Liza. I guess you've noticed these fellows don't take to Tennessee girls having ideas in their heads."

"They'll get used to it," Eliza snapped as the room was filled with the sound of knocking.

"All the same—" warned her father, going to the door.

Ben Solano entered first, removing his straw hat not so much in deference to Eliza or to her sex as to the custom itself. He was about forty, of middle height and lean build, and remarkable about him were the wolf-hide jacket he wore, as it was winter, and his tall melancholy face sided with lank brown hair, the palest of blue eyes that seemed to go dead when they rested on someone as if the face were immobilized by a rush of hatred to the brain. But for the color of his eyes he could have had Indian blood, but whoever told him so had better be ready to defend himself for Ben Solano hated Indians with the passion of a man who has found his own calling in life and it was a matter of honor to him that no man in the Territory hated them more. As John Hutchins had known for a long time, Solano was behind a number of the raids against Seminoles around Silver Springs. Just east of the reservation, he owned a log hut, twenty acres and three slaves, two of which were claimed by Indians as being their stolen property. After him came Jed Cunso, a tall gangly boy-man of thirty with outspreading ears, a permanent leaving of smile, whose pleasure in life it was to ride with Ben Solano. Then Tom Granger, an older man with a round face, thinning reddish hair, care-dulled eyes, who had lost a son, killed in a skirmish with Indians night-raiding his farm a year before. Granger was known to John Hutchins as a fair-minded man worn to desperation by grief and anxiety. The fourth, the stocky man, who held a new straw hat in his hand as Ben Solano motioned him not to hang back, appeared to be in his fifties, also a homesteader by his dress, ill at ease and angry.

Solano introduced him. "This here's Jim McKay."

"Pleased to meet you," said John Hutchins, shaking hands with the man, who did not meet his eyes, and as there was then a silence, broken only by a click of Eliza's knitting needles he asked Ben Solano what had brought them here.

"We got some more business to talk."

"Let's talk it then. Sit down."

Tom Granger and Jim McKay started to sit at the table but Solano motioned with his head to Eliza. Jed Cunso also made no move toward the table.

"I'll stay, Mr. Solano," said Eliza, not looking up.

"My daughter won't trouble us," Hutchins explained, and with a reluctant scraping of chairs the four men sat down as their host set out glasses and poured clear whiskey from a jug, refilling his own glass. This done, he sat with the visitors, three of whom looked to Jim McKay, who hung his head, the muscles of his mouth working nervously. No one spoke.

"Tell him, Ben," McKay said at last.

Solano fixed unblinking eyes on John Hutchins.

"Jim come down here a couple of months ago with his old woman, two kids, and all he had in the world including a nigger and five cows the nigger driv all the way from Carolina. Two nights ago the Indians come to the house he was half done building, set up a whooping, and by the moon made off with three of his cows before the neighbors come and scared 'em off. That's how settled down they are, Hutchins."

"Can't take no loss like that, Mr. Hutchins," said McKay.

John Hutchins looked from one tense face to another considering whether to ask if McKay was dead certain that the thieves were Indians, for some such night raids had turned out to be the work of whites disguised as red men, and he knew that Solano himself had been mixed up in such business; but he also knew that were he to ask the question he would only anger these angry men more and to no purpose. Besides, it most likely was the Seminoles; they were desperate enough.

"All I can do is report the incident to the Superintendent of Indian Affairs," he said.

"Government going to pay me for my stock?" McKay demanded, emboldened.

"I don't know," John Hutchins replied with a cautioning glance at Eliza,who had interrupted her knitting to glare at Cunso. "I don't think so. There's been talk but they haven't in the past."

Ben Solano turned his whiskey glass in the dying light, studying its contents, then looked sharply at John Hutchins.

"What's to keep 'em from coming back tomorrow and then the next day? How do we know they ain't at our places now? Is the government going to sit on its hindquarters till we're all robbed blind and massacred? Why don't they send soldiers and just plain clean 'em out? Why don't they send Jackson and get it done right? I hear you're some kind of kin to the general, Hutchins—only you sure don't act it."

Eliza was unable to keep silent any longer. "The Indians have rights too, Mr. Solano, and we've said that we mean to respect those rights."

"Who's said? We've all heard our fill about Indian rights." Ben Solano addressed her father as if she had not spoken. "Now we want to start hearing a little about *our* rights, and we want somebody in this agency who knows how to look after them. Listen, Hutchins, you better say in that report about Jim's cows that there's a hell of a lot of damned fed-up people in this Territory, white people with some say-so who's going to take matters into their own hands if the government don't do something and do it soon. We want those Indians out—and one way or another we're going to get them out—ourselves if the government ain't going to!"

68

"That's sure right," Jed Cunso echoed.

"Afraid it is, Hutchins," said Tom Granger.

Jim McKay, in possession of speech now, looked across the table at Hutchins with reckless defiance, as if the agent were the single source of all his troubles.

"Learned my lesson, I guess. Going to set my Negro to watching my place all night with a musket, going to tell him to shoot any Indian comes near there dead. That's what I'm going to do. Ain't no other way, I guess."

John Hutchins saw his daughter start forward in her chair to speak again but he stopped her with a gesture.

Tom Granger said, "Wish I'd done that one night a year ago. My son might be alive now."

"I guess that's your business, Mr. McKay," Hutchins remarked. Then, looking directly at Ben Solano, he added, "Only I'd tell that boy of yours to be careful not to make a mistake."

He got up to bring a lamp to the table as Ben Solano grinned at him as if he'd paid him a compliment.

"Why don't you let this bright gal of yours speak up again, Hutchins—since she's here and talking with us and all?"

"I'll speak when I've a mind to, Mr. Solano."

Her father set a lamp on the table and lighted it, sat down again. Solano fixed his wolflike grin on him.

"Maybe you figure what she might have to say'd be real unpleasant to us?"

Anger flared in John Hutchins.

"Let's go, Ben," Tom Granger said. "We said what we come here to say."

"Understand she visits the Indians regularly," Solano continued, getting to his feet as Hutchins rose and faced him over the lamp.

"She takes them food," Hutchins said. "Maybe if more people fed them they might not be out stealing cattle."

"Feed 'em!" Solano exclaimed. "Feed 'em they just get all the more hungrier afterwards. Anybody can tell you that."

"Let's go, Ben," said Tom Granger.

"By the way, Hutchins," Solano said, "hear that runaway of Mrs. Smith's—one everyone's been hunting so long—hear he got away from you."

"Well, you heard wrongly." John Hutchins fought the anger that pulsed in his head and hands. "That black never got here. He escaped from the Indians bringing him in."

"Oh," Solano said with a show of mock enlightenment, "escaped from the Indians, did he? Well now, that's not the first time that's happened, is it? Get's to the place a man wonders how hard those red skins are even trying to bring those niggers of ours in—like they agreed to do in writing." He narrowed his eyes and turned his head slightly toward Eliza, not so as to look at her but just to show whom he might be talking about. "Course that wouldn't matter to some, stealing another man's lawful property and his living."

In the silence that followed, the click of Eliza's knitting needles was loud in the room.

"Now Governor Duval," Solano went on, "he feels strong on that score. Oh, he's tried to treat them Indians as if they was civilized people you could make an honest bargain with and have 'em stick to their written word—or their marks anyway. Well, he sure seen daylight on that score. He never did have no toleration for them that disobeys the slave laws, be they red or white, don't make any difference to the governor, he's strong on the law. Hear the reward for Mrs. Smith's runaway's up to a hundred dollars. Now, that's almost worth a man's while, ain't it, Jed?"

"Sure is, Ben."

"I'd stay off the reservation lands if I were you, Solano," Hutchins warned. "That's the law too."

"Oh, now, you would?" He gestured toward Eliza. "What about her—she somebody special?"

"She goes on government business."

"Sort of your deputy?"

"That's right."

The lamp flickered, and meeting John Hutchins' angry

70

stare with a defiant smile, Ben Solano then turned to Eliza, who stood up and faced him, holding the knitting needles in her hands so tightly her knuckles showed white.

"Case you should ever get tired visiting Indians, Miss Hutchins, come over and visit us folks some time. Won't be much but I'll see to it the missus fixes up something tastier'n you're like to get with them."

Now, thought John Hutchins, *I shall surely have to fight this man. . . .*

Eliza's breath came fast, her eyes shone with fury in the lamplight as she faced Ben Solano. No one spoke. The whinny of a horse at the hitching rail made Hutchins think of the night that was settling on the swamps and hammocks.

"Thank you very much, Mr. Solano," Eliza managed to say at last. "I'd be pleased to accept your kind invitation one day."

"Hope you will," Ben Solano said. "Sure do."

And so with its honor secure the deputation left. Through the doorway Hutchins watched them go toward their horses, ambling as they had come, then mount and ride out into the dusk on the trail east. He closed the door and turned to find Eliza sitting by the fireplace, weeping into her hands. He found a taper, lit it from the lamp, and touched it to the laid fire.

"You did right," he said.

"Our people!"

John Hutchins filled his whiskey glass and sat again at the table.

"They're not all like Ben Solano, thank God; and most of their grievances are real enough."

She dried her tears, then said, "I do believe I could kill him."

"Don't talk like that, Liza," he told her. "You behaved like a lady when he was here. Now get us some supper and no more horsewhipping or killing."

How long could she stay here? he wondered, watching

her go to the stove and put in wood. Before long she should be going somewhere where there were balls and beaux, where she could be a proper young lady and marry when the time came; she was already twenty-five, more than pretty enough and clever, and warm-natured when her temper wasn't up. She should be in a fair-sized city—they had connections in Charleston and New Orleans as well as Nashville. It might so easily have been Washington. A single vote the other way in the House of Representatives and Jackson would be President now. It was not fair to let her stay here, even if she thought she preferred to stay, especially then, for the longer she stayed on, the harder it would be to leave. The troubles in the Territory were only beginning, it was all the more risky for her here because she seemed to have no fear of anything, least of all of the Indians. Alone she would ride to their villages, a sack of cornmeal slung over the back of her saddle and present the corn to the chief for his village, then talk with the women by sign language and the few words she had learned and tend any children who were sick. Often he had cautioned her about nursing the sick because should a child die the medicine men might set the whole village against her, but she did not heed him, nor would she hear any warning that the Seminoles were unpredictable and could in an instant turn hostile. Of course he could understand her feelings toward the Indians because they were very like his own when he had been a younger man trading with the Cherokees, as independent-spirited and confident of himself as she. Now the years had brought him perspective: He could see things from many sides now.

How long would he be here himself? Ben Solano and his friends were not the only settlers eager to see him out of his job. And the War Department was less responsive to his letters than ever. Now the governor had turned against him.

John Hutchins refilled his whiskey glass, aware of his daughter's frown as she set the supper table.

Did Duval suppose him to be a weak man? Rather it was

72

the governor who had gone back on himself and now contended with him because he, John Hutchins, had stood firm.

It was surely Ben Solano's day in Florida.

It was the day of cool speculators like John Eaton, his own cousin John Donelson, Duval himself.

And why should he be left out?

One morning only a month ago he had ridden over miles of savanna east of a place called Dunn's Crescent on the edge of the reservation, seen the lush virgin grassland under a slow-drifting archipelago of pink-tinged clouds that ended in a dawning burst of sun over the sugar plantations along the coast. *A man could own land as far as the dawn,* he had thought then. Someone would make a fortune from that land once the Indians were off it. Why shouldn't it be John Hutchins? A word to his kinsman. . . .

Why did he stay on in a job no one wanted him to do anymore, when there were profitable enterprises of every sort within his reach?

Was it really his concern for the Indians?

Or was it fear of risking failure?

Eliza brought their supper of cornbread and venison and sat across from him, moving the lamp aside. "The evil of that man clings in this room," she said.

"It's no place for you here."

She smiled. "Let's not talk about that, Father."

Hutchins smiled back, then after a moment said, "I'm not too sure how long I'll be here myself. Solano's right about the governor; he's had a change of heart. Now, I was thinking. . . ."

"Then it's all the more important that you stand by the Indians."

The girl has so little understanding of the world, thought her father, *and so little thought to her own advantage. Why, were I to make even a reasonable fortune here she could keep all the horses she wanted and when the time came have a fine trousseau. . . .* And he saw himself returning to Nashville as a respected man of property, standing at the bar at the Nashville Inn with Eaton and Donelson and their friends, with Andrew Jackson, no longer as a poor relation. . . .

The door swung ajar and he went to bolt and bar it, then he was closing the curtains at the window when in a vision he was in another house, with the curtains gone, furniture gone, even the doorknobs gone, everything gone to the creditors. He put his hand to his eyes to stop the memory of the bare room with his wife and daughter standing in the merciless sun.

Eliza half rose as he settled heavily into his chair, then she moved next to him.

"Damn Solano," he said. "Damn the Indians too. Maybe they should be sent west. Maybe it's the best thing for them."

"You know it isn't."

"All I know is three cows were stolen. Mrs. Smith's slave has escaped south. At Micanopy's village the newborn are buried with their dead mothers for lack of the grain we keep from them." He shook his head, seeing his sorrow reflected in his daughter's eyes. "There comes a time," he said then, "when a man has to look to himself—for his family's sake; when he has to look to the future."

She was smiling now, saying, "There comes a time when a man has to sleep." She turned down the wick of the lamp.

Enos

Abraham's Village
Harvest Offering Day

IN the middle of a warm gray afternoon Enos sat on a fallen log not far from the fire-hollowed tree where Abraham had found him hiding six harvests before. Back at the village he

74

heard the women calling out, heard the dogs, and he knew that Abraham and the others had returned from Micanopy's town.

Since the start of the harvest he had known that he had to leave the village soon, that Mrs. Smith would never rest until she had him back and that if he died her dogs would track his spirit, that she had advertised for him offering a reward of a hundred dollars, and that she had shamed men in the legislature telling them that he must be caught because their power was nothing while he was loose, and that they had gone howling to the governor, and the governor had gone in exasperation to the agent, telling him to make the Seminoles give him up as they had given their word to do at Moultrie Creek or give them no money or food and let them starve until they did. He knew these things from Abraham, who had gone today with his yearly corn offering and would speak about him with Micanopy. There was little corn to bring this year, and there was little to speak about except that he must leave.

He had stayed on in the village too long, always hoping that somehow one day he could stay here in safety, but as settlers crowded in around their boundaries until sometimes they heard the voices of the patrollers across the swamps, he had seen the faces of Abraham's people harden against him. Sometimes he slept with the charm woman, but no young girl would have him.

He spat.

Why had Abraham taken him to the village and let him sit with the others around the fire feeling the strength of his words entering him long before he knew their whole sense; why had he let him stay so long when all who had come after him were sent on to the big reservation to the south, if he must leave now?

At every harvest offering time, when the others left for their masters' towns, he had come to the forest because he did not want to stay in the village with the women. For no Indian had taken Enos to be his slave. He had come too late

75

even for that slight protection. None now dared to contend for him against the claimants, the bounty-seekers, the slave catchers, against the law that Mrs. Smith relentlessly invoked until it now seemed that the whole world was bent on his recapture, from the Great Father to those of the village who murmured that he would bring the soldiers down on them. So as on every year when Abraham and the other men took their sacks of corn to their Seminole masters— their only act of servitude—Enos had come to the forest alone and tried to think about what he must do.

But mostly he wrestled with his fear that the white slave catchers would rise up out of the saw grass, come out from behind trees, and take him to be chained and beaten and worked until he would die and then burn for the wrong he had done, until his fear became anger. And now, as Abraham and the others were returning to the village, the terrible idea sprang again into Enos' mind: Perhaps Micanopy and Abraham had agreed to let him be taken so that money and food would be given again. Would Abraham now betray him?

Then through the trees he saw Abraham coming toward him.

For an instant he thought of running; instead he stood up so that Abraham could see him. The old man came alone. He stopped at a little distance. He wore his bead-embroidered hunting shirt and his silver crescent gorgets that were as fine as Micanopy's. His squint eye gave him a fierce appearance. He approached Enos and put his hands on his shoulders.

"You cannot stay here anymore."

Abraham's grip tightened as Enos, though he had expected the words, felt his blood turning to water.

"Micanopy's braves will come for you. They will take you on the trail to the agency, and the agent will learn that you are coming there. But you will go no farther than the river to the east because there you will escape. It is agreed. You will go south to the big reservation where John Caesar and our people can keep you in their hidden villages in the hammocks. It is no longer safe for you here, and Micanopy must let the Americans believe he is trying to do as they bid him."

Abraham dropped his hands from Enos' shoulders.

"Tell John Caesar that you come because Micanopy can no longer keep fugitives here. Tell him he is dispirited now, his people are hungry and depend on the American's money. Tell him the governor no longer tries to protect their rights, that the agent cannot do much to help them, and that Micanopy looks to us, both as the source of his strength and the source of his troubles, and is perplexed. Tell him that we will talk again with the commissioners, many times perhaps, to know their thoughts and to resist them with words; tell him we do not look to them for justice anymore. Only time. Tell him that. And tell him he must stock arms and powder in the safest places.

"The old chiefs cannot be counted on. Micanopy is fat and fearful of war. New chiefs must be found whose will to fight is as strong as our own. Will you remember these things, Enos?"

"I know them," Enos said. "And I will tell John Caesar."

That evening five braves came with war whoops and cries and took Enos and led him to Micanopy's town where he spent the night in a well-guarded hut. The next day a runner started for the agency with the message that Mrs. Smith's runaway had been captured and was being taken there.

John Hutchins sent an express to the governor at once with the news.

Two days later another runner brought word that the fugitive had escaped.

Osceola

HE slashed the water, shattering his reflection. Across the dark river a jay screeched, a blue whir in the jungle. Overhead gravid rain clouds drifted. He found a piece of broken shell on the sand and drew it hard along his forearm. Then along the other arm. When the rain began, the drops blurred the sharp red lines.

An hour before, Osceola had sat with his following of twenty braves at his encampment a mile to the west listening to Holata Mico tell of his journey with the delegation to Washington City and of his meeting with the Secretary of War. When Holata Mico began his talk, Osceola's foremost feeling was pride that the older leader had come to his encampment, as he had come to Micanopy's village and as he would to the other chiefs'; it meant that in the prime of his youth he was already recognized as a leader of influence among his people. The older man had related that the Secretary demanded runaway slaves be returned, promising that the Indians' slaves taken by whites would likewise be returned; he had demanded that young Seminoles be restrained from stealing from the white settlements, all of which was reasonable and expected—but the Secretary had said something else.

He said that the Great Father wished them to move west beyond the Big River and receive lands there in exchange for their own.

When Holata Mico had finished, Osceola's only feeling was rage.

After the council he had seen Holata Mico on his way, then he had come to the river to rid his spirit of the numbing passion. To purify his blood. He welcomed the rain.

78

Once before he had felt such paralyzing anger. He had been a young boy then, traveling south with his mother and grandmother, with his great-uncle Peter McQueen leading two hundred southward from their Creek homeland, becoming, already, with each passing day, "broken-away people"—Seminoles, like generations of Creeks who had done gone south before them—when they had run straight into Andrew Jackson's army. The battle had been sharp. In the din and darkness, with nothing but a hunting bow and arrows, he had played no part in it. And in the chill, bleak morning he had stood with other youths, women, old men, and warriors who had not escaped with his uncle to the south—facing Andrew Jackson.

He had seen white men before (his own father, Powell, by then a dim memory) but never such a man as this, astride a huge gray horse, his face sharp as a tomahawk, holding Americans and Indians alike in absolute sway. The anger Osceola felt then was deepened by the fascination he felt in the presence of this destroyer of his people.

Then a miracle. Inspired by some vein of mother wit in her Scots or Creek ancestry, his grandmother, Ann Coppinger, had planted herself before General Jackson and begun a great harangue ending with the preposterous suggestion that if he let them go her brother McQueen would then give himself up with all his warriors. The Indians listened in amazement—but they were dumbfounded when Andrew Jackson appeared to take Ann Coppinger's proposal seriously, at least to accept it as a way out of a dilemma, for she had read in his restless glances eastward his desire to continue his march, unencumbered by prisoners, to his real quarry.

So Jackson had let them go free and marched on to Bowlegs' village, where he was to find the Indians gone, but where he captured Lieutenant Armbrister, the English agent who had warned them to flee.

Osceola remembered the reunion with McQueen and his braves near Tampa Bay, the festive reception by the Seminoles among whom they would settle; he remembered the joys of the new lands and the new life. He soon became renowned as an athlete; few could approach him in speed and endurance as a runner, in skill as a hunter, or in excellence in the ball games the young men played as if they were real battles; and he soon attracted the notice of the older men, the envious respect of the young; he was a great favorite of women; at the yearly Green Corn Dance he was the medicine man's helper, brewing and serving the "black drink" to the warrior celebrants as he sang the ritual song, thus receiving his adult name, Asiyohola, the Black Drink Singer.

After the treaty of Moultrie Creek, Micanopy, hereditary chief of chiefs, already obese and tortoise-brained, had employed Osceola in curbing the young men who hunted and sometimes raided beyond the set boundaries; nor was it against his inclination to act as a policeman then; he had been at Moultrie and judged the power of the Americans. In time they had employed him as a guide during the running of survey lines, and he had visited their forts and encampments, had wrestled with them, hunted with them, and made friends among them. Indeed, he possessed a keen desire to know this race whose blood he shared, and he studied them, but always with such conflicting feelings of wariness and attraction that they remained a mystery to him. "You are Muskogee," his mother had told him—and Muskogee he was by Indian reckoning, which accounted ancestry through the female line; with his white blood had come no heritage but a sense of apartness.

In the years following the Moultrie treaty, white settlers had crowded in along the northern boundary of the central reservation, the agency was established near Silver Springs, Fort King built nearby, Fort Brooke established at Tampa Bay, and the Seminoles had found that the land left to them was mostly poor, had not planted, and had soon fallen on hard times; and no Seminole had seen more warning signs of the storm gathering over his adoptive land than Osceola—yet he had failed to read those signs.

80

He had seen good and bad on both sides. He had believed in the ultimate good faith of the Great Father.

He had faith that the agent, Hutchins, would speak for Seminole rights and that his voice would be heeded.

He had visited many distant villages of his nation, smoked and talked with many chiefs; he had visited many American forts and encampments; he had journeyed far—and he had seen nothing. In the pride of his youth, in the joy of his being, the gathering storm had appeared as a passing cloud.

Until today. . . .

Again he drew the shell hard along his forearms; two more red-welling lines below the first.

He had gone among the Americans undaunted and had shown them that Seminoles were men too, with skills the white man could never match—then he had returned among his brothers proud of his reputation among the Americans.

Doubly proud, doubly deceived.

Now the rain had stopped and the sun broke through under the clouds to the west, flaring in the branches of the live oaks. Beyond the trees, an incalculable distance, beyond the Big River, was the dread, alien wilderness his people knew as the land where each night the sun dies, the cold, forbidding region from which there could be no return to their own lands where the sun was miraculously reborn each morning in the east. The Great Spirit had entrusted these lands to them, not to possess with papers and boundaries, but to use in their lifetimes, then to depart leaving them unspoiled for their descendants to use in their time. The Great Spirit did not wish them to leave. Yet some of the old chiefs, Micanopy among them, had grown bewildered by the incessant American demands and no longer could distinguish the voice of the Great Spirit from the voice of the Great Father.

Osceola raised his bleeding arms to the sun.

He would be deceived no longer.

Eliza

SHE tethered her horse where the trail opened into the village. In the warm clear morning the Indians were silent and no one came to meet her. Nearby a band of children watched her, then scurried away. From the council house at the center of the village she heard male voices rising in dispute; blankets hanging in the huts between prevented her from seeing who was with the chief. She waited; though Micanopy must have learned by then of her presence in his village, he sent no brave to take the sack of corn from her saddle and lay it at his feet.

Eliza started around the periphery of reed houses toward the great oak at the other side of the village where the women always gathered in the morning; from there she would be able to see Micanopy and whoever was with him and they would see her. In the shade of the oak women sat before stones pounding briar roots into flour; others squatted; some held infants who like their mothers appeared famished; all the women shunned her when she approached; her greeting met with only a grumble. She faced the council house and saw the four men on the raised floor watching her; Micanopy, Abraham, Jumper, and a young brave who was a visitor to the village.

She started toward the men, who sat cross-legged, so still that slashes of sun through the unmended thatch seemed painted on them. Passing the hut of the Prophet she glimpsed him rolling on the ground while a gaunt-bellied three-legged dog lapped at the soothsayer's drunken vomit. She walked on to the threshold of the council house.

Micanopy, chief of chiefs, sat in the center of the floor like a sullen potbellied idol. Abraham, upon her approach, whispered into his ear. On the chief's other side sat the man

82

the whites called Jumper, Micanopy's sharp-boned, fierce-eyed sense bearer, renowned for his eloquence in councils, now angry and avoiding looking at Eliza. The visitor sat a little apart watching her with a smile on his lips.

He wore a red turban with three plumes, one white and two black, arcing to his shoulder; a brown hunting shirt sashed at the waist over red leggings, moccasins; three silver crescents at his neck. His black hair flowed at the sides and over his high forehead; his skin was lighter than Micanopy's or Jumper's; his eyes black and commanding; his smile soft and insinuating, as if he was amazed by his own powers.

She turned again to Micanopy.

"I bring corn, and I bring greetings to Micanopy from my father."

Abraham interpreted; Micanopy acknowledged her words with a dour nod, issued an order; Abraham called to a brave in a nearby hut and the brave set off at a run toward Eliza's horse—but suddenly the visitor was on his feet with a shrill cry and the brave stopped dead in his tracks. The visitor spoke to Micanopy, insistently; the chief grunted assent and nodded to Abraham, who called the brave back; and the visitor came slowly down the steps of the council house, stopped before Eliza, then he turned and ran between the huts, returning a moment later with the sack, which he flung down on the threshold of the council house so that some of the corn spilled out before Micanopy. By then many villagers had gathered to witness the visitor's actions. Suddenly he threw himself prostrate at her feet. Leaping up, he ran up the steps, seized a handful of corn, ran down again, and flung the grains near her feet. Then, as the villagers looked on in silence, he stood before the council house, raised scarred arms toward the sun, and spoke in a strong, curiously shrill voice. When he had spoken he slowly lowered his arms and faced Eliza. Over Jumper's protest Abraham interpreted his words.

"He says that if the land that is left to us will not feed us then we will sleep in it forever, for we shall never leave it."

Jumper, irate, was exhorting Micanopy.

"Who is he who says this?" Eliza asked, not turning from the visitor.

"He is Osceola."

"Then tell Osceola that I come as a friend, that the small gift is a friend's gift."

The visitor, only a little taller than she, heard Abraham's interpretation, then replied.

"He says he scorns your kindness because it makes his people weak. He likes your threats and broken promises because they unite the Seminoles and make them strong."

Abraham's voice was resonant with his own feeling, his one good eye fiery; the villagers murmured. Despite herself Eliza felt a stirring of fear as she remembered her father's warnings, but angrily she suppressed the fear, meeting Osceola's smiling gaze, saying, "Tell him that I do not act for my people but for myself."

"We know this" Abraham said at once.

Just then Jumper, beside himself because Osceola had so usurped his prerogatives, leaped up and came to the threshold of the council house and addressed Eliza, holding before him an arrow in his two hands. When he finished speaking he broke the arrow and threw the tip with its sharpened steel head to the ground. Then, as Abraham interpreted, he handed her the fledged shaft.

"This arrow is straight and true. Micanopy is a great king. He sends the arrow to your father the agent so that he will speak straight and true to the Great Father about those he calls his red children and will tell him to honor his treaties with them and force them to make no more that are bad. He says he breaks off the head of the arrow because Micanopy sends it in peace."

Osceola's eyes were on her as she said, "I will take it to him."

In his hut the Prophet dragged himself to his feet, kicked

84

wildly at the three-legged dog, missing altogether, kicked a green rum bottle skating out of the hut, came unsteadily after it, and made a great remonstrance to the sky.

Osceola laughed aloud, and the villagers around him smiled. Jumper was more furious than ever. Abraham too smiled and when his master saw that his slave was smiling he permitted himself a regal softening of his fat lips.

As she was to remember it, five or six shots came first almost in a volley, then the woods to the east beyond the oak were full of yelping; the women were running toward the council house; Micanopy had risen to his feet; everywhere braves were shouting, running; Osceola had rushed inside, past Micanopy, seized a musket, at the threshhold uttered a shrill war cry, then ran toward the oak, past the Prophet muttering his magic at the yelping woods, past the approaching women, and other braves followed Osceola, Jumper among them exhorting others. The sky was full of screeching. Then Eliza heard bullets thudding into the hanging blankets as the second volley came and she saw the running woman fall and an infant slide from her arms through the dust. She heard nearer, answering shots as she ran to the woman.

She was about her own age; she lay with her head to the side, blood welling in pulses at her temple, flowing down across her eyes and spreading in the black pool of her hair. Then Eliza heard the receding shouts of the raiders, looked up, and saw horsemen galloping away on the trail to the east, Ben Solano rearmost spurring his dappled gray. The infant was crying. She picked it up and held it to her as the Prophet approached and spoke in a loud voice over the body of the woman, his eyes red, his broad pocked face menacing. Soon Osceola and Jumper returned with the other braves and all the village gathered around the dead woman before the council house. Osceola faced the Prophet and spoke to him scornfully but, after a moment's uncertainty, the Prophet stamped his feet and set up a loud chant over the body. In the council house, where Jumper had gone, Micanopy was conferring with Abraham, then Abraham came down the steps to Eliza and said, "Micanopy says you must leave the village, it is not safe for you now." At once Osceola came up to her and, as Micanopy and Jumper watched warily from the council house, he took the infant from her and holding it high over his head spoke in a strong shrill voice. Again the villagers murmured.

"He says, 'Who will feed this child now?'" Abraham told her.

Osceola made a gesture of dashing the infant to the ground.

"Tell him they are bad men!" Eliza said, fighting back tears.

Abraham interpreted and Osceola spoke again to the whole village, and Abraham, receiving a sign from Micanopy, said, "He says, 'Who will punish these bad men? We have bad men. They are punished by our custom. Who punishes yours? Does the governor anymore? Do the soldiers? Does the agent?' Now it is Micanopy's wish that you go."

An old woman took the infant from Osceola.

Eliza looked again at the dead woman. Near the spreading blood lay the broken arrow where she had dropped it.

"You must take it," Abraham told her.

She picked up the arrow and Abraham walked with her, making a path through the silent villagers, toward the place where her horse was tied. The birds were alighting in the trees again. Eliza walked in tears, feeling an anguish keener than she had ever known tearing at once at her breast and brain: horror at the sudden murder, murderous rage against Ben Solano and his riders—and shame for what Abraham had made her see in herself.

She had mounted when she saw Osceola approaching between the huts. When he reached her he looked up at her; he held out his closed fist, then opened his hand and spoke.

"He says it is a gift so that you will remember Osceola," Abraham told her.

In his palm was the broken-off steel-headed tip of the arrow.

He handed it to her.

Eliza to Laird

DEAR Laird,

I received your last favor after returning from a trip with Father to the main reservation south of here, so you must pardon me for the delay of this reply.

Yes, I remember I once said I was running away and now you write that it is time I stopped running and came home. Believe me, part of me longs for the care and the home you promise—but another part of me calls out warnings. You write of Emily marrying Andrew, of Phila Ann marrying Stokley, you write of Uncle Jackson and Aunt Rachel, of Uncle John and Aunt Mary and all the connections and friends; I see their faces, I remember the Hermitage—and Caffrey Station, the streets of Nashville, the river, forests, fields, everything—and the more keenly I remember the more I feel like a stranger there. Can you understand?

How could you when I cannot myself?

It would be heartless indeed to find fault with words that are tenderly meant, but the truth is that I read your letters over and over for some sign that you have a true acquaintance with me, some clue to my feelings, my thoughts—or even a token that you suspect I might have any worthy of serious attention. Why do I dread—while longing for!—your care and protection? Would it be heartless to suspect that the

87

portrait of me you carry in your mind is not me at all but an imaginary person, very much prettier, very much nicer, someone "spirited" but in reality meltingly tractable, a Bride ready to be molded by kindly admonition into a perfect Cumberland wife? Do you know that I wear buckskin skirts here? While not fashionable, they are excellent for walking through saw grass. I wear my hair shorter and tied up very primly (the other day I found a strand that was quite gray). The Florida sun has browned my face and arms. If anything, in two years, my disposition is more stubborn than ever; and I care no less about what matters to me; more, in fact. Of course my eyes are quite good. If you remember, they are blue.

When I wrote you of my efforts to help Father look out for the Seminoles' welfare you replied either with silence or else terse signs of your disbelief that I could have any useful place here, so far from ballrooms and "hearths"; so I refrained from burdening you with what is my constant care. I suppressed my "notions" in deference to your practical wisdom, for I could see you throwing up your hands when you read my first letters, exclaiming, "Dear Heaven, the poor addled girl!" And would it not be thus in everything if we were man and wife? Or do you suppose that one day I would sigh and come around to your way of seeing the world, even though I might relapse now and then into that interesting idiocy which is the ornament of my "superior" sex? I do not think so.

It may be heartless to respond so coolly to your renewed proposal—and it is very true that part of me longs to say yes—but it would be far worse to deceive you, or myself.

A few weeks ago I was visiting an Indian village nearby when it was attacked by men bent on terrorizing the villagers so that they would abandon their huts and fields. During the shooting at the village a young woman was killed. She fell near me. I saw her draw her dying breath.

I mean to stay here as long as there is any chance that I can be of any help to these people. I don't know what I can do. Every day I see the tragedy of what is happening here. I see it most clearly in my father's face. I shall stay with him for now.

You said once, when I "spoke up" for the Indians, that perhaps not the unkindest thing would be for Uncle Jackson to sweep with an army through their lands and drive them west without the pretense of councils or treaties. I was angry then; but the more I see here the more I believe that there may be some merit in your proposal—not so much on the Seminoles' account (for who can say which form of oppression is kinder—swift or slow?) as on our own. It would at least express the honest will of the Territory, the South, the West, and of the government, I suppose of the majority of the people. This present conquest by hypocrisy and outwaiting is ruinous to our race too.

I wish I could believe that we are on the side of God, as everyone here seems to do. I do not feel that we are, though we are certainly stronger and more numerous. I ask myself what in our nature makes us act with such mindless cruelty toward weaker human beings, as if there were no higher judgment of us.

You see I still "speak up." I am afraid that I shall never learn better.

Once I wept over your letters, so intensely did I long to become by some magic the person you thought you were writing—how I envied her!—but your words only told me how much a stranger I am to the world to which you would bring me. I am not cold or heartless, as you once said. Just now I feel alone and very sad. I also feel powers in me that I must not deny. That you will know me a little better from this letter, taking nothing in it as being discreditable to you, for nothing is so meant, is the earnest wish of your friend

                                        Eliza Hutchins

Hutchins

Government House, Tallahassee
February, 1827

THE rain had stopped and the late-morning sun was burning through the bluish mist in the courtyard outside the governor's windows. In the small anteroom John Hutchins sat as he had done for twenty minutes looking from a map of the Territory on the opposite wall to the desk where a sallow lynx-eyed young man sat scratching line after line, and from the secretary to the heavy square-carved doors behind which a drone of men's voices rose and fell, and from the doors to the open window where the mist drifted among the rain-bowed palms catching the first glints of sun, and from the open window back to the map.

Why had the governor summoned him to Tallahassee?

For it was a summons, though the letter was couched as an invitation, with the information that James Gadsden also would welcome his presence in the capital. Once, when the men's voices had flared up, he had distinguished the Commissioner's and the governor's, but who the others were he did not know. Twenty minutes became twenty-five. The secretary's pen scratched on—then stopped, and the young man looked up at the agent blankly, as if he were searching for a thought.

"My appointment was at eleven," Hutchins told him.

"I know it very well, sir," said the secretary. "The governor will see you when he's ready to. I have told him you're here."

And the youth had gone back to his writing. No doubt he had copied the governor's letters to him and noted their change of tone over the past months, and no doubt he knew very well what reception to mete out according to his estimate of the governor's disposition toward a visitor. Anger stirred in John Hutchins. To have ridden all the way to Tal-

90

lahassee to be received insolently by this prince of nobodies! He thought of leaving with a message to the governor that he might be found at his inn, awaiting Duval's better convenience; but on reflection he decided to wait several minutes longer, resolving instead to press the question of annuities with even more insistence than he had rehearsed on the long ride from the agency.

John Hutchins was now all too aware of the ironies of his situation. The government paid him an annual salary of $1,500 and travel expenses to tell it what it no longer wished to hear; the Seminoles no longer looked to him as their spokesman before the government but only as a bearer of more and more evil tidings, and the settlers execrated him both as a tool of the government and a friend of the Indians. Nevertheless, as the absurdity of his job became more apparent, Hutchins was spurred to perform it more resolutely, more conscientiously, now looking less to his instructions than to his instincts for guidance; yet always with the notion in the back of his mind that some day from his experience would accrue to him a share of the rewards which the Territory promised to all. Once, he recalled, Governor Duval too had ridden through Florida with a clear purpose, a sudden smile, a thousand good stories, and a mighty temper, seeking by face-to-face encounters to keep settlers and Seminoles from one another's throats, to see the law obeyed and treaties observed, and this one-time Kentucky hunter, judge, plantation owner had, as John Hutchins had done, sent letter after letter to the Superintendent, to Secretary Calhoun (and even once to President Monroe) acquainting them with the dire state of affairs in Florida. Had they submitted, Duval would have taken Commissioner, Secretary, President, and half of Congress on his back from Pensacola to St. Augustine to show them what they were dealing with; instead he had persuaded them to receive the chief Neamathla and other headmen in Washington, having let the Secretary understand that the savages would learn from the awesome size and magnifi-

91

cence of our public buildings (and from the Secretary's stern presence) the futility of resisting us—not adding that he and the President and Congressmen too might profit by looking once into the eyes of those their policies were destroying. Duval was not a fool. Neither was he a saint. He was a man willing enough to venture career, popularity, and even fortune to conduct the affairs of the Territory with respect for the rights of all free men and aboriginals according to the law as long as, but only as long as, that course seemed destined to succeed; for Governor Duval was not a man to play against the odds.

So the day had come when he saw that he had done his best to treat the Indians fairly, more indeed than any other man, and he resolved that nothing further could be done. Despite all his efforts on their behalf the Seminoles persisted in harboring fugitives, showing their contempt for American law and for the governor himself; so no wonder he had finally become exasperated and had listened to his cronies and constituents: As long as the Indians harbored black slaves, the obligation (had there ever been one) to treat them with Christian mercy and American law was suspended; they were hostiles until the day they could show that the last fugitive had been returned. And if they could not be educated to live according to the law of the land then they would surely be sent off the land, as a merciful alternative to their extermination.

Thus did Governor Duval, like other Territorials, justify by their possession of one race the dispossession of another, and adjust his mind to the drift of things. He had seen daylight. The noxious mother trouble in the Territory was the phantom blacks and ghost blacks whose liberty threatened the very integrity of law, robbed sleep, endangered property, and was by any standard intolerable to free men.

Suddenly the double doors opened and the governor came forward to greet the agent.

He was a short heavy-built man with broad rumpled fea-

92

tures, large humorously quizzical eyes, a balding head of phrenological interest, reddish tufts of hair flying over his ears; and dressed not at all for fashion but only for function: in shirtsleeves secured at his muscular upper arms by black garters, a brown waistcoat more unbuttoned than not, dun trousers stuffed into military boots; and he seemed to exaggerate his general homeliness by an aggressive gait and florid gestures, which added to the authority of his presence.

"Ah, Hutchins," he said seizing the agent's hand and clapping his arm simultaneously. "How are you? Come in!" He pressed his visitor to enter his office very much as if the agent had arrived late rather than been kept waiting almost a half hour.

Three men stood as they entered the carpeted room furnished with a massive desk and oaken chairs; two of these visitors he recognized at once; the third, nearest him, was a tall, exceedingly stout man attired in the blue field-uniform of a colonel of the regular army, about forty, with a candid rosy-gray face, graying wavy hair, and the most melancholy eyes Hutchins had ever seen. The sad officer offered his hand.

"Duncan Clinch, sir."

"What? Not acquainted?" Duval said.

"I've not had the pleasure. John Hutchins, sir."

The agent shook hands with the colonel and then with the two others in the room. The first: Captain James Gadsden, Special Commissioner of Indian Affairs, a powerful, choleric man also about forty, whose driven, impatient eyes reflected his dislike of the agent, being himself a man certain of his importance in the world, a loyal friend of General Jackson, his valor proved in battle at the general's side, his worth attested by the trust the general placed in him, a man whose vision (inspired by the general's) of a South cleared of the red man and prospering in peace was the touchstone of his career, a man who had every reason to hold in some contempt the general's once bankrupt kinsman with his concern for the Indian and his modest salary. John Hutchins remembered his face at Moultrie, twisted as he shouted in blind fury at the recalcitrant Indians; the Commissioner was not a graceful man when crossed. The second: a sour, imperious, elegant individual wearing the neatest of black coats, immaculate linen, his black curled hair pommaded, his head held back as if to assist him in seeing properly through his heavy-lidded eyes, his mouth fixed in a downcast line, his fine-featured face settled in a mask of scorn; born José Hernandez in the royal colony of Florida, having anglicized his first name when in 1821 the colony became a territory of the United States; becoming an American who never forgot that his blood was Castilian, and who by virtue of his wealth in land and slave holdings in eastern Florida and his skill in expressing the interests of the established planters (including Governor Duval and Colonel Clinch) became a general in the militia, a member of the Territorial legislature, and for some time a delegate in Washington, where he had quickly learned what could and what could not be expected from the central government; a Spaniard in his proud, dour alliance with God, an American in his ranging acquisitiveness and practical sense, Joseph Hernandez brought to the problem of the Seminole presence in Florida a clarity of vision altogether free of sentimentality; for years he had urged that they be removed. John Hutchins suspected, without proof, that it was Hernandez Ben Solano meant when he boasted that he had powerful friends.

The visitors took their places again before the desk, the agent sitting next to Hernandez; Colonel Clinch sat with a leg crossed, his mournful eyes fixed on his polished boot; Gadsden drummed his fingers on the arm of his chair, apparently vexed by the interruption and impatient to resume the business of the meeting. Governor Duval settled his homely gaze on the agent and asked for news of the Indians.

"I'm afraid it's worse than ever, Governor," John Hutchins replied. "They are bitter over attacks by whites, theft of their Negroes, and now are angered by the cuts in their rations and annuities. They say they are hungry and that some are starving. The chiefs insist that the money be paid as promised."

"Insist?" James Gadsden folded his arms and stared at the agent. "Have they been returning the fugitives as they were told, sir?"

"They brought in one—"

"One!" Gadsden exclaimed. "Why, there are scores, perhaps hundreds at liberty!"

"—and that one escaped."

"Another!" James Gadsden said. "From the agency?"

"Yes."

"How was it permitted to happen, sir?"

Hutchins forced himself to answer evenly.

"It was not 'permitted' to happen, sir. It happened. As you know very well, what serves as our jail was built as a schoolhouse. However in this case I have reason to think that the Negro was abducted by white men for their own profit. I have a good idea who might be behind it."

"Have you evidence?" Joseph Hernandez asked in a sharp precise voice, slightly accented.

"No, sir. It was night. And the only witness was an Indian."

The planter's eyes narrowed. He smiled slightly as he spoke. "Are you quite certain, Mr. Hutchins, that the escape could not have been the result of perhaps a lack of vigilance on the part of your own household?"

"Quite sure, sir. If you are referring to my daughter, she is not in the habit of breaking the law."

Hernandez shrugged and returned to the inspection of his sleeve.

"Gentlemen," Duval said, "the escape of the fugitive is regrettable, but it has happened, it is water over the dam; what matters now is that the chiefs must see they've got to turn over the blacks that don't belong to them. All of them—and all new runaways. They have not been doing

95

this. Now they must do it. That's why their annuities have been suspended, Hutchins, so that they will comply with the law."

Could he sincerely mean what he was saying? John Hutchins wondered, observing how Duval's face had aged in the single year since he had last seen him.

"Sir, you know the near impossibility of settling contested claims to Negro property with Indians. Every day they understand a little better that our law only works against them; and still, to appease us, the chiefs have made genuine efforts to bring in recent runaways—at least they did until we cut their food and money."

"Yes," the governor said. "I do know the difficulties of your position."

Hutchins smiled. "Until not so very long ago, Governor, I believe that my position was our position."

For a moment anger flared in Duval's eyes, then abruptly he leaned back in his chair and laughed.

"He's dead right, gentlemen," he said. "Why, I guess no man, including Mr. Hutchins here, has ridden more miles and knocked more heads together trying to keep the peace in this territory than I have. I have always done my damndest to deal fairly with the red man. I have rattled the beggar's cup for him. I've ventured my political future, my fortune, I have lost treasured friends in this endeavor. I have often offended Mr. Hernandez. I've decried the self-righteous hypocrisy of the federal government. And I have done these things with one thought in mind: that my efforts would be of some avail, some practical accomplishment. Now I believe that they have not been. The Seminoles have shown that they will not submit to our authority, and the people of the Territory have shown that they will not put up with lawless redskins in their midst. Sooner or later the Indians in Florida must yield to us, and I have lately come to the conclusion, Mr. Hutchins, that the Lord intends it to be sooner." His questioning eyes searched the agent's face for a moment before he continued. "Mr. Hutchins will ask

96

us: Is a course of deliberate bald-faced coercion right or wrong? I do not know the answer to that. I only know that the time has come when we are obliged to look after the lives and hopes of our own people and leave the higher justice of the situation in the hands of One who we may presume knows a hell of a lot more about it than any of us sitting here. The question, Mr. Hutchins, is no longer what is to be done, but how and when it's going to get done. At this moment Washington is working up its courage to put into law a policy that's pretty much settled on down here. I refer to the total removal of the southeastern Indian nations—including the Seminoles—west of the Mississippi."

"Should have been done years ago," Gadsden said, "when Calhoun first proposed it."

"Maybe," the governor conceded, "but Mr. Hutchins is going to ask us is it right or wrong? And I would have to allow that my own conscience is not perfectly at peace in the matter. But, Hutchins, I ask you very plainly: If we are wrong, do we then march into the sea to evade the burden of blame? Do we pack our families back to the farmed-out scrublands from which many of us came? Are we to manumit our Negroes and abandon our farms and plantations to the four winds? No, sir. What must be must be, and no man—red or white—can fight very long against what must be without destroying himself." The governor looked at the agent for a long moment, then abruptly turned to Colonel Clinch. "Colonel, would you inform our friend of the new military dispositions."

As if by prearrangement, the tall officer settled his doleful eyes on the agent and spoke in a formal manner.

"Sir, I have the honor to inform you that Major General Jacob Jones has ordered me to the command of all army forces in Florida. My responsibility will be to strengthen our military presence in the troubled areas until such time as the policy to which the governor refers can be put in effect. In the meantime we intend to keep the peace by a concerted show of force. Within two months, sir, a fort will be constructed on the promontory near your agency. This post will serve as a warning to the Indians that they cannot hope to defy us, much less meet us in open combat; and it should aid you, sir, in the execution of your duties. As for the recovery of the fugitives, I have no authority to order troops into Indian lands to apprehend them, but I venture that the Seminoles will be a little more disposed to comply with our demands when they will hear our bugles and drills from morning to night and see our colors flying over the fort."

"I hope so, Colonel," John Hutchins replied, "but I fear that it will take more than flags and bugles."

"I have no doubt," replied James Gadsden for the colonel, "that the mere show of our power will indeed have the desired effect—provided, Mr. Hutchins, that your diplomacy is as determined as the colonel's military presence. The days of the Indians in Florida are indeed numbered. John Quincy Adams and the present Congress hesitate—but there will be no delay when General Jackson is President, depend on it!"

John Hutchins remembered his kinsman's sharp face and steely blue eyes, thinking, *How many men like James Gadsden fashion themselves after him?* and he said aloud, "In the meantime, sir, they are still among us, still hungry and still dangerous. We have an obligation to feed them, as much for our settlers' sake as for theirs."

"I wonder," said Gadsden. "Who knows whether it's better to coddle now and root them out violently later, or to let them know, in ways they will understand, that it is in their own best interest to leave? I say the latter."

The Commissioner's restless eyes met the agent's for a moment.

"Are those official instructions, Commissioner?"

"They are suggestions, sir, intended for your benefit. Your instructions from Washington remain the same: See to it that the fugitives are returned and that they reach St. Augustine."

"I'll continue to do what I can."

Joseph Hernandez shrugged. "Mr. Hutchins," he said evenly, "the people of this Territory, including those I have the honor to represent, have reached the end of their patience, and the people through their representatives have now enabled themselves to act more effectively in defense of their lives and property. If you please, Governor, permit Mr. Hutchins to read the new legislation, so that perhaps he will understand the present mood of the settlers as well as he does that of the Seminoles."

Frowning, the governor took up a sheet of paper before him.

"Now understand me, Hernandez," he said as he handed it to John Hutchins. "I admire you gentlemen's forceful and manly lawmaking. However there's a certain language here that might be taken for a license to go out Indian hunting and raising hell; and as long as I'm governor I don't intend to preside over any wholesale Indian massacre, law or no law; any man who takes unreasonable advantage of the provisions here will have me to reckon with. "

And as the governor spoke, Hutchins read the new law. It provided that when a white citizen of the Territory found an Indian off the reservation he was empowered to seize him and take him to the nearest judge or justice of the peace, who could impose a punishment of thirty-nine lashes and take away the Indian's gun. There were other provisions of a similar sort.

"What do you say to that, Hutchins?" Duval asked when the agent handed him back the paper.

"Sir, I say that if the people act according to the letter of this law then there will be war in Florida."

"War?" Gadsden demanded in surprise, looking to Colonel Clinch.

The morose officer addressed the agent, speaking in a careful professional manner.

"War, sir, is an extended military conflict fought between the organized land and sea forces of civilized powers. That

99

is war. And all our experience has shown that the Indian, acting unaided on his own account, is by nature incapable of summoning the skills and effort necessary to mount and sustain a large-scale military campaign. At most we fight skirmishes against Indians; actions not wars. You will recall perhaps that when General Jackson led his troops here a decade ago he met what little resistance he did only because the Indians had been partially trained and supplied by British agents, two of whom he captured and, quite properly, executed. Today, to our knowledge, sir, there are no British agents aiding either Indians or Negroes, so we are confident that the Seminoles cannot muster and train an effective force. They cannot produce an effective leader. They lack the will—not the courage perhaps but the will—I draw the distinction; for they are not foolhardy and will see plainly that they can never hope to contend against us in the field."

Having spoken, the officer returned his gaze to his boot.

"Colonel," John Hutchins said, "with all due respect I don't believe the Indians would exactly choose to fight in the field."

"A figure of speech, of course, sir," Clinch responded, bristling. "A military term."

"Are you teaching us our profession, Mr. Hutchins?" Gadsden demanded with an unsteady smile. "I remind you, sir, that it is your duty to make the Indians aware of our strength and their weakness—not the reverse. And if you take our advice you will no longer conduct your agency as a charitable institution."

Governor Duval looked at the agent thoughtfully, his large searching eyes reading the distress in his face. "We are none of us insensible, Hutchins. We have the means to destroy an alien hostile force within our territory, yet we forbear to employ it. Even when our people are killed, their homes looted, we forbear. But now we want them out. And the government will indeed get them out—as humanely as circumstances allow. The point is, Hutchins, your job is not what it once was. Things have changed, and they will change more."

Colonel Clinch looked up. "Within two months, sir, the new fort will be built. The Indians will see for themselves that they must comply."

"We're trying to help you do your work, sir," the governor added, "not hinder you."

"Then I presume I'm to tell the chiefs there'll be no more annuities?"

Gadsden tapped his fingers on the arm of his chair and frowned, as if the question were out of place, then replied, "Tell them that when they've given up our Negroes that then the Great Father will watch over the needs of his red children. Tell them in the meantime to cultivate their fields."

"They have no more fields," Hutchins said. "Those few left to them are grown over. You see, they have some sense of their fate too, sir."

"Better that they do," Gadsden replied.

For a moment the five men sat in silence. Then Governor Duval asked if there was any further business which required the agent's presence.

There was none.

Hutchins

Hotel Jackson, Tallahassee
February, 1827

JOHN Hutchins left the anteroom, shown out by the arch stare of the secretary, descended temporary plank steps where stonecutters were setting the permanent staircase, and went out into the street where other black workmen were fitting curbstones. From all the hillsides of the new city echoed the sounds of hammering and sawing and the cling of stonecutters' chisels. On a knoll to the southwest, in full afternoon sun flooding through the closing clouds, Governor Duval's mansion stood nearly completed, a temple of prosperity. On both sides of the gullied street leading down to his hotel small frame houses and shops were going up on lots which last year went for eighty dollars and this year could not be had for two hundred, before the street was cobbled. On every mud-caked corner men of various qualities were talking land prices, titles, water rights, easements; while others hurried along the streets and diggings intent on deals that would not wait another hour, another five minutes. It was a paradise for speculators and sign-painters.

By the time he reached his hotel the clouds had closed and it had begun to rain lightly; he went inside, passing knots of men talking in the lobby; and he reflected that he felt no more community with the governor and his friends or these men of business than he had with the stonecutters. The voices, like the din of building, seemed part of his crushing depression.

This was a malady for which he knew the cure.

In his room, standing before the washstand mirror, he gratefully let the raw whiskey sear his throat. His long face looked drawn and somewhat puffy under the eyes; it had been a more handsome face a few years ago; yet somehow age had invaded it too stealthily to dislodge the open innocence which remained, unwanted, unneeded. He lay down on the bed to rest.

Some time later he awakened to a knocking at the door, having no idea at first where he was. It was raining fairly hard outside and there were no sounds of construction. He opened the door and a hotel boy handed him a folded sheet of notepaper and left quickly.

His mind clearing, John Hutchins read the bold, cursive hand.

Dear Sir:
I should be honored if you would join me in the barroom.

Joseph Hernandez

" 'Honored,' " the agent reflected, recalling the Spaniard's appearance of cold hostility in the governor's office. "Were it truly an affair of honor he would have sent a second." But despite this wry thought John Hutchins felt a certain exhilaration as he left the room.

General Hernandez was a powerful man in Florida.

Observing him seated at a corner table in the crowded barroom facing a rough-looking young man, the agent made his way over to him. With a wave of his cigar the Spaniard dismissed the young man and invited the agent to take his place, whereupon a waiter appeared instantly.

"Whiskey," Hutchins ordered, then met the planter's gaze. A silver cigar case snapped open. "Much obliged," he said, accepting a Havana and the flame of a match.

"I leave tomorrow morning with General Clinch," began Hernandez without further formality. "We will go to his plantation. Call will be with us. Then I will return to St. Augustine to resume my command. This is the only time I have and I want to talk to you."

"I also return tomorrow, sir."

"I suppose you know, Mr. Hutchins," the other said, as if the agent had not spoken, "that a good many people in this Territory would like to see you out of your job." His eyes narrowed against a curl of smoke.

John Hutchins smiled. "I know it very well, sir. In fact I believe that you are one of them."

"I am, sir," Hernandez agreed with a thin smile, "except that unlike most—in addition to other considerations—I'd like to see you out of that job for your own good."

"It's my living, General."

"They pay you fifteen hundred a year, I believe."

"Plus a pittance for travel."

"An honest living, at least."

"I try to keep it that way."

"They told me you were a difficult man."

"A fair description."

"Man of principle. Honest. Owing no one anything."

"Worse, I'm afraid."

"A sentimentalist. A humanitarian."

"Regrettably."

"Strange," the Spaniard said.

The observation floated in the slowly drifting smoke between them. John Hutchins drained his drink and asked what the other found strange.

"I saw someone different in the governor's office," Hernandez replied. He gestured again to the waiter that their glasses should be filled. Then, leaning forward across the table, he said intently, "I saw a man consumed by ambition."

John Hutchins leaned back in his chair and laughed.

"An exact description, General," he said, "of every man in this room!"

"True, Mr. Hutchins. But they're doing something about it. Taking risks. Betting on the future of this Territory. Betting on themselves. And they're not very understanding about anyone who'd want to upset the odds."

A brimming whiskey was set before the agent; he studied it a moment, then looked up at Joseph Hernandez.

"Perhaps you're right, General. But how is it that such an ambitious man would content himself with a modest government job?"

"Is he content?"

"Let's say that he feels a duty."

"Surely not to the government? To John Quincy Adams?" General Hernandez sighted down at a cuspidor placed conveniently near his boot and spat.

"Perhaps to those the government has made promises it is not keeping."

The planter looked into his own glass, swirled it, and drank. Then, turning his cigar between his fingers, he studied John Hutchins a long moment before he spoke again.

"I understand from Colonel Gadsden," he said at last, "that you were once in business for yourself in Nashville."

"I was," Hutchins answered firmly. "And no doubt he also told you how it ended. Bankruptcy, sir. Credit was my downfall. Credit and notes. Since then, though, I have managed to pay back all my creditors to the last penny. I owe no one."

"A hard experience, but a useful one, no doubt. A man would not be likely to make the same mistakes twice."

"You would think so, sir," said the agent expansively, beginning to feel the warmth of the whiskey, "but one always has one's nature to contend with. Though I do have plans—you were dead right there, sir. Ambitions." Hernandez smiled in a manner that now appeared to the agent as being remarkably amiable. "You saw it across the room."

"You'll need capital," the planter offered.

"Always the difficulty."

"Needn't be."

The planter summoned the waiter and requested that writing materials be brought.

"Look around you, sir," he said. "How many of these people have cash? You don't need capital, you need friends, Mr. Hutchins. You have not made friends in the Territory, you have made enemies!"

"Unavoidably, I suppose, considering my line of work," he said, thinking, *It does no harm to hear the advice of such a man.*

A pen, ink, and paper were set before Hernandez.

"And what would your future be if you lost that job?"

Just then the whiskey hit the agent's brain in a dizzying flood; and he was seized by the image of the barren sun-flooded house in Nashville.

"A great mystery, the future," John Hutchins muttered, trying unsuccessfully to stop his brain from reeling.

"Some of us do not believe it should be left entirely to chance." Hernandez held up the pen. "Here is your future, sir." Threat appeared in his eyes and faded as quickly as it had come. "Now let us get down to business. I make an early start tomorrow. Tell me of these plans of yours and we'll see what can be set up with my bank in St. Augustine." When Hutchins did not reply, General Hernandez tapped the end of the pen briskly on the table. "Come, sir, a moment ago you had plans but no capital: now you have a chance of capital and no plans. Think, sir, for your daughter's good if not of your own."

Eliza, thought John Hutchins. *I could make everything up to her. Everything I couldn't make up to my poor Mary.* He took up the pen, his brain clearing, telling the planter, "Yes, I do have plans." And then, feeling that he was committing some unpardonable betrayal, yet carried on by his thought of Eliza, he told Hernandez of the savanna where when the Indians were off it a man could own land as far as the morning; and even as he spoke he imagined his daughter riding over a vast estate, in velvet and a plumed hat, like a Sir Walter Scott heroine.

"Someday will be too late," the other said, matter-of-factly. "Of course you must write the President about it at once. Eaton and Call and others, myself included, owe Andrew Jackson much for seeing the Territory opened for acquisition. You as a kinsman are in an excellent situation, sir. Excellent. All you need is capital, and now you shall have that. Shall we say four thousand for a beginning? That should cover an option; then there'll be more needed later, for final purchase, improvements, seed, and Negroes. The first money is the hardest to come by, I assure you. Shall we say five?"

"I have no collateral," Hutchins protested, astonished that the other was treating his old dream as a perfectly realizable proposition, indeed was already writing on the sheet of paper. "Why are you doing this, sir?"

"For nine percent a year," the planter replied without looking up, "the interest to be deferred until maturity—say, four years? That is friendship, sir. A man can establish himself handsomely in four years."

"I must consider—"

106

"No time, sir. I'm offering you a chance to get started, to prove your worth; but it won't wait. I leave early tomorrow morning for Clinch's plantation." He finished writing and turned the paper toward Hutchins. "Besides, we need men of good reputation in this territory, men of your own kind to provide its growth and leadership. Leave the agency to Major Phagan. You are meant for better things, sir."

"I see," Hutchins said, reading over the paper, then looking up. "Major Phagan is the right man for the agency?"

"He'll do as well as the next, it matters little," Hernandez responded with great impatience, pulling out his pocket watch and glancing at it. "Now, come, sir."

John Hutchins took up the pen.

"The Seminoles signed away their future with a pen like this."

Now Hernandez showed the anger that John Hutchins had felt was growing on him.

"Sign, sir—for I'll think my trust in you has been misplaced—that your concern for the savages conceals a cowardly fear of looking out for yourself! But of course it's your affair."

In that moment John Hutchins saw clearly what course he must take.

"I appreciate your kindness, General," he said, "but I still have a job to do."

He placed the pen on the table.

Hernandez's face hardened. His eyes went cold, then blazed.

"Then, by God, sir, we shall see to it that you do it to the letter. You will see every Negro fugitive in the territory rounded up and delivered to St. Augustine if you have to drive them there yourself! You will see to it, on your personal charge, that not a single Indian sets foot off the reservation, as the law says. And any crimes—"

John Hutchins rose, making a great effort to hold himself steady and very nearly succeeding.

"As I said this afternoon, General Hernandez, so long as I

am in the government's pay I take my orders from the government."

Joseph Hernandez looked up at the agent, his face a mask again.

"Then we shall see exactly how long that will be. Good day, sir."

"Good day, General."

Only the next morning, upon awakening in his room to the new day's clatter of hammers and the shouts of hostlers below his window, and upon going to the window in time to see General Hernandez, immaculate in black frock coat and the whitest of linen, follow General Clinch and James Gadsden into a waiting carriage, did John Hutchins consider that he might have made a catastrophic mistake.

Eliza

The Indian Agency
April, 1827

ALL day now the woods above the agency echoed with the crash of felled trees and the ring of steel splitting wood, until at sundown the bugle called the soldiers to muster in the half-finished palisade on the wooded knoll; then Eliza could sometimes hear their voices, sometimes their singing, until the last bugle at night. Now, lying awake, she listened to the calls of the night birds, an animal marauding at the refuse pit. In her gauzy window-curtain shone moonlight and the dull glow of lamplight from the blacksmith's shop across the compound where the subagent Major Phagan now lived, with the young interpreter Steven Richards.

She closed her eyes and tried to sleep, to let her thoughts join with the sounds of the night, but through the thin wall she heard her father tossing and murmuring in the next room and she could not sleep.

She wondered if it was true, as he had said, that her staying on here with him was a pretext not to lead her own life. Two evenings ago he had declared she should marry, raise a family, and live with her own people by which he meant Donelsons and Caffreys, Tennessee gentry; saying that she needn't stay on his account, much as he wanted her here; that if he sounded harsh it was only because he loved her and couldn't abide seeing her spoil her life. It was the kind of deception John Hutchins depended on now, and it made her feel abysmally lonely, for he did love her, she believed, but his telling her he did not need her was for his assurance not hers.

Ever since his return from Tallahassee she had observed changes in him. Sometimes he appeared more determined than ever to shoulder the burden of the Seminoles. He would plead their cause in letter after letter to the department. Before the delegations of angered Territorials who came to the agency he would defend them with reckless defiance. She was proud of him for the stand he took but fearful too. For another John Hutchins had emerged since Tallahassee, a schemer of grandiose projects, who spoke of plantations to the east, of fortunes to be made, and when Eliza questioned him he only assured her that one day he would "make everything up to her." In these moods he would sometimes mention Joseph Hernandez, hinting that there existed between them a secret understanding relating to certain business. And it was in such a mood that he had made the accusation that she was using him as an excuse not to live her own life.

She herself sometimes imagined that a life awaited her in Tennessee like a coat hanging in a closet, which she had only to put on and be Miss Eliza Hutchins of Davidson County again. Her father encouraged this notion, speaking of old ties and kin as if nothing had changed in her or them in the years she had been away. The bundles of letters from Laird, from West Point and then one army post after another, were addressed to that immutable Nashville Eliza. On the other hand certain letters from a Lieutenant Lancaster in St. Augustine were addressed only to a radiance in Lieutenant Lancaster's brain; while the rare letters from relations and friends urging her to hurry home were more polite and perfunctory each year, Emily Donelson wrote her as if the Cumberland were the center of the world and she were beyond the farthest gates. Only Aunt Rachel wrote to her as she was. But lately Eliza had come to feel that the other Nashville girl had never existed, that the bonds her father spoke of were illusory or dead, and that in her twenty-seventh year her real life had not yet begun but was only hinted in certain talisman moments of the time already gone and could elude her forever. Rarely now did Eliza let her thoughts linger on her encounter with Margaret Timberlake, on the look that passed between them and the feelings which the beautiful girl had stirred in her; for what did it say of her life that that moment of meeting, so long ago, and which Mrs. Timberlake would doubtless have forgotten, remained one of her most precious recollections in all her twenty-seven years? Perhaps, she thought, her father was right after all. Perhaps her only life lay back in Tennessee, the life Laird promised. Perhaps it only seemed that another existence awaited her elsewhere.

Twice she had gone with John Hutchins to St. Augustine, where father and daughter stayed as guests of a Colonel Savage in a comfortable house on the post, overlooking a walled garden on one side and on the other the straits and the waterfront and, to the north, the stone bastions of the fort that guarded the city from invasion by sea. There she had made the acquaintance of the colonel's daughter Malvina, three years younger than she, engaged to be married and incredibly wise about life, clothes, and men. On the second visit Malvina had lent her a blue velvet gown for the dance to be given by the commandant and officers on the four-pointed-star roof of the fort; and on a balmy night Eliza had danced to fiddles under colored lanterns and garlands, with Lieutenant Lancaster, an Ensign Haight, Lieutenant Bradley, and others whose names on the tasseled dance card in her drawer meant nothing now. Malvina, she remembered, had been proud of her that night. And for a long time Eliza had dreamed of being part of the gay, worldly life of St. Augustine but she was never there long enough to be anyone but a stranger in a borrowed dress.

From the south an eerie yowl of wolves and the nearby screech of a bird sent a shiver through her. Never in the past had the sounds of the night disturbed her, but since her father's trip from Tallahassee and the building of the fort, the agency no longer seemed a sheltering home to her; there was threat now in the faces of the Seminoles when she rode into their villages, and in the faces of the settlers—and she could feel it now in the glow of light from the blacksmith shop.

Fat, bland-faced Major Phagan had come from Tallahassee three weeks after her father's return, accompanied by a beak-nosed white boy wearing a Seminole hunting shirt and riding an Indian pony. Eliza had disliked Major Phagan from the first sight of his heavy body slumped in the saddle of his mule-eared mare; of the boy she could make out little except that he was watchful, untalkative, and kept to himself. The major had presented to John Hutchins a letter from Governor Duval confirming the bearer's appointment as subagent, the hiring of the boy, Steven Richards, as interpreter, and warning that his instructions should henceforth be carried out to the letter, especially with respect to Negro property held by the Indians—

"On the subject of runaway slaves among the Seminoles it will be proper in all cases where you believe the owners can identify the slaves to have them taken and delivered over to the marshal of East Florida at St. Augustine, so that the federal judge may inquire into the claim and determine the right of property."

As John Hutchins had read the letter Eliza saw the bitterness in his face; then he had looked up at the new subagent and told him to make himself at home.

Major Phagan had done so. From the first days the subagent had taken up with men of dubious reputation, with traders in Negroes, with Indians, as well as with the traders of Forbes and Company and the sutler at the fort, with anyone with whom some deal might be struck. With John Hutchins he was circumspect; mealtimes passed with her father (in his high moods) holding forth on everything under the sun, Major Phagan eating and listening. As for Steven Richards, he spent whole days alone in the woods; and a week passed before Major Phagan chose to reveal that for five years the boy had been a captive of Seminoles who had murdered his mother, father, and sister while he looked on from a sleeping loft.

That horror, Eliza believed, explained why the young man seemed so mistrustful, why he avoided conversation with her—while watching her when he thought she didn't notice.

Then one evening the subagent told Hutchins he had spoken with Ben Solano, who mentioned that he and his friends meant to ride south to Big Cypress Swamp, to the Indian-Negro village where, reports said, Mrs. Smith's man was hiding, and bring him in; when Hutchins objected that the governor had barred whites from the reservation, Major Phagan said he reckoned it likely that the governor and most everyone else in the Territory would overlook any such technicality if only "the nigger Enos could be got back to Mrs. Smith and make her stop hollerin'," and that in any case there was no technicality because he, Major Phagan, as subagent had given Mr. Solano the necessary go-ahead. Hutchins replied heatedly that as long as he was agent he was the one who would give permission to enter Indian lands and that he did not intend to see the agency turned into a slave depot, whereupon Major Phagan had quite unexpectedly flown into a violent rage, cursing and shouting and turning very red in the face. John Hutchins had simply laughed at the fulminating subagent. From then on Major Phagan and the interpreter had taken their meals in the blacksmith shop.

As Eliza lay thinking of these things, unable to sleep, a shadow crossed the faint glow of light in her curtain and outside her window she heard the scrape of a boot.

In sudden fear she forced herself to go to the window and draw aside the curtain.

By the moonlight she looked a moment into the staring eyes of Steven Richards before he quickly moved away into the shadows.

The next morning Ben Solano and Jed Cunso brought Enos in. Solano led the pony with the Negro tied on by his feet under the pony's belly, hands bound behind him; he led the pony up before the main house, as Eliza and her father came out, then without a word he dismounted, untied the cords at the Negro's ankles, and pulled him out of the saddle onto the ground at John Hutchins' feet. Jed Cunso leaned forward on the pommel of his saddle, making a business of not smiling. Major Phagan, in uniform, came out of the blacksmith shop and started toward them; Steven Richards came out after him and leaned against the log wall, watching.

"Here's what we went for," Solano announced. "We been to a lot of trouble getting him, Hutchins; now it's up to you."

The black man lay still on the ground, staring dully. Eliza judged him to be about thirty; his face and arms were bruised and scarred; he wore coarse gray cotton pants and shirt, tattered and mud-stained. Eliza knelt and started to untie his wrists as the subagent came up.

"What exactly is up to me?" John Hutchins demanded of Solano. "You're in line for the reward, not I."

Solano smiled. "That's right. Me and Jed get what's due us—but you're getting him to St. Augustine."

When Hutchins looked at him narrowly, not replying, Solano added, "Course if you figure he's the rightful property of the Seminoles we took him from, you got a right to your opinion. We know he's Mrs. Smith's, but if you think differ-

113

ent all you got to do is prove it before the judge in St. Augustine. For that I guess you'd need some Seminole to testify—though on second thought it might not turn out to be worth the trouble dragging an Indian all that way to testify."

Jed Cunso laughed aloud. When John Hutchins asked Enos whether or not an Indian claimed him, Enos looked at the ground and almost imperceptibly shook his head.

"So there's no hitch there," Solano said then. "Only one thing shouldn't happen. If this Negro don't get to the marshal there'll be a lot of angry white people wanting to know why the government pays a man good money who don't give a damn for the law here."

Angrily Eliza remembered the governor's letter, whose contents were apparently no secret to Ben Solano. She was about to reply hotly when a glance from her father stopped her.

"The government pays others," he said, nodding to Major Phagan. "Major, I want you to take this Negro to the marshal in St. Augustine and bring me a receipt for him."

A quick look passed between the subagent and Ben Solano. Eliza saw it. Then, glancing at Steven Richards, she found that he was looking directly at her—then he shook his head once. No.

"If you say so, Hutchins," said Major Phagan, pokerfaced.

"Any way he gets there," Solano added. "It's your responsibility, Hutchins."

Eliza finished untying Enos, then stood up, glaring at the slave catcher, too furious to speak.

Solano grinned. "Now that you got him undone," he said in a hard voice, "you better see to it he don't run off, else your pap'll be the most unpopular man in the Territory of Florida."

On Hutchins' order Major Phagan led Enos across to the former schoolroom, now the jail. Eliza saw that Delia brought the captive food and water. Ben Solano and Major Phagan were standing by the door of the blacksmith shop in

114

close conversation, which they broke off when Eliza drew near. Steven Richards, seeing her approach, started away from the compound on the trail that led up toward the fort. Remembering the boy's sign to her, Eliza decided to follow him. When they had entered the forest of huge old oaks he looked back, then started to run. Eliza ran after him but lost sight of him around a bend; when she reached a place where she thought she must see him ahead, there was no one. She looked up. Directly overhead on a limb in the greatest of the live oaks he was scowling at her.

"Come down," she called to him. "I want to talk to you."

"No."

"Then I'm coming up."

"You can't in a skirt!" he said, and suddenly laughed.

"You just watch," she called back, and raising her buckskin skirts, she lifted herself to the arching limb and sitting, swearing not to fall, she edged herself sideways toward the boy's perch, far out where the limb forked. Grudgingly he made room for her.

From the fort they could hear soldiers' voices. Down to the north was the clearing in the forest where the agency compound was, and beyond, a sea of trees descending to the river.

"Why did you shake your head?" she asked him.

"Maybe I didn't."

"You did."

"Maybe for no reason then."

Eliza looked hard into the boy's troubled eyes. He said, "You followed me here because I shook my head."

"Then you admit it."

"Yes—and for a reason too."

"What reason?"

"I won't tell you."

"That's a lonely way to be," she said after a moment.

"I don't like to be followed places."

"Maybe I don't like to be looked at through windows at night," she told him gently, seeing pain fill his eyes.

"I like the night. It ain't just for you."

"You frightened me," she said. "I didn't know who it was."

He did not answer.

"Do you come here often?"

He looked away from her, out over the treees.

"You can see a long way."

Still he said nothing.

"Where do you come from?" she asked at last.

"A house burning."

"Before that?"

"Where the land gave out," he told her, nodding to the north, where a line of clouds stood on the flat horizon like hazy mountains. "Why did you trail me here?"

"Thought it time we made friends," Eliza said.

"I don't have white friends, just redskins." He reflected, adding, "Unless you call Major Phagan a friend." Then suddenly he looked at her hard, scowling, and asked whether she had ever heard of Osceola.

Eliza nodded. "I met him."

"How?" demanded the boy sharply. "You don't speak red-skin?"

"We understood each other." And Eliza told him how Osceola had given her the broken-off arrow tip.

Steven Richards' eyes now narrowed fiercely, his beak nose giving him a hawklike appearance.

"Someday Osceola will burn this fort and the agency and every white man's house in this Territory."

"Are you and he friends?" she asked.

"Brothers," the boy replied.

"I'm no enemy of the Indians," Eliza said, and seeing the boy's anguish she reached out and touched his clenched hand.

He drew it away quickly.

"You don't even know them! How could you even know them?"

"Maybe I don't," said Eliza. "But neither does your Major Phagan. He's certainly no friend of theirs."

116

"Someday they'll kill him," the boy said sullenly. Then he added, "You'd better not go to their villages anymore."

"They won't harm me."

The boy looked at his hand, clenching it into a tighter fist.

"My father used to ride alone to their villages, too—only he went to the worst Mikasuki ones—with presents, as their friend. At first what saved him was they thought he was a spirit to be so crazy. See, he'd built our house on their burial ground. He never did get to know that."

"Did they treat you well?" she asked after a moment.

"Redskin well. Why did you really trail me here?" He looked at her hard, smiling when he saw her hesitation.

"To find out what Ben Solano and Major Phagan are up to," she told him, exasperated by his suspicion.

"That's better," he said.

"Well?"

Again the boy narrowed his eyes with exaggerated ferocity—and he told her what was agreed between Ben Solano and the subagent.

That evening after sundown, when Delia had finished cleaning up after supper and gone to her cabin, Eliza told her father what she had learned. At first he had not understood.

"But if Major Phagan lets Enos escape," he said, "there'll be no reward for Solano and Jed."

"They don't mean to let him escape. Solano will take him and sell him to a trader. Phagan will say in St. Augustine that Seminoles ambushed him and stole Enos back."

"So they'll get his full price instead of just the reward."

"And the Seminoles will be blamed."

John Hutchins went to the window, looking out on the red afterglow beyond the forest to the west.

"Not only the Seminoles," he said quietly.

Then he lit the lamp on the table and took down the green whiskey bottle and a glass from the shelf; and as he poured the pale liquor and raised it to the light, even before drinking the transformation came over him. The tense lines of his face softened; his eyes filled with schemes; and as he drank Eliza knew that he was entering a world where she could not follow him and which she feared for his sake even more than his anguish.

"Well," he told his glass, "it's a lucky thing we found 'em out, Liza." He glanced at her briefly. "Now, you tell Delia to sleep up here while I'm gone. Only be a few days."

"You'll take him to the marshal?"

"It's my job," he said sardonically, admiring the slow syrupy swirls in his glass. "Just think what will happen if that fugitive isn't brought in. Why, the sun won't shine, birds won't sing, cows won't give milk, the whole country will be in lamentation until Mrs. Smith has her Enos back." He paused. "Besides," he added, "I've got business in St. Augustine."

"Father, I'm going with you."

He shook his head. "It's no trip for you."

"For you either," she told him.

She persisted and when, to win him over, she said she was afraid to stay at the agency without him, he yielded. They would set out together for St. Augustine with Enos at dawn a day hence.

Eliza

The Agency—St. Augustine
April, 1827

A draggle-eared yellow hound belonging to one of the officers at the fort followed them the first mile down the road through the forest before it calculated that they were going too far and turned back. The morning was windless, clammy; the sky a shifting luminous gray. Enos, unbound, rode ahead leading a packhorse; John Hutchins and Eliza rode side by side, for the road reaching north from Fort King had lately been widened by the army troops. Eliza and her father spoke little; at his belt was a holstered pistol, in his saddlebags leg and wrist irons (she had seen him put them there surreptitiously). Enos spoke not a word. By midmorning they emerged from the forest and passed along the edge of a swamp of fire-blackened tree trunks standing jagged against the lowering sky. At noon they stopped to eat on the bank of a lake bordered by thick hammock, but swarming mosquitoes forced them to move on; a mile farther on they came to an abandoned Indian cornfield and stopped there to take their midday meal.

In the afternoon the sky to the north darkened to billowing black; the air was heavy and oppressive. They passed through an abandoned Indian village, the reed huts with raised floors inhabited now by cawing crows. Beyond the village they came upon a log lean-to on the edge of a grown-over cornfield. A lone white man, wearing cheap trader's cottons and a straw hat with a broken brim, stood in the middle of the field striking at the soil with a heavy mattock, raising the iron high over his head and bringing it down with all his strength into the caked earth. He paused his work when the riders approached but did not respond to John Hutchins' wave of greeting except to return to his solitary labor with renewed anger against the intruders, the sodden heat, and, it seemed, against the earth itself. For a long time they could hear the thud of the mattock striking the soil, sometimes clinking against stone.

Entering a dense woods, they rode without speaking. After a time the trill and screech of the birds and the rumble of thunder ahead played tricks on Eliza's mind, so that when she first heard the delicate tinkling of bells it seemed part of the sound of the forest. Then from around a bend the first blacks appeared; she heard their humming and the bells, louder. There were a dozen in all, men and women, one a boy of fifteen or so, a woman with an infant slung at her back, all tethered in file by a rope joining leather collars, the last a tall young woman wearing on her head a sort of iron birdcage in which bells tinkled. Behind them rode a single horseman wearing a broad-brimmed white hat, and what struck Eliza at once was that his gray horse walked at an unnaturally slow pace, in step with the blacks. As the coffle came nearer and began to pass them, Eliza looked at their faces and saw that most moved in a sort of trance, lost in their humming; but one young man looked fearfully at her, then quickly to her father, as if still hoping for mercy from a white human face, as if rescue was conceivable; but the woman wearing the iron headdress walked erect as if proud of her punishment and whatever had brought it to be, determined to bear the pain, and when she came near Eliza she looked directly at her with a smile of murderous hate. The trader touched the brim of his hat; her father returned the gesture; and as the trader on his slow-walking horse passed them she caught a glimpse of his face.

Until the sound of bells died away they did not speak or look at each other; nor did Enos look back. Then her father said, "Headed for Tampa."

She dared not look at him.

"You shouldn't have come," he said. "I shouldn't have let you."

Rain began to fall.

When she did look at her father she saw that his eyes were as dead as the trader's.

"Have to find shelter," he said.

They passed the night in an abandoned cabin near the bank of a river, Enos in a corner ironed hand and foot. For much of the night father, daughter, and the slave lay awake without speaking; then, toward morning when the storm was passing . . . she awoke to see Enos kneeling in the doorway, silhouetted by the dawn sky, her father's pistol in his trembling manacled hands. Hutchins lay awake, half raised on his elbow, looking at Enos calmly; but when he realized that Eliza had awakened he looked at her with

120

great sadness and was about to speak—when Enos raised the pistol to his own temple and pulled the trigger. There was a dry click. Enos fell to the earth floor, moaning.

John Hutchins rose from his blanket roll and went over to the black man. He unlocked the irons first at his hands, then at his feet; then he took the irons and strode outside, and as Eliza watched through the doorway, at the river's edge he heaved the chinkling irons with all his force far out into the water, where the splash startled a while heron into flight. Then he came back into the cabin and told Enos that he would not be going back to Georgia. And Enos became frightened, kneeling before him with his hands raised in plea, as if he wished them manacled again.

"Seminoles never take me back! The white men catch me alone!"

"Do you want to be free?" John Hutchins demanded, taking him by the shoulders.

"No way to be free! Better I die!"

"There is a way."

Even as he spoke Eliza remembered Captain Wolfe of the black-hulled brig they had seen in Savannah.

"The *Northern Star*?"

Her father nodded, saying that he heard from Major Phagan that the vessel was in St. Augustine.

They rode three abreast now, still northward, skirting a vast dense forest, then across a flat country of lakes, hammocks, and sealike prairies where herds of wild Spanish cattle grazed, a mirage of the past, at the horizon. The sun was warm, the air fresh with shifting cool and warmer pockets, bearing the smell of the forest islands and the bright moist grasslands. Riding between Enos and her father, Eliza felt the black man's fear, far greater now than yesterday when he had been a captive of the Law; and sensing her father's exhilaration over having taken the fate of another from that Law and into his own hands, she did not yet dare calculate the risks they were taking.

By noon they reached the road from Pensacola which cut

through the jungle eastward. Now Enos rode behind them, as befitted a servant, for on this road they met other travelers; a family of settlers with their belongings stacked high on a wagon, a company of mounted troops, a preacher, and a party of men Eliza took for slave catchers by their looks of suspicion as they passed.

The sun was setting in the jungle behind them when they approached the orange and lime groves at the outskirts of St. Augustine; they were more careful now, leaving the road to ride through the orchards. When they came in sight of the first houses they waited for darkness to fall; the night seemed an endless time coming. Long ago her father's elation had passed, he was silent and anxious now; the three of them bound by the thought that it was still not too late to take Enos to the marshal. As the first lamps in the houses came on and the evening cold settled upon them, she found herself almost wishing that her father had remembered to prime his pistol before leaving the agency, hating herself for the thought, fearing that her father's plan was madness, that they would be unable to save Enos or themselves.

John Hutchins left their horses at the post stables, then together they proceeded through quiet back streets toward the seawall. Reaching a corner, they came upon a band of young serenaders under a window—and turned back quickly, taking a darker street. When at last they reached the quay Eliza at first saw only a sail-and-steam packet boat and a trim navy brigantine—then, far up the seawall toward the fort she saw in the beam from the lighthouse on Anastasia Island the *Northern Star.*

Watchful for anyone who might recognize them, they made their way along the quay, passing knots of sailors, strollers, carousers, and again as on the road it seemed to Eliza that these strangers must plainly see her father's anxiety and Enos' fear.

When at last they reached the *Northern Star* they waited in the shadow of the ship's hull until they were certain that they were unobserved, then climbed the gangplank.

A young black sailor met them on deck and at once motioned them to move inboard, out of sight. Hearing that John Hutchins wished to see Captain Wolfe, the young man glanced once intently at Enos, then disappeared down a hatchway ladder, where a few moments later the captain himself appeared.

By the dim light from the hatchway Eliza saw that he recognized them and took in the meaning of Enos' presence in a single swift glance, at once calm and intense, which nonetheless rested on her just long enough to revive sensations which had stirred her eight years before in Savannah, and which for some time she had experienced whenever she remembered that day.

Without a word he gestured to the hatchway.

At the foot of the ladder they entered a large low-ceilinged compartment, the full beam of the ship, curtained into partitions, where there were a number of blacks, men and women, some lying on bunks, a woman on a stool washing clothes in a bucket, a small girl peering around a curtain at them, a man tending a cooking stove. The captain passed among them aft, Eliza, her father, and Enos following, until they reached the small cabin, where he invited Eliza and her father to sit on the bunk, Enos on a sea chest, while he sat at a desk and set about regulating the wick of the gimballed lamp hanging above it.

"His papers?"

"He has none, sir," John Hutchins said.

"Runaway?"

"Many years with the Seminoles."

"Can't take him."

Enos began to tremble. Eliza saw the desperation in her father's face.

"You've been misinformed," Captain Wolfe pursued. "I've no respect for the slave law, but I cannot afford to violate it." He gestured into the hold. "I've others to think of, and others after them. Not to speak of myself." Then, after keen study of Enos, he asked, "Is there an Indian claimant?"

John Hutchins hesitated.

"No, sir," he said at last. "There is not."

Captain Wolfe smiled faintly. "Wouldn't matter, would it? In the event of dispute you're obliged to let the federal judge decide, I believe."

"Correct, sir. And if the past is any guide Enos would be returned to a cruel mistress whether or not an Indian claimed to own him."

"Enos? The Georgia woman's? Why, every bounty hunter in the Territory is after him! Mr. Hutchins, if I couldn't take an ordinary fugitive, think of what insanity it would be for me to take such a celebrated one as Enos!" Then, with a passing glance at Eliza, he asked, "By the way, did anyone see you come on board?"

As her father assured him that not a living soul had seen them, Eliza sensed that Captain Wolfe was playing a sort of cat-and-mouse game, that he did not in the least mind that they were very much in his power.

"We have twenty on board now," he continued, addressing her. "In my grandfather's day his captains took four hundred on this vessel—started out with that number, at least. Can you imagine it?"

"Yes," Eliza said.

"I do believe you can," he said slowly, his eyes brightening as he gazed at her. Then he turned to John Hutchins.

"In any case these twenty are free. That is, they are free to my satisfaction. All with papers." He paused, glancing again at Eliza, then, frowning, drummed his fingers on the desk. "Of course you can never be certain about papers. Devil of a lot of dishonesty about papers." Abruptly he looked up at her again. "Miss Hutchins, can you give me one good reason why I should venture my fortune and my reputation in every Southern port simply for the sake of this one human being?"

"Because we are asking you to take him," she replied.

When he leaned back in his chair and looked at her, smiling, she felt herself blush but she did not look away from him until he said, "Yes, that is a good reason."

124

Wolfe turned to Enos, who had not deciphered the captain's curious ways.

"Do you wish to go to Canada, Enos?"

For a moment the black man appeared bewildered, as if fearing some new deception; then he looked at Eliza and her father, understood, and sobbed into his hands.

Hutchins

The Agency
February, 1828

THROUGHOUT the sweltering summer of 1827 John Hutchins endeavored to conduct the agency according to his original directives, to safeguard Indian rights, to keep red man and white man apart, but that job was almost impossible now because the original directives were forgotten, and many in Florida now believed that the agent was their enemy, with no understanding of the interests of the Territory.

But such was John Hutchins' absorption in his own idea of what he was supposed to be doing there that it was September or October before he realized that among the influential men of western Florida he was an outcast.

He had not seen that Ben Solano was becoming a power to be reckoned with in Florida—and Ben Solano had not believed his story about Enos' escape en route to St. Augustine.

The rumor spread that the agent had sold the fugitive for his own profit.

In Georgia Mrs. Smith branded him a foe of the slave laws and probably a thief.

It was said in St. Augustine that he withheld other Negroes from their owners and worked them on some mythical plantation of his own. It was even said that he was in league with the Seminoles against the settlers. Some, old

125

enough to remember, went so far as to compare him, in treachery to his race, to the notorious English agents Arburthnot and Ambrister.

Governor Duval stopped writing him altogether.

Letters from groups of influential men of the Territory urged the replacement of the agent as a first necessary step to the removal of the Indians. A grand jury in St. Augustine issued a presentment against him and he spent the rest of the year defending himself against it, successfully inasmuch as no specific charge was sustained, and he was not brought to trial, though feeling against him ran higher than ever. The Adams administration sent a special investigator to look into the complaints against the Florida agent.

John Hutchins vigorously denied all wrongdoing, and even his enemies respected his performance in the federal courtroom at St. Augustine—but Eliza knew that he was deeply troubled.

To her he more and more often appeared unaccountably exhilarated, behaving with a strange secretiveness, after which he would fall into fits of dejection.

He had not dared tell her that he had filed a claim for the savanna at the east of the reservation. A week after the deliverance of Enos.

For Eliza the spiriting of Enos on board the *Northern Star* was justifiable because the slave had had a cruel mistress and should not be returned to her, law or no law. She told her father that she was never more proud of him than when he had cast the shackles into the river—nevertheless there was a barrier between daughter and father whenever they spoke of Enos' liberation. It became an uneasy, silent complicity. It weighed on John Hutchins as if he had done a shameful thing, the more because his daughter had witnessed it; he had broken the law; he had afterwards had to lie, and lie before a man like Ben Solano; he had had to put himself at the mercy of chance not to be found out and disgraced, conscious all along that when he searched his soul for the true motives behind his action none appeared clearly. How did they know that Mrs. Smith and her overseer were as cruel as they were said to be? People lied and exaggerated. Who was he to judge such a thing? Nor could mere compassion explain the sudden rage which he had hurled the irons out into the river. Perhaps it had been a flareup against his own race? A moment of pride? In any event the unlawful manumission of Enos had in no way freed John Hutchins from his demons but only put him in greater bondage to them.

Now, in filing a claim for the Indian lands, he was on the road to freeing himself from that bondage.

His whole life had now begun to seem like a journey toward possession of the land.

In 1827 John Hutchins did not suspect the onset of madness because it came upon him not frighteningly but like an old companion, easing his anxieties, turning his hopes into realities just around the corner. He saw pain in Eliza's eyes often now, and tried to assure her that all would be well at last, in a very short time; and sometimes he was tempted to tell her about his claim of the savanna but something always stopped him, a warning that she would not approve of what he had done, that she would not believe they were almost out of the woods.

Rachel

The Nashville Inn
December, 1828

NOT since General Lafayette's visit had Rachel seen so many people in Nashville, so many carriages and wagons and decked-out strangers, all come to celebrate her husband's triumphant departure for Washington.

All morning she had wrestled with her dread of leaving,

127

and none of the kind ladies with her, her friends, knew the calvary she had suffered in the dress shop, only her Hannah; for their sakes she had not let them see her anguish, allowing their fingers to straighten lace frills and do the buttons of the unwanted clothes. The worst moment of all had been fitting the white satin gown she was to wear to the Inauguration Ball, for with her friends chattering around her she had looked at herself in the mirror, ludicrous in the gleaming gown so ill-suited to her heavy body and rough dark complexion, and she had felt a dreadful presentiment.

For some time she had known what they were saying about her in Washington, her husband's enemies—though everyone at the Hermitage had tried to keep the truth from her: They were saying that she was a coarse-mannered country woman unfit to be mistress of the President's House. And they were saying worse things. In the shop, seeing herself in the white gown, her dread of going to the fashionable capital make her think of her own death and almost wish for it.

For the first time in their life together the general was powerless to protect her; the attacks against them both were vicious and cruelly calculated to arouse a response which would only serve his enemies' purposes; so for a time, wishing to shield her, the general had agreed that she might join him only after the Inauguration; but then good John Eaton, whose native judgment they both valued, had written from the capital that the storm of abuse had abated, the angry tempest ceased to howl, that ladies from remote parts of the Union would gather to pay their respects to her, and must not be disappointed, and that her persecutors must not drive her from her rightful place; so it was decided that she would come on with the general after all.

When the fittings were done with and the dresses chosen—they would not let her refuse the white satin—they had walked down Center Street, the ladies pretending not to notice the strangers stopping to point her out, until they reached the corner of the square where the stages stopped in front of the Nashville Inn. There she had managed to excuse herself from them, sending Hannah off to have Uncle James bring around the carriage, and went to her usual place in the inn for waiting, the back parlor.

There she had been seated only several minutes when three laughing young ladies entered the main parlor. Though she could not see them from her place Rachel smiled at their hilarity.

"Did you see her?" one asked.

"How could one not?" another cried, and all three fell to laughing again.

Rachel's blood froze. There was no way out of the back parlor except through the room where the young ladies were.

"They even say she was pretty once," the third said.

"Do you imagine she will smoke her pipe in the President's House?" inquired the first who had spoken.

"Only at state affairs," the second replied.

Again they laughed uncontrollably.

"But no one will laugh," the first said, "or else General Jackson will shoot them."

"In that case," observed the second, wriest of the young ladies, "I do fear he will have to shoot the entire country."

"I'm certain he wouldn't do such a dreadful thing," replied the first, lowering her voice to a whisper, "unless someone were to say she married him before she divorced her first husband."

"Who would dare?" asked the second.

Then the third girl said, "You're both too high and mighty for me. I think it's time the *people* were represented in Washington."

"So do I," the second young lady agreed. "And no question of it, they will be most *amply* represented now!"

Tears were streaming down Rachel's face. Her whole body throbbed with fear that the young ladies would find her there; she felt leaden and drained. At any moment Hannah would return and reveal her presence to the three, who

129

now stood chattering about what they would wear to the ball in the governor's honor. She prayed a childish prayer to God that He would take her then and there, great bulk and all, and enfold her to Him, so that she would not have to live another moment a disgrace to the great man she loved so dearly. Then she said another prayer for the young women in the next room, asking Him to free their souls from vanity and show them the path to His Heavenly Throne.

At last a clock in the main parlor struck twelve and the young ladies went out into the street, as the noise of an arriving stage drowned out their voices. Rachel sat absolutely still, the pain in her chest like a companion, until her Hannah came.

For a terrible moment she was unable to stand. She knew that she must pull herself to her feet and walk out of the inn to her carriage but she could not summon the will over her body.

"You all right, Miss Rachel?" Hannah asked.

"I've done my shopping," she said, delaying for time until her strength returned. "Is Uncle James outside?"

"Yes'm. Waitin'. Miss Rachel, you sure you're all right?"

"Just a mite tired from the shopping."

Her own voice sounded distant and strangely old to her.

Presently the travelers from the stage came into the main parlor, gaping at the fine furnishings, and when a man saw her and whispered to the others who she was, she told herself, *Rachel Donelson Jackson, your father founded this town with Mr. Robertson, these people have come here to honor your husband, and now with God's help, you are going to stand and walk straight out through that parlor to your carriage and go home.*

And so she did.

Eliza

ON a warm, pleasant day in early November an army courier had delivered to John Hutchins an express letter informing him that by order of the Secretary of War he was relieved of his post as agent to the Florida Indians effective February 1, 1829. In the interim he was to submit his final accounts and effect an orderly transfer of all agency business to Major John Phagan, who would then assume his duties until a permanent replacement was appointed. With respect to his application for a certain tract of land east of the reservation no action would be taken pending settlement of the agency's accounts.

Surprisingly, after the first shock of the news John Hutchins appeared elated by his "liberation" and seemed to believe that his acquisition of the savanna was delayed only by a technicality. As for Major Phagan, he accepted the news of his imminent advancement as being no more than his due. By then he was making no secret of the fact that no transaction of his was concluded without personal profit to himself, as if John Hutchins' opinion of his honesty would no longer be heeded in any quarter from which the major might suffer harm. The subagent had proved his reliability where it mattered and in the way it mattered by bringing in to the federal judge in St. Augustine a half-dozen valuable fugitives (not counting a half dozen more sold on his own account) and was known to be an advocate of the removal of the Seminoles, while in fact not wishing them gone until he had exhausted all possibilities of profiting from their presence.

Eliza had been expecting this day of reckoning for some time, and when it arrived she wrote at once to the one person in the world she felt she could turn to for comfort and

131

assistance, the person she had turned to once before in time of need—Rachel Jackson. She could no longer look to her father to manage for her or himself. He had begun to talk wildly of establishing a vast plantation in Florida but when she questioned him about it he would take offense and declare that she never understood him, that she would soon see for herself. So, anxious on her father's account, she had written Rachel and now six weeks later, on a chill January afternoon, two letters for Eliza arrived by the same express; one from Aunt Rachel, the other from Emily Donelson. With a sense of foreboding, she sat at the table by the fireplace and opened Rachel's first.

The Hermitage
December 16, 1828

My dear Eliza,

It is a Long time since I have written and it is a Sadness to me that I cannot reply but with a Heavy Heart. The enemys of the Genls have dipt their arrows in wormwood and gall and sped them to me. Almighty God was there ever aney thing to equal it? To think that thirty years had passed in happy friendship with society, innocent of any knowing wrong, doing or thinking no ill to no one, as my judg will know. Well the apostle says I can do all things in Christ who strengtheneth me, and my soul bears testimony to the truth of that Gospel for who has been so cruely tryed as I have. How many prayers have I ofered up for the repentance of the Genls enemys. Now I learn from your Letter that their vengance has not spared your own father. To remove a able man from his Post in the last monthes of their administration when the People have repudiated them is a unworthy thing but I fear only what we have come to expect of them. If God wills to preserve the Genls health (which has been poorly) he will soon be in Power and (always with His divin guidance) will right what Wrongs he can. When he is feeling better I will speak to him about your father. For me I would rather be a doorkeeper in the House of the Lord than live in that Palace in Washington but it is the Peoples Will that the Genl be President and while he has an ounce of strength in his Body he will serve them faithfuly. I had wished to stay on here as often before in the Genls absences but his friends through Mr. Eaton have urged me and I have agred to go to the Capitol if the Lord wills, my own Health has been poorly. Let not your Heart be troubled. I am on the rock of ages. In the world I have tribulation. In jesus I have peace. Emily and her husband will accompany us and it would be a Joy to me, dear Eliza, if you came on to stay in the President's House with us as part of our Family for a good long spell. The Genl joins me in this wish as do Emily and John. Sometimes it seems that this life is only partings and that reunions must wait untill the Everlasting City.

Your Loving aunt
Rachel

Then she opened Emily Donelson's letter, sensing before she read the first words what they would say.

The Hermitage
December 24, 1828

Dear Cousin Eliza,

We are all here deeply grieved by the sudden passing of our dearest Aunt on the 22nd of this month. Uncle is plunged into such a state of despair that at times we have been fearful that he would succumb. On the 17th while going about her household duties with Hannah she suffered a painful attack at her chest and left arm with palpitations of the heart. The General was called from the fields and Dr. Hogg and Dr. Heiskill sent for, who bled her profusely and by nightfall the attack abated and she was able to sleep. Uncle stayed with her in her room that night and for the next three days. She seemed to be steadily mending and became as cheerful as ever in the past, sitting up by the fire, enjoying the General's company and receiving a few friends. On Sunday evening she was taken with a cold and put to bed. The physicians and the invalid herself then urged the General, for the sake of his own health, to take to bed in the room across the hall, and he did so. Toward 10 o'clock Aunt had Hannah help her to her chair by the fire and fill her pipe. She told Hannah then, as she had told others, that she would rather be a gatekeeper in Heaven than live in that palace in Washington. Soon she called out "I'm fainting!" and fell from her chair. Hannah screamed and Uncle rushed in and they lifted her into bed. By the time the doctors had come from the other part of the house she was gone to her Eternal Rest. For a long time Uncle could not believe that she was taken from him. As the shrieking of the servants filled the house Uncle ordered the doctors to bleed her and they did so but no blood flowed. Still Uncle would not leave her side and stroked her brow very tenderly until long after it was cold. At last realizing that John Coffee was near him in sad attendance he said "John, can you realize she is dead? I certainly can't." Still he would not leave her. The next day, yesterday, she was buried at the eastern corner of the garden and never has such a funeral been witnessed in Davidson County. The news spread for many miles around and by one o'clock ten thousand people, they say, of every order, wealthy and poor, black and white, had come by every sort of conveyance, by horse and many on foot coming across the bleak winter fields, converging on the Hermitage, filling the garden, the drive, the surrounding field. Except for the moaning of the servants and hands the great throng was silent, standing reverently with bowed heads as Reverend Hume spoke the eulogy and no one present doubted it when he said that even then Aunt Rachel surely dwelt in the mansions of glory with the ransomed of the Lord. Uncle wept but with great courage found the strength to say "In the presence of this dear saint I can and do forgive all my enemies. But those vile wretches who have slandered her must look to God for mercy." Now as we prepare for a blighted journey Uncle is still sticken and utterly dispirited. Old friends beg him to think of his responsibility to the people who elected him President and to submit with philosophy and faith to this hard dispensation from the First Cause of All Things. I have no doubt that with the healing of time he will find his old strength again. Dear Cousin, before she was so suddenly taken from us Aunt informed me of her wish that you visit the President's House. Jack and I hope that this great bereavement will not prevent you from coming to stay with us, this is Uncle Jackson's wish also. We leave here on the 18th of January, accompanied by Laird and Major Lewis, and shall be in Washington City, if God wills, before mid-February.

Your cousin,
Emily Donelson

Through stinging tears Eliza reread the closing lines of Rachel's letter, then she heard her father's steps outside and quickly dried her eyes. John Hutchins came in with an armload of wood, noticed the letters and, in a glance, her distress, tumbled the wood into the bin, and went to the window looking out on the bleak compound.

"Nothing for me?" he asked.

"No, Father."

"Too early to hear. These things take time."

"Father, Aunt Rachel is dead."

He stood as if he hadn't heard, not looking at her. She wanted to go to him, to have him hold her as he had done when as a child she had needed comforting, but she sensed that the man standing at the window had no such strength left. So she started reading Emily's letter aloud, keeping her grief at bay because she had no idea how it would stop if she gave way to it.

"A calamity," he said when she had finished. "A terrible calamity." Then he turned and sat across the table from her, meeting her eyes but not the pain in them. "Of course you must go. Now more than ever." He folded his hands to stop them from trembling, then rose and went to the window again.

She thought, *Now I must stay more than ever.*

"The general will need Cumberland friends round him now. Of course you must go."

"It's so long he'd hardly remember me," she said. "It was Rachel I was to visit. I'd only be in the way there now."

Her father answered her sharply, "Emily says he wants you particularly! They all want you."

"It's Emily's kindness, Father," Eliza said with sudden bitterness against what or whom she could not tell. "Emily is always considerate."

"You mustn't stay on my account."

Hearing the false gentleness in his voice, she quickly rose and busied herself in Delia's pantry.

"I'll be traveling in any case," he added, pacing before the fireplace. "The time falls right. Of course Delia will go with you and when you come back—someday soon anyway—I'll have a real home for you."

"Where will the money for the trip come, Father?"

After a pause he said, "I still have savings. I can still support my daughter."

Eliza returned from the pantry and for a moment they faced each other. She saw unmistakably for the first time the stranger her father had become, to himself and to her; and knowing too the state of his reputation in Florida she realized that her visit to Washington City would perhaps be a last hope of defending his conduct as agent and securing him another post. And because he regarded the visit as her chance to return to the fold of Tennessee gentry (when all she had wished was to see Rachel again) her leaving would sustain him for a time, until somehow his future would be settled as firmly in reality as he had already settled it in his mind.

"I'll go," she said.

Then he smiled—and she realized that she had not seen him smile, except in bitterness, for a long time—and he came around the table to her, his face radiant as if he was recalling their past together, freed of sadness, and, taking her hands in his, said, "I'll miss you—but it's all for the best."

Eliza

Washington City
February, 1829

ON the morning of their departure, with Delia and all their possessions loaded into the wagon, Eliza's last impressions as she left had been Steven Richards' pained smile as he watched her go and, when they had started on the road north, Major Phagan entering what had been her home, while the new agent's dog hobbled into a patch of sun to scratch its ear with a fastidious hind leg.

In St. Augustine, where they had stayed with Colonel Savage and his wife, Eliza and Malvina talked long into the night about Malvina's forthcoming marriage to Lieutenant Belcamp and Eliza was struck by her friend's unromantic views of matrimony and her low opinion of the male sex. With the single exception of her father, Malvina found men to be rather comical and pathetic creatures, useful, if at all, only for marriage. Eliza was troubled by her friend's cynicism, but also intrigued. She herself—to her own annoyance—could not conceive of marrying except for love, and in the course of the night she confided more of her feelings than she had intended to her worldly friend, whereupon Malvina had been seized by the idea (after inquiring into the matter of fortune) that Eliza must marry Laird Caffrey without delay, and laughed at her protests that she was not certain she loved him.

137

"Love him indeed!" she said. "What an old-fashioned idea!"

John Hutchins accompanied his daughter as far as Savannah. True to his promise he bought her dresses, a gown for the Inauguration Ball, and himself a new suit of clothes. On the dock at sailing time they were the image of a prosperous father seeing off his fashionable daughter, and though the only witnesses were strangers to them John Hutchins seemed determined that no show of feeling would disturb this scene as he had conceived it.

"I've seen your trunk aboard," he told her. "Now write often, I want all the news."

"I will, Father."

"And my deepest condolences to your Uncle Jackson. You won't forget?"

"No, Father."

"Tell him how proud we are of him and how we stand with him. And remember me to Emily, Mr. Earl, and of course to Laird, all our good Cumberland friends." He gazed out past the prow of the vessel toward the open sea beyond the anchored ships in the river. "Tell them I'd be there myself but for business in St. Augustine. Perhaps in a month or two— Here, no tears. I'm quite all right." He paused, as if surprised by his own words, then pulled out his watch. "Almost sailing time. Best board now." He kissed her lightly on the cheek. When she threw her arms around him he drew away. "Now, now," he said. "Best get aboard. I've had a word with the captain. He'll keep an eye on you. You're in good hands."

Thirteen days later, as the packet was being warped into her berth at Alexandria, Eliza stood on the afterdeck looking out at a Washington City of great public buildings divided by spaces where sheep grazed in the fields around clusters of houses and shops, the Capitol on the hill catching the last light from the lilac sky beyond the rise of George-

138

town. Delia stood beside her, mumbling, frightened half to death; and just then Eliza wished that the voyage could have continued forever. She searched the throng on the dock, wondering if her letter had reached Emily before their departure from Tennessee, whether they had sent someone to meet her or even prepared for her arrival. Then at the edge of the crowd she saw Laird Caffrey, waving, smiling broadly when she saw him, handsome in his sky blue uniform. She waved across the closing water, taken unaware by the sudden joy she felt at seeing him.

On the pier he kissed her full on the lips.
"Hello, cousin," he said, admiring her at arm's length.
"Pier's rocking as bad as the ship," she told him foolishly.

In Uncle Jackson's carriage he held her hand under the folds of their coats, so Delia would not see.
"We've a lot of time to make up, Liza," he told her. She smiled without replying, then looked past him out the window remembering another winter night when she had come to this city with her father and mother to O'Neale's tavern when there had been nothing between them and destitution but a few dollars and the letter she had prodded Uncle Jackson into writing. The piles of stone were great buildings now.
"Can you make up time?" she asked then.
"Easiest thing in the world," he assured her—and the pleasure she felt at being with him surprised her.
"How is Uncle Jackson?"
"Holding on. He's a brave gentleman."
"I really miss Aunt Rachel," she said, biting her lip to hold back tears that sprang from nowhere.
"Everyone does," Laird said.

The street in front of Gadsby's Hotel was jammed with people and vehicles and as the President's carriage passed, faces pressed at the windows for a glimpse inside.

"Been like this since we got here," Laird explained. "Papers call it The Wigwam. People after government jobs, mostly."

Pressing through the crowd inside the hotel, past the self-appointed guards at the staircase, Eliza thought with dismay of her mission for her father, remembering his forced joviality at the moment of their parting, and was fearful for him.

Conspiritorially, Major Lewis opened the door at the end of the hall a crack, then admitted Laird and Eliza, shutting it quickly behind them. The President-elect sat in a high-backed wing chair staring into a hearth, the firelight wavering on his gray gaunt face. Emily Donelson, dressed in mourning, sat near him, while her husband, Jack Donelson, the general's ward and now secretary, stood on his other side. John Eaton sat before him, near the fire; he had been speaking and interrupted himself and rose as the newcomers entered. Seeing Eliza, Andrew Jackson slowly rose from his chair, heedless of Emily's protesting gesture. For a moment he looked at Eliza without seeming to recognize her, his grief-ravaged face aged, his bristling hair gone completely gray; then he took both her hands firmly in his.

"I am very glad you have come, Eliza Hutchins. She wanted you here, and so do I."

"I am glad to see you again, Uncle Jackson."

Then the drawn lines of his face eased and he smiled.

"How she loved them all," he said, shaking his head in admiration.

Emily Donelson nodded to Eliza when she thought it was time to leave the general, telling him that the visitor had journeyed a long way and was surely tired. Emily Donelson, eight years younger than Eliza, stood apart as Laird said goodnight to her in the hall outside the general's rooms. Emily Donelson, wearing a high-collared, long-sleeved black dress so finely cut it showed every movement of her frail shoulders, led Eliza down the turnings of the hall to a

140

room in the back. Her trunk was already in the room, a fire in the grate; Emily Donelson had seen to these things. Now she lit the lamp on the dressing table and glanced around with the eye of a practiced housekeeper.

"This little room was all they had left," she said. "It seems like just about everyone in Creation is coming for the Inauguration."

"It's very nice," Eliza replied. "You were very kind to invite me."

"Oh, I surely didn't mean *that!*" Emily protested. "Why, you're kin. Almost the very last wish of our dear aunt was that you be here. You *belong* here, Eliza Hutchins."

Almost indignantly she went to the window and closed it as if she were closing the subject. Eliza sat on the edge of the bed watching her, remembering a proud, delicate titian-haired girl of fourteen, who had been driven from her fine house to the Nashville Female Academy attended by two servants instead of one, reflecting that more than the difference of their fathers' fortunes and of their ages had always prevented any friendship between them; Emily had been born knowing that she belonged to the Cumberland, and never forgot it; Eliza had learned slowly and painfully that she belonged nowhere and to no one. Now Emily turned to her, her cool hazel eyes wide, serious.

"I always did regret," she said, "that you leaving Tennessee prevented us from really knowing one another." She smiled as if to show that no barrier stood between them.

"Perhaps there'll be time now," said Eliza, remembering Laird saying, "We've a lot of time to make up, Liza."

"I truly hope so," Emily said. "I truly do."

The sound of cheers rose from the public rooms below. With a final glance around the room Emily went to the door.

"Eliza Hutchins," she said, standing in the doorway with her hand on the knob. "You are welcome here and don't forget it. Do you hear?"

"Thank you, Emily."

"Hush now. Sleep well."
Softly she closed the door.

That night, still feeling the rolling of the ship, Eliza fell asleep to the sound of voices below. On the dressing table she had placed her silver box, her Spanish comb, and the broken-off arrow tip which Osceola had given her.

Eaton

Gadsby's Hotel, Washington City
February, 1829

AS a cheer arose in the street the general made a sign to his nephew, who nodded to Major Lewis, and both men said goodnight and left the room. John Eaton rose and went to the window where he stood with his arms folded looking down at the jubilant crowd. Snowflakes had begun to whisk the air.

"You have a thousand friends down there, General," he said after a moment.

Firelight wavered on Andrew Jackson's stricken face. "There is only one living friend I care about now," he said. "I want you to accept the secretaryship."

"You know my reasons for not accepting."

"I know them and I despise them!" Then in another voice he added, "Surely you will not desert me now, John."

John Eaton heard the appeal in his older friend's words.

For ten days he had put off this moment; now he must give his answer.

No doubts of his fitness to conduct the business of the War Department had caused his hesitation. Eleven years in the Senate had acquainted him with the tortuous operations of a peacetime army beset by public indifference, when the only wars fought were the paper squabbles of rival generals maneuvering for promotions, commands, and justifying their conduct in forgotten affairs. Only the problem of removing the southern Indians to the West was of any magnitude; and John Eaton suspected that, once recovered from his grief, Andrew Jackson, as President, would know how to carry out the policy he had advocated so long.

He had hesitated because he wished to impress deeply on Jackson's mind that he had not solicited the Cabinet post, but had ardently resisted it, suggesting other candidates who would be innocent of the charge, by any stretch of the imagination, of being friends of General Jackson. Especially he had made a strong case for his disqualification on the grounds of having married Margaret Timberlake, albeit with the President-elect's blessing, given upon his own solicitation of his elder friend's advice before proposing ("Marry her, if you will, and show there's nothing to their confounded gossip. For they know, John, that you would never marry her were their slanders true.") But now the very thought that his appointment bore seeds of trouble seemed to stir the general's spirits for the first time since the death of Rachel.

"I am only thinking of you, General," he said then. "Of you and the Presidency. Perhaps you underestimate the feeling against Margaret in this city, especially among the ladies—Mrs. Calhoun, Mrs. Branch, Mrs. Ingham."

"*I* choose the man I want. Mrs. Calhoun, Mrs. Branch, and Mrs. Ingham do not."

"They have great influence on their husbands, sir."

"Then the husbands are poltroons, sir!"

Cynics, John Eaton himself knew very well, might say that he used his knowledge of Andrew Jackson's temperament and his code of conduct to advance his own fortunes; but cynics, he also knew, misjudged the motives of honorable men, for cynics are blind to love, loyalty, honor; and John Eaton's profoundest thought at this moment was that if he accepted this high public trust it was out of devotion to this man. He could honestly say that he had no ambition but to serve his friend. He could as willingly return to his Tennessee plantation, his friends, his horses, his classic authors—but for Margaret. . . .

Gazing down at the crowd in the snowfall, he reflected on how he had come here, to this room, this moment.

He remembered Margaret at those first gay, intimate dinners at O'Neale's, after he had presented Andrew Jackson to her, and of how she had guided the general's fascination with her beauty to admiration of her wit, then to respect for her forthrightness, permitting his attentions peace only as admiration of her virtue. Never had the general cause to doubt her virtue. Together they had seen to that. For ten years they had loved each other with the discretion of Venetian assassins, and had married with the general's blessing, less than a year after her husband had cut his throat at sea.

He turned to his gaunt, grieving friend.

"I should never forgive myself were I to bring trouble to your administration."

John Eaton saw that Jackson had read the answer in his voice. The old warrior settled back in his chair.

"Thank God," he said. "I need somebody in this Cabinet I can talk to."

"I shall not desert you, General. I could not do such a thing."

And so John Eaton became Secretary of War of the United States.

And Margaret Eaton the Secretary's wife.

Eliza

.   Washington City
                                        March, 1829

FROM the first boom of the cannons in the morning Eliza was witness to the scenes of the Inauguration, yet she could not lose herself in the excitement of the day, thinking of the casualties of the general's march here, to this triumph which for him Rachel's death had made a calvary. Dark thoughts invaded her and the more she tried to capture the mood of jubilation the more they possessed her. With Emily and the ladies of the Cabinet she had seen Andrew Jackson walk up the long hill, accompanied by the gentlemen of his party, surrounded on every side by the crowd, in finery and in rags, and she had been moved by the tragic cast of his face, sensing his loneliness in this mass of people, the courage in each step of black buckled shoe, while the people claimed their hero, the champion they saw in the grim fighter, now fighting his bereavement.

And as that crowd cheered him, waving their hats and handkerchiefs, running to be near him, heard a lady say, "There is the old veteran. There is Jackson."

The portico where he would take the oath of office was filled with ladies dressed in scarlet, blue, yellow, and waving plumes amid the white marble pillars; in the center was a table covered with a red cloth; behind, the closed door leading into the rotunda; the grand steps leading down from the portico were also crowded with ladies and all around was a mass of living beings, thousands upon thousands as far as the eye could see; the sun which had been obscured by a morning mist now shone forth, and as the door from the rotunda opened, cannons thundered from the heights around Alexandria and Fort Warburton, and a great shout arose. Then, preceded by marshals and surrounded now by the justices of the Supreme Court, Andrew Jackson advanced to the table and bowed to the crowd. Breathless silence followed as he spoke, the pages trembling, his words inaudible.

Then the Chief Justice stepped forward to administer the oath, and when the marshal presented the Bible, Andrew Jackson took it from his hands, pressed it reverently to his lips, laid it down, and bowed again to the people.

As he left the Capitol and started down toward the gateway opening onto Pennsylvania Avenue the crowd closed around him, everyone eager to shake his hand. With difficulty he was able to mount the horse that had been brought for his return and ride through the crowd, which became an immense cortege following him: countrymen, farmers, gentlemen, mounted and unmounted, boys, women, children, black and white; carriages, wagons, carts all following him to the President's House.

That afternoon, with Laird, Eliza saw a sight she would remember all her life. For the crowd soon became an unruly mob, and the mob a rabble which invaded the President's House, ran wild, and nearly pressed the President to death before John Eaton and Jack Donelson could fight them off and spirit him out the back and to Gadsby's. No police had been provided; the Donelsons had never imagined that any but ladies and gentlemen would attend the reception. Cut glass and china worth several thousand dollars were smashed in the struggle for the refreshments; punch, lemonade, ice cream, and cake were carried out in tubs; ladies fainted, men were seen with bloody noses; it was the People's day and the People's President, and the People ruled.

And there were ladies and gentlemen heard lamenting the departure of John Quincy Adams, proclaiming the end of an era. The shutters of neighboring houses were slammed shut, the doormats taken up.

That evening, after their party had narrowly escaped being crushed by the celebrants downstairs at Gadsby's, Eliza and Laird, following the Donelsons, entered the double doors of Carusi's grand ballroom; and Eliza was surprised to see in the helter-skelter capital so many people of fashion, splendidly dressed women, men in evening dress, scarlet sashes, uniforms, at tables with candelabra and hothouse flowers, so much expanse of gleaming floor, laden refreshment tables, musicians, garlands, patriotic bunting, the re-

146

splendent scene endlessly reflected in mirrors. Here was no repetition of the afternoon; here invitations were taken and intruders turned away; and though a vibrant excitement filled the room, heightened by the music, there was decorum and elegance.

The center of attention was Emily. As she entered the brilliant room there were gasps at her youth and proud bearing, her amber satin gown with off-the-shoulder sleeves, all embroidered with rosebuds and violets and set of with artificial flowers at the bodice and skirt, her mass of titian hair crowning her small fair face; and many present were thinking, *What if it had been Rachel?* and were secretly thankful that Providence had spared the nation a First Lady who was stout, wore a bonnet over her sunburned face, and smoked a pipe. Upon Emily's entrance it was apparent that, after all, American Society was not about to be disgraced, that, despite her youth, the new mistress of the President's House possessed natural poise and dignity that would enhance Society in the Republic before the eyes of the world. And moments after her entrance many present were comparing her favorably not only to the specter of Rachel but to chilly Mrs. Adams, with her fondness for foreign nobility. Emily Donelson of Tennessee was an American aristocrat—a natural aristocrat. As she advanced into the room ladies of her acquaintance hastened to press around her, Mrs. Calhoun, Mrs. Branch, and Mrs. Ingham; and already many present were glancing to the table not far from the places reserved for Emily and Jack Donelson, where Margaret Eaton, simply yet dazzlingly attired, sat with her husband and some of the diplomatic corps; and when Emily passed the Eatons, she looked neither at them nor away from them, while Margaret Eaton, engaged with a besashed gentleman on her right, looked neither at Emily nor away from her, so that it was impossible to say that a snub had been given or received by either, only that there had been no greeting.

147

Then Eliza, on Laird's arm, passed the Eatons' table; Margaret Eaton looked directly at her—with no sign of recognition; Eliza looked quickly away.

"Looks like it's Tennessee's day!" Laird said, leading the applause as Jack Donelson and his Emily opened the dancing.

Watching Emily, Eliza remembered how she had always thought of her cousin as a Cumberland girl acting the part of a lady; now she realized that it was she, Eliza Hutchins, who was out of place here. As Aunt Rachel would have been.

She dared not glance again at Margaret Eaton.

Gentlemen of rank and station vied to dance with the President's kinswoman.

General Alexander Macomb, commanding general of the army, portly, with a red, jovial face and agreeable manners.

"Will there be war in Florida?" Eliza had asked him.

General Macomb, unaccustomed to discussing military topics with ladies, at first had not understood.

"With the savages?"

"With the Seminoles."

"Oh, no indeed, my dear. We won't fight them—we'll remove them—for their own protection."

"And if they won't leave willingly?"

"Then we will be obliged to remove them by force," explained the general, marveling at the waywardness of the female mind.

And Secretary John Eaton, as collected as ever, pleased by the frowns of the other Cabinet wives directed at his wife as she danced with a handsome naval officer.

"We have missed you in Nashville, Miss Hutchins."

"You are kind, sir, but Florida is our home now."

148

John Eaton raked over his memory for a moment, then said, "A man of consummate humanity, John Hutchins. Consummate humanity."

"Then it would seem that humanity is no longer wanted in Florida," Eliza said.

"Everywhere, Miss Hutchins. As much of it as possible."

"Perhaps you are not aware, sir, that my father was replaced as agent of the Florida Indians."

John Eaton paused in the dance with a show of concern.

"I was not, Miss Hutchins. The matter had not come to my attention. A very great pity." Resuming the dance, he said, frowning, "No doubt that rascal Clay planted one of his following in the post. Same thing all through the country. Unconscionable. Still, Miss Hutchins, your father may be better off. The people of Florida no longer view the Indian question reasonably—no more than do the Indians themselves. They have no notion of our power. I believe that the situation there will be a great deal worse before it is better; so it may be that Henry Clay, without meaning to, has saved your father considerable distress and possibly his life."

"My father must earn a living, Mr. Secretary."

"Have you brought the matter to the general's attention?"

"I've not wished to burden him now. He has already been more than generous to our family."

"Admirable, Miss Hutchins. Now is not the time. However, men of your father's quality will not be forgotten by this administration, and I shall absolutely make it a point to give the matter—my fullest attention—at the earliest possible moment—"

Even as he spoke Eliza saw that John Eaton's attention was drawn to his Margaret being seated at her table by the naval officer, while across from her the Dutch ambassador was starting to rise, evidently with a view to asking her to dance, and the Dutch ambassador's wife was trying to tug

149

him by the sleeve back into his chair. Meeting Eliza's eyes again, John Eaton seemed to recollect, through a maze of other considerations, the drift of their conversation.

"A truly difficult situation in Florida," he said and, glancing at Margaret, added, "One can sympathize with the Seminoles—they didn't ask to be born in the path of civilization."

The dance ended.

"Do call on us while you are here, Miss Hutchins," Eaton said as he led her to her place. "I'm certain that you and Mrs. Eaton will find much to talk about, and we can pursue at leisure—the subject of our conversation."

And Jack Donelson, in the kindest possible way, told her, "Emily and I both hope you will stay with us just as long as you can, Eliza," somehow making her feel more than ever like a poor relation, a burden on the household of the President of the United States.

"What's wrong?" Laird asked her when Donelson had seated her at the table.

"May be Tennessee's day, it ain't mine."

"Could be," he said, "and mine too."

When she understood that he was asking her to marry him she felt the old urge to refuse him, as always before, to escape as she had escaped Davidson County, to go on running, as he called it, toward whatever destiny or blind road was before her, possessed by no one; but as she searched his face the loneliness she had always warded off coursed through her and she felt a longing to be cared for, and to care for this stranger she had known all her life.

"Marry me, Eliza," he said, and she said yes.

Eliza

ABOUT the time the windows of the President's House were thrown open on the first warm days of spring Eliza discovered that she was in love with her future husband. Her cousin and companion since childhood, whom she feared to marry because she feared she did not love him, could suddenly flood her with pleasure merely by walking into a room. Now her care was whether he loved her. For he took all of life as he found it, as he was now taking her to wed; and although she had lingering thoughts that to marry him would be to betray some childhood trust with herself, all she knew for certain now was that she loved the look of him, the touch of him, that being with him was all she lived for. They argued often.

In April on a stroll along the Potomac he told her that when his assignment in the capital ended in September his next post would be St. Augustine.

"You'll be down there running the Indians off their lands," she said.

"Indians! I thought Florida was like home to you. I thought you'd be pleased." When she didn't answer he gestured toward the President's House. "I'll be down there obeying orders, that's all. Anyway, I thought we weren't going to talk about Indians. It's one subject you never have been reasonable about."

"And never will," Eliza replied. "I suppose you'll find there's no end to things I'm unreasonable about."

"Who cares?" he said with a sudden grin.

"You mean because I'll change," she told him. "You mean that though I can't change the shape of my nose to suit you I can certainly change any of my ideas you don't care for."

151

He appraised her profile judiciously.

"Your nose ain't so bad. I do believe in time I could learn to like it."

Amused but wary of the game, she pretended to be offended and walked faster. He caught up with her.

"Liza," he said, now with no banter in his voice, "I have a feeling right now there's a whole other woman locked up inside you without a bother in the world—just trying to get free."

"And she's the one you're marrying?"

"I'm marrying you."

"For the other."

"I do believe I want both of you."

Three days later they had another, more serious argument—about Margaret Eaton. Laird maintained that in defending the Secretary's wife Andrew Jackson was really striking back at the calumniators of Rachel, to the great advantage of Mrs. Eaton, who did not merit such gallant defense of her virtue. Eliza asserted that Mrs. Eaton was innocent until proved guilty—until the argument grew so bitter that it was an entire dismal hour before it ended.

This incident determined Eliza to overcome certain disturbing fears and to call on Mrs. Eaton. By an exchange of notes a visit was arranged for the following Sunday.

Standing at the entrance of the Eaton's brick house opposite the British Legation, attended by Delia, Eliza felt as if she were entering a forbidden domain; the memory of her first encounter with Margaret Eaton, revived by glimpses of her at the ball, was still vivid.

An elderly black butler opened the door, admitting them to a mirrored foyer beyond which was a broad hallway with a gracefully curved staircase. On a Chinese table in the foyer stood a silver bowl for visiting cards. Delia having been directed to the servants' quarters below, Eliza was escorted into a splendid parlor, where a fire burned in a black marble fireplace. The room was papered in deep blue, curtained in red, furnished with a shawled piano, a harp, a bust of Caesar on a pedestal, a loveseat, red velvet settees facing across a low table set with a silver tea service in front of the fire, Oriental carpets on the polished floor. In the corner by a tall window hung a filigree birdcage in which two canaries twittered. Narcissuses bloomed in a Chinese bowl on the piano, their vibrant aroma mixing with the smells of wax, wood fire, and a lingering scent of rose water. A footfall on the stairs and the Secretary's wife entered.

In the eleven years since Eliza had first seen her, Margaret Timberlake Eaton was perhaps more beautiful than she had been then; her figure was slightly fuller and for this the nearer to statuesque perfection; but it struck Eliza from the first moment that this perfect beauty no longer seemed enlivened from within; when she smiled Eliza experienced a brief stir of remembrance; but when Mrs. Eaton greeted her in a way that seemed to ask why she had come at all, the memory was gone, and the Secretary's wife was a lady of the world.

"Have we met before?" Margaret Eaton asked, as they faced each other over the tea things. "I saw you at the ball, but I have a feeling we have met before, long ago."

When Eliza reminded her of their encounter at O'Neale's Mrs. Eaton reflected, then laughed.

"Of course! I do remember. You were so very serious. I remember that. Very serious. So you see—my memory is not so bad as all that."

The canaries chattered.

Eliza forced herself to smile and sipped her tea. The Secretary's wife inquired after her parents and upon Eliza's telling her of her mother's death, said, "What a great pity. A dear quiet lady. I remember her too, though of course only vaguely. And your father?"

"My father resides in Florida. He had been agent of the Indians there." She had not meant to say "resides," but the Secretary's wife possessed the power to coax false manners from her.

"Indians!" that lady exclaimed with sudden animation.

"Why, they're my husband's responsibility. I ought to know because—you'll never believe it—I've had Indians in this very house. I've *received* Indians, my dear. Lemons! said my husband one fine day, send out for all the lemons in the city and make the largest quantity of lemonade possible, we have made a treaty with some Indians and I have invited them here to smoke the peace pipe, and I said no, my friend, I shall never permit dirty tobacco-smoking Indians to enter this house, and he said that I must, that we must treat our red brethren civilly, and I said plague take your red brethren but my husband insisted that I must be very good and treat them nicely and what was more that I would have to smoke the peace pipe with them, and I told him not for anything would I put that nasty thing in my mouth. Well, he said that I had to or else there would be war with the Indians, I said very well there will be war with the Indians, but of course he knows all the ways to get around me and I finally consented. I sent out for lemons and two kitchen tubs and on the appointed day had more lemonade prepared than has ever been seen in Washington City. Well, they trooped into these very rooms, a hard-looking lot, I must say, all dressed up in the fantastic style of the forest. Of course I tried to behave but I can tell you I did not feel very heavenly then; besides, from the look on my husband's face and the way the savages kept glancing at the door I could tell that some horrid surprise was in store and I dreaded what it might be. Well, they wheeled in a cart with something on it covered by a cloth and when the cloth was removed there was this tea service—isn't it handsome?—they were presenting it to me, you see; because my husband had treated them well but as Secretary would accept no gratuities, so they'd gotten together and decided to present a tea service to his wife. Well, of course I melted. I kicked off my shoes and stood on that chair and made a little speech—I've forgotten what I said but it seemed to please them immensely; then the pipe was prepared and I whispered to my husband that I meant to wipe the mouthpiece with my lace

154

handkerchief and he whispered back that I might do so if I wished both of us murdered on the spot, so I smoked the pipe and it was not so bad and we were all great friends, the red brethren and I; I believe some of them even had tears in their eyes as they left, I daresay from the smoke. In any event, that's my story of the Indians."

During this narration Eliza tried to find excuses for the Secretary's wife. Surely the lady was in no way to blame for the disenchantment which Eliza felt now, the realization that nothing had ever passed between them, not even for a moment, and that it was only her beauty which was so deceiving. Then she was aware that all through the telling of her "story of the Indians" Margaret Eaton's eyes remained shrewd.

"Of course one pities them," she went on, as if in deference to her guest's sensibilities. "As my husband says, they didn't ask to be born in the path of civilization."

"In Florida they are starving," Eliza said quietly.

Margaret Eaton's slight frown conveyed equal concern for the plight of the Indians and for the propriety of a reference to it.

"Really? I thought we fed them."

"Too little. And too little of that actually reaches them."

"Indeed?" Mrs. Eaton said. "Cannot your father do something to remedy that? I suppose it's terribly difficult." The shadow of a smile showed through her concern. "More tea?"

Eliza declined, then told her that her father had been dismissed from his post.

"Oh, I *am* sorry," the Secretary's wife replied. "Though I'm not surprised. Politics is a heartless business. I've known politicians all my life, of all parties and persuasions—though only gentlemen because only gentlemen were welcome at my father's tavern. Andrew Jackson was one. My husband was another. When Andrew Jackson and John Eaton were with us it was as if we were receiving members of our own family." She smiled, remembering, then frowned. "I imagine that your father should have no difficulty in securing another post?"

Eliza explained that the President had been too deeply affected by Rachel's death to attend to appointments—she did not add that more recently the source of his distraction was the attacks against Margaret Eaton herself.

"The cruelty of people has always amazed me," the Secretary's wife said with a sigh. "A more virtuous woman than Rachel Jackson never lived. We were well acquainted, I believe I can say that we respected one another. Now they have destroyed that excellent woman and they are at work on me. You know of course that I am not welcomed in the company of certain ladies of this city?"

"Yes, I do know."

"And you came to this house—no doubt at the President's suggestion?"

"No, madam. I requested this visit on my own account."

"Then I am doubly grateful for it. Dear little Mrs. Donelson, I fear, had to be fairly pushed through that door—and I think that by mutual agreement she will not appear in it again. The poor thing is not to be blamed, she is very much the victim of her own inexperience and has chosen to believe the tales of those so-called ladies who have so degraded themselves as to envy a tavernkeeper's daughter. Would you believe such a thing? Some of them still turn green when they remember Mrs. Madison publicly praising me at my first ball, and now my marriage to Mr. Eaton and my friendship with the President have them quite beside themselves. Shall I tell you a secret? My one real sin, to which I plead guilty, is never to have been ashamed of my parentage. And for a very good reason. Because it was every bit as good as the best of theirs and better than most—in fact my mother's sister was married to the governor of New Jersey. But for me not to be ashamed and bow my head because my father accommodated gentlemen visitors under his roof, that is what my enemies find unforgivable. That is why they invent scandal, to justify their spite."

As she spoke her eyes flashed, then abruptly she smiled at Eliza with a show of warmth.

"But this is such a tedious subject. Do tell me about yourself, Miss Hutchins. I hardly know you."

As the canaries chirruped, Eliza's mind raced over her life for something to share with her hostess—and she told her of her engagement to Laird. Mrs. Eaton found this subject to her liking, asked several direct and sympathetic questions, then for the next fifteen minutes recounted the story of her reception at the Timberlakes' aristocratic Virginia home when she was first married.

Eliza made no further effort to return the conversation to her father, nor did Mrs. Eaton allude again to the former agent of the Florida Indians.

The door closed behind Eliza and Delia as they started down the street toward Pennsylvania Avenue. They had gone a block before Delia broke the silence.

"So that's what all the fussin's about."

Eliza was near tears. She spoke harshly. "What do you know about her?"

"'Nough."

"You hardly caught a glimpse of her."

"Don't take but a look to tell trash."

"Delia! That's plain insolence and I won't have it."

"Ain't neither," the other said, as determined. "It's the truth. 'Bout half the truth."

"Delia, that woman is Senator Eaton's wife and the President's friend."

"Ain't my fault."

Eliza stopped. Delia went on a few steps, then halted and turned to her. For the first time in her life Eliza found herself raising her voice to a servant.

"I won't have you speaking against her—you hear me?"

"Yes, ma'am, I sure do."

They walked in silence until they came in sight of the President's House. Then, remembering the "Indian story,"

Eliza smiled at her own disillusionment, and she was thinking how to make up with Delia when the other spoke again.

"All I knows for certain is that Gen'l Jackson's makin' hisself a big mistake."

Jackson

The President's House
September, 1829

THE President sat perched on his clerk's high stool, wearing his full-dress, gold epauleted, general's tunic over his plain riding clothes and muddy boots, staring at the gilt clock on the mantle as the painter had directed him to do. Between the subject and the windows was the large oval table at which the special Cabinet meeting would take place. Throughout the sitting the President's face had been a sea of moods from fury to satisfaction, amusement, then back to fury. Tonight he intended to put an end to the Eaton trouble forever.

For of all the battles of his life this one was the most trying to his spirit. It was a war against barroom wits, women, clergymen, political enemies, whose weapons were whispers; a war against the traducers of Margaret Eaton and her husband, his friend. But now, tonight, the President was confident that it was in his power to end the whole vile conspiracy.

He was absolutely certain that the Eatons were innocent—as certain as he was that he and Rachel were innocent before God for having married, through an honest mistake, before Rachel's divorce decree was final.

Yet his enemies had hastened Rachel to her grave with their caricatures of that best and noblest of women as a gross, immoral character. He had raged in the restraining

158

hold of his friends, John Eaton foremost, but did not punish the slanderers because, his friends said, there was no way of identifying them. Yet he had let a grievous wrong against Rachel go unpunished, and that failure to act, even rashly, even madly, now filled him with remorse such as he had never felt over any who had met a just death on his order or on the field of honor.

No! President of the United States or Emperor of China— he would not abandon his friend and let an honest woman's reputation be destroyed. No matter if the affairs of government had to wait; he would win this battle too!

Tonight if possible.

There had been little warning of the storm that was to break over the Eatons' marriage; but from the day of that marriage, the first of January, to his Inauguration on the fourth of March, the winds had freshened. Ladies of the capital stopped calling on Mrs. Eaton, and by summer all Society was in a furor over her right to admittance in it. Newspapers called her Bellona, the goddess of war. The Cabinet was divided: the President, Martin Van Buren and Eaton against Branch, Berrien, and Ingham—and John Calhoun, whose brooding presence filled the President with presentiments of treachery. His own household was bedeviled. His friend Major Lewis was a staunch Eatonite, but his own niece Emily, the mistress of his house, had, at his urging, called on Mrs. Eaton and returned saying flatly that she would not call on her again, that the woman had prattled of nothing but her intimacy with the Jacksons; and his nephew Jack, loyal and invaluable in other matters, sided finally with his wife. Political friends had proposed that Eaton be offered an ambassadorship overseas, but Margaret had rejected any such project, saying that her enemies were here and she would meet them here. Andrew Jackson had liked her fighting spirit. John Eaton would remain Secretary of War.

In his campaign in the Eatons' defense no one now stood closer to the President's side than the dapper, genial, astute

Secretary of State, Van Buren. He visited the Eatons frequently and had only agreeable things to say of them. A bachelor, he entertained them handsomely. Others might find the New Yorker devious, conniving, but the President was discovering that the Secretary was a man of excellent judgment. Lately Van Buren had even purchased a great bay gelding so as to accompany the President on his brisk daily ride along the Potomac. To be sure, the diminutive Secretary cut a comical figure, for he was no horseman; his hands were bad and his mount was already jittery from puzzling out what its rider expected of it; at a trot he was more off the saddle than on, landing at one angle only to fly off at another; at a canter his lurches forward and back were alarming to see—*but he hung on.* And his readiness to risk his neck and dignity was the latest proof that the Secretary of State was a loyal and serviceable ally, whom the President would be glad to have at his side tonight.

How had the storm arisen?

The most stubborn charge against the Eatons was that they had slept together while she was married to Timberlake, Timberlake being at sea. To this the President could state that—at least when he was staying at O'Neale's—nothing of the sort had ever happened: Eaton's room was next to his own, Margaret's in a distant part of the house down a creaky corridor, up groaning stairs, and no mortal being could have traveled that corridor and those stairs without Andrew Jackson knowing about it. Moreover, Eaton was a Mason, as was Timberlake, and no Mason would ever so flagrantly violate his vows unless he had been infected by a moral depravity entirely foreign to John Eaton. Rather, Eaton had always helped Timberlake, aiding him discreetly with substantial sums of money, making it possible, when ill luck cast a shadow on his friend's career as a naval purser, for him to go to sea again.

Gossip would also have it that Margaret was promiscuous with other men, indeed many other men, and there were even those now in Washington City who let it be understood that they had enjoyed her favors—every last one of

160

these so-called gentlemen a known braggart and a liar. Let them ask his friend General Richard Call about the matter of Margaret's promiscuity. The President well remembered the night at O'Neale's when Call, a young robust man then, inflamed by whiskey and tales of Margaret's availability, had followed her into a sitting room, determined to join the ranks of contented gentlemen who (as he had heard) were enjoying her ultimate gifts. Under the impression that the surest way to her bed was a bold expression of manly ardor, he had approached her breathing "Margaret, my beloved!" and taken her in his arms when to his utter astonishment she had screamed. Far from melting in his embrace she had then drawn away and quite unexpectedly seized a poker from the fireplace and chased him from the room, to the amusement of O'Neale's guests. When General Call of the Florida militia had recently presumed to express doubts about Margaret Eaton's respectability, the President had been pleased to remind him that he had special reason to know of her virtue, and no more was heard from General Call.

Still, nothing could induce the ladies of the capital to call upon or receive Bellona.

And as her cause appeared more hopeless the President's will to see her vindicated strengthened. Jackson men despaired over his obsession, which left him little time for their business with him. His enemies were delighted. The Eaton Malaria, as the papers called it, soon spread from the capital through the nation.

Tonight the President had set the stage to stamp out the epidemic—by exposing as false the tales of two men of God.

A black servant opened the double doors and began to light the lamps. Major Lewis entered then, followed by Martin Van Buren, none the worse for his morning ride. As they were greeting the President, Messrs. Branch, Berrien, and Ingham entered in close order, startled by the sight of Andrew Jackson in full-dress general's tunic. The painter quietly left the room. The President and his guests had

161

gathered to inspect the portrait when a creak of the stair announced another arrival. John Calhoun came in, sweeping the company with his dark gaze. Again, as they greeted each other, Andrew Jackson felt an instinctive mistrust of the Vice President, a warning against this man of Carolina birth, of Scots-Irish blood like his own, with his intense manner, this brilliant, morose, ambitious man whom he had once admired but now sensed was no friend of his.

The President led the others to the table, directing Major Lewis to take John Eaton's usual place next to the Secretary of State, on his own right; John Calhoun was on his left; Branch, Berrien, and Ingham took their places toward the foot of the table, at the very end of which, facing the President were two extra chairs. No sooner were they seated than the Irish doorkeeper ushered in, with no especial enthusiasm, Reverend Dr. Ely and Reverend Mr. Campbell.

Both reverend gentlemen appeared at first somewhat struck by the sight of the President of the United States in uniform and the gentlemen of the Cabinet in black seated watching them. Andrew Jackson rose to greet them, Dr. Ely warmly, Reverend Campbell coolly, then introduced them to all present and bade them be seated.

Dr. Ely was a tall elderly man with tufts of white hair jutting over his ears and a gentle narrow face pinched with concern, a concern, it might be guessed, not for himself but for the affairs of others, temporal as well as spiritual. Reverend Campbell was a much younger, shorter and stouter minister. His hair was red, his face pink and freckled; and it would have been a more pleasant face were it not fixed in an expression of truculent piety. On his short nose he wore thick round spectacles in the lenses of which his green suspicious eyes swam slowly. Throughout his parish he was noted for his lofty disdain of wealth, position, and worldly achievement, a sentiment all the more noteworthy because he ministered exclusively to those most burdened with exactly these spiritual liabilities. He took his place beside Dr. Ely and carefully folded his small hands.

"Gentlemen," began the President in his commanding rasp, "I have asked Dr. Ely and Reverend Campbell here so that you may listen to what they have to say on the subject which has lately agitated our city—also so that you may hear what Major Lewis will report on the same subject, Major Lewis having at my request assembled facts—I repeat the word, gentlemen—facts, as well as testimonials from persons of the highest character. Also you shall hear what I have to say on the matter, as a witness to events alleged to be illicit but which were not illicit, gentlemen, as I am prepared to swear on the Holy Book.

"John Eaton is not present here. I have not asked him here because I wish this meeting to proceed unhampered by considerations of John Eaton's feelings—I want the truth in this room. Nor does John Eaton need to speak in his own defense since there is no case against him, as the facts will show—but there again I leave the matter of judgment to you."

Now the President turned his attention to Messrs. Branch, Berrien, and Ingham, who sat very erect, keeping their faces as blank as possble.

"It is well known," he went on, looking from one to the other, "that certain ladies have refused to show Mrs. Eaton the ordinary courtesies due her. Indeed, my own niece has fallen under this influence. Now there may be little that can be done about this, gentlemen. I do not know. I do not wish to legislate whom they or you, sirs, will see or not see; this is entirely your personal affair. All I know is that John Eaton is an able member of this Cabinet and a friend of mine for many years and John Eaton will remain a member of this Cabinet and there will be harmony and courtesy in this Cabinet or by the Eternal—" Checking himself, the President looked at Dr. Ely, then with an expression of distaste at Reverend Campbell. "Let me say only that it is my heartfelt expectation that this whole business wll be ended once and for all—tonight, gentlemen.

"We ask ourselves how the rumors about the Eatons be-

163

gan. We shall never know. In a barroom, no doubt. The quip of some inebriate trying to earn a reputation for wit. Or some lackey of Henry Clay. Let us not speculate, the poltroon has done his work and we shall never find him out. However, gentlemen, when his foul fabrications assume the colors of truth and respectability, are propagated even by ministers of the church of Jesus Christ, then, my friends, we are witnessing the ravages of rumor upon reputation, especially upon the always fragile reputation of a woman. And this is when all of us who esteem honesty over sensation are bound to cry stop! How in fairness do we know these things to be true?

"Dr. Ely, gentlemen, I know from personal acquaintance to be a devout Christian of irreproachable character. Therefore when I received from Dr. Ely a letter, written obviously with the best of possible intentions, urging me for my own sake, that of my dead wife, for the sake of my administration, the credit of the country, not to countenance *a woman such as Mrs. Eaton,* only then did I conceive the full extent of the mischief; for if Dr. Ely could be so imposed upon by the calumnies as to advance, as he did, certain arguments which I personally know could not be true, then I could well imagine how readily less scrupulous men and women would credit the same stories.

"As Dr. Ely is now aware, there is no truth whatsoever to the report that Mrs. Jackson put the seal of reprobation on Mrs. Eaton. On the contrary she believed her to be an innocent and much maligned woman. As for the tale of there being too intimate relations between Major Eaton and the then Mrs. Timberlake under her father's roof while Mr. Timberlake was in his country's naval service, in all the years I shared from time to time the same quarters, I never once observed the slightest sign of there being any such intimate relations and am positively convinced that there were none.

"Dr. Ely also reported certain stories of Mr. Eaton and the then Mrs. Timberlake traveling to New York City and regis-

164

tering together at the same hotel as man and wife. Since I wished to investigate each accusation made by the traducers of female reputation I asked Dr. Ely to oblige me by personally traveling to New York City for the purpose of making inquiries at the hotel in question. Dr. Ely—"

"Yes, Mr. President."

"Did you travel to New York City?"

"I did," the minister replied carefully, "for the purpose you name."

"Did you make inquiries at the hotel?"

"I did, sir."

The President leaned forward, riveting the clergymen with his intense blue gaze.

"And did you discover any evidence that Mr. Eaton and the then Mrs. Timberlake ever registered at that hotel or at any other hotel in New York City?"

"No, sir. Nothing. Though of course—"

"Nothing!" announced Andrew Jackson, leaning back in his chair with satisfaction. "There you have it, gentlemen. Close inquiries are made in New York City by an ambassador of Christ and what is revealed? Dr. Ely, you who have traveled so far; for the benefit of these gentlemen kindly say again exactly what it was you found."

"Nothing."

"Exactly," agreed the President. "Nothing. And why nothing? Simply because there was nothing and there is nothing—nothing except a sort of fever affecting people's minds. Margaret Eaton is chaste as a virgin!" Turning his attention sharply to Reverend Campbell, he added, "I am disgusted even to loathing at the depraved state of society. It needs purifying."

"I should think it possible, sir, and with all respect," put in the younger minister, "that the hotel's records of a time so long ago have disappeared, and with changes of staff any witnesses too. I believe that Dr. Ely himself—"

"Dr. Ely needs no one to put words into his mouth, sir!" declared the President firmly. "Yes, I allow that what you contend is possible, sir. However, what matters far more is that Christian charity and justice may have disappeared, that witnesses to Christ's Divine Errand may have disappeared! That is what has disappeared here, sir!" The President paused and gazed again around the table, then continued in an abruptly milder voice. "Gentlemen, we are all too familiar with the nature of the stories about the Eatons, the common gossip. However, there is one tale—most damning were it true—which I believe is not current. Dr. Ely reported it to me as coming to him from another clergyman, and I confess that I was pained to learn this and advised Dr. Ely to remind that clergyman of the precepts of the Book, which he himself would know where to find, and I thought no more about the matter. Several days passed. Then the very clergyman in question presented himself to me in this very room and I was amazed to find that he was no other than Reverend Campbell, whose sermons I have often heard with profit. Reverend Campbell related the tale, and while I was a second time greatly struck by its patent absurdity, I shall not insist upon my own response, gentlemen, but will ask Reverend Campbell kindly to relate it now so that you may form your own opinions, which I urge you to do in as fair and unprejudiced a manner as possible. Reverend Campbell."

Thus presented, the younger minister, very determined not to be discountenanced by the President, began warily, as follows:

"Some time ago, gentlemen, I chanced to meet a certain Dr. Cravan, who was attending a parishioner of mine in his last illness. Somehow our conversation turned to the Timberlakes and the doctor informed me that he was acquainted with them, very well acquainted indeed, he assured me with great amusement."

"Amusement, sir? In the presence of a dying man?"

"We were downstairs, sir, perhaps even in front of the house."

"Which?"

"I don't remember, Mr. President," replied the minister

166

resolutely. "What matters is that the doctor then related to me that he had once been summoned to attend Mrs. Timberlake, having been told that the lady had been thrown from her carriage—only to discover upon examination that Mrs. Timberlake had not in fact—miscarriaged but rather—miscarried."

Here Reverend Campbell paused, looking owlishly around the circle. Only Van Buren let appear a measured smile.

"Rubbish!" said the President.

"And this when Mr. Timberlake had been at sea for more than a year," put in Campbell, adding, "Not long afterward I learned that Dr. Cravan had died of apoplexy."

"Laughed himself to death, no doubt," responded the President, then leaning forward, asked, "In what year, sir, did Dr. Cravan allege that he had attended Mrs. Timberlake?"

"1826, sir."

"1826! You originally said 1821!"

"So you have told me, sir. I do not recall doing so, though if I did it was a mistake—but only about the date."

"Sir, were I to ask you the year of Creation and you told me first one year, then another, then perhaps a third— which would I believe? Indeed, would I believe any?"

The minister clamped his hands together more tightly and replied that he would not mistake anything so important.

"Ah?" pursued the President. "Then to you the reputation of a defenseless woman and the good name of a member of my Cabinet are not important?"

"Most certainly, sir. That is why I felt obliged to tell Dr. Ely about my interview with Dr. Cravan, knowing that Dr. Ely was acquainted with you."

"And why not inform me directly, knowing me to be one of your congregation?"

"Because, Mr. President, I entertained the strongest suspicions that you might not believe me."

John Calhoun's baleful regard softened into a smile;

Branch, Berrien, and Ingham appeared to relax for an instant.

"Nonsense!"

But Reverend Campbell would not be intimidated.

"I thought Dr. Ely better fitted than myself for the task of presenting the facts."

"Facts? What facts? Is 1821 a fact?"

"Sir, in the opinion of both Mrs. Cravans, whom I interviewed this very morning—"

"We are not interested in the opinion of both Mrs. Cravans. We are interested in evidence. Hard evidence, sir, such as the sort Major Lewis has collected. Major Lewis—"

But to the surprise of all present Reverend Campbell rose to his feet and spoke as follows.

"Sir, the only purpose in all I have done was to preserve this administration from reproach and the morals of this country from contamination. I have tried to make known to you the event Dr. Cravan told me of, which I honestly believe to be a true account of what happened in a year— whichever year it was—when Mr. Timberlake was out of the country. I furthermore believe that the accumulation of circumstantial evidence against the Eatons is sufficiently convincing; for as it is commonly said, where there is smoke there is fire, and here, no one can deny, there is a most unusual quantity of smoke."

"From Hell, sir!" said the President with great asperity. "You were summoned here to give evidence about what you know, not to pass judgment on what you don't know. Kindly be seated, sir."

Reverend Campbell, however, remained standing.

"Then I perceive that I have mistaken the object of your *invitation* to come here. I shall only say that as for the affair of the late Dr. Cravan I stand ready to prove what I have said in a court of law—where I should hope, Mr. President, to receive a fairer hearing than I have tonight. Good evening, gentlemen. God be with you all."

So saying, Reverend Campbell turned and left the room,

which then became silent as the sound of his footfalls on the stairs died away and were heard no more.

Andrew Jackson stirred uncomfortably in his chair.

"So much for the dead doctor," he said. Then, with a fiery glance around the table, he demanded to know if anyone ever had heard such a cock-and-bull story in his life.

At first no one replied. Then Martin Van Buren raised his brows and examined his manicured nails.

"I for one certainly never have."

"Absolute nonsense," the President agreed, mollified. "Major Lewis."

Major Lewis then read a dozen testimonials to the good reputation of the Eatons and was beginning the thirteenth when Andrew Jackson interrupted him to declare the Eaton affair conclusively settled, harmony restored, and the meeting adjourned.

Hutchins to Eliza

St. Augustine
June, 1829

MY dear Eliza,

I rejoice at the news of your forthcoming marriage to Laird Caffrey and offer all the blessings a father can bestow upon you both and my wishes for your happiness and prosperity together. The Caffreys are a fine Tennessee family and I am confident that Laird will provide well for you and for any offspring God may bless you with. For my part I am cruelly disappointed that I shall not be able to journey to Washington City for the wedding but in the coming months will be at a crucial juncture in my affairs here, so that to leave would be impossible without grave risk. I take comfort in the fact that you will be settling in St. Augustine within the year and look

169

forward ardently to a reunion with my beloved daughter and her husband. By that time I shall be established in a new and most promising enterprise, a trading post on the St. Johns. This very day I have engaged with General Hernandez for the necessary capital for purchase, improvements, and goods. But I write of my business affairs when you are starting forth on life's greatest adventure! If I am not wrong the circumstance that you and Laird have known each other all your lives will not make that adventure any less hazardous—or less rich in rewards. Only one thing do I fear for you. That old differences, imagined or real, will in marriage harden into barriers to the full and loving discovery of each other. Only now do I realize that with my preoccupation with work and hopes I never really knew your mother, except as I chose to know her, and that, I see now, was not at all as she was. I would die content if I knew that in another life I could make up to her and to me that self-imposed blindness. See through to the inner being in Laird. Let him know yours. Look to the day when you can love each other as if the human race had no shame to hide.

With my blessings,
John Hutchins

P.S. I have it on General H's authority that within a short time Congress is certain to pass legislation to remove the Indians and the exodus of the Seminole people will at last commence. I have come to believe that this course, tragic as it is, is the only one possible and that in any case nothing can prevent it, if indeed to prevent it would be anything but a cruel reprieve.

Eliza

ON a clear September day Eliza and Laird were married in the Presbyterian Church in Washington City. Under a bower of swords they left the church and were driven in Andrew Jackson's carriage to the President's House where Emily Donelson had arranged a small reception. Uncle Jackson himself led the toasts, wishing them, God willing, long life and happiness. John Eaton had raised his glass to Tennessee woman, "the fairest and purest in the United States" and to Tennessee men, "whose honor it was to protect their good name"—his own wife being at home with the vapors. All through the reception Eliza had unconsciously been searching the rooms for her father, and the handsome cavalry officer who was now her husband, and whom she was so in love with, had never seemed more a stranger.

Their honeymoon was on board a packet and in a Savannah hotel with a balcony overlooking a garden square. Laird bought her gowns, and a splendid green riding costume, soft leather boots and a matching plumed hat.

"You'll spoil me," she had said.

"Exactly what I mean to do, Mrs. Caffrey."

The evening at sunset when they disembarked from a smaller packet at St. Augustine, Eliza had felt that she was living a dream lodged deep in her imagination ever since she had come with her father to this seashell-mortared town and danced on the roof of the fort in a borrowed blue dress.

It was a homecoming of someone she had never been.

She searched the waterfront for her father but he was not there. At the post they learned that he was traveling in western Florida.

171

They had taken a house at the south end of town near the post, with a view across the straits to Anastasia Island and north to the seaward bastions of the fort. Early mornings, Laird sleeping beside her, she would awaken to dawns breaking over the island, smells of fresh sea air, of the walled garden below the windows, of coffee, bread, and bacon fixed by Delia, and then too she felt that she was awakening into the life of another person, with no cares, that in the role of being Laird's wife, kept in comfort, she was drifting off the true course of her life, and there were things she should be doing which she was not doing. Nor was it enough that from the start she understood that Laird was trying to strip from her the independence of her maidenhood, leaving a perfect lady for him to be proud of, willingly submissive; his contented smile as he slept vexed her beyond reason—until he awoke and took her in his arms.

Her days were free. With Laird at the post, a lieutenant with a cavalry company to command, she shopped at the marketplace on the plaza with Delia, strolled on the seawall past the vessels at the wharves, in the narrow streets of white walls and shuttered houses with the ambling crowd of Spanish, Minorcans, Americans, French, sailors and traders from everywhere, blacks; worked in her garden; read Scott; visited Malvina, now Mrs. Belcamp and wiser than ever about men and more amusingly acid; rode the Arabian mare Laird bought her, drove a lacquered phaeton; and it required Malvina's exasperated explanations to teach her that such luxuries were not to be had on Lieutenant's pay and that Laird—who never said a word about such matters— was very well off, and doubtless had even greater expectations.

That first winter, with the Belcamps, a certain merry Captain Appleton and his Charleston-born wife, and young bloods among the Spanish and French who did not scorn American company, Laird and Eliza attended the fiestas, the masking parties, the dances at the fort, and, afternoons, the horse races at the popular-ringed track south of the post, which became their regular gathering place. For the first time in her life Eliza knew the feeling of being part of a sporting, reveling crowd; but the more she tried to lose herself in Laird's unreckoning world, the more she felt like an outsider; and the mild winter days passed, leaving no trace, obliterated in gaity.

Sometimes, alone, she strolled in the Minorcan quarter north of the plaza behind the fort, envying the contentment of these olive-skinned people, once bondsmen, now fishermen and graceful women, to whom each sunrise was the promise of a day of life, until vespers, and for the young the night's festivity. She would search for some secret in their faces as they gazed at the raised outdoor altars, each with a copper Christ in candlelight; she would listen for it in the Mass that filled the plaza like a serenade under God's window; as within the church, lovers bowed their heads and flirted stealthily, and outside along the church wall the day's dead lay in open candle-decked caskets, dressed in their best for strollers to see. There was no secret.

It was November before John Hutchins visited them. Eliza found him greatly changed. His lean, proud face was drawn, his hands trembled, and his whole manner with her was evasive. With Laird he was deferential, sometimes siding with him in his disagreements with her; and while at first she had been pleased that her husband and her father got on well together, she soon sensed that their friendship was fed by the idea that there were flaws in her that it was their business together to mend. In vain did she look for the John Hutchins of the wedding letter in this man who supported her husband's reproaches. Least understandable to her, her father seemed to find a connection between the imagined failings in her upbringing (whence sprang the flaws) and his own failure to make his fortune—as if she had somehow stood in his way. On the November visit she

173

thought little of such matters, but one day in January something happened which caused her to search more deeply into them, only to discover more questions without answers.

The three of them were returning from the weekly market on the plaza, taking the seawall (as far as possible from the slave auction on the other side of the plaza); they had just passed the wharf where the *Northern Star* had been berthed when she saw a party of Indians approaching them, six Seminoles. Leading them was Osceola. He was dressed as she remembered him, a red turban from which trailed two black plumes and one white, three silver crescents at the neck of his long tunic, a faded calico sash at his waist, leggings and moccasins. The five braves with him were similarly attired, except that they wore no plumes, and beads instead of crescents hung at their necks. All six carried bundles of doe and raccoon pelts slung over their shoulders.

When the Indians came almost abreast of them Osceola halted his braves and stood facing John Hutchins with the smile that Eliza remembered. John Hutchins spoke words of greeting and Osceola replied, then looked at Eliza, an intense look undimmed by any constraint of race or sex. He greeted her and Eliza returned the greeting, then Osceola glanced at Laird, sweeping his uniform disdainfully, then returned his attention to John Hutchins, who asked him about the Seminoles in the central villages.

"Why does he who was once the Seminoles' friend ask about us?" he said.

"I am still the friend of the Seminoles."

"Of our lands, not of us. Your friendship is as yesterday's sun."

The braves murmured in agreement. When John Hutchins did not reply Osceola turned again to Eliza.

"You once brought food to our villages. You taught us to wait for your gifts. Then you came no more."

"Osceola showed me he did not wish me to come," Eliza said.

"It was too late," the other replied. "Now our women and children are starving."

"Where are those who have come with you?"

"On the road south. Where your horses run."

"Then I will take them food."

"It is not safe anymore. Our bad men have short memories just as yours do."

"I'm not afraid."

"It is not safe for our people. If you were harmed your husband would lead many soldiers against us. And how could we tell him that only our bad men would harm a woman, when he doesn't understand our language?"

"I shall not be harmed."

He looked at her steadily a long time.

"Remember my gift," Osceola said then, and for an instant the smile was gone and she saw fury in its place, then with a word of parting Osceola led his braves past them toward the plaza.

When Eliza had told Laird what had passed between them (omitting Osceola's words to her father) he looked back at the Indians striding down the seawall.

"Bad men, indeed! He's the worst of the lot."

"If anyone can get the Seminoles to resist it's he," said John Hutchins.

"And you're taking food to them?" Laird demanded of Eliza.

"Yes," she told him. "They're starving. Their children are starving."

Laird walked in silence, then looked back to the plaza and stopped.

"Looks like they got other ideas than food."

The Indians were throwing their pelts down at the gunsmith's stall.

"They need powder and lead for hunting," she told him.

"Maybe," Laird said. "I'm thinking of you. A lady doesn't go riding around the countryside by herself."

Eliza looked to her father, hoping he would offer to ride with her but he did not. And so they returned down the seawall and turned into the street to the house, walking apart.

Eliza

Caffrey Station
May, 1830

IN March came the news that Laird's widower father had died and Laird had come into his full inheritance, Caffrey Station, with the house, 500 acres of cropland mostly planted in cotton; woods, and 150 servants and field hands. Laird had secured a leave and by stage and steamer they had traveled to Nashville, where a swarm of chattering Caffrey kin were on the wharf to greet the lieutenant and his wife; and they had driven up the long, cedar lined drive to the house, her home now, Laird told her, letting her know he had no doubt she would be worthy of it.

As their first months in St. Augustine had seemed like the enactment of an old dream, this sudden return to her birthplace was the realization of another, deeper presentiment, full of threat.

The Cumberland received her well, as the new Mrs. Caffrey and the President's kin. Obliterated was the memory of John Hutchins' daughter with her too private, too independent ways (sharp-tongued and tending more to her horses' grooming than her own looks); the girl who had lived with the Indians; the Cumberland now laid claim to Laird's wife as one of their own. Women were all kindness to her, the men courtly. The girls she had known at the Nashville Female Academy, most married now, gathered around her to hear of the Inauguration, every utterance and

176

gesture of Andrew Jackson, every detail of Emily's ball-gown, how darkly handsome John Calhoun was, how lively Justice Marshall, how sure and self-possessed John Eaton, how beautiful and fascinating his new wife (Eliza did not reveal her disenchantment over Margaret to these ladies). They listened, asking question after question, their eyes never straying from her—as if they were watching for signs that she was a stranger to them.

Not once did they ask her about her life at the Indian agency or mention her father. Only old Mrs. Donelson, rocking imperiously in her sun-drenched window corner, had broken the interdiction.

"John Hutchins is a fine man in many ways, Eliza," she decreed. "In some too good for this world."

The women had pressed around her avidly like children with a pet to teach, as if being Laird's wife she was in their charge now, with no chance to escape but by cleaving to their ways.

Laird had been proud of her.

He had taken to calling her Mrs. Caffrey, even during their lovemaking.

And she had tried for a while to act as the Mrs. Caffrey he seemed to want, offering a meek replica of herself as a trophy to his mastery, her gift, while yielding nothing of her true being; but her efforts to content him in this way somehow always ended in disaster.

The worst was the trouble about Lucy.

Soon after their arrival she had found comfort in the company of the house servant who had been Rachel Jackson's Lucy, bought from Blair, traded to the Caffreys after Rachel's death. In Eliza's sitting room they talked and mended together, about Rachel, and Uncle Jackson in Washington City, about Pensacola, a city which Lucy even now remembered as Bab'lon where all the mens had badness in their head. Eliza took Lucy with her marketing in Nashville. And soon in their talks Eliza began telling Lucy about the world beyond the Cumberland, where the oceans and continents were, the Pacific beyond the great unclaimed plains and mountains to the West, where the sun set, and under the dawn the Atlantic, Europe, Africa. And she told her also about the things she could not share with white women, about her father and the Indians of Florida. Once she caught herself about to tell Lucy about being with John Hutchins and Enos in the storm, before Lucy's wondering eyes stopped her.

Lucy listened, unable to keep her mind for long on anything she was hearing, so amazed was she to be hearing it at all.

At first Laird had approved of his wife's familiarity with Rachel's former servant. It spoke well of her that she treated the house Negroes as family. But as their stay neared its end Eliza saw his face grow set whenever Lucy was around or mentioned. Then one evening, after he had been drinking with friends at the Nashville Inn, while they were sitting in the big front parlor after supper with a driving rain at the windows, she learned what was on his mind; part of it right away, the rest a little later.

"Honey, about Lucy," he had said very gently.

"What about her?"

"All those things you been teaching her."

"What things?"

"Geography," he told her, frowning judiciously.

"What else?"

"History," he said, raising his brows, still determined to be gentle. "Natural science, for all I know. Maybe Greek? Honey, it doesn't do to tell her things she can't possibly understand. Already she's getting airs."

"What *can* she understand?" Eliza asked.

"For one thing," Laird replied sharply, "she can understand she's not meant to go lording it over the other people talking about *Africa!* Besides, she's got the world all scrambled up. North Pole in the middle of the Pacific Ocean. China out somewhere east of Natchez. It ain't a kindness to fill their heads with stuff they can't make sense of."

"Perhaps I should be learning from Lucy."

Laird looked at her a moment, letting pain creep into his face.

"Honey," he said, "I hate it when you go acting like a visitor here. The Cumberland's yours as much as mine."

"Seems not," she said, surprised by the sadness she felt then.

"You're what you're born to, like anyone else, Liza. You're home, Mrs. Caffrey."

Eliza stood, facing him, her sadness gone in a rush of anger.

"I am not *home*, Mr. Caffrey!"

Laird's look turned hard and he said very quietly, "No woman has ever raised her voice in defiance to her man in this house since my grandfather built it."

"Then it's surely high time!" Eliza said. "I'll not be told where I'm home or who I am by anybody!"

"And no grown-up woman," he went on in the same dead-quiet voice, "has ever been seen walking in Nashville with her servant *hand in hand*."

Eliza was stunned. Her thoughts raced—if she had ever taken Lucy's hand casually in the street she had thought nothing of it at the time and completely forgotten it—but it was not thought that directed what she did next but rather a power within her that ordered her to do exactly the thing that had to be done. Obediently she went to the window at the corner of the room where Laird had told her his father had spent every afternoon of his last years gazing out at his busy fields and game-stocked woodlands, and she raised the window, gratified to see rain driven by the wind onto the painted floor, the wing chair, and the polished round table. Then she turned to her husband, who watched her now with a calm, settled look.

"Laird Caffrey," she said, "as long as you live you will be dirtied by that remark and so will whoever tattled to you about nothing but the sick evil-mindedness of this place!"

"Shut the window, Liza."

"I am airing this house!"

"Shut the window."

She felt the strength in his quiet command, and she resolved then that no matter what happened to her, no matter what became of them both, she would not let him subjugate her.

"Never!" she said.

Slowly Laird got up and came toward her, the liquor showing in his face—then walked on past her and closed the window.

"Looks like you been living with the redskins too long," he said, with a faint smile.

"I lived with my father," she said, feeling the power that told her what to do leaving her, "—who had feelings he wasn't afraid to live by, not by everyone else's damned code!"

Now when he smiled again she swore she would never forgive him.

"You better start getting used to that code," he said. "Someday we'll be back here for good."

"Never!" she said again and, answering the rain, "And I'm leaving now!"

"Where to?"

"Any place. It doesn't matter."

"Any place's noplace."

"Any place but here." Abruptly she sat down again, wiping her eyes with the back of her hand. "I'm used to love—not being blamed for not being someone I'm not."

Desolate, she wept; for she was not really used to love.

"Stop bawling," Laird said. "Can't talk to you while you're howling like that."

Hearing the tenderness in his voice now, she tried to stop her sobs.

"Who said I wanted to be talked to?" she said, meaning just that; but then, despite her every effort not to, she answered his smile.

"Fair enough," said Laird.

He led her up to the bedroom and to the sound of the rain slashing at the windowpanes they made love; and for the first time in her life Eliza felt not merely mastered and pos-

180

sessed but loved with a full and giving love and she responded fully.

A week later they started on their return journey to St. Augustine, leaving the plantation in the care of cousins of Laird, William and Clara McAndrews, and the overseer.

Eliza

Buloff Plantation
January, 1831

ON the day the Caffreys reached St. Augustine the news arrived there from Washington City that Congress had passed an Indian Removal Act.

Its provisions were simple.

Cherokees, Creeks, Choctaws, Chickasaws, and Seminoles now dwelling in the southeastern United States were to be granted lands west of the Mississippi in exchange for the extinguishment of all claims to lands east of the Mississippi. They were to be protected in their new homes forever. For the expenses of their removal the sum of $500,000 was appropriated.

Proposed to Congress in the twilight of the Adams administration, and one of the rare measures about which Andrew Jackson concurred with his predecessor, the act stirred feelings of relief and optimism among Southern white Americans, the majority of whom greeted it as a statesmanly alternative to the extermination of the Indians, and the best means of ridding the country of them promptly, practically, and humanely.

All that remained was that the provisions of the act be executed.

However, in Florida the summer passed with no commissioners arriving, no orders being handed down from Secretary Eaton, no call for parlays with the chiefs, in fact no sign at all of effort on the part of the administration to set the clockwork of the act in motion there.

September.

October.

The papers were full of something else altogether; a curious epidemic which had stricken Washington City called the Eaton Malaria.

For not merely had the President failed in his efforts to quarantine that disease, but he had managed to spread it across the country; and now not a preacher or editor, and scarcely a citizen in the land, lacked an opinion on Peggy Eaton's virtue. Undaunted, the President had pressed his case all the more vigorously until it was said that Margaret herself now regarded his fanatical chivalry as being something less than gratifying.

The business of government languished.

And the removal of a single wretched band of Indians in Florida was but one of countless affairs that would have to wait upon the vindication of Mrs. Eaton.

November passed.

December.

Since her return to St. Augustine Eliza had been drawn deeper into the society of the Belcamps and the Appletons until she almost persuaded herself that she belonged to their circle, in which the rule was that nothing be taken seriously. At the racetrack, at dances on the roof of the fort, they were the center of fashion, and Eliza now blamed some flaw in herself for finding their hilarity joyless, their wit foolish and cruel, their lives senseless. More than ever she tried to free the uncaring person Laird told her she held captive, and perhaps she very nearly succeeded—until a certain day early in January, 1831.

On a cool blue-sky morning they had driven south for a shooting party at the house of Jacob Buloff, and whose plantation was among the few in that coastal area south of Moultrie Creek still worked despite Indian raids and losses of Negroes. Its master was a big, full-faced, barrel-chested man of about forty with a loud laugh and intense never-resting eyes hooded by bushy brows. After a midday meal at which the men drank much wine, the host had led his guests along the sea cliff and then to a shooting range, with stands and targets, near a wooded area running parallel to the shore—Laird and Eliza, Lieutenant Belcamp and Malvina, Captain Appleton and his young wife, the party followed by four plantation hands brought to tend the targets.

A herd of cattle was grazing on the range. When Buloff sent the blacks to drive off the herd, two young Seminole youths holding coiled ropes broke from the midst of the animals and ran for the woods.

Buloff raised his rifle and fired. One of the Indians fell sprawling, Lieutenant Belcamp's rifle misfired.

Major Appleton shot the second Seminole at the edge of the woods. As Eliza looked on, horrified, Laird approached the first, writhing in mortal agony, and fired into his head. Captain Appleton went over to the second and with his boot ascertained that he was dead, then returned.

"Thiefs!" Buloff shouted, his face empurpled.

Then he sent one of the blacks back for shovels with an order to bury the two dead where they lay and shouted to the others to set up the targets.

"I regret that ladies must see this," he said then.

"You didn't have to shoot them," Eliza said. Laird came up to her and took her arm; she pulled away.

"You didn't have to shoot them!"

"Easy, Eliza." Laird calmed her.

Out of finer feelings Captain Appleton and Lieutenant Belcamp turned away and engaged each other in conversation. Whatever shock Malvina and Mrs. Appleton had felt over the shootings was at once dissipated by their concern over Eliza's outburst.

"They surely were stealing cattle," said Malvina, frowning at her friend.

183

"I regret," Buloff repeated. "It was not something ladies should see."

"It was not something anyone should see," said Eliza.

"Remember yourself, Eliza," warned Laird.

"That's exactly what I'm doing," she said. Then she turned and started walking toward the dunes at the edge of the beach. Laird called to her once, then let her go. She sat on a grassy knoll watching the green combers breaking, the blue horizon beyond. Soon over the sound of the waves she heard the crack of a rifle. The shooting party had resumed.

For weeks afterward she could not shake off the memory of that afternoon. She became silent and distant. For a while Laird had treated her with the consideration due a woman's frail sensibilities, but when her spirits did not respond he told her one night that it wasn't natural to carry on so about a couple of Seminole cow thieves.

"It's not them," she said. "It's you."

"The boy was finished," he replied. "I just put him out of his misery."

"I didn't mean that. I saw how you looked then. You felt just as I did yet you sided with Buloff."

"I sided with a man protecting his property."

"And Buloff loved the killing. He especially loved showing off to his female guests—that best of all."

"Those things happen in border country. Can't let it get to you."

She searched his face. "You think I behaved badly that day?"

"Nobody blamed you. Everyone respected your feelings."

"Laird—" Suddenly his look then, determined yet lost, filled her with pain. She went to him and he held her lightly.

"I guess we can't get to each other, either. Not in border country."

He said nothing, holding her close now until she was herself again.

Hutchins

ABOUT the time John Hutchins' two-year note to General Hernandez came due the former agent of the Florida Indians rode to St. Augustine confident that the note would be extended. He judged that about everyone in Florida was in the same fix; many coastal plantations, among them General Hernandez's, were deserted, new settlement near the Indians' lands was at a standstill, losses of livestock by Indian raids were costly; and the whole Territory was waiting for the administration to get on with the removal of the Seminoles. John Hutchins was now in a good position to capitalize on that eventuality and had persuaded himself that General Hernandez looked on his note and partnership as a fine investment in the future of Florida. Therefore he was greatly surprised when General Hernandez informed him that on the day the note had come due he had discounted it to an individual he had often done business with in the past, someone known to John Hutchins; and on the same day General Hernandez had also dissolved the partnership agreement, according to its provisions; so that John Hutchins now had the option of redeeming the note with interest or entering into a new partnership with its holder, who now drove around town in a fine brougham, dressed in gentleman's broadcloth, and styled himself Benjamin Solano, Esq.

So it was (John Hutchins being unwilling to turn to anyone for assistance) that the trading enterprise of Solano and Hutchins was formed.

And because misfortune seldom falls singly but, one rock loosening the other, in a very avalanche, on the same visit to St. Augustine John Hutchins learned from the federal judge that his request for the grant of the savanna was still refused, pending Mr. Hutchins' response to certain allega-

185

tions presented by Major Phagan concerning his use of government funds during his incumbency as agent. Knowing that the charges were false, designed to becloud Major Phagan's own peculations, John Hutchins also knew that he was in no position to defend himself: a debtor known to white Territorials—falsely in the end—as a friend of the Indians.

While staying with Eliza and Laird he said not a word about these reverses, out of pride and in the belief that somehow the last word was not said.

But one evening on the side south to the trading post (his mind troubled by Ben Solano's injunctions to recover trade lost on account of the Indians by cheating them ruthlessly) John Hutchins gazed up at the stars overhead and for the first time in his life realized that they were not cast for him.

Eliza

St. Augustine
November, 1831

IT was Laird who broke the news, giving her the following letter which the express rider had found beside John Hutchins.

Dear Eliza,

What will be done when you read this is for the best and you must never grieve. God knows I do not leave this world a better place for my passage through it but perhaps not much the worse; and I depart from it now as would a traveler from a passable inn, with no complaints but no intention to return. I have always tried to follow my own road, and stand up for what I believe. But I have also sought worldly success, imagining that the world had some use for my independence and that someday gold would be showered in my path. This fancy I now bequeath to

186

an institution for the incurably insane, in the belief that better use will be made of it there than I have been able to do.

Yesterday some thirty Seminoles came to my store, men, women, and children, saying they were starving and asking for something to eat. I asked what they could give me in exchange and they said nothing. Their miserable condition spoke for them. I gave them food and told them to go away in the morning. Though they could have overrun the store they made no hostile sign—but in the morning they were still there. They stayed the next day too. I did not feed them again. In the afternoon I was overcome by a sort of fit: I shouted at them, called them beggars and told them to leave, to find game, to plant crops, only to leave—but still they would not go.

On the third day one of them died, a young girl of twelve or so. She looked mummified.

What I did next must appear to the world as an act of madness and perhaps it was, but I do not regret it. I threw open the door of the store and called to the Indians to take all they could carry away. They did not believe their senses so I began hurling kegs, sacks of grain, blankets, everything, out to them. Then they came and carried out all the provisions and trading goods in the place. I stood at the door urging them on. When they could carry no more I told them to take my wagon and horses and they filled the wagon and drove off with it, taking the dead child. So I got rid of them.

Now it is late afternoon the following day. With the provisions and the value of the blankets and tools a handful of Seminoles will live another month here before facing starvation again, so nothing much has been accomplished except the demise of the house of Solano and Hutchins, not to be regretted.

How much there is to say—yet I will write no more. Only—do not grieve. I feel a certain peace and do not believe that my life has been for nothing.

Your affectionate father,
John Hutchins

P.S. I leave you my gold watch. It loses two minutes a day. Take care not to overwind it.

With the chaplain at the post Laird had arranged for John Hutchins to be buried at the edge of the savanna east of Dunn's Crescent and a service read. Only he, Eliza, Delia, and the chaplain were present. Laird had then settled John Hutchins' last affairs and paid his debts. He had been tender and considerate to Eliza—until several weeks passed and there was no abatement of her mourning. Then it seemed to her that Laird was subtly teaching her by looks and silences how many tears a Cumberland lady was supposed to shed. She was herself amazed at the reach of her pain, and she realized that she had given the only key to her being to John Hutchins; and perhaps—the thought was unbearable—he had pulled the pistol's trigger, in a tragic misjudgment, to free her to live the unburdened life he had always wished for her.

Then in time the grief dulled and Eliza seemed to yield to Laird's patient program for her improvement—or, as he viewed it, her natural flowering as a married lady. They seldom argued. Her flare-ups were rare and passed quickly. Thorny subjects were skirted; he was especially careful not to allude to their childless state, or to the very changes in her comportment which gratified him. She no longer set herself apart from their friends—the Belcamps, Buloff, Major Appleton. She tried to act as he expected her to act. However, Laird's pleasure in her transformation began to wane even before she herself understood what was happening in her. Laird became moody; for he had perceived that his wife's transformation was not a flowering at all but a dying off.

"I'll be exactly as you wish," she told him one evening.

"Just be yourself. That's what I wish."

She resolved not to struggle against him anymore, not so as to please him but to close doors between them in order to save herself. If he could not accept her as she was, with her emotional nature and unfashionable cares—and with longings she could scarcely define herself—she would withdraw from him, leaving him with the wife of his desires, never again venturing her true self to be unwanted. In the mirror she had found two gray hairs, tiny lines at her eyes, a slight severity in the set of her lips; but at thirty-two she was still young-looking and pretty. She would close doors between them until the time she looked to, when they would find their way to each other. She was no stranger to loneliness; but she felt now that retribution was being asked for her having relied too much on herself, given herself too little into the hands of others—a retribution which she was determined not to pay.

Jackson

The President's House
February, 1832

THE President, being in excellent humor, studied the reports from Florida while awaiting the arrival of the new Secretary of War, Lewis Cass. Only the earlier visit of John Eaton had momentarily dampened his high spirits. Eaton did not look well. In the full daylight from the window behind the President's desk his friend's face had appeared ravaged, his eyes staring gloomily from dark circles, his fingers trembling. There were reports that he was drinking. Andrew Jackson acknowledged that these had not been easy times for his friend.

All in all however the Eaton affair had been resolved satisfactorily, and the President was well aware from what quarter that resolution had come. Martin Van Buren had quietly stepped forward and with a wave of his wand removed the dissension in his Cabinet by the simple means of removing the Cabinet itself. Offering his own resignation, Van Buren had thus nudged Eaton into tendering his, leaving the President the welcome opportunity of obtaining

189

the resignations of Messrs. Branch, Berrien, and Ingham. Now a new Cabinet was formed, Van Buren was the new ambassador to England, and Eaton—would be assured a further term as senator from Tennessee. What vexed the President passingly was the memory of Margaret's cold reception of him and Van Buren when they called on her—and this morning John Eaton's curious apathy when he had assured him of the senatorship. He appeared to covet higher honors, a governorship, an ambassadorship.

Had the President not done enough for the Eatons?

Now, in any event, the administration could move again. There were fights spoiling to be fought.

With France over the 25-million-franc obligation to the United States.

With Nicholas Biddle and his damnable Bank of the United States.

And Florida. Reading over the army reports the President marveled that the Seminoles had been permitted to aggravate the affairs of the Territory so long.

He would swat that fly first.

He would have Secretary Cass send a special commissioner to Florida to read the riot act to the Seminoles and get them on their way west.

And who better to send than James Gadsden, author of the Moultrie Creek treaty? Gadsden knew the Seminoles. Better yet, he knew the President's wishes with respect to them.

By the time Secretary Cass entered, the President had to his satisfaction settled the question of the Seminole Indians once and for all.

Steven

Payne's Landing
May, 1832

IT was not much of a place. Sun- and shadow-swept marsh and vagrant dune between the pine forest and the river. On a rise of sand, a pavilion of brown canvas. Nearby, in a hollow, four soldiers tending a cooking fire. The west a wall of rumbling black.

In the pavilion Major Phagan's beak-nosed interpreter sat cross-legged on a campstool, watching the faces of the nine Seminoles and Abraham. To Steven Richards' right sat Eustace Rodgers, man of trade, the sutler at Fort King; to the boy's left, Major Phagan, sitting with a placid look which gave no clue to the anger he was prone to. Next to Major Phagan, standing huge in the cramped pavilion, Commissioner James Gadsden, his closed fist suspended over the treaty on the table before him. Next to the Commissioner, his young secretary, the son of the commandant at St. Augustine, sitting before the ink bottle, paper and pens that he had not touched all morning. Behind them all stood young Lieutenant Russell from Fort King, his hands locked behind his back, feet planted apart, studying the Indians and their black interpreter as if they were a problem in artillery.

The Commissioner's fist crashed down.

Steven watched the secretary quickly reach to steady the ink bottle, as he had already had to do several times that morning, for Colonel Gadsden was in a high temper and had sworn to Major Phagan that he was goddamned if they would leave this sorry place without the Indians' marks on the agreement, and would Major Phagan, who presumably knew the Indians' disposition, be so good as to put his mind to work; and Major Phagan had. As he spoke now, the Commissioner struck the table repeatedly to stress his words.

"We cannot feed you anymore! We cannot help you any more! You must go to the new lands or die here!"

191

Abraham met the Commissioner's angry glare, then faced the two rows of Seminoles and interpreted, adding, as Steven alone understood, "So speaks the sense bearer of the Great Father."

The delegation of chiefs grumbled; Jumper, his eyes wide with rage, was suddenly on his feet shouting, "Never! Never will we be slaves of Creeks! We will starve first!"

James Gadsden, who had heard these words so often he needed no interpreting, shouted back, "You will be given money, tools, guns, everything you need to live on the new lands. Everything the Creeks were given. Are you so afraid of Creeks?"

Jumper sat down again, glowering and muttering to himself, finding no reliable voice to his anger. He was fierce and brave in battle and intelligent in council; yet before this white man whose power seemed to flow up his arm from the paper he struck he was weakened by his own fury.

Then Charlie Emaltha rose to his feet. Steven saw the face of his own dead father; for though of different races his father and Charlie Emaltha had the same troubled eyes that hunted for reasons behind things when there were none, for outcomes that would never be, for hope, for some answer to the cry of their own anguished sanity; eyes that seemed to Steven tragically innocent as the Seminole began to speak in the formal manner of council.

"We have grown weak," he began. "There is no use saying we are strong. We are hungry, and if some of our braves have raided outside the lands you left to us at Moultrie Creek, it is because those lands are too poor to sustain us. Now you wish us to leave even these lands for others we know nothing of, except that our old enemies live there. You say you cannot protect us from bad men of your own race or feed us here. What are we to do? Our women look at us to know what will become of us tomorrow, while our infants die." Abruptly he turned to the Indians. "I say that we must go. That is all."

He sat down, and as Abraham interpreted, the Indians argued heatedly among themselves, Jumper angrily raising his fist against Charlie Emaltha, Micanopy preening with indignation that another had ventured to speak for them; but some of them were troubled by what had been said.

"He speaks wisely," Gadsden said to Abraham when the black man had translated. "He speaks for the Seminoles—not for their counselors."

"That will be seen," said Abraham, and he spoke to Micanopy as the old chief glared at the sacks of corn stacked by the table, the side of beef crawling with flies, scratching his hungry belly. Major Phagan whispered to the Commissioner, both watching Micanopy and Abraham.

To Micanopy this place on the river was his; his forebear King Payne's place, through whom he was descended from the legendary Cowkeeper, patriarch of the Seminoles, whose many tribes and clans had so little common history; and all the other leaders who had come here knew this place and its meaning, that though it might change with the wind and water, becoming less a certain place than a notion in the mind, it reminded this fat carbuncled king that he still wielded power, that he was still wealthy, that his fields still produced some corn and cotton—more than many of the white man's farms to the east and north; that he still owned some hundred slaves, though the whereabouts of many he did not know. The worse it was for his people the more he believed that the bad times could not in the nature of things become worse still but were passing, and he believed that by preserving in his person his noble line, by preserving his wealth, he could someday see his people through to the return of times as they had been. Only the fear of being forced onto strange western lands where the Creeks had gone, and losing slaves, possessions, independence, to their ancient brother enemies—so much more numerous than they and some with long alliances with the whites—only this fear troubled Micanopy deeply; for he wondered if indeed the Great Spirit had not abandoned the Seminoles and breathed the secret of their destruction to the Great Father in Washington City. But then he always assured himself that this threat too would pass, that they would never go west, no matter what words were said or written on paper, for the land here was his and his people's; Abraham would advise him shrewdly, he knew the white man's ways; Micanopy depended more and more on Abraham, and it satisfied him to take counsel from his slave; in times when little was of avail in any case it made him free to be a king.

Now he rose and spoke to the Commissioner and the agent just as Abraham had advised him to speak.

"At Moultrie Creek we were promised twenty summers on the lands left to us. Eight remain. When they have passed we will talk again."

As Abraham interpreted no one moved or spoke. The sky was darkening and thunder crackled in the west; smells of beef and corn cake from the fires stirred in the wind. Major Phagan studied Abraham, calculating. James Gadsden, who owned many slaves, also contemplated this crafty son of Africa in Indian garb who counseled his master to defy the United States government, defy Andrew Jackson himself, at any cost.

Any cost?

The Commissioner turned to the agent.

Steven Richards observed the look that passed between them, then he looked away to where the trail from the south emerged from the saw grass and pine forest.

The one Seminole who could speak for his stricken nation was not here.

Osceola.

All morning Steven had looked for him, desiring him to come until his desire turned to shame and then to hate; and he deliberately thought of his mother, father, and sister, seeing again their faces through the screaming terror in his body and hearing the war cries as the tomahawks fell on them; but he still could not free himself of his longing for Osceola.

Suddenly, as Steven watched him, James Gadsden seized a sack of corn, set it on the table, and spilled it out over the treaty.

"There will be no more food!" he shouted. "Tell them that, Abraham. Tell them there is no more time; they must sign. Tell them that the Great Father will send soldiers against them if they refuse but that he will be most generous with them if they do his bidding."

As Abraham spoke Major Phagan whispered to the Commissioner, who nodded, then when Abraham turned to him again said, "And he will be generous with you too, Abraham, if they sign."

The black man and the Commissioner regarded each other a long time, then Abraham spoke softly to his master and Micanopy, blinking his fleshy eyes disdainfully, replied.

Again Abraham addressed the Commissioner.

"Micanopy asks how the Seminoles are to know if the lands are good."

A faint smile crossed Gadsden's pursed lips.

"Tell him that ways can be found. Tell him that ways can be found to satisfy him that the Great Father is a generous friend. But first we will have food, for our guests are hungry."

Then the Commissioner, in close conversation with Major Phagan, led the assembly over to the cooking fire.

Steven Richards took his tin plate to the riverbank, a good distance from the fire where the Americans sat in a circle, the Indians in another a little apart. When he finished eating he washed his plate in the river with sand, then lay on his back on the still-warm tufts of grass looking up into the threatening sky, thinking of Osceola.

The Indian knew his secret.

Soon after he had taken him from the Mikasukis, out of captivity, he must have known; there was no hiding anything from Osceola. For a time Steven had been content in his village, desiring no more than to be near his deliverer,

195

never thinking of going among white men, until one day Osceola came upon him and told him in the presence of other braves that he might sit with his wives. The braves had laughed at the insult and Osceola had looked at him as if he wished him to know that he cared nothing for him, that he was not a man in his eyes, and for the second time in his life Steven felt his inner self die.

He had stayed on for a time in the village because he had nowhere to go, now bearing a hatred for Osceola that grew greater for not ending his love but making it also greater; and when his dark brooding looks drew Osceola's subtle mockery he swore terrible vengeances on him, even as he longed that by some miracle he would come to him as his brother. Only after weeks of pain and abasement did Steven finally leave the village, with Osceola's indifferent farewell in his ears, and offer his services to Major Phagan.

Through blades of grass Steven saw the Commissioner's young secretary get up and approach him. Major Phagan was sliding through the sand on his bottomside to where Abraham sat. Thunder rumbled beyond the pine forest to the southwest. The secretary came up to Steven, looked out at the river and remarked as he had prepared to do, "Thought there was supposed to be a landing here."

"What's your name?" Steven asked him.

"David Stockton."

Steven lay back and shut his eyes. "You ain't writing anything."

"The Commissioner said not to. He said it wasn't needed."

"He's right. What matters is their crosses on that paper—not how they get there."

The boy sat down at a little distance from Steven, then asked the real question he had come to ask.

"They say you were a prisoner of the Indians."

Steven smiled, not opening his eyes.

"They say right," Steven told him. "I was a captive of the fierce Mikasukis who killed my mother, father, and sister, but didn't kill me. Why? Tell me that." Steven abruptly

196

opened his eyes, scowling at the boy, then added, "I wouldn't lend Major Phagan money if I were you."

"I wasn't," the boy answered, surprised. "Does he borrow?"

Steven lay back again, closing his eyes. "Major Phagan has big notions for his future. He's all schemes and no money. He even owes Abraham thirty dollars."

The boy looked over to Major Phagan, who was sliding himself back to the Commissioner's side. "He just spoke to Abraham. Now he's talking to the Commissioner again. Is he borrowing money from the Commissioner?"

Steven laughed. "What's Micanopy doing?"

"Eating like a wolf, like he hadn't eaten in days."

"He's always hungry. Have you ever heard of Osceola?"

"No."

"You will."

"Who is he?"

"A redskin."

"A chief?"

"Yes and no. What's Abraham doing?"

"Looking at Major Phagan and the Commissioner."

Steven smiled. "No wonder. They're fixing his price."

"Bribing him?" asked the boy, pained at the idea. "I thought Abraham was on the Indians' side."

"He is," Steven replied, then he opened his eyes, sat up, and glared at the boy. "Osceola's war cry'll be the last thing you hear on this earth," he told him, then looking past the boy's shoulder added, "You'd better go. I think the Commissioner wants you to write something now."

Indeed at that moment Colonel Gadsden, walking toward the pavilion with Major Phagan, beckoned to the secretary. Steven watched the boy hurry toward them, then he lay back in the sand as the rain began.

When the talk resumed, the rain was pelting the canvas on the pavilion and Colonel Gadsden now spoke in a different voice, no longer intimidating but commanding.

"The Great Father does not wish to drive you to inhospitable lands. To go or stay will be your choice. He cannot support you here anymore but he understands that you fear to go to an unknown country. Therefore he will let you choose a delegation to visit the new lands and so it will be decided whether you go or stay. Is this not just? Look into the eyes of your women and children, then ask yourselves if you can refuse?"

And Abraham also spoke commandingly, showing that he stood behind the words.

"Never!" Jumper cried, but there was no conviction in his protest.

"We must choose a delegation," Charlie Emaltha said. "It is a fair offer."

Then Abraham stood before Micanopy, who was torn between his desire to delay the moment of decision and his desire to be the one to make it.

A young war leader rose and asked how the delegation would know the way to the new lands. James Gadsden told him that Major Phagan himself would personally accompany them and show them the way.

Everyone now looked to Micanopy. With all the regal bearing his short gross body was capable of he rose and looked to Abraham, who slowly nodded to him, then he spoke: "Let the delegation be chosen. We will sign."

Eliza

St. Augustine
October, 1832

LIEUTENANT Belcamp was a madcap. Malvinia had married him because he "refused to take life seriously" only to discover that if the lieutenant was frivolous he was also immune to passion and yet able to detect the subtlest symptoms of such disarray in others. Try as she would, Malvina found it impossible to make a fool of him. Mischief, pranks, teasing wit were his elements. He walked with a springy, unofficerlike step, on the balls of his feet, his round boyish face expectant.

When in the summer of 1831 Malvina had taken to favoring Major Appleton with her company her husband had followed the course of the flirtation with avid appreciation. And when, stung by his unnatural behavior, Malvina had shared the secrets of her deeper nature with the major, only to discover that he was quite stupid, Lieutenant Belcamp manifested signs of physical distress which turned out to be laughter; for in this respect he lacked the instincts of a man of honor. Then, in the spring and summer of 1832, when Malvinia had tired of Major Appleton to the point of disgust, and, throwing caution to the winds, had set her cap for Laird Caffrey, the lieutenant was even more entertained.

With the onset of summer came the sweltering morning sun, afternoon haze darkening to incarnadine gray, thunder, sometimes before nightfall the clearing sun, and it was on such an evening in August, during a stroll along the seawall, that Eliza had suddenly become aware of the attraction between Laird and Malvina. A quip of Lieutenant Belcamp's had aroused such anger in his wife and such precaution in Laird that Eliza, as she watched them walking together, discovered what Belcamp later assured her she might have observed all summer had she been less in the clouds. Jealousy only strengthened her will to give nothing of herself for nothing, certainly not tears or reproaches; and yet the flirtation between her husband and her friend (for she had always regarded Malvina as a friend despite her faults) filled her with a new kind of loneliness, neither benign nor indifferent, but which clawed at her heart and her head mercilessly.

Already by September the attraction was waning. Perhaps Laird had let himself be drawn to Malvina as a way of reaching out to Eliza; however, when at the end of the month it was over, she found him no nearer than before.

On the fifth of October there was to be a military ball at the fort. Lieutenant Belcamp was in charge of entertainments.

The morning before the ball, a clear, blue day, she had been helping with the decoration of the roof of the star-shaped fort when from the seaward bastion she saw a ship rounding the headland of Anastasia Island.

She recognized the *Northern Star*.

All afternoon, long after the black-hulled brig had been moored at the wharf, Eliza debated whether or not to pay a call to inquire about Enos and express her gratitude to Captain Wolfe. All afternoon she hesitated. Of course she would send her card aboard first, and Delia would accompany her—though Laird must never know the story of Enos' liberation. Why did she feel such hesitations? Annoyed, she shook the truth from herself. She wanted to see Captain Wolfe again. She wanted to see him very much, enough to make her wonder whether she could even conceal that desire. She could seldom fool Delia; and Captain Wolfe she feared would see right through her. Perhaps on the other hand he would not remember her. She herself could not recall his features clearly. Perhaps it was not even Captain Richard Wolfe in flesh and blood she wanted to see, but only someone she had dreamed about who did not exist. And that would be the worst of all. She resolved to postpone the visit at least until after the ball.

Lieutenant Belcamp's first entertainment was a cannonade which was fired under the northern bastion of the fort after supper at precisely ten, when the dancing had just begun. Eliza was with Major Appleton on the roof, decorated with lanterns and colored streamers, when the stupendous concussion shook the night. Women screamed. The music faltered. A second mighty detonation. The music stopped. Smoke curled over the northern parapet. Between the reports Lieutenant Belcamp could be heard below the wall, howling with laughter. Major Appleton, unapprised of the project and finding himself the senior officer present, excused himself to find out what was happening. When the echoes of the last report had died away over the water and the music resumed—Eliza was dancing in the arms of Captain Wolfe.

"I'd hoped to find you here."

"I'm glad to see you again, Captain," she said, meeting his steady eyes. "I've wanted to inquire about Enos."

"In safe hands in Boston. Bound for Liberia, I believe."

Then he asked about John Hutchins and Eliza told him that her father had died.

"I'm truly sorry," he said. "He was a man of compassion—though he tried to hide that disability. One knows of his work with the Seminoles."

"As one knows of your work, Captain."

"Not at all the same thing!" the other protested vehemently, adding, "Some years ago I did imagine I was performing a service to the black race—improving my soul and expiating my grandfather's sins into the bargain."

"You were not?"

"I've ferried perhaps two hundred to a somewhat better life—and perhaps the same number to worse misery than they'd ever imagined—freedom with no means to live, no protection or hope. In the process I've come to realize that my grandfather's blood and mine are the same."

"You judge yourself harshly."

"Yankees do. It's our secret pleasure." He smiled, then asked, "And what of Eliza Caffrey?"

Amid the gay voices of the dancers she heard Malvina's laughter and the female training of a lifetime told her to reply evasively to the question she most wanted to hear.

"You learned my married name."

"I have thought of you often."

"Not unkindly, I hope?"

He paused a moment in the dance.

"I thought I'd imagined you."

"Perhaps you have."

"No," he said, "you're as I remember."

When she answered, her voice belied the coquettishness of the only words she could find.

"And what of Captain Wolfe? Do you always speak so agreeably to married ladies?"

"Never," he said. "Nor to unmarried ones—not as I'm speaking to you."

"You'd be disappointed if you knew me better," she told him. "I'm impossibly willful, they say."

"Knew it at once," he said. "So am I." Then he added, "I wish to God we'd met sooner."

"As I recall it, sir—we did."

The dance ended.

Lieutenant Belcamp now had stationed himself at a little distance from them on the roof and was announcing his second sensation of the evening—in the person of a fiery, handsome young Seminole wearing a plumed turban, silver ornaments, embroidered hunting shirt, and beaded sash. Eliza recognized him as Coacoochee, known as Wild Cat, son of King Philip, the leader of the St. Johns River Seminoles. He stood beside the lieutenant with a look of fierce arrogance—though, Eliza observed, unsteadily—as a crowd of couples gathered around them. Only a bribe of whiskey, she was certain, would have induced this young war leader to let the lieutenant show him off as a curiosity to the celebrants at the ball. Then, among the onlookers, she saw a young girl of seventeen or eighteen, the bride of an ensign, her face shining with pleasure at seeing such a young and beautiful creature of another race. Coacoochee, apparently enjoying the general attention he was receiving, strutted and postured, taking no notice of the girl. Lieutenant Belcamp, however, observed her and pointed her out to him, saying aloud, "Prince! The fair young person who stands before you is a new bride. This is her husband. Would you give them your royal blessing?" Then, seeing that Coacoochee had not understood, he took the girl's hand, showed him her ring, and by other signs made him understand. The

Seminole then approached the girl and appraised her from head to toe. She lowered her eyes in confusion. He slowly circled her, raised her chin, and looked directly into her eyes. His inspection of her done, he considered the bridegroom with a brief glance and a scornful sniff. Then he pointed at the girl and said, "Now she give him much pleasure. When she have a few children she will give him none." Eliza saw the girl's face dissolve in dismay. Coacoochee, highly satisfied, suddenly laughed wildly and some of the crowd laughed too. Lieutenant Belcamp was reassured.

"Not very gallant, Prince. Expected better of you somehow. Great disappointment."

And putting his arm around the Seminole, he went off with him.

Eliza let Captain Wolfe lead her in the dance. For a time neither spoke; then she asked how long he would be in St. Augustine.

"We sail tomorrow on the tide."

"Where?"

"Philadelphia, then Bristol."

"To your wife?"

"I have no wife."

"You'll return?"

"This is the last voyage of the *Northern Star*, Eliza. My capital's not unlimited—and in any case nothing can be done this way." He searched her eyes and in another voice said, "I wish you were sailing with me tomorrow."

Before she could answer, the dance ended and Laird was approaching them. She introduced them. They conversed for several minutes, then the captain excused himself, bade them both good-bye, and departed. Laird took her in his arms as the next dance began.

After a silence he looked at her and said, "Your eyes are still shining for that abolitionist."

She drew away from him and went to the parapet facing the silvery black of the open sea north of the lighthouse. She was aware of him coming up beside her.

"Getting to where a man has to court his own wife," he said at last.

She turned to him. "He certainly does!" she said, and reaching for both his hands held them tightly. "I love you," she told him; then she was talking in a rush. "Let's start now—let's start yesterday. Let's make up for keeping apart from each other. You said we could make up time. Let's do it!"

"Liza," he said softly, "I hardly know you this way."

She released his hands and turned again to the sea.

Then suddenly she was letting him take her in his arms and kiss her hard, and she returned his kiss. When he looked at her again she felt that he was seeing her for the first time in their lives.

Jackson

The President's House
June, 1834

"FIVE thousand regulars!" marveled Andrew Jackson, scowling at the letter before him on his desk. Then he looked up sharply at the Secretary of War.

"Most of the army," said Lewis Cass.

The President's stomach hurt and his head was beginning to ache again. In the two months since he had appointed John Eaton governor of the Territory of Florida he had sensed that he had made a mistake, and here before him was the damnable proof of it.

"Still—" ventured Cass.

"Mrs. Jackson used to say that no Christian could endure the climate of Florida. She was referring especially to the spiritual climate, sir, and she was right. It seems that our friend Eaton has been touched by it. Here he's cautioning us that this so-called leader of theirs, this—Osceola—may one day be a match for the best of our generals!"

"An exaggeration, of course. Still—"

"Two companies!" the President broke in vigorously. "Give me two companies of Tennesseans—damn the regulars!—and I'd soon have every Seminole in the Territory quick-marching west. What's needed is not five thousand regulars but persuasion, sir. Seminoles are Creeks, and Creeks are not fools. Show them a clear proposition and they'll not resist when they see they haven't a prayer in Hell. But instead of telling them in plain terms what lies in store for them if we leave them to the mercies of Territorial authority, Eaton warns *us* that we'll need five thousand regulars to root them out. On top of it he suggests that we've let the treaties lapse and they're invalid. By the Eternal, I—"

"The Attorney General assures me that the treaties are quite valid."

"Of course the treaties are valid!" The President stared at the offensive letter. Then, exacerbated, he rose and went to the window where he stood with his hands locked behind him, looking far down to the river where a gang of young boys were diving from a boat landing. He was ailing and longed to return to the Hermitage. When he spoke again his voice was weary, old.

"For years, sir, I have taken it for the certain will of Providence that Indians east of the Mississippi must move west of the Mississippi, and for as many years John Eaton has known my opinion and professed to share it. Why then does he write me now of lapsed treaties?" He turned to Lewis Cass, adding, as if to nullify some indiscretion in the former question. "What is happening to people, Mr. Secretary?"

A military man, reflected the President; *one can talk to a military man.*

"In point of fact, sir," said Cass, "that letter being addressed to myself, Governor Eaton could have intended no personal slight. As for his military opinions, sir, while exaggerated of course—"

"Slight, sir? I was referring to the treaties, to five thousand regulars."

The President turned again to the window. He had never expected gratitude from the Eatons—never! His defense of their reputations was a matter of plain justice, the ordinary duty of a friend. He had not expected gratitude but neither had he expected icy receptions or Eaton's sulky manner when he offered him the governorship. With all his strength he had defended them and somehow in the course of it he had lost their friendship. In penning this overbearing letter to the Secretary, the governor had surely meant every word for him. The question which lately had tormented him in the night assailed him now; the question he hardly dared let enter his mind: Had the Eatons deceived him?

Worse—since in fairness neither had made any express claim of innocence—had he deceived himself?

Even as his early memories of Margaret at her father's tavern remained like a flame in his spirit, his blood ran cold when he remembered that he had compared her in virtue to his dearest Rachel.

Had Eaton's friendship been all it seemed?

Had these friends betrayed him—or was he, even now, in the spiteful vanity of old age betraying them?

Nothing was revealed to the President then. Even his vision of the boys swimming off the pier was blurred by his failing eyesight. He turned again to face the Secretary.

"The Seminoles will go west, sir," he said. "We will send men to Florida who will know how to enforce the treaties. Appoint a new agent, sir; Major Phagan thinks of nothing but his pockets."

Even as he spoke Andrew Jackson recalled that it had been his own kinsman, John Hutchins, who as agent, an appointment recommended by himself, had for years countered the removal policy. And suddenly, across the years, he remembered little Eliza Hutchins at the Hermitage, before all his guests, saying, "But the lands are theirs." And now his friend Eaton.

He handed back the letter to Lewis Cass as a sign that the interview was over.

"Send someone who can do the job, Mr. Secretary. Send someone who can show this Osceola who he's dealing with. Five thousand regulars indeed!"

Thompson

The Indian Agency
October, 1834

IN contrast to Major Phagan, General Wiley Thompson brought to the post of agent to the Florida Indians a high conception of his own standards of conduct and for the first time faithful representation of the real interests of the United States in dealing with the Seminoles. Two heads taller than his predecessor, he was a powerful man of military bearing; a full, florid face; sharp, direct eyes; whose years as a representative of Georgia in Congress had honed his sense of justice and of how things got done. The very fact that he now found himself at the half century of his life a general in the militia, with no fortune to speak of, in a $1,500 post that he was grateful for, was perhaps ample testimony to his honesty and dedication to public service. In all his fifty years there had never been any question about his personal integrity. Yet if he was totally innocent of that spirit of peculation which had brought Major Phagan to a provisional sort of downfall, he was even more innocent of that rarer failing, conscience with the balance wheel gone, regulated by neither religion nor common sense, only in the end by pride on the borderline of madness, which had brought on the dismissal and perhaps the death of John Hutchins. General Thompson steered a course between venality and idealism; or rather, put another way, since he was a militia officer and by no means a seafarer, he strode the highroad of circumstance and thoughtfulness to friends wherever it led him. He knew the pitfalls. He never doubted that his star was rising. As an officer under General Jackson in the Creek campaign and in all his service in the Georgia militia and in Congress he had never been known to commit a notable blunder.

He was the man for the job.

This, then, was the officer who rose to address the assembled chiefs of the Seminoles on the morning of October 23, 1834, in the cool palm shadows of the agency council ground. Flanking him at the table, facing the seated rows of Indians, were young Richards, the interpreter he had inherited from Major Phagan, and Captain Russell from Fort King. Abraham would interpret the Indians' talk and Steven the agent's, and as he began, and Steven picked up his words in Muskogee, Wiley Thompson was aware of the searing black eyes of Osceola fixed on him.

"Friends and brothers," he began, "On the ninth of May, 1832, you entered into a treaty at Payne's Landing. Under that treaty, in exchange for lands here, you have acquired a country west of the Mississippi which your delegation found to be a good country. I come from the President to tell you that he has complied with all his promises and that you must be prepared to move as soon as the winter cold shall have passed."

The Indians sat still and silent while for a half hour General Thompson discussed the fine points of the proposition; then he met Osceola's eyes again.

"In conclusion, as your friend and brother, I say to you that Captain Russell and myself are to accompany you to your new home, and we pledge ourselves to be your friends, to share your toils and hardships, and your sufferings if unfortunately you should undergo any.

"Retire now and enter into private council. Should you want explanations on any point, send for me; I will attend you, then retire immediately, so as not to be an intruder on your private councils. You are at liberty to leave."

Then Charlie Emaltha was on his feet addressing the assembly of Indians.

"My brothers. We have now heard the talk that our father in Washington has sent us. He says that we made a treaty at Payne's Landing, and that we have no more excuse for not doing what we promised. We must be honest. My brothers, let us go and talk it over, and don't let us act like fools."

As Steven Richards interpreted these words Osceola stood up, glared at Charlie Emaltha a moment, then strode away from the council; and when he had gone about twenty paces he turned and faced General Thompson, raised his right arm defiantly; then, as the other Seminoles left the council he walked at their head, leading them away on the road northeast to Silver Springs.

When they had gone, Wiley Thompson, in Captain Russell's presence, ordered Steven Richards to follow the delegation to their encampment by the springs, keeping out of sight, and overhear what they said in council. The boy scowled at Wiley Thompson and the agent was made uncomfortable and felt that he was about to become angry (he knew himself very well on this score); however before he did become angry the beak-nosed boy smiled, his eyes creasing oddly, and said, "Depend on me, General."

"Strange lad," he remarked to Captain Russell when Steven had gone.

Late that night General Thompson had searched the dregs of his glass for an answer to the question why Andrew Jackson wanted the Seminoles rejoined with Creeks, when there was land enough out under the setting sun for ten nations. He didn't see the percentage in it and concluded that something was going on over his head. One thing was certain (as he replenished his glass for the last time): Though the Creeks were not likely to slaughter the arriving Seminoles (as many of them feared) the Creeks might, as was known from past experience, seize their human property, and here General Thompson hewed to principle. He had always stood up for the Florida Indians' right to their Negroes, even knowing that there were fugitives among them, that titles were often faulty, that the blacks were becoming dangerous allies; for what mattered to him was that *there were some just claims,* and it was nowhere in Wiley Thompson's code to deny the rights of any man, white or red, to his lawful property. No matter that the majority of settlers held that the savages, being heathen and improvident, had no rights to slaves worth honoring, Wiley Thompson believed that because the red man walked the earth upright and spoke in words he must be accorded the same fundamental rights as white men, if Law itself were not to be defiled.

The next morning General Thompson learned from Steven Richards that Osceola was going among them usurping the powers of the chiefs, counseling resistance, dividing the whole delegation into rival factions for and against emigration. Most striking of all was the fulminatory character of his language and his open hostility to Wiley Thompson himself: "I have a rifle," he had said, "and I have some powder and lead. I say we must not leave our homes and lands. My brothers, when the agent tells me to go from my home, I hate him, because I love my home and will not go from it!"

Thus Thompson learned the identity of the one he must bear down on. Already, he had closely observed Osceola at Fort King, where the Indian was a frequent visitor, showing none of the diffidence of his people before the white officers and men of the garrison but rather an inclination to show himself off, whether by the sweetness of his smile or in bold feats of horsemanship and his marksmanship which, considering the antiquated Spanish rifle he used, was extraordinary. This was Osceola, all grace and bearing and a shameless poseur for all that, now appearing as the spokesman of resistance. From Steven's report General Thompson learned too that Jumper had spoken for emigration, but Osceola had replied in fiery language and carried the assembly; and Jumper himself was then induced, because of his eloquence and rank, to present the arguments against their going.

Thus forewarned, General Wiley Thompson faced the chiefs on that second morning, Friday, October 24, under a dull, windless sky. Holata Mico, an elderly chief, rose and made a flowery speech about not letting blood rise against one another during which Osceola whispered to Micanopy, and when Holata Mico sat down Micanopy rose and said, "When we were at Moultrie we made a treaty and we were to be paid our annuity and live on our lands for twenty years. That is all I have to say."

Then Jumper spoke: "At the treaty of Moultrie we were told that should we die it would not be by the violence of the white man but in the course of nature, that lightning would not rive and blast the tree, but the cold of old age would dry up the sap, the leaves should wither and fall, and the branches drop. At Payne's Landing we only agreed to send a delegation to look at the land and report to the nation. That is all. We went and saw the land. It was no doubt good, and the fruit of the soil may smell sweet and be healthy, but it is surrounded by bad and hostile neighbors, and the fruit of bad neighborhood is blood that spoils the land and fire that dries up the brook. The Pawnees stole our horses. Major Phagan told us there would be no warring, that a treaty of peace was being made between the nations. I do not know if this was done. The government would send us among tribes with which we could never be at rest. Does the Great Father know this? When we saw the land we said nothing, but Major Phagan made us sign a paper at Fort Gibson which you now say signified our consent to remove; but we thought we only said we liked the land and that when we returned the nation would decide. We had no authority to do more. My people are not willing to say they will go. If our tongues say yes, our hearts cry no, and call them liars."

By the time Jumper sat down General Thompson's blood was beginning to boil. He looked from one impassive face to another—then at Osceola, who was smiling at the agent's irritation.

"This is the talk of children!" he told them. "This is foolish talk, unworthy of chiefs. I want answers to my questions: Will you go by land or water? Will you sell your cattle or take them with you? How many are your people so that the government can provide for you? The talk I have given must stand!"

Jumper answered: "This was our home when the game was plenty and the corn high. If the deer have gone and the corn tassels withered it is still our home, and we love it and prefer it."

Then Alligator spoke: "I agreed to go west and did go west. I went in a vessel and it made me sick. The land is very distant and I think that for so many people to go there would be very bad."

Then, just as General Thompson's exasperation was cresting, Micanopy, following a whispered conference with Osceola, rose and declared that he had never signed the treaty at Payne's Landing in the first place.

"Micanopy lies!" the agent shouted.

"I never touched the pen," said the chief, blinking stubbornly.

"Here is his name!" Thompson held up the treaty of Payne's Landing and struck it with his hand. "His mark is on this paper!"

"I never touched the pen. I only pointed to it."

The agent now found himself short of breath; his face reddened; his indignant gaze ranged the rows of silent Indians, until Holata Mico rose and declared again that they were all of the same father and there was no reason to get mad.

"I AM NOT MAD! I AM YOUR FRIEND!" the agent shouted, his voice echoing in the forest.

Steven Richards smiled as he interpreted the words.

Osceola smiled.

Micanopy.

Jumper.

"YOU WILL GO WEST!" said the agent then, mastering himself as his anger found release in the threat. "You must stand up to your bargain. Your father, the President, will compel you to go. Therefore do not be deluded by any hope that you will be permitted to remain here. I must tell you the plain truth as your brother and your friend, and the plain truth is that, were it possible for you to stay here, certain disaster would overtake you. The Congress of the United States has granted the territories the same jurisdiction as the states have over the Indians: Indians will be subject to the white man's law in the white man's courts, and even the President, your friend, with all his power and kindness toward his red children, cannot promise equal justice for them when the laws are kept by men who do not regard themselves as your brothers and friends. To think otherwise is to dream. The President wishes to save his children. He wishes to settle you beyond the states and territories where the white man's law will never reach you and where you and your descendants will possess the land as long as the grass grows and the rivers run. He feels for his red children as a father should feel. It was to save you that he will compel you to comply with it. Already Cherokees, Choctaws, Chickasaws, and your brothers and Creeks are going, as you must go, as leaves in winter must go; there is no choice."

The agent paused. As Steven Richards finished interpreting his words the Indians were silent, affected by what they had heard. Only Osceola met General Thompson's glare— with an answering look of challenge. Micanopy swayed with indecision.

"You can see," the agent continued, addressing himself to Osceola, "were it possible for you to remain here you would be reduced to hopeless poverty. And when you would be forced by hunger to beg a crust of bread from the same man who took your house under his law he would call you an Indian dog and order you to clear out!"

It was then, for the first time in a council with white men, that Osceola rose, glaring at General Thompson, and spoke for all the Seminoles.

"The sentiments of the nation have been expressed! The people in council have agreed. The chiefs have spoken. The nation has declared; it shall perform. The truth must not be broken. If I speak, I shall do as I say. What should be, shall be. NOTHING REMAINS WORTH WORDS." Then he raised his clenched fist against the gray sky and shouted, "If the hail rattles, let the flowers be crushed. The oak of the forest will lift its head to the storm, towering and unscathed. The leaves will remain!"

He brought his arm down in defiance and the Indians murmured as one.

Micanopy rose to his feet beside him.

"I do not intend to remove," said the chief of chiefs.

Steven

Fort King
June, 1835

HE had not minded spying on Osceola during the October councils. His attraction to the Indian was now all but dead though it had pleased him to watch him secretly in the night by the fires.

He reported on Osceola's activities to Thompson, who himself, though quite incapable of acknowledging the fact, was affected by the Indian leader in ways which did not appear in his reports to the Secretary, yet which were no secret to his interpreter. Indeed, for some time Steven had observed the intense relationship which had grown between the war leader and the agent, a bond in which, in the agent's case, it was impossible to trace the frontiers between duty, curiosity, and ardent, yet by no means affectionate, attraction. Though Thompson spoke of his bond to one and all as "a friendship based on mutual trust and respect" it was clear to the interpreter that he was in fact proud of having (as he believed) overawed an extremely complicated and volatile Indian by means of crafty personal diplomacy in the service of the United States. As for Osceola, his feelings toward the agent were less legible, being neither so hypocritical nor so candid; certainly he was not indifferent to the general's endeavors to maintain a manly, straightforward understanding between them; nor did he welcome any less than his host their being closeted together and, better yet, their being seen together strolling in the stockade and outside under the pines, sometimes down to the sutler's house and back, with Steven their shadow. However, since last October the interpreter had understood that Thompson, caught in the turbulence of novel affections, assumed that Osceola would eventually submit to the winning combination of real friendship, intimidation, and hard reason and was thus laboring under a catastrophic illusion; for throughout the bitter winter Steven had seen unmistakable signs that the Seminoles were secretly preparing for war.

Then in June General Thompson made a very serious mistake.

By then Osceola had formed another friendship at the fort. He had struck up an acquaintance with a young West Pointer named Graham, which was remarkable for being, on both sides, entirely spontaneous and innocent of any motive but warmhearted interest in another human being.

As springtime came Osceola made a habit of spending more and more time with Lieutenant Graham before and after his sessions with Thompson; they taught each other phrases in their languages and got on together with perfect trust and amiability. One morning Osceola brought his pretty four-year-old daughter on his shoulders and showed her off to Graham and other officers and men, but not to Thompson. That same afternoon Lieutenant Graham requested Thompson's permission to accept Osceola's invitation to visit his village and make the acquaintance of his two wives, whereupon General Thompson had promptly granted the request saying that as far as he was concerned

Lieutenant Graham might go wherever the devil he wished. The return of hot weather had found the agent in an unusually poor temper.

Now although Steven himself was not quite so indifferent to Osceola's friendship with Graham as he would have wished to be, he was a keen student of theatrics, whether on the itinerant stage or in life, and was therefore sufficiently absorbed in the drama unfolding between the Indian and the agent to welcome any circumstance which heightened it, and on June 2 General Thompson committed the blunder which was to alter the "friendship," fatefully.

Angered because Osceola had tarried in conversation with Lieutenant Graham before coming to his office, thus keeping him waiting, General Thompson, after a grudging salutation, addressed his visitor as follows:

"For many weeks, months in fact, Osceola has come to me with professions of friendship which I have most willingly and indeed wholeheartedly reciprocated. He and his following have been treated with unstinting hospitality. He has purchased—for skins not always of the first quality—large quantities of powder and lead from the sutler. Yet when I ask him to sign the agreement ratifying the treaties made openly and fairly by his brothers, when I do him the honor of asking him to put his mark with such far-seeing chiefs as Charlie Emaltha and others, Osceola refuses. Is this the act of a friend?" Here the agent pushed the document in question across his desk toward Osceola. "Now I am asking him once again to sign the paper. If he refuses I must ask myself whether his friendship is everything that it appears to be."

When Steven finished interpreting, Osceola sat motionless a moment, then in a movement too rapid for the eye to follow, drew his hunting knife and stabbed the paper precisely where the line was drawn for him to sign, leaving the knife planted in the desk.

"There is my mark!" he declared. "There will be no other."

Thompson's full florid face became plum-colored. Then he exploded.

"There will be no more purchases of powder and lead!"

With an exhalation of rage Osceola drew the knife from the desk and for an instant seemed about to plunge it into the general's breast, and it appeared to Steven then that the general was daring him to do so.

"Am I a slave forbidden weapons?" Osceola demanded. "I am an Indian—a Seminole! The white man will not make me black! I will make the white man red with blood and then blacken him in the sun and rain, where the wolf will smell of his bones and the buzzard live on his flesh!"

With a violent movement Osceola sheathed his knife, turned, and stamped out of the office. For a moment General Thompson stood at his desk, paralyzed with surprise and fury. Steven let himself smile thinly at the agent. Thompson stared at him a moment as if the floor under his feet had suddenly given way, then he lunged for the doorway.

"Arrest him!" he bellowed after Osceola.

That was at noon.

It had taken four husky infantrymen to carry out the general's order, and two of them had afterward required the attentions of the surgeon. Confined to the guardhouse in leg irons, Osceola raged like a wild animal and swore vengeance against Thompson the entire afternoon, his shrieks still filling the fort when the last bugle sounded. Later that night the prisoner fell silent.

In the morning Steven, at the general's request, went to Osceola in order to determine whether or not the night of confinement had had a beneficial effect upon him.

As the interpreter entered the guardhouse Osceola stood at a barred window, apparently composed. Steven sat on a bench. The Indian in leg irons made him think of a trapped wolf he had once seen knawing at its bone. When the captive spoke his voice was gentle and beguiling.

"Tell General Thompson that Osceola will sign the paper. Tell him that if he is released he will agree to move beyond the Big River with all his following."

It was then that Steven realized that the agent was marked for death.

General Thompson, while gratified by the prisoner's show of submission, demanded assurances. Steven went again to the guardhouse.

"Tell him to send for Charlie Emaltha and the other chiefs who have agreed to go west," Osceola said. "Tell him I shall speak to them and if they believe me they will intercede for me and I shall bring my following in and many others as well."

To Steven's astonishment General Thompson agreed to this proposition at once.

Three days later Charlie Emaltha and four other chiefs, all in full regalia, stood before Osceola. Steven, who on Thompson's order was sequestered in an adjoining storeroom, heard Osceola address them as follows:

"Brothers, listen. I have done what I thought best for our people. I saw that we were divided among ourselves and tried to join us as one nation to resist the Americans. Now I see that this was a foolish dream and would only bring destruction down upon us. I have suffered for what I believed and am not ashamed. I know now that I was leading our people toward ruin. Brothers, your course is the wise one. It is now mine also. We must submit and go to the new country, for if we do not we will all be in irons as I am now. Go and speak to the agent and tell him that I will bring my following in as I have promised, with others too, and will agree to go west."

Charlie Emaltha had pleaded Osceola's case so impressively that General Thompson, very moved, had let his prisoner go with a manly embrace and the promise of a fine new rifle when he would live up to his end of the bargain.

Colonel Alexander Fanning, a wiry, blunt-spoken regular

218

officer with an arm missing, watched Osceola go out of sight on the trail to the southwest.

"You've made a bad mistake, General," he said.

"I believe not, Colonel," Thomspon replied, his broad face suddenly clouding with doubt. "Charlie Emaltha will keep him in line."

It was then that Steven knew that Charlie Emaltha too was doomed.

Exactly a week later, to the surprise of everyone at the fort—with the exception of Lieutenant Graham, who believed that his friend would keep his word—Osceola appeared at the gates leading some eighty of his following, including his two wives and two children.

General Thompson, jubilant, greeted him warmly. He felt that his judgment was vindicated and that same afternoon he wrote the Secretary, "I have no doubt of Osceola's sincerity, and as little that the greatest difficulty is now surmounted." Colonel Fanning remained skeptical. The first night there was feasting and band music, then speeches and a ceremonial exchange of gifts, at the height of which Thompson, who had exceeded his normal ration of whiskey, held over his head the breech-loading rifle with silver chasing and carved walnut stock which he had ordered from New York, then addressed the assembly.

"Osceola and I have had our differences, as good friends sometimes will, but now we have buried the hatchet deep in the ground. Osceola has promised to lead you to the land beyond the Big River and I, acting for your Great Father, have promised to see you safely to your new homes with all the presents and money and other property as promised. This rifle signifies our trust in you, as you by coming here have signified your trust in us."

Receiving the rifle, Osceola too held it high overhead, saying, "This is a good gift. It means that the white man trusts the Seminoles as the Seminole trusts the white man."

219

"No doubt of it," murmured Colonel Fanning.

The next morning Osceola announced that he was leaving the fort with his following for the purpose of bringing in many more who were occupied in hunting. General Thompson hesitated. "Should not some be left behind? Why take all your people since they will be returning?"

"Is this trust?" demanded Osceola, instantly flying into a rage. "Are these the words of a brother?"

"Go in peace," said Thompson then.

As the last of Osceola's party filed out of the stockade, Colonel Fanning, standing with the agent and Steven, remarked that in his considered opinion General Thompson was making his worst mistake yet.

"He came back before," Thompson protested, "as I was certain he would."

"For the rifle. To buy time. To win your trust. Now he'll come back only as your sworn enemy."

"No, Colonel. I know the man."

Just as he spoke the woods were filled with a blood-freezing scream.

"His war cry," Colonel Fanning remarked when the shriek had echoed away. "We'll be getting used to it."

Osceola

Southwest of Fort King
November, 1835

A week after his release from Fort King Osceola caused Micanopy to hold a council at Big Swamp, north of Osceola's village and west of Fort King. There Osceola, Micanopy, Jumper, Alligator, Cloud, Sam Jones, and a half dozen other leaders and warriors opposed to emigration met and decreed

220

that henceforth any Seminole who would sell his livestock and agree to go west would be declared an enemy of the nation and be put to death. And all that summer war preparations were made, directed by Osceola who by now had become the chief strategist of the Seminole defense. He was now a leader of great influence, the more so because he acted with deference to the hereditary leaders, relying on clear, forceful argument, initiatives and deeds which spoke for themselves. He still visited Fort King, leading Thompson to believe that he was actively, though against obstacles, rounding up his warriors; whereas in fact he was assessing the Americans' readiness for war and gaining time. Thompson of course had to die; that had been certain from the first pressure of iron on Osceola's flesh; but he lived because according to the plan agreed among the chiefs Osceola's act of vengeance would be the sign for his people to rise against the enemy, and the time was not yet right.

Summer wore on into autumn.

On the twenty-sixth of November two of Osceola's warriors reported that they had seen Charlie Emaltha driving his cattle into the pens set up by the soldiers to receive Indian livestock and was already at the fort collecting money for the animals. The chief had made no secret of his intentions; a man of fierce independence, he had resolved to emigrate with his following in defiance of the death edict. At once Osceola called twelve of his warriors to follow him. The leaders had spoken. If Charlie Emaltha lived, the defense which had been prepared would collapse. Others would drive their cattle to the pens; others would accept Thompson's gold and consent to go west. Charlie Emaltha must die.

By midafternoon Osceola and his warriors were concealed in a thicket on either side of a turning in the trail about five miles southwest of the fort. The day was clear and cool and each leaf glowed with golden light. Soon Osceola heard horses up the trail, then a man's deep voice

221

crooning a tune; when the first rider appeared Osceola's grip on his rifle tightened—into view came one of Charlie Emaltha's slaves, in full Seminole dress, cradling between his braceleted arms Charlie Emaltha's two young daughters. From their hiding places Osceola's men were looking to him for the signal to attack. Charlie Emaltha appeared, also in full regalia, riding a black horse. Now the Negro was abreast of Osceola. The scouts had said nothing of the chief's daughters, who were the ages of Osceola's own. Osceola let the Negro pass. His men were looking to him anxiously. Then he noticed the coin bag slung around Charlie Emaltha's neck. With a cry he leaped into the trail before the chief and pulled him to the ground. He shouted to the Negro to go on. The rider hesitated. Half-rising, Charlie Emaltha motioned to him to obey.

"You know the decision of the chiefs!" shouted Osceola then.

Charlie Emaltha got to his feet and faced him.

"I know the decision Osceola forced on them. I believe what I believe. I think it foolish for our people to resist. I have said so many times. Now if I must die, I must die."

In sudden fury Osceola raised the rifle. "Who speaks for our people who wears the agent's money at his heart?"

Charlie Emaltha showed no sign of fear. "Who speaks for our people who threatens his brother with the agent's rifle? Your pride will doom the Seminoles, Osceola."

Osceola fired at his chest. The chief fell and the warriors fired nine more shots into his body. Osceola gathered the bloody coins which lay on his chest and on the ground, then stood and held up the coins in his palms.

"This gold is Seminole blood!" he cried.

Then he flung the coins far into the thicket.

When what the wolves and vultures had left of Charlie Emaltha's corpse was discovered three days later, panic spread through the white settlements of Florida.

General Thompson set an admirable example of calm.

Laird

WHEN the news of Charlie Emaltha's assassination reached St. Augustine Laird was ordered out with two companies to protect the settlers along the west bank of the St. Johns and to show the Indians the army's presence. Six days later he returned to report that he had encountered no Seminoles but had heard many an angry tale of recent raids. The Indians no longer showed themselves or visited the forts and there was apprehension about what this new behavior might mean. And though the patrol itself was uneventful, something happened to Laird in the course of it: certain thoughts and feelings met in an illumination so clear that he wondered that it had not happened long ago: He loved Eliza, never in his life more than now, yet out of old habit he had been holding back his love for her. No longer had he any wish that she change. Indeed, he had come to share the concerns he had once tried to shake out of her. Returning to their house on a warm evening late in November, he was determined to make her know this.

As he approached, crossing the street, the door opened and he saw Eliza showing out a man he recognized as the interpreter Steven Richards. Eliza called to Laird in pleased surprise. The interpreter passed by him with hardly a nod. In the doorway Laird embraced his wife—but not the way he had planned to only a moment before. He glanced down the street as Richards went around the corner. Everyone at the post knew that the interpreter lacked a man's desire for women. Still. . . .

"He's an old acquaintance," explained Eliza, reading his look. "Sometimes he comes calling and we talk." Then she added, "Somehow I thought you'd be a little more pleased to see me." He held her close again. There was nothing wrong, he told himself, only that he'd never imagined her entertaining any young male visitor while he was away, then he felt desire for her, even before his doubt had passed. "More like it," she said.

Muttering as she set the dinner table, Delia was in bad humor.

"Sure glad *you're* back, Capt'n Laird," she said with a dark glance at Eliza. "Hope you cleaned out them Seminoles too, every one of 'em."

"We're not at war with them, Delia," he told her. "Nobody's cleaning out anybody."

"Too bad," she declared and went into the kitchen.

"What's going on in this house?" Laird asked, as they went into the living room.

Eliza drew him down beside her on the settee. "You're coming back to it, that's all."

"I missed you," he told her after a moment. "And I've been thinking a lot about us, what you said at the ball, about keeping apart—and how you said it and how I pretended I didn't know what you were talking about. I got to realizing how much I care for you." Delia stamped into the dining room and set out plates noisily. "What's troubling her?"

"Steven talking about the Seminoles. Laird—"

"He comes often?"

"Almost never." Delia went back to the kitchen. "Laird, I've been thinking about us too, and I've decided I'm ready to go back to Caffrey Station, as the wife you want. To stay."

"Never doubted it. And you are the wife I want, always were. Just as soon—"

"I mean I'd hoped we could go now."

"We can't now. You know that."

"There's no war. Nothing keeps you in the army."

"It's just no time to resign now."

"Matter of honor?" she asked with a trace of bitterness.

"Nothing like that."

"And what if I were to ask you straight out to do what I want?"

"I'd hope you wouldn't."

"I don't want anything to happen to you."

"Can't say as I do either. 'Specially not now," he said as Delia came to call them to supper. "Don't worry, we'll be home again before you know it."

Osceola

Fort King—Fifty miles southwest of Fort King
December, 1835

IN the concealment of the thicket he waited with his band for the agent to take his after-dinner stroll outside the fort. The log doors of the palisade stood open, no guard was posted, the garrison suspected nothing. The distance from the edge of the thicket to the agent's usual path was about twenty-five yards. Two hundred yards down the wooded knoll was the sutler's log dwelling and, just beyond it, another dense thicket where a second force waited for the signal of the first shot to attack the house. Inside, the sutler was at dinner with his two clerks and a boy. The day was cool and clear.

Osceola, his face streaked with vermilion and black, glanced up to the sun raying in the branches of the pines, well on its downward arc. Fifty miles to the southwest Micanopy, Jumper, and Alligator would be tracking the American relief column working northeast from Fort Brooke at Tampa Bay; and if all went according to plan Osceola would kill the agent and then ride with his force to be present at the ambush.

An instant after Osceola glanced at the sun in the branches Wiley Thompson appeared in the compound inside the gate smoking a cigar. With him was Captain Rus-

225

sell, and for a long time the two men talked. Then Lieutenant Constantine Smith, a frequent companion of the agent on his strolls, joined them, and General Thompson and Lieutenant Smith left Russell and came out of the gates.

Osceola let them come abreast of his hiding place. Then, kneeling, set the bead in the V, tracked the agent's temple, and fired. General Wiley Thompson fell at once; and in the volley that followed Lieutenant Smith stood for a second or two, bewildered, before bullets spun him down beside the general. As the first fusillade echoed away Osceola uttered a war cry that was answered down the sutler's house by yells and cries of the second party as they burst from cover and fired through the open windows of the log house. The door flew open and two clerks stumbled out, sprawled, picked themselves up, and began to run for a nearby thicket; four shots from the attackers cut them down. Osceola, anticipating a counterattack from the fort, now deployed his men behind trees and ordered up the second party, whose work at the house was done.

Then the great log doors of the fort creaked closed and the massive latches were thrown home.

Osceola stood over the agent's body. It lay full length on the ground bleeding from fourteen hits, staring at the sky. Osceola took the scalp, a two-by-three-inch oval tuft of thinning reddish-gray hair, fastened it to his sash, then took the general's bloody coat from his body and put it on, as the braves shouted the victory cry. Not a shot had been fired from the fort.

With his warriors Osceola galloped southwest, racing the setting sun. He felt at one with them now, as he did with all Seminoles, from the eastern shore to the Apalachicola, from his birthplace in the north to the great swamplands south, for today they were one people joined no longer only by the memory of King Payne and Cowkeeper, but by a common determination to fight for the land flying beneath his pony's hooves.

In four hours he reached the main force, as darkness fell. The stretch of road through the pine barren and palmetto where the ambush had been sprung was alive with torches of Negroes moving up and down the column of fallen soldiers. About twenty yards to the left of the road more torches swarmed inside a low prowlike log breastwork, and Osceola saw that here those who had not fallen on the road had made their last defense.

Indians wandered amazed among the bodies. Most had been on raiding parties, some had taken white scalps, but this day was altogether different: Never in memory had there been such a slaughter of those who claimed mastery over them. There was no looting, no spree of mutilation; only the Negroes went about the usual business of victors. As Osceola dismounted, the only celebration was the torches and the cool wind seething in the pines.

He started toward the log bastion, four feet high and studded with lead that shone in the moonlight; near it he found Micanopy sitting on a log, his head in his hands; Jumper and Alligator came up behind the chief, who looked up and seeing the bloody coat Osceola wore said, "Now they will destroy us."

"Micanopy has done well," Osceola said. "He has won a great battle. Where is the victory dance!"

"They are too many and too powerful," protested the old chief. "They will destroy us."

Jumper said, "This was the plan and we must go by it. We must not lose heart. If we are afraid of winning we are cowards."

As Micanopy gazed gloomily around at the corpses, both Jumper and Alligator looked to Osceola for the first time openly as their leader.

They sat in a circle and Osceola related the events at Fort King. Then Alligator, as measured in speech as he was frenzied in battle, told of the massacre.

For four days they had tracked the two companies of Americans northeast out of Fort Brooke on Tampa Bay.

There had been favorable opportunities to attack but, according to plan, they were waiting for Micanopy from the north and Osceola from the northeast to join them. When Micanopy did reach them, Jumper (since Payne's Landing firmly against capitulation) urged that they strike at once, since he thought the opportunity was then too good to resist; but Micanopy insisted that they wait for Osceola. However, when the sun began to sink below the treetops and Osceola still had not come, Jumper and he, Alligator, had pressed Micanopy to order the attack and the descendant of Cowkeeper had done so, firing the first shot, which killed the American leader.

Major Francis Dade.

In the volleys that followed Micanopy's shot, nearly half of the American force of more than a hundred had fallen in the road behind the major.

Many died with their coats still buttoned over their cartridge boxes.

Others were cut down as they ran for thickets that came alive with Seminoles.

A remnant found cover in the deadfall and managed to raise the crude prow of logs from which they returned the Indians' fire and even managed to get off several rounds with the six-pounder they were taking to Fort King.

During the engagement a short, stout little officer known by the chiefs as Captain Gardiner rode furiously through the smoke and hail of bullets, shouting, "God damn! God damn! God damn!" ordering the wounded dragged into the log defense and directing the Americans' fire; and it seemed that no bullet could touch him until one caught him over the eye and dropped him from his mount.

The dwindling remnant fought until dusk when almost all were wounded or dead and their powder was used up, much being wasted in firing the six-pounder with solid rounds and little effect; then the blacks had overrun the log breastwork and sought out the living among the corpses.

When Alligator finished his narrative Osceola looked

around and saw that the Indians were still awed by what they had done.

"What is this?" he cried to the chiefs. "Are we mourning these dogs?" Then he stood and let the woods ring with a triumphant shout, then leaped up onto the breastwork.

"Is this battle lost?" he demanded. "Will we be driven from our lands? Will the sun not rise tomorrow?"

The Indians murmured and drew closer. Osceola, seeing among them Hillis Hadjo, the most respected of the prophets, dropped from the breastwork and handed him the agent's scalp, saying, "Gather the trophies of the day's victories and let us celebrate according to our custom."

A bonfire was built near the battleground and a ten-foot pole implanted on which were hung all the scalps taken that day; and Seminoles and their black allies were soon dancing in a circle around the trophies, chanting and dropping out often to refresh themselves at the kegs. Soon Micanopy was staggering among them regally, at peace with his ancestors. Osceola, wearing the agent's coat, was now the acknowledged war leader of the Seminoles.

Near the dead Americans red man and black man danced and drank and shouted until at last Osceola, who had also drunk freely, solemnly approached the pole hung with scalps, General Thompson's at the top, and raised his arm for their attention. When the dancing had stopped and all eyes were on him he puffed out his cheeks and raised his hands in mock supplication to the agent's scalp.

"I AM NOT MAD! I AM YOUR FRIEND!" he shouted.

A moment of astonished silence was followed by whoops and wild laughter.

"IF THE INDIANS DO NOT LEAVE PEACEABLY, THE GREAT FATHER WILL REMOVE THEM BY FORCE!"

It was more than mimicry: Thompson's ghost inhabited his assassin; Osceola was expelling from his spirit the last drops of poisonous fealty to the white man, distilled from his own blood, now purified.

"YOU WILL COME FOR BREAD TO THE MAN WHO

TOOK YOUR HOUSE AND HE WILL CALL YOU AN IN-
DIAN DOG!"

Through Osceola the Indians saw the dead agent for the
first time clearly as their enemy. They believed then that
the American, for all his soldiers and gunmen, his writing
that was to him Creation's law, was alien to the elements,
his spirit false, his friendship a lie—and they believed then,
through Osceola, that he was also weak.

When Osceola stood before them no longer as General
Thompson but as himself, there was a roar of jubilation.

All night the celebration lasted, until the drunken victors
fell across the dead.

So passed the first day of the war.

Osceola

Withlacoochee River
December, 1835

THE next morning buzzards wheeled over the site of the
massacre as the chiefs met in council. Within the hour
their plan was formed, for it had long been anticipated that
once open war commenced, the Americans would move
down from Fort Drane on the village strongholds in the
mazy wilds along the southern bank of the Withlacoochee
River, where no white man had ever penetrated. Osceola,
with Alligator second in command and a detachment of 250
warriors, would ride north to intercept the southward-mov-
ing army at the river in order to prevent them from reaching
the sanctuaries. Already the scouts had reported that the
enemy was approaching in a large force, mounted and afoot
but moving slowly, encumbered by its baggage train and
numbers.

Riding swiftly through oak-dotted rolling hills, hammock trails, and lake country familiar to Osceola, they

230

reached their destination by nightfall, the single ford on the river where General Clinch could easily cross his army. There Osceola made camp and sent out scouts to learn of the enemy's progress, then he rolled himself in his blanket and lay awake for a long time gazing up at the stars, thinking that tomorrow when the sun was born again would come his first trial as a leader in battle against the Americans.

But at dawn the scouts reported that General Clinch was still a day's march away, his wagon train bogging down in the swamps, so Osceola spent the day preparing an ambush at the ford—only to learn late in the afternoon that General Clinch's force was not making for the ford but preparing to camp three miles upstream. Realizing that the north bank was impenetrable jungle except where the trails intersected the river, Osceola ordered his warriors upstream to the place where, the next morning, Clinch would emerge from the jungle—and face fifty yards of deep water.

"How will he cross here?" Alligator had asked.

"We must help him find a way," said Osceola.

The next morning, incredibly, a bugle at the American camp shattered the predawn silence. Across the river, a hundred yards from the bank, Osceola's warriors were arrayed at the perimeter of a horseshoe-shaped clearing where the only trail passed, an even more perfect ambush than the first. Osceola, his face painted for battle, wearing General Thompson's bloodstained coat, waited with Alligator, watching the river as the Americans reached the narrow beach where the trail ended. He recognized the big-bellied officer in sky-blue and white who rode up, dismounted, and scanned the water. General Clinch. Presently another general, also a big man, rode up and dismounted beside Clinch. Now the two officers studied the river. Pressing behind them, far down the trail, there must have been a thousand men. The generals were arguing. At last General Clinch pointed across the water and issued an order. Osceola smiled at Alligator as two swimmers started across for the bark canoe he had had planted there the night before.

It took the Americans all morning to ferry, seven or eight at a time, furiously bailing the leaking canoe, more than 200 regular troops to the south bank. Directing the operation was another officer Osceola had seen at Fort King, Colonel Fanning. At last General Clinch swam his horse across. The other general remained on the opposite bank with the main force, the citizen soldiers. Without a sound, Osceola and Alligator returned to their places in the ambush.

From behind a tree at the apex of the horseshoe Osceola watched the soldiers file into the clearing and, on their officers' orders, stack their arms. It seemed to him then that the Great Spirit was directing the Americans' every move to favor the Seminoles, yet even so he felt trepidation; the council had directed him only to protect the villages; the provocation to battle was his initiative, because he feared that if they did not engage the Americans now the spirit of resistance born at the victory celebration might as quickly die.

His war cry froze the soldiers in their places. His first shot sent General Clinch's cap flying. Then the officers were shouting and the troops were running for their weapons. As he reloaded, the forest came alive with the cries of his warriors and a volley of shots. General Clinch's horse fell. The general picked himself up, drew his sword, stepped up on the heaving side of his fallen steed, and shouted orders for his troops to fall into ranks. Colonel Fanning was riding wildly up and down rallying the troops, his one arm flailing the air with his sword. Americans were falling; the rest were now returning the fire and the woods began to sing with bullets. Colonel Fanning rode up to General Clinch apparently exhorting him to order a charge. By now the clearing was filling with acrid smoke and Osceola showed himself, shouting at his braves to redouble the fire. Now the enemy troops were formed in ranks, firing, falling, but holding. For a long time they sustained the punishing attack, neither charging or retreating. Through the gray-blue haze General Clinch, now mounted on a fallen officer's horse, rode among them, a huge ghostly target seemingly invulnerable. Colonel Fanning galloped up to him again, then was off leading a charge against the Seminole positions to the rear, guarding the escape route to the river. A third of Fanning's troops fell in the assault but the rest forced the Seminoles to give way. Now the militia general rode up at the head of a number of his mounted men, all dripping wet. In the dense smoke the muzzle flashes were like fireflies. Suddenly Osceola felt a sharp pain and seizing his forearm felt blood welling through the thick cloth of the coat. Alligator ran up to him and led him to cover.

"It's nothing," Osceola insisted. "Is the militia crossing?"

"Only a few," Alligator said. "The rest are cowards. Their horses can swim but they turn their backs to the river."

"These are not cowards," Osceola replied, as through the clearing drifts of smoke he watched the soldiers carrying off the wounded and dead, General Clinch and Colonel Fanning directing the retreat.

The Seminoles had won the field and inflicted many casualties. Osceola told Alligator to order the warriors to break off the engagement and return to the villages.

That night around the fires there was no victory celebration. They had killed and wounded many more enemy soldiers than their own three dead and five wounded, including Osceola; they had turned the Americans back to Fort Drane and saved the villages; they had observed the foe's weaknesses, their slow noisy movement, how the militiamen and regulars could not work together; but they had also seen that the Americans could fight bravely and that they were as numerous as stars. Osceola remembered General Clinch, capless, standing on his fallen horse waving his sword in the air in the midst of flying bullets and, staring into the fire, he realized that the war would be long, desperate, perhaps finally hopeless, but he swore that he would lead his people through it to whatever fate was theirs, as long as the Great Spirit gave him breath.

Laird

FROM besieged St. Augustine the smoke of burning plantations rose as a pall over the southern sky. And now to the west the Seminole war parties under King Philip and Coacoochee were raiding the settlements up and down the St. Johns River. Newspapers throughout the South echoed the appeals of Governor Eaton, General Clinch, and Colonel Gadsden calling on gallant young men to save the Territory from the savage attacks of the red man and the renegade black. And they came; from Georgia and the Carolinas, Alabama, Mississippi, and Louisiana, even from more distant northern states, overland and by sea they poured into St. Augustine, Picolata on the St. Johns, and Tampa, a thousand strong in January alone, militiamen and new volunteers, proud young officers of the landed gentry, enlisted sons of farmers and tradesmen, all eager to prove their courage, avenge the murder of General Thompson and the massacre of Major Dade and his men, subdue the Seminoles, and, foremost in many ardent hearts, to teach the rampaging blacks a lesson that would never be forgotten.

By early February the harbor was thick with masts and the town crowded with soldiers mingling with a citizenry relieved at least of fears of being murdered in their beds. The town drew comfort from the rows of tents extending south from the post to the racetrack, from the quantities of arms and military supplies unloaded along the seawall, and from the news that one of the four highest-ranking generals in the army, Major General Winfield Scott, was now on his way to marshal this force, and thousands more, and lead them against the enemy. Where before there had been fear and disarray now there was confidence in an early victory.

In February Laird Caffrey was assisting unseasoned militia officers in forming and drilling their arriving companies. A veteran now, he had received his baptism of fire when his patrol flushed a war party south of Buloff's now-deserted plantation; and he had fought again on the main road to the garrison at Picolata, eighteen miles west. During the second encounter a private had been killed. On both occasions Laird had observed the same pattern in the way the Indians did battle, never fighting in the open but whenever possible from cover—and only then when they were sure of achieving surprise or were surprised themselves; sometimes they fought, then retreated to a prepared position and fought again; other times they simply vanished into the forests, swamps, and jungles; melted away. One afternoon, watching an eager young Georgia officer putting his men through an intricate close-order drill, Laird found himself wondering whether the army in Florida should not be learning an entirely different sort of warfare—but he put the thought out of his mind. Civilized men did not fight like savages. Certainly, from what he had heard, General Scott did not.

A week later, early in the afternoon, approaching band music and the guns of the fort dueling with the thunder of a storm receding northeastward to sea announced the arrival of General Winfield Scott. When the band marched into the plaza, the sun came out as if on command, and the gathered citizens applauded the general, riding a white horse surrounded by his staff officers. Attired in a full-dress uniform of blue, white, and gleaming gold, he was six feet four, powerfully built (one shoulder slightly stooped from an old wound), with the imperious face of a Caesar, the very commander they had been expecting. As the troops followed into the plaza, the town cheered and the church bells rang out in jubilant dissonance with the marching band.

Among the officers rumors had preceded General Scott concerning the magnificence of his field headquarters and his grand style of living when on campaign, but the truth belittled all reports. Within an hour a great tent was raised south of the post and special wagon trains drawn up and unloaded. Polished furniture and Oriental rugs were carried into the tent, fancy lamps and books set in place, French wines and delicacies stored in sideboards, and only then was the general's personal pennant raised on staff in the parade ground below the national ensign, and the officers of the post requested to attend the general and his staff.

"Where in hell is Gaines?" demanded the major general when introductions were done and the visiting officers seated around the towering officer, who stood before a map of Florida unrolled on a map stand: General Eustis, Major Appleton, Captain Caffrey, and Lieutenant Belcamp.

"Tampa, sir," General Eustis replied.

"With his *troops?*"

Major Appleton undertook to relieve General Eustis of bearing the brunt of the attack.

"According to the express, sir. Yes, sir—with his troops."

Looking to his staff officers seated on either side of him, then to the visitors, he tapped the pointer he held on the back of the chair before him, ominously.

"What in the name of God is General Gaines doing in Tampa with his troops? He was ordered to *Texas.*"

"Perhaps his orders did not reach him in time, sir," Laird observed. The major general contemplated him critically.

"He had none to go to Tampa, Captain." The major general turned to the offending place on the map.

"He'll exhaust our rations in Tampa. He is raising havoc with my campaign."

For another five minutes General Scott vituperated against his rival, declaring that should his own campaign go awry they and the War Department would now know exactly who was to blame. Then with the pointer he described three lines on the map, from south, north, and east, converging on the area of General Clinch's engagement on the Withlacoochee.

"They're massed here," he said, tapping that spot. "We shall strike them with three forces simultaneously. Clinch from the north, Eustis from the east, and Colonel Lindsey from the south—from Tampa." He gazed around the half-circle. No one spoke. "The main objective is that the enemy be contained and not permitted to scatter to the south. General Eustis, you and Lindsey will join forces—here—to prevent their escape, and then drive them north into Clinch's arms."

General Eustis considered the area on the map from Volusia on the St. Johns westward, the line of march indicated by the major general.

"Sir," he said, "there are no roads or known trails west of Volusia. That whole region is unexplored wilderness."

"Then," Scott replied, "you will have the honor of exploring it, sir, and rendering that service to your government, in addition to subduing the hostiles."

General Scott then demanded to know if there were further questions; and because his gaze rested on Laird, Laird posed the question that was on all their minds.

"What part will General Gaines play, sir?"

"I thought I informed you, Captain," came the reply. "General Gaines is ordered to Texas. General Gaines will play no part in the Florida campaign." With the pointer he rapped a portfolio on his desk. "My orders are clear, gentlemen. We are to crush all Seminole resistance. We are to crush Osceola. No negotiations will be opened until they have surrendered unconditionally." He paused and looked from one to the other, stopping at Laird. "And that means, gentlemen, surrendering not only themselves and their families but every Negro in their possession—in all cases where there is a *lawful* white claimant." Still looking at Laird, he added, "That is the order. I assure you it comes from the very highest authority. Any questions, Captain?"

"No, sir," replied Laird, who nonetheless had a number of questions about carrying out such an order; but he chose not to ask them just now.

Addressing the map, Scott again drew three converging lines. "From north, south, and east," he said. "This attack has served the English handsomely against Napoleon. I venture that it will do well enough against Osceola. Good day, gentlemen."

Turning to an aide, he ordered the band to resume playing.

Laird

IN their bedroom bureau she had a special drawer for mementos. As he was packing to leave he found it open.

There was a small oval portrait of her mother, her father's watch, his own letters to her, Rachel's, the engraved invitation to the President's Ball, tasseled dance cards, yellowing notices of their wedding, jewelry—and a book.

From its black covers he thought at first that it was a Bible. He picked it up and read the title page. *The True Face of Slavery* by Harrison Philips, and the handwritten inscription, "For Eliza Caffrey, in friendship, Richard Wolfe, Bristol, R.I."

When Eliza returned home from marketing with Delia Laird was downstairs pacing the red tiles of the cool dark parlor, the book in plain sight on a round table in the middle of the room. By now he was certain that a guilty liaison existed between his wife and Captain Wolfe. What else could "friendship" mean? As Eliza entered the room he stood in silence until she recognized the book. Her smile of greeting faded.

"What right have you to go through my things?"

"Who has a better right, Mrs. Caffrey?"

"Nonsense," she said, proceeding to unpin her hat in a most unrepentant manner. "A gentleman I've met twice in my life sends me a—"

"*Twice!*"

"Once with my father, since you're interested."

"I might have expected."

"Don't you dare speak against my father!"

"You had precious little respect for mine!"

"All I did was let a little rain in on his pet chair once."

"Deliberately!"

"Maybe I wanted you to look at me and see *me* just once—even in anger as you're looking at me now."

"You have always resisted being my wife." He struck the book. "Now this!"

"Now what, exactly, Laird Caffrey? If you mean your own foolish temper over nothing at all, I cannot accept the blame for that."

He remembered to speak to her as to a child. "Eliza, do you know what's in this book?"

"Of course I do. I'm not a fool."

"Do you believe what it says?"

"It says some things I believe, yes. Have you read it?"

"I've read enough to know that the author is an ignorant scoundrel and the man who would send a lady such a book is a damned reprobate!" He went to the garden doors, looked out, returned to the table, and picked up the book again. "It's as if you were taking revenge on your own people."

"For what, Mr. Caffrey?" she demanded sharply.

"It's how it seems."

"Say it! You mean I'd see things in their proper light if I'd been born landed."

"I meant no such thing."

"Then explain yourself, please!"

"Explain myself! It's you that has the explaining to do."

"Will you stop striking that book, Laird Caffrey, and listen for once. I have not resisted being your wife. The fact is, when I found out you weren't about to take me as I am I tried to pretend to be someone more to your liking—except it didn't fool either of us. I can't change, Laird, and I'm through trying. That other girl you married doesn't exist, never did, and you'd better forget about her."

"I told you that's all past!"

"You told me no such thing."

"I let you know in every possible way. What does it take to reach you?"

Suddenly she drew a deep breath, studied him a moment, then spoke softly.

"First you could put that book down instead of waving it in my face. Oh, that damned Caffrey pride."

He looked at her in amazement. "Caffrey pride! Why, Caffreys are humble besides Hutchins. At least we live in the world God gave us without trying to turn it around to suit ourselves. Pride indeed!"

"Second, you might try holding me instead of fighting me."

He took her in his arms. She looked up at him, smiling, and said, "Trouble is there's a lot more Hutchins in you than you're ready to admit."

He took her to bed feeling both ardor and the distance the war put between them. The next morning he marched his companies out on General Scott's campaign.

Steven

Fort Drane
March, 1836

SILHOUETTED against a bleak white midmorning sky, General Clinch eased his heavy bulk up the last rickety lad-

240

der to the windlass platform high above the rum distillery, then carefully stood erect. Far below, in the bed of a hay wagon, Steven Richards lay watching the general. Near him, stretched out so that the sides of the wagon protected them from the eyes of any passing sergeant who might order them to work, lay Privates Eldon Washburn and Ned Dudley, also watching the general.

"Why's he gone up there?" asked Ned, who at fifteen was the youngest regular soldier in the regiment.

"To piss," said Eldon.

Steven smiled faintly. In the week since the interpreter had been at Clinch's sugar plantation, Auld Lang Syne, now in government service as Fort Drane, Eldon Washburn was the only person he had found among the 400 men in the stockade half worth talking to and the only person in the world to whom he had confided his ambition to leave the army and join a theatrical company. Ned was in the wagon because he followed Eldon around.

A distant boom like faraway thunder made Ned sit up.

"Get your dumb head down," Eldon ordered. Ned obeyed.

"General Gaines must be in bad trouble," the boy said after a moment. On the tower the general was sweeping the southern horizon with a pocket spyglass.

"What's *left* of General Gaines," Eldon corrected. "Can't be much left by now, can there, Steve?"

The interpreter sighed. "Steven," he said. "My name is Steven."

"Listen to His Lordship," said Eldon, impressed.

Ned asked why General Clinch had not yet ordered a march south to lift the siege.

"Tell him—Steven."

"You tell him. He follows you."

"I don't follow anybody," Ned declared. "Anyway, I know why."

"Then why ask?" said Eldon.

Ned shook his head as if the conversation had taken a thoughtful turn. "I just can't figure it out. Why would General Scott order Clinch not to rescue General Gaines when General Gaines is surrounded by Seminoles? Hell, it's our troops dying over there."

"Keep your head down," said Eldon.

Steven squinted to make the figure of Clinch waver. "Scott doesn't like Gaines," he explained. "He especially doesn't like him spoiling his campaign."

"Will he let General Gaines' men get wiped out for *that?*"

Now General Clinch had put away his spyglass and stood with his hands locked behind his back, gazing at the milky horizon.

"Don't worry," Steven said then. "We'll march, order or no order. Clinch is just up there agonizing with his angels."

Eldon looked doubtful. "How do you know we'll march?"

"Clinch wants another crack at Osceola. He thinks he can beat him this time. Now he's just waiting for a sign from God. Clinch is crazy."

"I think *you're* crazy," said Eldon.

Moments later the three in the wagon heard the sound of flapping wings and, looking up, saw high over the general's raised head a squadron of cranes, their long necks pointing due south.

Eaton

Governor's Mansion, Tallahassee
May, 1836

HEARING his wife's steps clicking across the stone hallway, John Eaton set aside the letter he had been reading and took up his book. Margaret entered the library and without a glance hurried to the window to wave good-bye to the escort whose carriage had brought her back from the race-track. She was wearing her new red satin from Paris, a matching hat, matching parasol. During her farewells at the window John Eaton read. When at last she lighted in a chair facing him, twirling her parasol in the carpet, he looked up at her and smiled.

"Was it hot?"

"You're mightily pleased with yourself," she said.

"I am."

She glanced scornfully at his book. "Are the Greeks as heavenly as ever?"

"Romans. How did our horses place?"

She sighed. "First, of course. Is there something wrong with my dress?"

"On the contrary, it's amazingly well fitted to your figure—where there's dress to fit at all."

She smiled mirthlessly. "Oh dear, the governor of Florida is becoming a wit. And in such heat. Well, you should know that I'm ordering two more from the same maker. Of course I must send my measure since I'll never see Paris myself"—she glanced around at the book-filled shelves—"not in *this* life."

"How can you be so sure?"

"Because we are in exile. First the general makes it impossible for us to live in Washington City, then he banishes us to this hideous place where nothing but nothing ever happens."

"There is a war."

She glanced again at the book. "I see it occupies you mightily. No, it's exile. It's punishment. As for the war, it's a wretched war, you said so yourself. You said it wouldn't have happened at all if the general had occupied himself more with the government and less with my virtue." She stood restlessly and went to the window. "We are exiled here forever. We shall die in this heat. He's a ridiculous old man."

243

"Margaret!" said Eaton firmly. "He is still my friend. He meant what he did in friendship to us both."

She turned to him quickly. "Then if he's our friend why aren't we in Paris? Why is Mr. Van Buren in London? Anyway, you've said far worse about the general when you're drunk."

Governor Eaton leaned back in his chair, placed his fingertips together, and smiled. "You'll regret what you've said."

His wife shrugged. "I've made it a rule in life never to regret anything I say—no matter how high the station of the person I'm saying it about."

"Spoken like a true niece of the governor of New Jersey."

"If you start!" she warned. Then, touching her temple with a lace handkerchief, she said, "It's too hot to argue." And appealing to his sympathy, "What I cannot stand is the way the riffraff of this place stares at me wherever I go."

John Eaton reached for the decanter on his desk and, replenishing his glass, looked at her over its rim.

"Wait till they stop."

For the first time Margaret Eaton rewarded him with a faint smile of amusement. "I swear," she said, "there is something on your mind, and I don't think it's Romans."

He took up the letter, glancing over it. "Mm."

When she came near he quickly held the letter away from her.

"John, I won't be teased. What is that letter?"

He looked her up and down, admiring the full curves of her body, then said quietly, "Margaret, what if I were to tell you that you are going to Paris—not to stay—only long enough to buy dresses before traveling to Madrid—where I shall present credentials as our country's minister to the Queen?"

When the servants in the kitchen below heard their mistress shriek, they ran upstairs thinking some accident had befallen her, to find the governor and his lady laughing and dancing in wild circles through the halls.

244

Adams

HE sat with his hands folded over the petition of the ladies of Dorchester as the majority of members applauded the gentleman from Georgia, taking his seat. The ex-President, now representative from Plymouth, Massachusetts, remained unmoved by his colleague's praise of the heroic exertions of the citizen soldiers in Florida, defending American lives and property against the savage tide, and particularly unmoved by the gentleman's appeal for new appropriations, once again, to sustain the war in Florida.

In the first place the military situation there appeared to be abysmal.

More important, for some time now the member from Plymouth had formed the opinion that the conflict was a war promoted by the South—with broad Northern sympathy—for the entrenchment of slavery; and for some time his inner voice had been telling him that that institution was a great and foul stain upon the nation—but he had heretofore kept silent. As President he had never raised his voice against human bondage in the United States, believing that incontinent strife over the issue would endanger the Union.

Yet the inner voice was persistent.

As President he had written in a secret sonnet,

> Roll, years of promise, rapidly roll round,
> Till not a slave shall on this earth be found.

But he had said nothing. He feared that the inner voice might be illusory—even diabolical; the Founding Fathers had wisely avoided confrontation over the institution; and today the plain political reality was that in Congress as

245

throughout most of the nation abolition was germinating not as a sacred cause but as a radical novelty feared by citizens of property and standing. To the attacks of abolitionists the South was responding with a determined defense of her institution: Black laws were tightened, white terror swept the South enforcing them with lynching and burning, and most ominous of all was the entrenchment of proslavery power within the federal government; in the Senate where John Calhoun now defended the institution as a positive good, feeding Southern pride in the evil it was wedded to.

As the gentleman from Georgia spoke on, John Quincy Adams envisioned the Florida war as a part of a greater movement to spread slavery, even to Texas, eventually to the Western Territories, in which legions of Mexican peasants and Plains Indians, as well as Southeastern Indians, would be sacrificed at federal expense so that slaveholders might invade their lands to establish a whole continent of shame.

Slavery was evil!

Yet were it only a moral matter John Quincy Adams might have gone on writing furtive sonnets, voting for the restitution of fugitives, confining the subject to the pages of his memoirs—the worst was that slavery was fatally injurious to the Union!

He could be silent no longer.

For he was now aware that the best and deepest feelings in the nation on the most important issue facing it were without an effective voice in the federal government.

Henceforth his must be that voice.

The gentleman from Georgia concluded his speech with a motion that the appropriations for continuing the war in Florida on a larger scale be approved, and took his seat.

John Quincy Adams voted Aye—for to terminate that conflict in mid-course by a denial of funds could only outrage the South, punish the soldiers, and lead to greater harm; the stand to make was against the annexation of Texas as a slave territory, against war with Mexico, against all aggrandizement which would implant slavery under the Stars and Stripes—and *for* the constitutional right of the ladies of Dorchester to petition against slavery.

Knowing that he was too old to witness the triumph of freedom over bondage which must come one day, he resolved to devote the rest of his life to fighting slavery by every lawful means at his disposal, as long as he was granted strength and a seat in the House. He would fight not as a partisan but as a man for the whole nation, as a politician with a clear purpose whose time had come. He would fight as an Adams: with intellect and unswerving loyalty to the Union.

The Ayes carried.

John Quincy Adams was on his feet, shaking the petition of the ladies of Dorchester over his head, shouting, "Mr. Speaker!"

Laird

Withlacoochee River
October, 1836

OSCEOLA'S war cry split through the wet forest, a howl rising to a bone-chilling screech which seemed to come from just ahead, but when Laird led his exhausted troops forward at double time they reached the river only to find the Indians already on the opposite shore, across fifty yards of forbidding black water, firing from the cover of trees.

Laird's instinct was to ford the river; if the enemy could cross, they could, and here, within reach, was the main Seminole force—but General Call's order was not to carry the pursuit south of the Withlacoochee River.

Reluctantly he ordered his men to take cover and resigned himself to wait for General Call to arrive with his troops.

The rain which had stopped began again.

A minute later, upstream, Major Stonewall Quirt, leading an advance column, came out of the forest and, hearing the enemy fire, raised his sword, cried "Forward!" and splashed into the river, his men following; he went about six paces, then fell and slowly began to sink. His men seized him and dragged his body across the sand to cover.

Laird watched the major's forage cap float past in the rain-pocked river.

It was still raining when the new commanding general rode up at the head of his main force and demanded to know where the hell Major Quirt was.

"Dead, sir," Laird told him. "He started across and the Indians shot him."

"My orders were to stay on this bank," said Call, studying the river.

"He must have forgotten, sir."

A bullet skirred through the leaves overhead.

"Damn fool thing to do," said Call. "That goddamn river looks deep as hell."

"The Indians made it—Osceola's main war party. We may not have another chance at them for a long time."

General Call scowled at the river, raindrops peeling down his broad face. "They'd never make a stand. We'd be chasing them halfway to Key West."

"Maybe," Laird said. "They seemed pretty ready to fight."

"Well, we're not, Captain," Call declared. "We're not going to let Osceola draw us into a goddamn debacle."

And he called back the order for a return march north to Drane.

On that march the image of Major Quirt splashing into the river repeated itself in Laird's thoughts until the senselessness of it staggered him, yet he himself had felt the same instinct to cross the river and now regretted that he had not followed it.

Osceola

ONLY when the scouts reported that the entire American force was retreating northward did Osceola yield to the waves of fever he had struggled against since dawn. He knew that had the Americans crossed the river in pursuit they would have soon overrun them and discovered the secret village, occupied since the start of the war by 400 Seminole warriors, 200 Negroes, and women, children, old people—more than 1,000 in all.

Three miles from the river.

Had the Americans crossed in full strength Seminole power in central Florida would have been broken. The entire enemy force would have then turned eastward against Philip and Coacoochee; the war would have soon been over.

An important victory had been won yet in this war even victory was bitter.

For Osceola knew also that the Americans would return in even greater strength, more determined, and that the village, miraculously saved today, could not be saved tomorrow, and that now they must move farther south toward the great swamplands, living with no shelter, scant food, like hunted animals.

As he returned through the forest, the sweeps of fever so weakened Osceola that he had to walk with the help of two warriors.

He had recognized the American captain across the river. He was the husband of the former agent's daughter who had once come to the central villages with food, the blue-eyed woman whose kindness he remembered as being like the fever that now weakened him, whom he had wanted to kill in revenge for the Seminole woman murdered in cold blood by the Americans. In his weakness he had only given her

249

the arrow tip, a symbol of their people's enmity; and today he had shot at her husband without the bullets finding their mark.

Entering the village Osceola forced himself to walk unaided. In silence the women and children searched for their own among the returning braves, helping the wounded. To the west the sky was a blaze of red and in the eerie light Osceola saw written in the faces he passed, their misery, their trust in him—in his reeling head, his weary, trembling body.

Inside his palmetto-thatched hut his wife Morning Dew was tending his second wife, Star, who lay on a bed of rushes gravely ill with the fever.

"Will they come?" asked Morning Dew, looking up at him. Her beautiful face was ravaged with exhaustion and near starvation.

"Not now," said Osceola. "Maybe a week. Maybe a month. We must leave the village. They are too many to fight."

"Then we will leave."

He looked at Star. Beads of sweat stood on her black skin. She smiled faintly. He took the cloth Morning Dew held and wiped Star's forehead. Morning Dew took his hand.

"You too are ill," she said.

"It will pass."

Morning Dew rose, took General Thompson's coat, and put it over Osceola's shoulders. His daughter entered the hut, came to him, and without a word put her arms around him. He felt the thinness of her shoulders.

Fires were lit in the pits as he walked through the village; women were cooking for the warriors, using almost the last of their stores. The western sky glowed red over the dying sun. Walking among his people, observing their wretchedness, Osceola felt that their hope too was now dying. He wore Thompson's coat now not in defiance but to keep warm—yet the cold that shook him came not from the night but from within.

A full moon had risen in the east when Morning Dew found him by the stream. Through the trees firelight wavered as she approached and sat beside him. He picked up a handful of sand, let some sift through his fingers, then threw the rest seething on the water.

"They are too many."

"We will move south," Morning Dew said.

"They will follow us. They will never give us peace here." And suddenly he remembered Charlie Emaltha's last words. Could it be true that his own pride—his, Sam Jones', Coacoochee's, Alligator's—the pride of warriors—was condemning all who resisted with them to extinction—old ones, women and children, his own among them?

"Perhaps it is time to go west," he said softly.

"And Star?"

"She is too ill to travel south. Many are too ill."

Then, even before she spoke again, Osceola understood her meaning—and was filled with new anger.

"Would Star come with us? Would they let any of our blacks come with us?"

Laird to Eliza

Fort Brooke, Tampa Bay
September, 1837

DEAREST Eliza,

I deeply regret that this war separates us just when I feel that we have found our way to the threshold of a new life together. I see now how many of the faults of the past are mine and am amazed at the predeces-

251

sor in my hide! He was sometimes mean, jealous without reason, possessive yet inattentive, critical yet unobservant; and the worst of it is that I suspect I may still bear some likeness to the fellow. But fore-warned is forearmed.

Do not however imagine that I have grown over-fond of your "rival" as you once called this war. Like most other officers now, I am on a very cold footing with her. We fight without passion or reflection. Up before dawn. March. Skirmish. Attack. Tally the day's casualties. Throw ourselves into the sleep of the dead. If one of us were to speak (as we once did) about the reasons we are fighting he would be accounted a lunatic. You may judge our mood by our reaction upon learning that a gentleman of St. Augustine proposed a toast at a large gathering to the "gallant and undefeated Osceola" and was promptly rebuked by another gentleman for expressing a thought which might dampen the patriotic fighting spirit of the army. We laughed heartily at the innocence of the second gentleman! We too have come to respect Osceola and the other resisting chiefs. Their will to fight against ultimately hopeless odds is extraordinary, and almost all of us—including our commanding general—would be glad to see his people permitted to stay in Florida "for as long as the grass grows." But as long as it is the government's policy to get them west we will see the job done. For almost a year, since General Jesup replaced Call, we have from time to time held hopes of an imminent capitulation—only to see them dashed by Osceola and the other diehards. General Jesup however is most determined. He is methodical and will not repeat Call's tactical mistakes, but the man is also driven by a rage to succeed that in any endeavor but this war would be accounted insanity. Having sought to steer the government toward a more humane policy, he has now *done what he could* on that score, and the Seminoles have never faced a more formidable adversary than General Jesup now.

252

Since I began this letter the express has brought news that Osceola has requested a meeting near St. Augustine under the flag of truce. Jesup is removing there at once and I rejoice that I shall soon be with you, at least for a time, since this "talk" like others may be merely a stratagem for gaining time.

Your loving husband,
Laird Caffrey

Jesup

AT four o'clock in the afternoon General Jesup sat at his desk at his St. Augustine headquarters, turning in his fingers a fancily beaded peace pipe. On the maps that covered the desk lay a white egret plume, a sign of truce, Jesup had no doubt. The smooth beads covering the pipe in patterns of blue, brown, white, and yellow had the slick feel of treachery. He set it down on the maps next to the plume and folded his broad hands.

Osceola was encamped to the south asking for a meeting with General Hernandez, daring to ask it on his terms: General Hernandez was to come to his camp, a few miles below Moultrie, unaccompanied by an escort, under the white flag.

What they were to talk about, what the Indians were prepared to ask for or offer, Osceola had not deigned to say. Coa Hadjo, the older chief, would also receive General Hernandez. With Osceola and Coa Hadjo (his spies had found) were about a hundred armed braves.

Thomas Jesup rose and went to the French windows of his second-floor office and opened the shutters. Four fishing boats in a line rode at anchor in the glistening straits. Below, a wagon rumbled along the embarcadero toward the

253

center of town where the streets would be coming to life again after the midday repose; St. Augustine was prospering on his campaign and this was the high season of fiestas and dances on the roof of Fort Marion; the shops and groggeries were crowded; there was an air of festivity in the town after the summer, as if the war were already over, or had never begun.

It was different with the landed men who met to drink coffee and converse at the cafés, the proprietors whose plantations to the south were idle, some abandoned, and whose blacks had run off; the friends of General Hernandez, himself one of them, their champion in the war. It was different with Jim McKay and his family, driven from their precarious claim in a wilderness clearing where now tendrils entwined a scratched field and climbed from ashes around black timbers. It was different with Maria-Isobel Fuentes, a slender eighteen-year-old with moist hunted eyes, whose soldier boy from Georgia had left her with memories of kisses and a promise of marriage and who would not come back. It was different with legislators and land speculators in Tallahassee and with men and women all over the Territory, bitter over losses and the frustration of their plans, and over the nightmare of vengeful black fugitives nesting in the forests and jungles, as the war dragged on.

Women and tradespeople of St. Augustine might still wave at his carriage, but General Jesup knew that most white territorials looked upon him as the symbol of a federal government that could not drive the Indians west or restore slave property because it had never made up its mind to do so.

As he turned back into the room General Jesup caught sight of his reflection in the wavering glass pane of the French window. Though the fatigue of mounting the campaign showed around his eyes and in the lines of his face, it was still a commanding face. None of the general's kindness showed in it, buried deep in him, only perhaps the

merest trace of sadness that the world had not yet permitted him to be more kind, but nowhere a trace of the genuine
feelings of humanity and compassion which troubled him,
though less of late.

For a while he was convinced that the war was all but
won. After taking over the command from Call (at the in-
stigation of the President, who could not understand why
his old friend had stopped just short of victory), Jesup had
organized his forces into well-supplied, mobile forces capable of engaging the enemy whenever it chose to fight,
which unfortunately was not as often as General Jesup
would have wished. In fact it had occurred to him that the
pursuit could go on for a very long time, if not forever. His
greatest success had been on the diplomatic front.

By early spring he had managed to persuade several
chiefs, including Jumper, chiefs who claimed to speak also
for Micanopy, to agree to emigrate. King Philip was also
said to be ready to capitulate if Micanopy so ordered. A
stumbling block as always was the blacks.

General Jesup thereupon hit upon the plan of permitting
the Seminoles to remove *with* their Negro property.

While Floridians vented their outrage against what appeared to them as theft by military edict, Jesup nevertheless
managed to induce 700 Seminoles, including Micanopy, to
gather at a detention camp near Tampa. Others had indicated a willingness to come in later—including Osceola and
Sam Jones. Then, on June 2, catastrophe!

On that night Osceola and Sam Jones, with 200 warriors,
surrounded the camp and marched all 700 of their people—
including a rueful chief of chiefs—back into the wilderness.

The war was where it had been a year before.

General Thomas Sidney Jesup had not been the same
man after June 2. Until that infamous date it never occurred
to him that he was not fighting a war, however ill-starred,
from which, with strenuous negotiation backed by ample
troops constantly engaged, a victory could be wrested with
honor. In this spirit he had taken on the conflict whole-

heartedly. His officers learned to read in his stride and in the set of his expression how it was going. In time he had acquired an attitude of possession about it, which did not prevent him from calling it "unholy" in his officers' presence. "By God, this is an unholy war," he would say, and for a time the officers shared with him a warm esprit de corps to be fighting such a war; but it was only after June 2 that he really did believe that the Florida war was indeed unholy and utterly so.

The complete collapse of his expectations was a great shock to General Jesup. His dispatches before and after the escape describe a rising curve of optimism followed by a plummet into the blackest dismay checked only by the general's suspicions of far-reaching betrayal. For the worst was that the commanding general had anticipated precisely what had occurred, having received warning, and had taken countermeasures to prevent it from occurring, whereupon it had occurred anyway. He had ordered any Indian found outside the detention camp captured; he had sent Creek spies among the interned to learn when the rescue was to be attempted and report to him; he had put a trusted lieutenant colonel in command of this careful surveillance operation with the result that the warriors led by Osceola and Sam Jones had liberated the 700 Indians without a shot being fired.

In that first wave of disappointment General Jesup had suspected the Creek spies of betraying him; he had suspected the trusted lieutenant colonel of neglecting his duty; he blamed the War Department for its vacillation, the press for disparaging the War Department; he blamed white traitors whom he would surely hang once their identities were established; he blamed agents of foreign powers working clandestinely with the hostiles; and his rage against the hostiles themselves for breaking their pact would have known no bounds were it not for the thought that he should never have trusted them in the first place.

Only the most imperative duty brought any officer near

him now. He would be found sitting at his writing table staring into space, his eyes wide and haggard, his mouth set in a downward crescent of gloom, collar undone, fingers drumming relentlessly, ears now deaf to the drums and bugles of Fort Dade where he had heard the news of the escape. He took his meals alone, spoke little, his lamp burned late, and even those officers who did not know him from the past could see that a change was occurring in him. On the bitterest dawn of his career, walking alone in the flat pine-forest near the fort, General Jesup concluded that he had been ordered to fight a war which could not be won by honorable means. And though he was a Jacksonian, General Jesup found himself, on that bitter morning, suspecting that the ex-President was somehow the author of the whole mess.

Three times the Stars and Stripes were raised and lowered before Jesup recovered himself sufficiently to write the department informing them that the Indians had all decamped and that there was no end in sight to the conflict. Where before he had taken all responsibility on his shoulders, now he dumped it on the department's doorstep. His report was an avalanche of bad news, beginning with the statement that the campaign insofar as it related to Indian migration had entirely failed. If it were to be continued, he wrote, it would have to be as a campaign of extermination and as he wanted no part of that he asked to be relieved of his command.

Having purged himself, General Jesup concluded that he could best serve his government by advising it of the lessons to be learned from fighting Seminoles in an unhealthy climate on terrain poorly suited to fighting any enemy much less one whose favorite tactic is to vanish into thin air. Nor were his reports limited to military considerations but ventured, with the independence of spirit characteristic of General Jesup (who did not regard his superiors as being necessarily his betters) into areas of policy, even into philosophy, suggesting that the wisest course for the government might be, after all, to let the Seminoles stay in Florida.

So when letters reached him which were not only unresponsive to his humane counsel but critical, and sharply so, of his management of the Florida war, General Jesup was stunned, enraged, then stunned again—and readier than ever to fight. His eye became flinty. His look of dismay disappeared. He spent hours at his desk preparing a fall campaign which, he swore, would introduce an entirely new kind of warfare never before fought on American soil. Instead of treating the enemy as a military force to be fought in battle, Scott fashion, he would treat it as quarry to be found and destroyed by any means that would do the job. He had tried fighting it his way, by civilized rules, now he would fight it the government's way. He thought of Andrew Jackson smashing into Spanish Florida in '18, not caring a damn for the ambiguity of his orders; and the image of Andrew Jackson, enjoying a hero's retirement on his Tennessee estate after eight years in the nation's highest office, was very much in General Jesup's mind as he prepared his new campaign.

He informed General Hernandez and his colonels that any methods they might find expedient in dealing with the Indians were acceptable.

Mikasukis and Tallahasses, the fiercest of the Seminoles, were to be shown no mercy.

New enlistments of Indian allies were to be taken from the northern tribes known for their readiness to kill Seminole men and enslave their women and children.

As for the hostile blacks, in the first wave of his outrage after June 2, General Jesup had issued an order that all persons of color found in opposition were to be hanged on the spot, but he soon rescinded this decree in favor of a more serviceable one. Before, only Indian allies had been allowed to keep Negroes as bounty taken from the Seminoles, but now General Jesup extended that boon to the citizen soldiers and to the regulars. The result was a field day of red men, militiamen, regulars grabbing blacks leaving their villages for freedom—followed very soon by an abrupt disappearance from circulation of the Indians' blacks. By now it was clear to General Jesup that the Seminoles would resist as long as their black allies were a power among them; and so in September he ordered that Negroes taken in the war no longer be treated as private spoils (with the risk of their escaping back to the Seminoles) but be held in escrow by himself on the government's account. In Washington City the Secretary of War read Jesup's letter twice before he realized that the government of the United States had entered the slave trade.

Oddly, it was at this juncture that General Jesup again suffered one of those curious crises of conviction to which he was subject. It had again struck him that there were areas in southern Florida, some above the surface of the water, where Indians might settle with no great harm to anyone; and having been visited by this thought, the general promptly set it down in the form of a letter to the Secretary, who ten days later received it and was greatly amazed.

Perhaps it was time after all, the Secretary reflected, to relieve Jesup, for it appeared that he had lost his wits in the summer heat. How much had gone into the making of the Florida Indian-removal policy! how many years of deliberation, how much eloquence and persuasion! And the war itself: how many wounded and dead; how much planning, sweat, sickness, hardship, material. Above all, how much public money. Ten million dollars or more. And now General Jesup, on the very eve of his renewed campaign, was once again inspired to suggest that they simply give it all up and inform the American people that American lives and money had been squandered, because the commanding general in the field had hit upon the solution of allowing the Seminole Indians to stay where they were.

The same instinct that had worked before, however, prevented the Secretary from relieving General Jesup of his command. Rather, he wrote him reiterating the government's policy and advising him that, far from winding down the war they would wind it up; the commanding general would have additional troops in order to mount an even more formidable campaign to be launched against the hostiles on or before November 1. And again the Secretary's instinct proved true. For the second time in a year, rebuked, countered, his statesmanlike proposals belittled, General Jesup was steeled to fight with blind determination.

All through the hot, sickly summer difficulties thwarted his efforts. Troops fell ill, troops' enlistments expired. Florida militiamen mutinously refused to operate outside a certain sector, and the consumption of horses, by glanders, worms, and sheer exhaustion, had exceeded anything the general had ever witnessed before. Nonetheless he rallied the Floridians, obtained horses and mules, requisitioned acres of material, from haversacks to Dearborn wagons, saddlers' tools, hospital tents, medical supplies, rifles, shotguns, Cochran's repeaters, Colt's revolvers, flat-bottomed Mackinaw boats, India rubber pontoons (with special gum to repair them), stores of rations distributed among the forts to the south, and a thousand other necessities of war from darning needles to river steamers.

By October, before the launching of the main thrust, several raids on Indians south of St. Augustine had already been successfully conducted by General Hernandez. Negroes, many hungry and disgruntled by the fugitive life, were deserting the Seminoles, singly first, then by tens and scores. One had led the Americans to an Indian camp where a hundred hostiles were captured, including King Philip. Other camps were surrounded and more quarry taken; for General Jesup now threatened his captives with summary hanging if they failed to reveal Indian positions, and the new policy netted results. Every time he fought the enemy *in the new way* he gained; and now, having captured Philip, he determined to capture other leaders by any means in his power.

He told King Philip to send for his son. In time Coacoochee came, with Blue Snake, under the flag of truce. Ignoring the white flag, Jesup ordered them both held, then directed Coacoochee to bring in his followers, assuring him that the father would pay with his life if the son did not return with his band.

Nor did his disregard of the flag of truce trouble General Jesup excessively. After all, Europeans had taught the Indians the use of the white flag in the first place. It was not *their* custom he was violating; they had merely borrowed it to serve their own purposes, often abusing it shamelessly. Besides (and this was the argument that settled the matter in the general's mind), he had had Coacoochee in his power in any case, with Philip in captivity; Coacoochee knew this, and his marching in under the white flag meant nothing.

More villages were taken, more captives.

Then the main campaign was ready to be launched. In place of Scott's strategy of advancing three columns simultaneously southward into territory of unknown character, there to converge upon the Indians and force them to fight, General Jesup's plan was to move *seven* columns south into the same territory, in the configuration of a seven-branched candelabrum with each branch moving not simultaneously but at a speed determined by the terrain encountered and, as in Scott's plan, then converging on the Indians. The advantage of Jesup's plan over Scott's was that if a single one of Scott's columns were delayed, say, by a swamp, his opportunity to converge on the Indians was at once reduced by half; if two were stopped the remaining one had the option of stopping also or advancing lancelike into a wilderness with no end to it, having by itself no capability of convergence; whereas in Jesup's plan, one, two, or even three columns could stall and there would still remain more, advancing smartly southward, than General Scott for all his experience had fielded in the first place.

Such was the state of affairs when shortly before four in the afternoon of October 27, 1837, at the commander general's St. Augustine headquarters, the duty sergeant had

261

brought in Osceola's messenger and the interpreter Steven Richards, and General Jesup had accepted the offerings and heard Osceola's proposition.

His first impulse had been to send the messenger back to remind Osceola and Coa Hadjo that he had declared already there would be no more talks unless the Indians agreed beforehand to emigrate, but then he had another thought. He directed Richards to take the messenger downstairs. Feeling a curious excitement, he picked up the peace pipe again, seeing Osceola's face as if he were in the room with him, his eyes subtly taunting, savage. The assassin of General Thompson, shot from ambush in cold blood. The treacherous liberator of the seven hundred. The firebrand who stirred up the young men and terrorized the moderate elders. The Seminoles' most skillful strategist. The counselor of Micanopy. The wrecker of all Jesup's plans, who moved from place to place with diabolical swiftness to work his mischief and then disappear. Why was he asking for a parley? Surely not to say they had quit. He had come with Coa Hadjo to make more promises that would never be kept, to receive gifts and food and whiskey, to refresh himself as he delayed the campaign.

Setting the pipe aside, General Jesup drummed his fingers on the wood. Then his hand was still.

He thought of Coacoochee, safely imprisoned now at Fort Marion.

From Washington City the response about the method of his capture had been no response at all. Silence. Only his humane proposals had met with reprimand. There were generals in the capital ferreting for his command. He slammed his open palm on the maps. Was he to play into the hands of devious Indians on one hand and devious rivals on the other? Were all his plans, promises, campaign, command, career to be jeopardized, the damnable hide-and-seek war to go on indefinitely—all for the sake of a damnable white rag?

What would Jackson have done in his place?

The question answered itself.

General Jesup sent for the messenger and told him through the interpreter that Hernandez would meet with Osceola and Coa Hadjo on the day and at the place proposed.

Then he wrote out his orders for General Hernandez, who would not, he was sure, be displeased to receive them.

Osceola

OSCEOLA stood apart, watching the four braves raise the white flag on a tall pine pole so that General Hernandez could find the encampment. Most of the night he had sweated and shivered with fever; only toward dawn had he fallen asleep and dreamed strange dreams filled with voices he had not heard since his childhood; now the fever had abated, leaving his body weak but his spirit calm and curiously detached from what was happening around him. Other braves were covering stashes of rifles with deer skins. Coa Hadjo was directing the four as they wedged the pole upright in a hole dug at the edge of the clearing, near the path where the Americans would come. The morning was clear and windless; the white muslin hung limply in the first sunlight. Osceola smiled at Coa Hadjo's exertions to have the work done right; then, feeling weak, he sat down on a log and began to dress himself in the oddments of finery he had carried with him: a turban of blue figured cotton, a shawl of the same material thrown over the shoulder of his hunting shirt, red leggings.

In all there were about eighty warriors at the encampment, all but a dozen of them Coa Hadjo's St. Johns River Seminoles; six women, and four Negroes, these last part of

Osceola's remnant force, so many times dispersed, decimated in fights and by sickness and reformed again, always with blacks but lately with recent runaways from the seaboard plantations, and they had not been good fighters or trustworthy. Used to working in fields from sunup to sundown, they had no heart for sharing swamps with cottonmouths and alligators, living on handouts of briar-root meal, for being scorned by the long-time Indian-Negroes, driven by Seminoles, hunted by Americans. It was no kind of freedom for most of them, and many had chosen to return to the overseer's mercies and the protection of their masters. Some had betrayed the Indians, with disastrous results to the latter. Thus King Philip had been captured; Yuchi Billy and Jack Billy too, and many braves with them.

Osceola finished tying up his leggings and glanced up at the white flag, thinking of how they had come to be at this place today, waiting for the Americans.

Coacoochee had come to them on the St. Johns River, sent by the Americans, who had let him know that his father would hang were he not to return to the fort by such and such a day; but instead of urging them to give themselves up and come in as the Americans wanted, he told them that the defenses of St. Augustine were weak, that with so many troops campaigning in the interior the fort and the post were poorly garrisoned and that it was within their power to take the town and the fort and rescue Philip and the others. So Osceola and Coa Hadjo had come north with their warriors to attack St. Augustine and its moated fortress—only to learn on the way that General Jesup had strengthened his forces, that there was no more hope of success.

So, three days before, to the south by a marsh near a burned-out plantation house silhouetted by the morning sea, they had held a council, Osceola and Coa Hadjo taking the lead in the talk, Osceola the outlander whose gift for war was proved by many victories, who more than anyone had united the Seminoles in resistance; Coa Hadjo, chief by hereditary right who now commanded the greater force. There was some jealousy on Coa Hadjo's part, and Osceola had tried not to wound his pride—but they had not agreed on the matter of the hundred or so Negroes in the St. Johns area still in their hands.

Coa Hadjo had spoken first:

"The Americans are sick because the Negroes are with us. They are sick and they are powerful and so they fight us. They want us gone so they can have the Negroes. Let us give them up and maybe they will forget us and let us alone."

There was a murmur of assent; then Osceola spoke:

"These are the words of a wise leader who wants to save our people. It is true the Americans are sick. I know them and I have seen it. But their illness will not be cured as Coa Hadjo hopes; for if a man gets sick from drinking too much strong water, drinking more will not cure him. If we bring in twenty Negroes he will demand a hundred; if we bring a hundred he will say a thousand. I say the Negro has been our ally in many battles. Because of him the white man fears us more. I have fought at his side. I say that Coa Hadjo's words are good but the white man is bad and cannot be satisfied. I say the Negro is our strength and we must not give him up."

An uncertain grumble met these words and Coa Hadjo spoke again:

"The Negroes on the St. Johns are not those Osceola has fought with. They are not Abraham's people. They are not John Caesar's. Few have lived with us very long. They are of different minds and spread trouble among each other. They are not warriors. They eat our food and when there is none they get hungry and betray us. I say that we must turn over all except those who have taken Seminole wives and husbands. Then we can justly ask the Americans to let us stay here in peace because we have done what they want. I have spoken."

The voices of Coa Hadjo's braves had risen in agreement

with their leader and Osceola signified to his own following that they would not contest the proposal, though he knew that it would not satisfy the enemy. For Osceola too was tired of fighting and sick with the fever he had caught many years ago, and which returned when he was tired. He knew that in any case it would not matter very much whether they turned over the Negroes or not. He felt ill and heavy-hearted.

That same day an interpreter had been sent to General Jesup with the message that they were returning seventy-four blacks and that they were willing to meet General Hernandez south of Moultrie Creek on October 21 for a talk under the flag of truce.

When he had dressed himself Osceola felt very uneasy. He went over to Coa Hadjo and proposed that they set out an armed picket but Coa Hadjo replied that they must not show bad faith lest their deliverance of the Negroes go for nothing. The Americans would not violate the flag of truce. Moreover, their rifles, under the deer skins, were their protection against treachery.

Again Osceola stood apart, feeling warnings which he took for symptoms of his sickness.

An hour later General Hernandez and his officers entered the clearing at the head of a double column of armed horsemen, which swiftly, no order being given, divided and entirely surrounded the encampment. Coa Hadjo was bewildered, uncertain whether to order his braves to rush for their rifles, but Osceola smiled seeing this, for it was too late, and because he suddenly could see this moment with perfect clarity, as from a great distance. As General Hernandez approached him, he saw a vulture sitting on the general's cap plucking at his brains. The other officers approached and shook hands with him and Coa Hadjo, showing signs of friendship, but Osceola saw the ravens picking at their eyes.

When the general spoke and the interpreter rendered his words, Osceola nodded to Coa Hadjo signifying that he should answer because he could not speak himself.

"What people have come with you?" the general asked.

"All that are well and that we could gather."

"I speak as a friend—what made you come?"

"We come for good."

"What do you expect of me?"

Coa Hadjo looked to Osceola but Osceola gave him no sign.

"We do not know," Coa Hadjo said then.

"Have you come to talk. We want to make peace."

"In what way make peace?"

"We have come to talk peace, with liberty to walk about."

"Are you ready to give up all the property you have captured?"

"We already sent you many Negroes yesterday. We intend to bring in what is due to white people."

"Why have Micanopy, Jumper, and Cloud not come here?"

"They all got the measles."

"What word did they send?"

"When they feel better they will come and see you."

General Hernandez's face hardened.

"I am an old friend of Philip's and wish you all well, but we have been deceived so often that it is necessary that you come with me. You may send out a messenger. You shall stay with me and none of you will be hurt."

"We shall see about it," said Coa Hadjo, stepping back.

General Hernandez moved his hand to his sword.

At once the circle of riders closed around the Indians, as a company of foot soldiers moved swiftly into the clearing and began to seize the braves. In less than a minute all were captives.

It happened as Osceola had foreseen from the instant General Hernandez had ridden into the clearing.

He smiled.

He smiled at Coa Hadjo's helpless anger; at the cavalry captain who stood by him, distressed, the man he had almost shot, across the river.

He smiled because at the moment of being taken captive, for the first time since he could remember, he felt free of this mighty and infamous race; because he remembered his own wild rage that made him an animal when General Thompson had seized him and locked him up and how he had bided his time and killed General Thompson.

He smiled because at the moment of being taken captive by this treachery he felt a new strength in himself.

He smiled because he knew that long after this day would be forgotten the shame of it would be felt by white men, until the land would grow barren under his tread, the leaf wither at his touch, the river dry up when he put his mouth to it, until he would stand with his woman and children under a dead sun amid a destitution of his own making, deserted by the Great Spirit.

He felt no more hate for this race whose blood he shared.

And he felt no more love for it; for it had always been that impure love, used, mocked, and defiled, which had most blinded him to the spirit of his own people.

He knew now that the Great Spirit would avenge them as would a father the murder of his son.

He smiled at the white flag.

He smiled at the captain who laid his hand on him.

The captives walked in file between the two columns of horsemen; only Osceola and one brave rode because they were sick. At noon by the new log works on Moultrie Creek, upstream from the site of the first treaty talk, they stopped to eat army rations.

It was midafternoon before they started north again, almost sundown when they reached St. Augustine.

Eliza

ALL day since Laird had left before dawn Eliza had felt uneasy, and as the afternoon hours wore on she was sure that something had happened to him; he had left with a kiss and a smile but she had let him go with no kind word, because she was thinking of the Seminoles the soldiers were going after; and by late afternoon she was certain that he lay wounded or had died remembering her cold farewell. Three times she sent Delia to the post to ask for news of General Hernandez's companies; the third time, toward sundown, she had returned with news that the soldiers were returning with Seminole captives.

"Captain Caffrey's all right?"

"They's all all right. Everybody's going to the plaza. They's bringing the Indians up to the fort. Osceola, him too."

Five minutes later Eliza and Delia entered the plaza where the crowd was gathering, lining both sides of a path along the seawall where the cavalry men would pass with their prisoners. Sailors on the yards of berthed vessels in the last glaring flood of amber sun catcalled and Indian-whooped. At the south end of the plaza an idiot boy stood on the roofed-over slave-auction block, entertaining a gang of boys with mimicry; but the crowd was mostly silent; their steps scraping on the cobbles in the shadow of the church. By the church wall a Minorcan widow sat by her husband's candle-decked bier.

As Eliza moved through the crowd toward the seawall she saw Ben Solano and some men with him appear from behind the auction block walking in the same direction. Often before she had seen him in town, but not since her father's death had she spoken to him, always keeping her distance; now they were on a collision course and she resolved not to give way.

In the years since she had first seen him at the agency Ben Solano had changed his dress from a wolf-skin shirt to a suit of white linen and a broad-brimmed white hat; he was stouter now, his long face settled in hate. No longer was his following of gunmen, bounty hunters, uprooted settlers, the outcasts they had once been. They were now a new class, with new power, in Florida; for where once their nightriding bespoke the secret fears of the Territory, now it expressed its open demands; and their number was increased by ambitious, exasperated men, dispossessed plantation owners, land speculators, family men from Georgia and the Carolinas desperate to settle, all looking to a Florida swept clean of the red man and worked by Negroes. They were the community now, the law of the Territory bent to their will; their strength was felt even in Washington City; in eastern Florida their leading spirit was Ben Solano, who was a friend, as was well known, of General Hernandez. Eliza recognized Jed Cunso and Jim McKay among the men. Ben Solano tipped his hat.

"Evening, Mrs. Caffrey."

"Evening, Mr. Solano."

"Expect the news today ain't too pleasing to you, considering your feelings."

She remembered the Seminole woman falling, the infant rolling from her arms into the dust.

"The army's only doing what you and your friends make necessary, Mr. Solano." The other smiled, glancing at Jed Cunso, then with hostility at Eliza.

"That ain't the way it is, Mrs. Caffrey. The army's doing what *your* friends made necessary. Instead of fretting about Seminoles, you should be proud of your husband today."

Seeing Cunso and several others grin, Eliza hesitated, the uneasiness she had felt all day suddenly returning.

270

"Maybe you ain't heard?"

When she didn't reply he said, "Jesup had General Hernandez take 'em under the white flag. Your husband had the honor of taking Osceola personally." He smiled faintly. "Only right, too," he pursued. "No use being too particular with Indians."

The idiot boy pranced ahead of the foremost cavalrymen, rolling his head and clapping his hands. "Boy's got the haunts in him," Delia was saying, but Eliza, now standing with the silent crowd lining the path along the seawall, scarcely heeded her. She prayed that what Ben Solano had just told her was not true.

General Jesup and General Hernandez rode abreast near the head of the riders. Jesup's heavy face was set in determination, in contrast with Hernandez's look of aloof indifference. Following them rode two militia officers leading the long twin columns of 250 horsemen; between the columns walking by twos were the eighty braves of Coa Hadjo's and Osceola's war parties, dressed in faded tatters and finery. Behind the braves walked Coa Hadjo, grim and proud; then came Osceola, riding his war pony, his face drawn with illness, a smile at his lips, riding with uncanny grace to the clapping of hooves on the cobbles.

Following him, flanked by two Florida cavalry officers, rode Laird.

Four of Osceola's Negroes came next, then a score of Seminole women, in rags, two in army blankets drawn around them, and bringing up the rear, mounted Floridians leading horses.

It was two hours before Laird returned to the house. While Delia fixed supper Eliza went upstairs and opened the bedroom windows on the water glistening under a half-moon over the island. Remembering Laird's look as he rode past her through the hushed crowd she felt a sense of deliv-

271

erance: He was safe—he surely needed her now. When she heard the front door open she started downstairs, decided not to let anything stand between them tonight.

She went to him, he kissed her then held her at arm's length searching her face.

"Gallant day," he said at last, then turned from her and went to the window, looking out on the moonlit garden.

"Laird—"

"Guess you heard."

"It wasn't your doing." She wanted to let him know that she stood by him now. When he turned to her again and she saw in his eyes the same lost, remote look she had sometimes seen in her father's, she said, "It was bound to happen."

"Bound to happen so as even Laird Caffrey'd get it through his head what a rotten war this is."

"I didn't mean that. All day I was afraid something had happened to you."

"Something did."

She read his meaning. "I saw it when you rode through the plaza."

"They taught us 'Duty, Honor, Country' but there's no chance for that in this war. We're not soldiers, we're hunters. Treacherous hunters at that."

"Not if you feel that way."

"I feel no way. Not even shame. Just dead inside."

Then he took her in his arms. "I guess I've always fought hardest what I favor most about you," he told her.

"Never loved you so much as now," she said, finding then that even if this moment was bought with all the blindness, bigotry, and greed of her race and it was in her power to forgo it as atonement, she would never give it up.

During the next weeks she was to know with Laird a closeness she had only imagined before, the love she had first felt for him in Washington City was now answered with a strong tender caring that was no longer an escape from lonely need, claim to her body, but ardent discovery of her entire being.

Yet always in the end there seemed to be one final bridge between them which neither could cross. She was to remember the day of Osceola's capture with anguish and gladness, dread and promise. In November Laird left with General Jesup's staff for Tampa Bay.

Jesup

Fort Brooke, Tampa Bay
January, 1838

BY November, 1837, with more than half the United States army in Florida—almost 5,000 men—and as many citizen soldiers, General Jesup was poised to launch the greatest military offensive of the war. He was optimistic. With Osceola locked up the fort at St. Augustine along with Coacoochee and other chiefs and braves, the Seminole fighting force was now weak, leaderless, and must soon yield before his forces—seven lumbering armies to be set adrift on independent southerly marches like logs after fish.

Then, on November 29, appalling news.

Somehow Coacoochee, sixteen braves, and several women had managed to slip through a ten-inch-wide loophole, down a sheer wall, and were now reported to have joined with the veteran firebrand Sam Jones in rallying the Seminoles to resist to the last man.

Laird observed the commanding general's optimism fade. The prospect of his campaign failing half maddened Jesup, and it was not until after Christmas that his gloom was somewhat lifted.

On that day Colonel Zachary Taylor, lately arrived in Florida eager to fight, and having led more than 1,000 troops south to Lake Okeechobee, there engaged the forces

273

of Coacoochee and Sam Jones. Finding the Indians in the cover of thick woods, with a half mile of swamp and saw grass between them and his forces, Colonel Taylor ordered an attack straight through the swamp. In two and a half hours Taylor's losses were 26 killed and 112 wounded; the Indians' 11 killed and 14 wounded. All other Seminoles escaped. Nevertheless it was to be noted in the capital that Seminoles could after all be induced to meet American forces willing to lay down their lives for their country. Okeechobee restored a measure of confidence to the Florida war. It was something real. Zachary Taylor was breveted a brigadier general. General Jesup's hopes began to rise again.

By January still more promising news. Several Seminole bands had voluntarily given themselves up for emigration. Micanopy and his counsellor, Abraham, were taken by treachery. But Coacoochee, Sam Jones, Halleck Mico, and others continued to elude Jesup's troops.

Outside Florida many Americans had come to view the Seminoles not as savage murderers but as freedom-seeking victims of a grave injustice.

In Congress a representative of Virginia called the Florida war a disgrace.

The Florida delegate replied that sentimental concern for the Seminoles had greatly prolonged the war.

The representative for Plymouth, Massachusetts, permitted his remarks on the subject to stray in the direction of abolition and was promptly ruled out of order.

In Florida General Jesup was moved to pen yet another appeal to the Secretary to allow the Seminole remnant to remain in the Territory, arguing that the war was virtually won as it was. Again he was reprimanded, the Secretary concluding his letter, "It is to be hoped, however, that you will be able to put it out of the power of these Indians to do any further mischief. They ought to be captured or destroyed." In response the general ordered the capture of more than 500 Seminoles whom he had requested to remain near his army pending the government's decision on his humane proposal for them. Uncooperative Indians and Negroes throughout Florida were to be hanged.

At last General Jesup saw the light. Henceforth he would satisfy the government's real wishes—as Jackson had done in Florida. Henceforth let Seminoles be taken by any means, fair or foul; but thereafter let all promises made to them be observed—by others—west of the Mississippi.

As for Osceola and the other captive chiefs, General Jesup resolved that they would be sent far from any chance of escape. He issued orders that they be transported from St. Augustine to the fort on Sullivan's Island in Charleston Harbor, there to be held until arrangements could be made for their removal west. As his special aide in charge of the escort detachment and liaison with the fort's commandant he chose Captain Caffrey.

Laird

AT dawn on the twenty-ninth of December Laird had seen Osceola, Micanopy, Philip, Coa Hadjo, and Cloud, with 200 warriors, women, and children, file on board the steamer *Poinsett*; and as the vessel had cleared the straits he had observed Osceola standing at the aft railing, gazing out over the water as the headlands of Anastasia Island merged into the coastline reaching southward into the mist.

Three days later the prisoners were disembarked at the brick fort on Sullivan's Island.

Osceola was ill; so was Philip. Jealous of both, Micanopy was most jealous of Osceola, who with his family and following was assigned a large room with a fireplace, where he was attended by his wives, a medicine man, and Dr. Weedon, who having befriended him in St. Augustine had

275

accompanied him from there. Visitors came to the prison, always to see Osceola. Micanopy sulked, more withdrawn than ever into regal isolation.

Laird had welcomed his orders. Since Osceola's capture he had felt a deep unrest which he could not escape, and which had to do with the Indian leader, as if their encounter under the white flag was more than chance, was indeed a moment in a far greater mystery. He told himself that everyone who met Osceola was affected by him, yet the feeling stayed, even when during the voyage and the settling in at the brick fort Osceola seemed hardly to notice him, as if he had no recollection of their meeting on the seawall or of the capture.

Under bleak winter skies the island fort was a dismal place, its two interior levels connected by a central stone staircase on which all day boots reverberated in cold, cavernous chambers. Warriors were confined on the lower level, women and children near them in other rooms; the chiefs lodged on the upper level, where the officers slept, and had the run of the fort. Laird and Dr. Weedon shared quarters next to Osceola's.

From the first an uneasy decorum existed between captors and captives, though the atmosphere was tense: The Indians gave no open sign of hostility or resentment, the blue-uniformed officers regarded the chiefs with deference and Osceola with awe, as the master spirit of the Seminoles; the days settled into military routine; but at night sometimes the chants of the warriors carried Laird's thoughts into regions he had never visited before. One night he awakened from a dream into terror: Someone was standing in the blackness of the doorway. The figure remained still until the lantern light of someone on the stairs revealed the shawled silhouette of Osceola, turning back to his room. . . .

On the sixth day the atmosphere at the fort began to ease, following the arrival of a stranger. The visitor's letters introduced him as George Catlin, an artist lately returned from eight years of travels among the Western Indian tribes. Presented to the officers and chiefs, the painter at once set to work on a portrait of Cloud, and before long the man and his canvases drew officers and prisoners to the large room where Catlin had set up his easel. All day he would paint, one chief after the other (Micanopy refusing until he was offered a bottle of whiskey for his trouble) and in the evenings the chiefs, Laird, Dr. Weedon, and officers of the post would gather in the painter's room where until late at night the Indians would tell of their people's past, of the war, of the treachery of their capture. They talked freely and sometimes, with the help of liquor, their tales would become plaintive or angry—until with a word Osceola would remind them of their pride as Seminoles.

One night when the painter and Laird were talking alone, Osceola had come in, accompanied by the black interpreter, and without a word stood before the nearly finished portrait of himself, luminous even in the dim light with its strong reds, browns, black. Though Osceola could not have been much older than thirty Laird had observed in the days the painter worked on the canvas the metamorphosis of the Indian's flesh, wasting from disease; and Catlin had painted his face in the colors of youth and life, yet with a vision of tragic destiny in the haunted eyes. Osceola had stood a long time in thought then asked what would become of the painting when it was finished. And George Catlin told him of the exhibition he was preparing of all his works, which would be shown in New York and other cities to let the white man see for the first time the true face of the Indian and his manner of life.

"Why should the white man wish to see the face of Osceola?" the other had demanded.

"Because he is famous among us," Catlin replied.

Again the Indian studied his likeness.

"This is not Osceola," he said then. "This Osceola will never raise his knife, never howl in chains, never utter a war cry, never look into his enemy's face when he lays treacherous hands on him. This Osceola wears no war paint. He is *yours!*" Facing the painter with blazing eyes he suddenly turned to Laird, and touched his own breast. "*This* Osceola will never be yours." Then he had walked out of the room.

During the next week Osceola's health worsened, and twice—as Catlin was preparing to leave for New York—Dr. Weedon had announced that the Indian leader was dying and that if they and the officers of the fort wished to be present at the end they must lose no time; twice they had gathered in his room, and twice Osceola had disappointed the surgeon. Then George Catlin had sailed for New York with his new paintings.

It was Osceola himself who knew when his death was near.

On January 31, the third evening after Catlin's departure, he sent Dr. Weedon again to summon the chiefs and officers to his room. As Laird entered with the commandant, Osceola rose up in his bed, which was on the floor, and put on his shirt, his leggings, his moccasins, his war belt, his bullet pouch and powderhorn, and laid his knife by his side on the floor, near four candles which cast his huge shadow on the walls frescoed with reddish mold. Then by signs to his wives, for he could no longer speak, he called for his red paint and his looking glass, which was held before him, and he painted one half of his face, his neck and throat, his wrist, the backs of his hands, and the handle of his knife, red with vermilion, a custom, as Laird knew, practiced when the irrevocable oath of war and destruction is taken. His knife he then placed in its sheath, in his belt, and he arranged his turban and his three plumes, two black, one white. Thus attired in full dress he lay down a few minutes to recover his strength, then he rose up again on his bed and with a smile reached out for Laird's hand, took it and held it, looking at him as if from another world, pulling him gently toward him, then released his hand. Then in dead silence he shook hands with the other officers, lastly with Dr.

Weedon, and with signs bade farewell to the chiefs. Lastly he made a sign to his wives to ease him down on his bed, which they did, then he slowly drew his knife, holding it in his right hand, laid it across his left hand on his breast, and in a moment he smiled away his last breath without a struggle or a sigh.

Four days later Laird was ordered to Fort Brooke for combat.

Laird

Southeast of Fort Brooke
February, 1838

HE opened his eyes to darkness. Gradually the rhythmical croaking of frogs, the snores of the lieutenant in the next cot, a triangle of gauzy starlight at the tent opening reminded him where he was: the bivouac at the edge of the cypress swamp, a mile from the village they would attack at dawn.

Outside his troops slept, some perhaps lying awake wondering if they would see the end of the coming day. All would look to him tomorrow, young men, family men forced into service by the hard times; they would look to him for crisp orders, the flash of the sword that would inspire them to fight well; and he would lead them as bravely as always before, but not with the blind belief that had once inspired him. He knew now that no sense could be torn from Major Quirt's death; that no glory would attend the fallen in this war; no recompense but the camaraderie of the veterans of Death: Major Quirt striding into the path of the bullet, Captain Gardiner riding in a storm of lead, shouting "God damn! God damn! God damn!"

At dawn he halted his extended lines a hundred yards from the hammock where the Indians were. Tensely his

279

men awaited the order to charge, most knowing as he did that the Seminoles were not about to run but had taken up a defensive position in the dense woods. If Laird charged they would return fire until his front lines were cut up, then would retreat and stand again, before disappearing altogether; and if he himself survived, Laird would be left with many of these brave, scared men dead and groaning on the grassy sand.

No deliberation guided what he did next.

He told the lieutenant at his side to hold fire unless he was fired on—then he walked out slowly, alone, toward the edge of the woods.

Twenty yards away he stopped. He could see Seminoles' painted faces down rifles leveled on him, steadied in notches cut in the trees.

"I come for a talk," he called out.

Silence.

Then from the woods before him appeared a tall elderly Seminole chief whom Laird recognized from counsel meetings at Fort King as Halleck Mico; at the chief's side, remonstrating with him, was a powerfully built black, his slave and counselor John Rainbow. Halleck Mico, followed by the other, advanced toward Laird, stopped at arm's distance, then spoke.

"Halleck Mico asks why you put your life in his hands," John Rainbow began in a deliberately insolent manner.

"Tell him to show we do not wish to fight, only to ask him to come in for a talk with the general."

As the black man interpreted, Laird watched for signs that he was falsifying what was said.

"He says General Jesup captured Osceola and others who came for talks. He would be foolish to go."

"Seminoles have broken promises."

"Only to live on their lands a little longer."

"We wish to give you new lands, where many of your people have gone already."

At this, John Rainbow spoke heatedly to the chief and an

argument between them followed; at last, grudgingly, the black man asked Laird what assurances Halleck Mico would have that he would not be seized.

"Let him come alone or with only a few," Laird said. "The Great Father wishes all his band settled on good land in the West. Let him come alone, as I come before him now, and hear the general's talk; let him bring his people only when he has agreed to the terms."

"And if he does not agree?"

"Then he will return to his people and the fighting will go on."

"How can he know he will be allowed to return?"

Ignoring the black man's deliberately hostile manner, Laird looked directly at the chief and said, "He has my promise."

John Rainbow spoke on his own account. "It's a trick! Another lie!"

"He has my promise."

For several moments they stood without speaking, Americans facing Seminoles across the grassy dunes, then suddenly the old chief with both hands seized Laird by the hand and elbow and shook his arm violently, speaking to him.

"He says he will come in for a talk in a few days," John Rainbow said—with every guarantee in his scowl that no such thing would ever happen.

Yet it did.

Laird

Fort Brooke
March, 1838

THE sky was a leaden dome over Tampa Bay. Outside the fort on the hill Laird sat beside General Jesup at the council

281

table facing Halleck Mico and John Rainbow. All morning, item by item, they had debated the terms under which Halleck Mico would bring in the rest of his band and leave for the new country. Would they have their own lands, forever separate and distinct from those occupied by Creeks? Yes, said the general. Would he swear to it? The Great Father in Washington City had sworn to it; in the name of the United States they would have exclusive right to their own lands as long as the grass grows and the rivers run. Then could they take their horses to these lands? No, said Jesup, there was no room for horses on the boats, but they would be paid a fair price for them. How much? After some haggling a price was reached. And their dogs, of course, they would take their dogs. No, said Jesup. Then, declared Halleck Mico violently, they would not bring in the others, they would not go without their dogs. Very well, said Jesup, they might take their dogs. Then John Rainbow, speaking for Halleck Mico, said,

"And all Negroes, as agreed? Under the protection of the Great Father?" Jesup tapped his pen on the table.

"Promised," he said.

All during the talk Laird and John Rainbow had crossed glances now and then, and Laird had felt anger against this black who dared dictate terms (for they were his own as much as the chief's) to a general officer of the United States, and he knew that he had not disguised his feeling; therefore he was greatly surprised when, after a further conference with Halleck Mico, John Rainbow suddenly fixed Laird with a hard smile, then told General Jesup that one more condition must be met if a bargain was to be struck.

"What is that?"

"That Captain Caffrey lead us to the new lands."

Laird to Eliza

Fort Brooke
March, 1838

DEAR Eliza,

I write these lines on the eve of our departure if, God willing, there are no more delays. Halleck Mico brought his band in this morning, not all of them but all we are likely to get, 80 Seminoles and 32 Negroes the chief claims are his, men, women and children of both races. Now they are encamped all around the fort and quiet but you cannot imagine what a scene it was this afternoon; at midday we heard them coming by the shouting of their women who walked along beside their men scolding them for agreeing to go, Halleck Mico and John Rainbow getting the worst of it, and as they entered the fort the women refused rations and at first even the blankets and sacking we offered them, some not being decently covered, as if to demonstrate that immodesty and wretchedness were trifles compared to the shame of their capitulation. The braves and especially Halleck Mico were grim and sorry-looking, obviously surprised by this latest humiliation (the women generally defer to their men), and the old chief soon retired, reappearing in the finery he had demanded as part of the agreement, black frock coat, beaver hat with a red cockade, Irish linen shirt, superfine pantaloons, thinking I suppose to regain his dignity but only throwing his band into more dismay and confusion, seeing him so outlandishly attired; and all avoided him except his slave-counselor John Rainbow. This Negro, who dresses as a lesser Seminole leader, much like Abraham whom he resembles though a few years younger, is now I believe the effective leader of the entire band, exercising power through his master, and the one with whom I shall be dealing on this journey.While an officer was paying off the owners of the few half-starved horses which had been brought, most of the little population of the Bay had gathered to watch the proceedings, and they were joined by two strangers from a vessel, shady-looking personages, one a very fat man, and on seeing them approach, John Rainbow came to us in a great state insisting they were slave traders and all the Negroes became very fearful and the Seminoles uneasy, some yielding to their wives' objurgations, whereupon General Jesup went over to the intruders and parleyed with them forceably, being anxious that nothing go wrong, and they reluctantly departed, though their vessel still lies at anchor in the Bay. Now my charges are fed and issued blankets and lie under discreet guard in and outside the stockade under their last Florida night. A little while ago when I walked among them I found that many were gazing up at the stars as if they and everything else dear to them would be gone tomorrow and they were determined to experience each moment of the time remaining, for there is surely a magic in the land of one's birth which the red man I think feels as keenly as we. I have killed many of them in battle as these know, and there are officers better disposed toward them (though others less so), so I do not know why they insisted that I accompany them; strangest of all I think John Rainbow had a hand in it though he knows that I am as committed as any Southerner to defending that institution which Providence made ours to prosper with or perish without. Perhaps they merely wanted the honor of a captain as escort instead of the lieutenant Jesup had picked. Anyway at daybreak tomorrow we sail from New Orleans, then will steam up the Mississippi, northwestward on the Arkansaw to Fort Gibson, in Indian Country; from New Orleans a distance of *one thousand miles,* or to give you a more vivid reckoning of it, three times the distance Moses led his people from Egypt to the Promised Land, a mere step for an American. Do not imagine however that I have formed any vainglorious idea of

my mission, it is a military duty; but I am determined to conduct these people to their new home
under the terms agreed and with the least possible
suffering. One hears of hardships endured by the first
Creeks and Chocktaws sent west,the result of poor
preparations; General Jesup, despite his failings, is an
able quartermaster and this journey has been
planned with the greatest care, from the advance
chartering of a suitable steam vessel in New Orleans
to ample provisioning at every stage of the way. Indeed, though the plight of these Indians may seem pi-
tiful now, on the eve of departure, when one reflects
on the brutal course of mankind's history, on foreign
wars, barbarous conquest and the treatment of captives by heathens, one may count these people com-
paratively fortunate—yet this thought is of little
comfort when one looks in their faces. General Jesup
believes that the war is near its end. He has believed
so before but now he may be right. At least such is
my prayer because I believe now that when this in-
glorious conflict is over a new life awaits us in which
all that has kept us apart may now join us closer than
ever before. I long to be with you again.

Your affectionate husband,
Laird Caffrey

Eliza

St. Augustine
March, 1838

ONE last time she read the closing lines of the letter, then
folded it and tucked it through the ribbon holding all the
letters he had ever written her, thinking, *This one is
different.*

Then she placed the thick bundle in her drawer next to
the thin pile of Captain Wolfe's letters.

Two piles of letters.

Two parts of herself.

Though she treasured the intellectual and guardedly sentimental correspondence with Captain Wolfe, it was since that correspondence had begun, and perhaps in part because of it, that she realized how much she loved Laird and how much he loved her. To return to Caffrey Station with him was now her greatest wish and, dreading more then ever that he would be killed in the war, she was relieved that the escort mission would take him out of the fighting for a time.

Laird

At sea on board the schooner *Lochinvar*
March, 1838

THE first three days of the voyage were clear and pleasant, light easterly breezes furring long blue swells, but from the morning the schooner headed into the open sea the Seminoles were silent and downcast. They had stood together, some shading their eyes, watching the land disappear, until the sun stood high over an empty sea; when Laird had gone among them he found them dispirited and John Rainbow told him that they believed they had left their spirits on the headlands of Tampa Bay. That evening they had sat together as near the afterdeck as the captain permitted, their backs to the twilight, staring into the darkness aft.

Captain Beaumont, a red-bearded Charleston man, assured Laird that such behavior was usual, except that he had seen much worse, had seen some jump overboard, one fine-looking girl he remembered particularly, in fact for her he'd even brought the vessel up into the wind and lowered a boat but they found no trace of her; others had died on board for no apparent cause; Negroes, he'd observed, had more resistance, no doubt from being bred from survivors of the Middle Passage but for the same reason they had a powerful mistrust of the sea, a spoiled memory of it, so to speak—some fine specimens in this party, he'd noticed, very marketable in New Orleans. Then the captain had taken his glass and swept the horizon, stopping at a point astern of them and handing Laird the glass with a nod.

"The traders' ship," said Laird, handing him back the glass.

"After your blacks," Captain Beaumont remarked. When Laird asked if they might attempt to board them at sea the other laughed. "Not them," he said. "They're land pirates. Their Jolly Roger flies over the New Orleans courthouse. An hour after we make port they'll be all over your people with lawyers and affidavits."

"These are the Seminoles' Negroes."

"All are, aren't they?" replied the captain. Then seeing that Laird took offense, he added, "Can they prove it? Can they prove it against respectable gentlemen with claims in legal form? Can they prove it against Major Phagan of the Indian Office?"

And he said that even if they kept out of the hands of such persons there were others less scrupulous ready to seize them on no pretext at all, beyond a common repugnance at the sight of a valuable Negro going north with an Indian master; oh, yes, Negroes *had* passed through the city on no better than an Indian's claim but such oddities were less and less frequent; and when Laird said that he meant to honor General Jesup's promise Captain Beaumont was thoughtful for a long time.

On the second day out the captain told Laird that he had been giving more thought to the question of the Negroes, and it had occurred to him that since it was next to impossible to pass such a handsome lot through New Orleans, the best thing would be to see them delivered into kinder hands than those into which they were bound to fall in the ordinary course of events. It so happened that he knew a certain trader. . . .

"I mean to get them through," Laird told him again, keeping his voice matter-of-fact.

"Suit yourself, Captain," said the genial Beaumont, also showing no offense. And it seemed to Laird that the other drew as much satisfaction from contemplating what lay ahead of them as he might have from any accommodation.

By the fourth morning the wind had freshened and shifted northerly; black curds of scud kited across the eastern horizon where in the last flare of dawn under a lowering sky the following vessel heeled, holding the same course; by midmorning the sky had closed around them, rain began to pelt, and soon the storm was on them. At the captain's order passengers were told to stay below in their tumbling confines, many being seasick and all terrified as thunder boomed around them and the vessel reeled in the waves. Laird stood on the afterdeck near Beaumont, who had taken the wheel (seeming well pleased by the tempest); the bow rose dizzyingly, hung for a moment, then plunged into the trough. The forwardmost hatch opened and Halleck Mico clambered determinedly onto the levitating deck, stood precariously erect for a moment, then pitched to the lee railing as the bow abandoned its search for the sky and skewed into a mountainous wall of green.

Miraculously, when the lee deck shuddered out of the sea Halleck Mico, spitting water, was still clinging to the railing; the captain shouted but Laird was already making his way forward, as other figures popped out of the hatch like jacks-in-the-box. He shouted at them but his voice was lost in the wind. When he managed to reach the bow he found Halleck Mico standing again, clinging to the railing with one hand, John Rainbow beside him, two Seminoles hugging the captain, three holding onto stays, and yet another floating down the lee scuppers, barely managing to save himself from washing over the railing; and two more clambering out of the hold, terrified, finding nothing more substantial to hang onto than one another.

"Get below!" yelled Laird to Halleck Mico, but the chief stood defiantly, then said something to John Rainbow, who shouted as spindrift drenched them,

"He says you brought him to his death but he will die his own way!"

"Tell him nobody dies if he goes below."

As John Rainbow spoke Laird realized that the chief was was determined to refuse. His knuckles showed white as he clung to the railing but from his expression Laird was certain that he would throw himself over the side rather than give in. Over the roar of the wind John Rainbow called into his ear.

"My master says he has obeyed a white man for the last time."

"Will he obey *you?*" Laird demanded at once, then as the other glared at him defiantly, he took him by the arm and said, "If he dies, you'll have no master in New Orleans. I get him west and you with him—but only with him! We're partners, John Rainbow."

Then Laird turned and made his way aft along the windward railing.

By the time he reached the captain at the wheel, the last of the Indians had returned to the hold and John Rainbow was pulling the hatch closed.

The next morning the wind had dropped and to the west the sky began to clear over tumultuous slate-colored waves. The day following, the sixth out of Tampa, they entered the smooth water of the sound, navigated the passage into Lake Borgne and were soon in sight of the steeples of New Orleans.

Laird to Eliza

New Orleans
March, 1838

DEAR Eliza,
    Although we reached this port three days ago I have not found a moment to write, as you will readi-

ly conceive when I relate what has befallen us since our arrival here. From the first moment we have been set upon by unscrupulous men of every description whose sole occupation is preying upon the Indians and Negroes who are brought through this city. Each vulture has a specialty perfected by practice on earlier victims; one will engage to separate the Seminoles from their notes for coins at huge discount, another will peddle watered whiskey, another useless trinkets, while two actually attempted to spirit off one of the blacks during the confusion of debarkation. This villainous pack was our reception committee and has dogged our steps to the New Barracks on the river, where our party joined some 800 other emigrants already here, and it besieges us now, leaving only when word spreads that a vessel bringing fresh quarry is sighted. And yet if this rabble of thieves and sharpers were our only harassment we could account ourselves fortunate—a far more formidable foe besets us. They appeared in the commandant's office at this barracks, the morning after our arrival, having tracked us by ship from Tampa Bay, a large individual with sartorial pretensions which confirm his low breeding, accompanied by a fierce little lawyer who very soon produced an affidavit which was the subject of their visit. The big man declared himself to be the business agent of a "number of prominent gentlemen of Florida" including (to give you an idea of the quality of his clientele) Mr. Benjamin Solano of St. Augustine; the affidavit stated that the Negroes in our party were claimed as the lawful property of Mr. Solano, by right of purchase from certain Creek Indians. The Creeks were alleged to have received title to them as recompense for military services rendered to the United States government *under the authority of General Jesup.* I then threw my orders from the very same officer on the table, declaring that the Negroes in my charge had never been owned by Creeks, that others must be referred to (the affidavit being wonderfully vague as to numbers and descriptions), and that I intended to

290

obey my orders from General Jesup to the letter. At this our commandant Major Duncan frowned some, looked uncomfortable, and at last announced that he could not find it in his conscience to let the Negroes proceed north until the claim was settled one way or another in the courts, in Mr. Solano's favor or not, it did not matter to him. Without delay I took the case to Major Phagan, now lording over the Indian office here, and found him to be every bit the blackguard you have described and worse than no assistance, indeed apparently persuaded that any claim against Indian-held Negroes by respectable whites must ipso facto be valid. All in all, there seems to be a great reverence for legal form in New Orleans but very little for justice. My representations to civil authorities also proved fruitless, and Major General Gaines, the one man who could clear the way with the stroke of a pen is absent from the city.

So our argosy is halted, the commandant adamant, the Indians miserable and plagued by the human jackals who never sleep, and our situation grows less promising by the hour. The steamer *James Monroe*, chartered to ferry us to Fort Gibson, awaits at the wharf, but the term of the charter will expire in a few days and her captain will pocket the government's payment for the voyage not made and strike a fresh bargain. Halleck Mico and his band are very low and John Rainbow watches me like a hawk for the sign that I have decided to abandon the blacks (as other officers have done in the same circumstances), but I have resolved not to do so, being convinced (though without proof) that Solano's claim is fraudulent. I now pin my hopes on General Gaines returning before the agent can press the claim through the courts.

(Just after sunset.) Past the window where I write flows every sort of river traffic, flatboats, keelboats, steamboats, barges, one or another perhaps laden with cotton from Caffrey Station or the Hermitage, and viewing this scene I am struck by the contrast between the Cumberland and the city just down the

291

river where its produce is marketed. At home a man lives by his word, his honor, his reputation; here success, wealth, power alone are respected and sharp practice and mistrust are the rule. At home the Negro labors hard but in return is decently cared for and valued; here he is merely an expensive work animal to be traded, with no value but his price. It is as if there were two distinct systems in the Southern states, as different as night and day yet coexistent, one depending on character and kindness, the other on cash and cruelty. Were it ever to be necessary I believe that I would readily defend with my life our right to enjoy the fruits of the former, but I will have no part of the other.

Indeed, since I have been in this place I begin to suspect that there may be more evil in the world and more trouble in avoiding it than I had ever imagined. Even now, through the open door, John Rainbow has his eyes on me. The river is settling down for the night, leaving me restless. I'm aware of having let my life go by unrecorded, unfelt. One must learn to see, even the surface of things. One must learn to love. Since the mails on the Western rivers will be irregular I have resolved to set down these trials and adventures in a journal, and bring it home to you. Tomorrow I shall learn if General Gaines has returned or not.

Your affectionate husband,
Laird Caffrey

Laird

New Orleans
April, 1838

ON the seventh of March Major Duncan informed Captain Caffrey that General Gaines was detained for an indefinite time and ordered him to proceed north to the Indian lands without delay, leaving the Negroes "to be adjudicated" and in the event the court were to favor the Indians' claim over Mr. Solano's (here the major stifled a smile) sent on afterward. Citing his orders from General Jesup, Laird declined, whereupon the major informed him that he would sorely regret his refusal. That night, in the crowded barroom of a riverside tavern near the barracks, Laird observed at a table, absorbed in close conversation, Major Duncan, Major Phagan, the business agent, and the lawyer; and that night after leaving the tavern without being seen, he made a decision.

A full moon lighted his way along the cobbled wharfside to the *James Monroe*. Finding the captain in his cabin preparing to retire for the night, Laird informed him that he wished to embark his party and sail the next morning.

"How many'd that be?" inquired the other, raising bushy brows.

"Hundred and twelve."

"That'd include Negroes?"

"As the contract says."

The captain shook his head firmly. "Contract can't make a man break the law. I heard about the claim. Besides, we should have sailed two weeks ago; Arkansaw'll be shoaling soon. Course now, if it was just Indians I'd naturally stick to my bargain."

Laird descended the gangplank of the *James Monroe* without an inkling of what he would do next and was about to turn back to the barracks when he noticed a familiar vessel moored astern of her just up the quay—a steamboat, but a steamboat like no other now seen on the rivers in twenty years (except in the ignominious role of delta towboats)— the *Victory*, the faded painting of Andrew Jackson on the wheelhousing still visible in the moonlight.

As Laird approached, a figure appeared at the pilothouse door, bone-lean, wiry.

"Laird Caffrey?" The voice was humorously insinuating.

"Will Hollis!"
"Come right on board, Laird Caffrey."

Now nothing in Laird's past relations with the riverman's son (as he thought of him, though the father had died long ago) could account for his gratification at seeing him now, insofar as he did see him against the light of the moon; for in fact relations between him and the little veteran of Jackson's campaigns hardly existed, except that little Will Hollis had shipped some cotton from Caffrey Station, though Laird had seen him maybe a hundred times around Nashville, remembering him most vividly out on the river atop the pilothouse of the *Victory* hoisting the French and American flags the year Lafayette had visited. But when Laird stepped on board and climbed the ladder to the pilothouse, seeing the other's narrow, crisscross smile as if he was saying, "Now ain't this the damndest joke?" he suddenly realized that what separated them was like sand on an endless shore compared to the one pale grain of their common birth in the Cumberland.

Yet that grain was enough.

Laird

On board the *Victory*
April, 1838

EARLY the next morning, his deal made, Laird loaded Halleck Mico and his band on board the *Victory*, which by daylight appeared even more ramshackle than in the night, every plank, bolt, valve, pipe, lever, brace, fastening appearing worn yet essential to the vessel's holding together. As Laird boarded, the only crew, a boy called Dan, heaving wood into the fire door, briefly showed a sullen face not so dirty as it was permanently the color of dirt, but white nonetheless, for Will Hollis owned no Negroes.

When all the passengers were aboard, Dan cast off the mooring lines, Will, Laird beside him in the pilothouse, opened the throttle valve, the wheels began to churn, Dan poled the bow clear of the *James Monroe,* and Will sounded the whistle, a wheeze becoming a stunning blast that floated in easy echoes across the river; Will, looking well pleased, grinned at Laird, who smiled back, marveling that the other had consented so readily to make the voyage.

All Laird was certain of was that Will had agreed for more reason than the four hundred dollars from the government he had promised him on his own guarantee; people in Nashville were awaiting the cargo the *Victory* was to bring: ax heads, French wines, furniture, calico, engine parts, even a piano, all yet to be put on board in New Orleans, and the extra trip west would hold up those consignments by perhaps a month, a serious inconvenience to his customers, most important in the case of the piano, for it was going to the Hermitage; and Will had at first stated (over a whiskey jug) that he would not let General Jackson down for anything, much less for a passel of redskins and niggers, though he'd surely like to accommodate Laird. Besides it was a fact that the western rivers were entering a low stage early this year. So what it was during the hour's talk up in the pilothouse that had changed his mind as Laird related the story of Halleck Mico's band, of Jesup's promise and the rest he could not tell; they had passed the jug; sometimes Will pulled on his cigar, his eyes steady in the lighted circle of his sharp-boned face, listening shrewdly, showing not a flicker of interest in any hint of appeal on the grounds of need and justice; in fact what seemed to strike Will was that Laird Caffrey—all well-born, educated, landed as he was—had somehow managed to commit himself to a foolhardy course leading nowhere, imperiling his career and reputation, all to honor the promise of a general who had proved himself famously capable of dishonor, a promise to Indians concerning Negro property at that. Nevertheless, at a certain moment Laird caught the first sign of Will's interest, ironical it seemed at first, for why indeed should he risk jail or a fine (Laird had not concealed that hazard), why should be risk running his one proud capital in the world on a sandbar, why should he disoblige Andrew Jackson? Certainly not for four hundred dollars. Nonetheless at the end of the hour the riverman had grinned, shaken his head at the folly of what he was doing, spat into the dark, and agreed.

The first three days, the weather holding fair and pleasant, they had made good time; Laird had stopped glancing astern for a pursuing vessel, setting his mind on reaching Vicksburg, where rations were ordered, those he had obtained in New Orleans being almost exhausted. All day they steamed, anchored at twilight, made camp along the bank, replenished the wood, and embarked at the first light of dawn. All day Laird sat with Will in his aerie, the two getting better acquainted, at first with each other's silences.

The trouble had come from Halleck Mico. Having sensed that his authority was waning with every passing mile into unknown lands, perhaps remembering the jeers of the women (who now seemed more reconciled to their fates than the men), the old chief had decided to conduct himself with olympian contrariness, as if to set himself aloof from the whole enterprise of emigration. He complained of everything: that prayer was impossible because the Great Spirit would not hear over the sound of the steam engine; that his braves were made to gather wood with the women; that they were all too crowded on the boat and some were getting sick; and even that the countryside was never the same and the sun was in some new place in the sky whenever he thought about it. He insisted that they stop more often to rest and walk around; and when Laird through John Rainbow told him that the journey would only be more painful and dangerous if dragged out, that they must reach food and start up the western river before the water ran low, Halleck Mico drew himself up and declared that if he could not live like a man then he would die.

The chief's obstinacy strengthened the alliance between Laird and John Rainbow. Between them—the Negro counseling Laird about how Halleck Mico was likely to react to a given proposition—they managed together to defer to the chief just enough to prevent him from jumping overboard without letting him halt their progress. Of course the chief observed this collusion, scornfully, as if the connivance of his slave and his captor was to be expected in a world where the sun would not stand still. Will Hollis observed it too. And their alliance, expedient and provisional though it plainly was, made Will less than charitable about the chief's "acting up."

"Who does he figure he is?" he demanded, when they were together in the pilothouse.

"He's not sure anymore," Laird told him.

"Getting free government land, ain't he? And Negroes?"

Laird explained that the Seminoles were fighting a war just to stay where they were and that the blacks were mostly theirs to begin with. Will considered this.

"Never did think much of Indians owning Negroes," he said at last. "Just never took to the idea." Then with a frown he asked if they worked them.

"Hardly at all."

"Well, hell," said Will, spitting out the window, "that's what I mean—they got no business owning Negroes."

Over ricefields to the west turkey buzzards slowly spiraled under a mottled sky.

"Some say nobody does." Laird thought of Eliza. Will cast him a sharp look.

"Well, the hell with 'em," he remarked in a general way, standing up to judge the water ahead, turning into the channel. Laird did not reply. They had steamed another mile when Will spoke again.

"Guess if a man's got land and Negroes to work it and ain't sure who he is, then there's no way he's about to find out."

There were no rations at Vicksburg. There had been but

there weren't now, the lieutenant told Laird; other emigration parties had requisitioned what the contractors had provided, which was only a fraction of what General Jesup ordered. That afternoon, from certain civilians in Vicksburg fattening on the Indian removal, Laird purchased beef and flour at four times the price in New Orleans. When he returned to the landing he found the same lieutenant with four men eyeing the blacks on board the *Victory*—and Will Hollis in the pilothouse with a rifle in plain view.

They left the inhospitable town that evening and made camp at a deserted landing above the Yazoo.

The next day it became clear that Halleck Mico was not "acting up" but was dying. His face was gray and gaunt, he no longer complained but would eat nothing; all morning he sat cross-legged gazing out across the moving water, insensible to the packets passing upstream with white migrants to the western lands, the families on flatboats, the new towns at the landings, the clattering of hammers, the planted fields, woodland being cleared; insensible to the smoke and din, to the strange world he was leaving.

Will Hollis remained critical of the chief, telling Laird that it was beyond his understanding how a person "could just cave in like that." Toward afternooon when mares' tails began to lick the sun Halleck Mico, his family near him on the deck, sat immobile while John Rainbow told stories of his master's past bravery and services to his people. From the pilothouse Laird watched the dying chief, thinking of Eliza, of how she would feel toward Halleck Mico—until he glanced at Will and found the riverman studying him with a fine, crooked smile and narrowed eyes as if there was some secret between them.

That evening, by lantern light in his cabin, Laird began his journal for Eliza:

April 14, 1838.
    Halleck Mico died today. Showing no sign of disease or pain the chief expired in the evening soon af-

ter we made camp in a sycamore grove on the eastern bank near the settlement of Greenville. John Rainbow heard his last words and related them to us. I think you will find them affecting, as I did. (Even Will relented a little though it is plain that he did not make this trip out of love for redskins). I set down what I remember of the chief's dying words:

My leaves are fallen, my trunk is dead and my branches break in the wind. My bones will be buried here, but my spirit will follow my people along the dark and crooked path to the land of dreams, where we will be together again; and the star of our success will come out from behind the cloud and shine again. Do not mourn for me. We go to a land we know little of. Our home will be beyond the river on the way to the land where the sun dies. There we will build our house, in another country from the one we have known.

He was buried in Seminole garb, with what remained of his possessions, and mourned by his family, his people, and his slaves. At dusk the obsequies were rudely interrupted by the arrival of an express rider who, having spotted the Victory and found our fires, delivered a letter to me from a colonel of General Gaines's staff informing me that by court order the Negroes in our party are to be delivered into the hands of Solano's agent and his lawyer, said gentlemen following on board the steamer James Monroe; I am to await them and take a receipt for the Negroes, before continuing on to Fort Gibson.

I am certain that John Rainbow's grief over the passing of his master is genuine but now he has a further reason to mourn him; for just before his death the chief granted him and the 31 other Negroes their freedom, an act no doubt inspired by generous motives, but which removes the slender protection of Indian ownership. John Rainbow's eyes were scarcely dry but were on me again, warily, as I conferred with Will, reading him the letter.

Plain enough, says the riverman.

I mean to go on, I tell him.

With the Negroes?

Yes.

No reason now, says Will. They ain't theirs any-more.

Of course he is right. In fact there is now every rea-son to give the Negroes up—except that I feel it would be wrong to do so. I tell Will that I respect the law too much to see it twisted around so and that I am going on, on the authority of General Jesup, over-land if need be.

He looks at me a moment, then investigates the ground at his feet, then looks up at me again with a sharp smile.

What's the matter with the Victory? he asks. Ain't she getting us there?

You could lose her, I tell him.

He glances over at the old vessel which I believe he prizes more than anything else in the world, shrugs, and says, She ain't exactly brand-new.

For a passel of redskins and Negroes? I ask.

Oh, hell, it ain't them, he says scornfully, then looks at me with a smile just around the corner.

April 15.

What an admiral is Will Hollis! Under his able hands the Victory has lived up to her proud name to-day. But to relate the events in order, we left the grave of Halleck Mico before dawn this morning, steaming against wind and current into a rumbling black curtain embroidered now and then by light-ning bolts, and had progressed only a few miles when from downstream, over the sounds of wind and en-gine, we heard two quick blasts of a steam whistle, and we saw the James Monroe heeling round the bend in full pursuit. Will looked, made a judgment, directed Dan to move the weight on the safety valve lever out some, had me set two braves to helping the boy stoke the fire, opened the throttle valve, and set-tled down to steering.

Now Will already had told me that the Monroe can

outrun us easily in deep water; our advantage being shallow draft, permitting us to make a beeline course, staying out of the main current. This we did. He had also let me know that our pioneer boiler was made to operate at a hundred; information of vital importance had the pressure gauge been working; Will reckoned that we were no more than about 115 or 116 and had nothing to worry about because, he said, she shouldn't go unless we hit 120, which reassured me some, though not much, since the furious hiss of steam at each rapid stroke convinced me that we were no more than a square inch or so from Eternity; still, despite Will grazing the bulrushes on the bends, and the extra speed, we were not holding our distance from the pursuing vessel. I must have shown my concern then but Will was busy studying the squall we were headed into, and when it hit he executed the maneuver which ranks him with naval immortals. One minute the broad river was before us, flared by lightning under the engulfing black, then all was hammering rain; but in the instant of the flash I'd seen that Will was looking to the right of the main current to the mouth of a small tributary, up which a quarter mile or so was a landing and a settlement; and when the rain caught us he yelled to Dan and his crew to leave off stoking and stand some Indians around to hide the light from the firebox. Then he wound the wheel over hard to the right, and through sheets of rain, navigating by memory, feel of the water, and some star in his head, Will eased the Victory into the smaller stream and up to the landing; a few minutes later, when the squall passed, we heard in the distance two faint blasts of the Monroe—far, far up the Mississippi.

We went ashore, Will and I, to see about purchasing rations, for we were near the end of our food supply. The settlement was nothing much; rain dripping from a half-dozen eaves and porches into one mud street; not a soul in sight; not a sound but the rain dripping, the departing wind. Eerie place, says Will.

A faint light in in a window, I rap on the door, no answer, Will raps on the window, Get the hell away, says a man's voice, I state our business, Go away, says a woman's voice, you'll bring the disease. We try two other houses. The same. There is cholera on the river.

April 16.

Laid over, departed at dawn, our passengers hungry and apparently dazed by the loss of their leader. The beauty of the day, early springtime with a warning of summer heat, seems to mock our plight; we are a day's run from the mouth of the Arkansas and we must have food soon, but fear to stop to forage since at any time the Monroe, undeceived, may return. In any case the landings fly the yellow flag of quarantine. We are on our own, Will and I—and John Rainbow. At noon I make a decision: we will make a landing at Fort Davis that afternoon, fifteen miles upriver, and take our chances; if the order to stop us has reached them we will play our cards as best we can—but, I am determined, without going back on General Jesup's orders.

(Later.) God Bless Lieutenant Cabot.

I ask him if the James Monroe put in here lately.

Might have, he says with an up-east accent and a wise look.

Will has his number right off

Lots of vessels on the river.

Can hardly tell them apart, the lieutenant says, except that crackerbox of yours. He turns to me. Now, Captain, do you want rations? We've not many but I've held onto what I could, sir, and I advise you to take them before I recall something I heard this morning.

I truly believe that we were dealing with a dyed-in-the-wool abolitionist—who no doubt took me for one of his breed!—but under the circumstances I made no objection and thanked him warmly.

April 17.

Today we reached the Arkansas and start north-westward—the water even lower than feared. Will and I got a little better acquainted today. Often his mind (and so his conversation) runs to superlatives—the fastest time he's ever made the run to Nashville, the greatest man alive (Andrew Jackson), the most land a man could own in Texas.

April 18.

Low water. Low rations. Low spirits.

April 19.

Hard aground. Will says we could be stuck for a week or more, until the river's next stage. Rations gone. In the afternoon I send a party ashore to forage for game. At nightfall the braves return with dressed meat, grain, even bread—and an unsettling tale: they came upon a farmhouse stocked with food and every sign of habitation—except human beings. Outside—two fresh graves marked with wooden crosses. I look at Will. He has the same idea—but our passengers are already feasting.

April 20.

What I have witnessed today will not find its way into any history book. Except in these lines it will pass unrecorded, and yet it was a truly memorable, American in its high proportion of craziness, proving nothing in the end except that Little Will is more of a man than anyone in Nashville imagined.

At dawn we discover that an Indian boy is gravely ill and we fear what his ailment may be. Again our food is nearly gone and it is clear to me that we can't stay here but must take our chances overland. I tell Will my decision.

River's up a bit, is his answer.

I tell him that, this being the case, he can soon back off and head back down the river; we will pro-ceed on foot, for the plain fact is that a bar without

303

two or three feet of water in the deepest places blocks our passage upstream. Will studies the bar, squinting as if to figure out its secret.

Deep water yonder, he says at last, stating a fact which seems indisputable but under the circumstances irrelevant. Then he looks at me and says, I said I'd get you to Fort Gibson.

You've done your best, I tell him.

He looks at me a long time, as if we'd known each other all our lives.

Not quite, he says.

By midmorning all passengers are ferried ashore. From the bank we watch Dan stoking the fire until the steam is escaping like banshees; on Will's signal he's hopping in the boat and rowing toward us for all he's worth; Will is slinging the lead weight far out on the safety lever—then he's up in the pilothouse opening the throttle valve. Slowly the Victory backs off, finds deep water—I wave urging him to turn downstream, but he reverses the engine.

For a moment it looks like he might make it. More like a mud turtle than a steamboat the Victory churns halfway across the bar. When she begins to lose way, Will is down slinging that weight all the way to the end of the lever. He has just time to get back to the pilothouse, the Victory gives one last lurch, then shudders into the sand. Then with a deafening blast the boiler goes; the air is filled with flying iron and splintering wood; the cabin bulkheads go outward taking the wheelhousings into the river; but most amazing the pilothouse goes straight up, Will still hanging onto the wheel and throttle valve, arcs back and falls with a great splash astern.

When John Rainbow and I get Will ashore he looks finished. But in a minute or so he comes to, looks at me for quite a time, piecing things together, then sits up painfully and studies the wreck in the river, spits, grins, and says, By God if we didn't damn near make it.

April 22.
   Rains. Many ill. Feel the onset of fever but must go
on to Fort Gibson. Should I not return let this be the
sign I so wanted to give you in this world.

Eliza

St. Augustine–Caffrey Station
June, 1838

SHE learned of Laird's death by a letter from a Nashville
boatman she had barely ever spoken to. Soon other messages reached her, from Caffrey kin and from acquaintances
she barely remembered from the past, offering condolences
and assuring her of her place among them; even a note from
Andrew Jackson asking her to bear her loss in the knowledge that her husband had served his country bravely and
had been taken into the Kingdom of Heaven.

Twice she went to the church on the plaza to pray but
dared not test her faith. That Laird was gone filled her with
a grief beyond all consolation. Instead she busied herself
selling the house they had shared.
   A week before setting forth with Delia she wrote Captain
Wolfe telling him the news and of her decision to live at
Caffrey Station.

Will Hollis was at the Nashville landing. As the McAndrews and other Caffrey connections greeted her, showing a
new deference, and servants hoisted her trunk on the carriage, Hollis watched from a distance, until she excused
herself and went over to him.
   "Mr. Hollis, I thank you kindly for your note," she told
him, struck by the intense look in his narrow face.

305

"Most welcome, Miz Caffrey."

"You were with my husband when he died?"

"Yes, ma'am," he said, adding, "And I got something of his for you. A journal he wrote. Said it was for you and that I was to bring it myself."

For a moment she hesitated, then asked, "Will you come to my house?" And she saw that the invitation was what he expected.

"Yes, ma'am."

They agreed on the following afternoon.

In the eight years since Eliza's visit Lucy had grown heavier and grudgeful. She and Delia became enemies on sight. The first morning passed with commotion in the kitchen and a constant stream of callers in the parlor, so that it was afternoon before Eliza had a moment to herself. Exhausted, she was about to sit in the chair by the west window where Laird's father had sat, but she chose a hard settee. A few minutes later the bell rang again and Lucy, openly disapproving, showed in Will Hollis.

He stood in the doorway from the hall, the notebook in hand, looking straight at her without a word, then slowly took in the room with a sidelong but careful eye. Then, remembering the notebook, he came to her and presented it, saying, "This here's what he meant you to have. Guess it tells what happened to us up near the end, though I ain't read it 'cause I can't."

"Your letter?"

"Writ for me." He glanced at the books in the shelves. "Mean to learn reading and writing someday, maybe surveying too." Then looking at her intently, frowning slightly, he said, "Captain Caffrey was an uncommonly fine man."

"Yes," Eliza agreed softly, and suddenly looked down at the notebook, opening it. A blue pressed flower fell from the pages. Will picked it up and handed it to her.

"Captain Caffrey picked that special for you. Don't go losing it, now."

For the next hour, seated in the chair by the west window, Will Hollis told her about the last weeks of Laird's life and how he died. He told her about the rains they met when they went overland, the mired roads, the sickness that took eighteen lives on the way. He told her about how, even though sick himself, Laird had cared for each stricken emigrant, red and black, citing many proofs of Captain Caffrey's kindness and bravery. He told her about the captain's rage when he led the survivors into Fort Gibson only to find Seminoles by the acre encamped there, refusing to go on to the lands the government assigned because Creeks were already settled on them. And he told her of Laird's decision to go on with his party west until they found unoccupied land as they had been promised; exceeding the obligation of his orders, indeed violating them; and about the last hundred miles of the trek across rising prairies, when Laird was so ill he was carried on a litter. Finally he told her about how he had hung on by sheer willpower until the Indians came within sight of the magnificent valley where they would settle, even pointing it out to them from the ridgetop, before passing on peacefully.

Only when Will had gone did it occur to her to wonder if it had really been that way.

For the first weeks Eliza lived by the idea that the Cumberland was where she belonged now, but as the numbing grief of bereavement turned to pain and the pain finally began to ease, she was aware that her life here was becoming an enactment of what was expected of her, that she had thrown herself into the role of the Widow Caffrey with a determination which had mystified her household and the Caffrey kin; and as the pain lifted she found that she had been breaking old trusts with herself, acting a travesty of

307

Laird's old ideal of what his wife should be. She remembered long ago Aunt Rachel asking, "Ain't our horses good enough for you?" realizing that now she had horses of her own and miles of fields and woods, a fine house, John Hutchins' dream for her, but that none of it was her own or ever would be. And she knew that once Laird's estate was settled she must leave.

At the end of the fourth week, just before sundown, at his special invitation, she called on Andrew Jackson at the Hermitage.

As her carriage drew up at the portico the old man came out himself, greeted her saying that he had other visitors, unexpected, who would soon be departing. In the parlor she said little, listening to the general as he entertained his guests, complete strangers it appeared, who had come to pay their respects. Only when they had gone and Andrew Jackson returned to the parlor did she see the ravages of weariness and age in his face; and, reading the thought, he smiled and said, "Think they're visiting a confounded monument," adding, "Let's take a walk in the garden."

At the far corner of the fragrant spring garden Rachel's columned tomb stood against a pale rose sky over the darkening fields beyond, where the hands moved as pieces of the dusk toward the smoke of their cabins. At the tomb Eliza stood with the general in silence, and the old man with his head bowed, leaning on his cane, until he turned to her and, by the failing light, she thought for a moment that he was searching for words to speak of her own loss but then realized that in the world he had entered she had no place; he was trying to remember who she was.

"Garden used to be better kept," he said, starting back toward the house, then stopped by a small gravestone. "James Earl used to keep it up. Course nothing like she could."

As they walked on she was aware of his efforts to place her. Then he paused, turning to her, seeming to remember something.

"Lincoyer's gone too, you know." He indicated a nearby gravestone with his cane. "Consumption took him. Boy had never come to feel like one of us here, though we loved him like a son."

After a silence she said, "I'm leaving the Cumberland, Uncle Jackson."

He looked bewildered. "Where to?"

"East. I'm putting Caffrey Station up for sale."

Then he remembered.

"Fine place," he said, relieved, as they walked on, "but these are bad times to sell. Cotton's down but nothing like land and Negroes." He smiled at her. "Anyway I remember Rachel saying Eliza Hutchins always knew her mind. And Rachel was never wrong about people."

Then as they reached the house he said in sudden anger, "You know they drove her to her grave with their damnable lies! By the Eternal, I would rather burn in Hell than forgive them!" And turning to the darkening western sky he raised his silver-headed cane, calling across the empty fields, *"He may show them mercy but I shall not."*

In the twilight she saw pain fill his drawn face as his thin lips formed the words: "I truly miss her."

And with a courtliness that brought tears to her eyes he added, "Just as you must miss your husband."

Then he handed her into her carriage.

Will

Caffrey Station
November, 1838

SIX months later, on the eve of his leaving the Cumberland, Will Hollis came back to Caffrey Station, the now untenanted white house at the end of the cedar lined drive, silent fields beyond, the low sun inflaming bolls, briar, and thistle against the violet hills west of the river. He went up on the portico, recognizing the sign on the door (as he might recognize a jay or a quail) which meant that the plantation was up for sale.

Why had he, a dreamer admittedly, but not a man given to doing things without a reason, come to Caffrey Station now, on what would be his last evening in Davidson County in a long time? He had thought of going to the smaller white house nearer town, where passing by an age ago he had seen her as a young girl in riding skirts holding the reins of a pony, and again sitting up in a pear tree in wintertime, but new people lived there now (as they had done for twenty years); or he might have just walked through Nashville, down certain streets, at the landing, or out certain roads, remembering each time he had seen her, riding with her father, later with Caffrey, and once driving in Rachel Jackson's carriage. Never had she suspected, not in all these years; not even when he had sat across from her in the parlor, telling her about Captain Caffrey's death; he had made certain that she would not, even though inwardly he had still responded to her, a woman not far short of forty, much as he had done when he first glimpsed her as a girl in riding skirts holding the reins of a pony; not that she was so especially pretty then or now; and the fact that he had known from the beginning that she was kin, even distant, to Andrew Jackson maybe had something to do with that first infatuation, not to mention the evidence that she owned her own pony, but each time he saw her, even at a distance, his original impression was strengthened, and all that he heard about her, her difficult nature, her independence from the other girls of the Nashville Female Academy, added to the portrait of a girl the mere thought of whom released within Will Hollis powerful though unsorted notions about himself and the future.

When he had learned of John Hutchins' bankruptcy he had felt heartened, supposing that some fatality was at work breaking down the barriers which separated them;

but the misfortune only took her away from Nashville, East, then to the wilds of Florida, and when at last she did return it was as Laird Caffrey's bride, one day to be mistress of Caffrey Station, so remote from him then as to make a mockery of his feelings about her; yet even then he could not have freed himself from them even if he had tried.

When Captain Caffrey had taken her back to Florida and gone off fighting Indians Will had often imagined him getting killed. He did not wish him dead, he had nothing against him, in fact of the Nashville plantation gentry Caffrey had always been the one in particular Will took every occasion to study and he regarded him all the more highly for marrying Eliza Hutchins. Still it was well known that there were natural hazards to Indian fighting.

All such notions Will himself recognized as being fantasies—until the evening in New Orleans when Laird Caffrey in flesh and blood stood on the cobbled wharfside looking up at him. For Will that moment was perhaps the strangest in his life and yet, strangest of all, expected; it was as if the world and his dream were suddenly one, resolved as an endless, spacious future in which everything was possible.

Will came up to the shuttered parlor window and peered through a crack into a dark of shrouded furniture, light-specked wisps of cobweb hanging motionless; she was somewhere East now, they said, having manumitted all the Negroes who wanted to be manumitted (some did not since it meant leaving all they had by way of home) and shipping them East. Other, vaguer reports came down the Ohio: Some of the Negroes sent off had chosen to emigrate to the new colony in Africa and Eliza had sought the assistance of a certain New Englander, a sea captain, an antislavery man. And Will understood that kin and friends of the Caffreys were incensed over the rumor that Eliza, not six months widowed, had "taken up" with the Eastern abolitionist, not to speak of their resentment because, having borne her husband no children, now she was selling Caffrey Station and

311

packing off house servants and hands to the four winds, with no consideration for the McAndrews or anyone else. Certain predictions of old Mrs. Donelson were recalled, and the balanced judgments of Emily Donelson, now two years in her untimely grave. The story of how as a child Eliza had spoken up to Andrew Jackson was remembered as her "talking back" to the future President; in fact nobody could recall when there were not signs of her waywardness; some said that she had made Laird Caffrey's life a calvary, her never wanting to come home, her barrenness, her ungiving nature, her never knowing just how to conduct herself with colored, and that that was why he'd stayed on in the army so long, till he found himself fighting a misbegotten war; the best that could be said of her—and most were fair enough to remember it—was that Rachel Jackson had favored her.

Will Hollis was not troubled by the censure of her. To him the talk had yielded the discovery that she was a born outcast in the Cumberland like himself. As for her supposedly taking up with an abolitionist sea captain he discounted that tale as an ignorant fable, considering its source; and even if it were partly true it didn't matter much to him; she had been gone a long time before, been married to Caffrey; and as for freeing the Negroes he hardly held that against her, they were hers after all; in fact he even liked the idea for the consternation it caused. Indeed, he felt as ardently toward her now, peering into the lonesome room, as he had sitting with her in that same room six months ago, or even when he had first seen her as a proud little girl with a pony—maybe more. All that he had feared was that one day she would come here, to his house to settle for good with Laird Caffrey and be lost to him forever.

Now everything was possible.

Time and distance, likelihood, had nothing to do with it. For some time his wife and kids had begun to look scraggly to him walking in Nashville; he had been thinking of leaving the river and moving to the Western country, not for-

312

ever, only long enough to establish himself and return to Nashville as a man of property. On each trip with the *Victory* the rapid settlement on the Western bank of the Mississippi made him more restless, and the chance meeting with Laird Caffrey had happened when he was never more ready for it. It meant a chance to look over the Western lands. And it meant a chance to study the master of Caffrey Station, Eliza's husband, up close.

On the journey Will had pondered the way Captain Caffrey had set himself to keeping a promise at any cost that was not worth keeping in the first place; such impractical will had struck the riverman as being both crazy and admirable. Especially dying in the course of it just as if he were dying for some high cause.

Not once did the running of the *Victory* across the bar strike Will as being of the same order of madness. He had survived in one piece. And with a purpose. After the Indians found their land he had gone on beyond the reservation and found himself a fine section just west of the Seminole lands, a tract he had later been able to purchase thanks to the mistrust of banks and paper money he shared with Andrew Jackson. Always Will had put his steamboat earnings into coin, even while the whole country was busy trading paper with nothing to back it for real estate at wilder and wilder prices—until Andrew Jackson had a law passed requiring that public lands be sold for specie, thereby causing the bottom to drop out of the land market and permitting Will to get his section for a few gold coins—with enough left over for building and the purchase of Negroes to work it.

So, soon he would be five hundred miles west, Eliza Caffrey a thousand miles east; yet the space between them made no difference nor did the years it would take him to make good and return here someday, perhaps, he considered, to this very house; for nothing was out of the question. In the meantime, later on, he might even try his fortune in Texas for a while.

313

The sun was down, flaming the distant ridge, the air was turning chill. Will took a last look in the dark parlor, then touched his two hands to the painted wood of the shutter, just as Caffrey had told him the Seminoles touched the walls of their houses, the trees, the ground, to take through their fingers the memory of the home they were leaving forever.

Only Will Hollis was not leaving forever.

He would be back someday.

Turning down the long drive he smiled, remembering how he had exaggerated some to Caffrey's widow about the captain's last day, how he'd borrowed from things he'd done himself; and about the ridgetop and the magnificent valley, when the fact was that Caffrey had died in considerable agony three days before they ever reached the scrawny draw the Creeks had overlooked; and about the cornflower he had pressed in the journal himself, after Laird's death, and forgotten.

He would be back here someday.

And maybe Caffrey's widow would too.

THE Second Seminole War did not end that year, or the next, or the next, or the next after that. The longest, costliest, bloodiest Indian war in America history did not end until August 14, 1842, six years, eight months, seventeen days after General Wiley Thompson was shot by Osceola and Major Dade's force was massacred; after 1,500 American soldiers had lost their lives and $40,000,000 been expended. In nearly seven years, under seven generals, the army had killed an unknown number of Seminoles and moved more than 3,800 on their Trail of Tears to the new lands west of Arkansas, which they were to possess not for as long as the rivers run and the grass grew but only until the grass and the rivers were coveted by new generations of white settlers; yet a tenth that number, old Sam Jones' band among them, were never captured; and though years later many of the survivors were persuaded to emigrate, a hundred remained in southern Florida, where their descendants live today.

Osceola's remains were never returned to Florida. Dr. Weedon, having gained possession of his corpse, severed the head, mummified it, and sometimes would hang it on the footboard of his children's bed to frighten them into obedience. Later, as a gesture of professional tribute, the physician presented the head to the celebrated New York surgeon Dr. Valentine Mott for his museum of curiosities. In the course of time the museum was consumed by fire.

After the capture of Osceola the principal prize sought by the Americans was Coacoochee. From all evidence Philip's fiery, antic son had at first regarded the war as a fine sport and had been known to burst out laughing at the sight of troops struggling through a swamp under fire, forgetting to fire himself; but after his escape from Fort Marion, angered by the treachery of his capture, Coacoochee and his band had gone on a rampage of bloody attacks on soldiers and civilians alike, spreading terror through northeastern Florida. Most bizarre of these actions was an ambush of an itinerant theatrical company in which the former interpreter Steven Richards was slain and the Indians came into possession of a magnificent wardrobe of Shakespearean costumes. On March 5, 1841, responding to a request to come in for a talk, Coacoochee attired as Hamlet, accompanied by Horatio, attended by Richard the Third robed in ermine and with murder in his eye, entered Fort Cummings and at the talk spoke as follows:

"The white man has dealt unjustly with me. I came to him, he deceived me. The land that I was upon I loved, my body is made of its sands; the Great Spirit gave me legs to walk over it, hands to aid myself, eyes to see its ponds, rivers, forests, and game; and a head with which to think. The sun, which is warm and bright as my feelings are now, shines to warm us and bring forth our crops, and the moon brings back the spirits of our warriors, our fathers, wives, and children. The white man comes; he grows pale and sick. Why cannot we live here in peace? I have said I am the enemy of the white man. I could live in peace with him, but first he steals our cattle and horses, cheats us, and takes our lands. White men are as thick as the leaves in the hammock; they come upon us thicker every year. They may shoot us, drive our women and children night and day; they may chain our hands and feet, but the red man's heart will always be free."

He was to be, a second time, captured by treachery, threatened with hanging, and by such means induced to persuade other chiefs to bring their bands in. Many were to do so.

In the spring of 1845 Andrew Jackson, in his seventy-eighth year, lay dying at the Hermitage. As his last act of service to his country he succeeded, through letters and emissaries, in persuading his old friend Sam Houston to agree to the annexation of the republic of Texas to the United States. Texas would join the Union as a new slave state—strengthening the nation in the coming contest with

Mexico for an even larger prize: the Southwest to the Pacific Coast.

When John Quincy Adams learned that Texas would be annexed to the United States he wrote to a friend: "Our Country, if we have a country, is no longer the same . . . the polar Star of our Foreign Relations was Justice, it is now Conquest. Their vital spirit was then Liberty, it is now Slavery. As our Dominion swells she becomes dropsical and by the time our Empire shall extend over the whole Continent of North America we shall be ready for a race of Caesars. . . . Liberty has yet her greatest warfare to wage in this Hemisphere." He who had been the staunchest supporter in Monroe's Cabinet of Jackson's incursion into Spanish Florida, architect of the annexation of that Territory, principal author of that President's doctrine asserting America's right to an equal place among great nations, had in his later years viewed territorial expansion that spread slavery as a cancer ruinous to the nation.

In 1846 the United States declared war against Mexico. Veterans hardened in Florida fought in the mesquite deserts of Nuevo Leon, at Veracruz, Cerro Gordo, Chapultepec; and in 1848, after that war was won, a resolution was proposed in the House of Representatives tendering the thanks of Congress to the generals for achieving the triumph. But when the vote was called John Quincy Adams responded with a resounding "No!" For, brave as the generals might have been, he would not see them honored for winning what he considered to be a most unrighteous war. That "No!" was the last intelligible word Adams uttered. Moments later he seized his desk, started to rise, his lips framing the words "Mr. Speaker," then fell to his side and was dead.

And so the once-fanciful vision of Jefferson of one nation under one flag to the Pacific shore would become a reality, but at a cost undreamed of; for in Florida were sown the dragon's teeth of ruthless conquest and fratricide; and

317

young Lieutenant William Tecumseh Sherman, who brought in Coacoochee, became the general who in 1864 burned Atlanta and marched his army to Savannah, leaving a swath of destruction that would scar the nation long after the countryside had healed; the same officer who in 1869 at Medicine Lodge, Kansas, told the Indians, "Our people East hardly think of what you call war here, but if they make up their minds to fight you, they will come out as thick as a herd of buffalo, and if you continue fighting you will be killed."

So the land would be won, but with no clear title to it. And when the roads were built which all the old politicians thought would bind the nation together in prosperity and peace they were traveled by strangers and gunmen. Ties between the living and the dead were severed. Only a few held some memory of what had happened and of who they were because of it.